BETRAYAL

JULIAN STOCKWIN

BETRAYAL

HODDER

First published in Great Britain in 2012 by Hodder & Stoughton
An Hachette UK company

First published in paperback in 2013

1

A CIP catalogue record for this title is available from the British Library.

ISBN 978 1 444 71202 5

Typeset by Palimpsest Book Production Ltd, Falkirk, Stirlingshire

Printed and bound in the UK by Clays Ltd, St Ives plc

Hodder & Stoughton policy is to use papers that are natural, renewable
and recyclable products and made from wood grown in sustainable forests.
The logging and manufacturing processes are expected to conform to the
environmental regulations of the country of origin.

Hodder & Stoughton Ltd
338 Euston Road
London NW1 3BH

www.hodder.co.uk

'The repossession of Buenos Aires has been stained with such deliberate acts of treachery and perfidy as are not to be instanced in the annals of history'

Commodore Sir Home Riggs Popham,
HMS Diadem, *Río de la Plata, 1806*

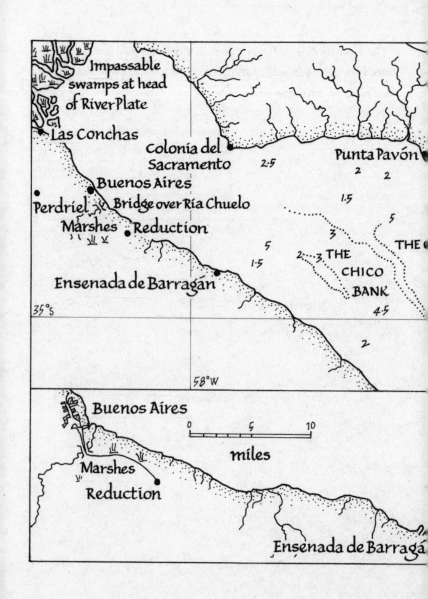

Impassable
swamps at head
of River Plate

Las Conchas

Colonia del
Sacramento

2.5

Punta Pavón

2   2

Buenos Aires

Perdriel   Bridge over Ría Chuelo

1.5

Marshes   Reduction

5

3

2...3 THE

5

THE

Ensenada de Barragán

5

1.5

CHICO

BANK

35°S

4.5

2

58°W

Buenos Aires

0   5   10

miles

Marshes

Reduction

Ensenada de Barragá

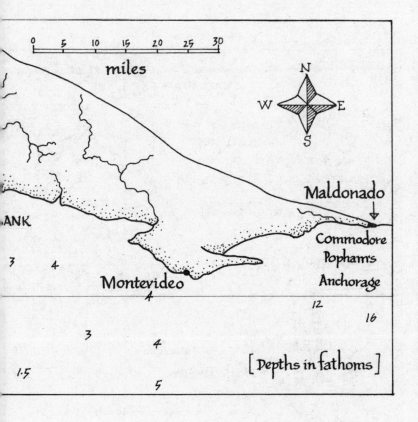

miles

0 5 10 15 20 25 30

N
W   E
S

Maldonado

ANK

Commodore
Popham's
Anchorage

3   4

Montevideo

4

12

16

3

4

[Depths in fathoms]

1·5

5

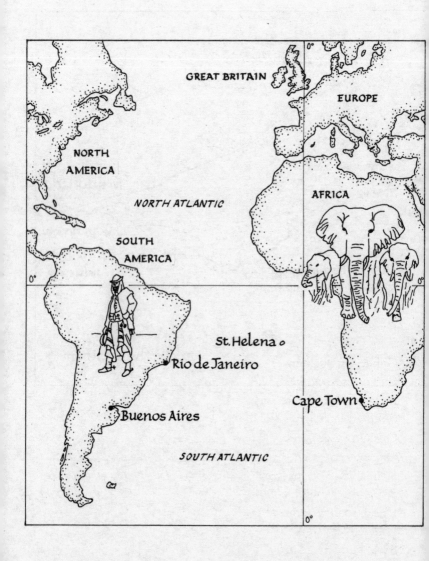

Dramatis Personae

(* Indicates fictitious character)

*Thomas Kydd, captain of *L'Aurore*
*Nicholas Renzi, his friend and confidential secretary

L'Aurore, ship's company

*Gilbey, first lieutenant
*Curzon, second lieutenant
*Bowden, third lieutenant
*Clinton, lieutenant of marines
*Owen, purser
*Oakley, boatswain
*Kendall, sailing master
*Searle, boy volunteer
*Dodd, marine sergeant
*Poulden, coxswain
*Stirk, gunner's mate
*Collas, carpenter's mate

*Legge, carpenter
*Doud, seaman
*Pearse, master's mate
*Cumby, boatswain's mate
*Wong, seaman
*Saxton, signal master's mate
*Tysoe, Kydd's valet
*Calloway, midshipman

Officers, other ships

Commodore Home Popham
Lieutenant Herrick, duty lieutenant
Lieutenant Davies, *Diadem*
Captain Downman, *Diadem*
Captain Byng, *Belliqueux*
Captain Honyman, *Leda*
Captain Donnelly, *Narcissus*
Captain Audley, *Ocean*
Lieutenant Godwin, *Encounter*
*Lieutenant Garrick, *Dolores*
*Lieutenant Selby, *Staunch*
*Acting Lieutenant Hellard, *Stalwart*

Army

Captain Arbuthnot
Erskine, aide
General Lord Beresford
Major General Sir David Baird
Colonel Pack

Others

*Beekman, midshipman
*Bolt, petty officer
*Dougal, master's mate, *Stalwart*
*Ribeiro, Portuguese trader
*Geens, pest control
*Cuthbert Richardson, cocoa planter
*Ditler, ivory trader
*Scholes, passenger
Captain Waine, *Elizabeth*
*Hardiman, *Justina*
*Maycock, supercargo, *Justina*
Jed Russell, a.k.a. Crujido, senior pilot for the viceroyalty
Lord Grenville, prime minister
Charles Sidmouth, Lord Privy Seal
Charles Fox, foreign secretary
Viscount Howick, first lord of the Admiralty
Patton, governor of St Helena

Buenos Aires

His Excellency the Governor of Truxillo
The Virrey Diputado Quintana, deputy viceroy
*Don Baltasar, Hidalgo de Terrada, paramount leader of patriots
*Manuel Bustamente, patriot deputy
Martín Miguel de Güemes, cadet-lieutenant in Spanish Army
*Barreda, Popham's envoy
*Rodriquez Corazón, merchant and host at Kydd's billet
*Dona Rafaela Callejo, lover of Vicente Serrano
Rafael de Sobramonte, viceroy over the viceroyalty of the Río
   de la Plata
Martín de Álzaga, wealthy merchant
Don Santiago Liniers, military leader
Colonel General Pueyrredón, commander of the gauchos

Chapter 1

In the dilapidated office Mr Owen looked up from his reckoning. 'Bananas at eighty *reis* the quintal seems a little excessive, Mr Ribeiro,' he said slowly, mopping his brow. The humidity was formidable, the dull heat like a suffocating blanket, but the purser of a frigate of His Majesty's Navy had his standards and he sweltered in coat and breeches.

Shrugging, the fat Portuguese trader leaned back in his chair. 'You think? I sell you green ones, not go rot, best in Mozambique.'

Tugging at his clammy neckcloth and dismissively eyeing the hand of half-ripe fruit brought for his inspection, Owen looked pained. 'My captain wishes only to serve his worthy crew with a mort of sweetness in their diet, but if the price is beyond my allowance . . .'

'Then I help! I can find th' red banana, very creamy, very cheap and for you—'

'No, no, Mr Ribeiro, the crew would think it sharp practice. Were you to vary your price to accommodate a larger order – say, five quintals – and payment in silver *reals*, then . . .'

1

Nicholas Renzi, sitting to one side of the table, fanned himself with a palm leaf. The negotiations dragged on and his attention wandered. The doorway was jammed with wide-eyed children, fearful but entranced by this visitation from the outer world. Beyond, in the harsh sunlight, was the noisy ebb and flow of an African market town. The world of war with Napoleon Bonaparte might have been in another universe but it was precisely why he was here. Hove to off the river mouth and enjoying the fresh oceanic breezes was HMS *L'Aurore*, a thirty-two-gun frigate whose captain was his closest friend, Thomas Kydd.

As his confidential secretary, Renzi had an unquestioned right to come and go on ship's business; in these last weeks he had often landed with the purser but not to lend his presence for business negotiations to secure fresh foodstuffs. He had every sympathy for the dry Welshman who, as a man of independent business aboard ship, had to balance his costs at supplying stores and necessaries with fairness at the point of issue yet leave himself with sufficient profit to weather financial storms. In the absence of an agent-victualler this meant making a deal with often unscrupulous local merchants that might well be repudiated later by an officious Admiralty functionary in faraway London.

The purser probably suspected but had never enquired the real reason why Renzi so often accompanied him: if there was one thing a scouting frigate needed from the shore even more than fresh victuals it was information. With an infinite number of directions to sail off in, even the tiniest whisper was better than nothing, and Renzi had personally witnessed the effectiveness of Admiral Lord Nelson's network of merchant intelligence in the Mediterranean before Trafalgar, overseen, it was rumoured, by his own secretary.

The current mission for *L'Aurore* was an important one. Only a few months before the British had taken Cape Town, the Dutch settlement at the tip of Africa at the Cape of Good Hope, to secure the all-important route to India. With slender military resources, it lay vulnerable to a vengeful counter-attack by the French, specifically by Admiral Maréchal, who was known to be at sea with a battle squadron greatly outnumbering the few ships of the Royal Navy on station there.

L'Aurore's orders were to follow the coast around the south of the continent and up the Indian Ocean side, stopping vessels, seeking word. As far north as Lourenço Marques, there had been not even a rumour, but Kydd had pressed on, if only to prove the French absent from the area. He knew that on the other side of Madagascar the French had strong island bases in a direct line from India, which could well be sheltering a battle group. *Leda*, the larger fellow frigate to *L'Aurore*, was sent to look into these, so *L'Aurore* had sailed on into the Mozambique channel, past hundreds of miles of the frightful remoteness of the dark continent to the foetid flatness of Quelimane, an ancient Arab slave market but now a lonely outpost of the Portuguese empire, itself dating from the daring voyage of Vasco da Gama in the 1490s.

'Five quintal?' Ribeiro came back with a frown. 'We just quit o' three cargo for Zanzibar, not so many left. Cost me more to find.'

Idly Renzi looked out at a grove of densely clustered scrub palms nearby. To his surprise he made out arrays of the unmistakable yellow curves of magnificently sized fruit. More than enough, surely. 'Er, may we not avail ourselves of those fine bananas yonder, or are they spoken for perhaps?' he enquired.

3

The other two men turned to him with surprise. 'Do allow I should conduct my business without your valued assistance, Mr Renzi,' Owen said huffily. 'Those are not bananas, rather plantains, which every soul knows may only be suffered to be eaten after cooking.' He turned back to Ribeiro and stiffly concluded arrangements for a delivery of three quintals of standard bananas.

As Renzi rose with the purser, he offered casually, 'Then your trade prospers, Mr Ribeiro?'

The man looked up guardedly. 'As is always the chance o' luck in these days. Why you ask?'

'Oh, just that Mr Napoleon is stirring up trouble in these parts. Has your business suffered at the hands of the French at all?'

'They don't trouble as we,' Ribeiro replied.

'Then you haven't heard – his ships of war are at sea. He seeks bases for his privateers, territory to add to France. Should he decide on Quelimane, well, as you have no friends . . .'

'Er, no friends?'

'Those who will rid you of him, should you tell them in time. You haven't seen any French ships – big ones, I mean to say?' Renzi added.

'Um, no, not b' me.'

'Perhaps have had word of such?' It was a last try. So far north and failing any intelligence, *L'Aurore* must now cease her search and put about for Cape Town with nothing to report.

'No.'

Renzi shrugged and turned to go.

'Wait.' Ribeiro hauled himself to his feet, snorting with the effort. 'I not seen, but the fishers? They on the sea, they will know.' He went to the doorway and called over a wizened man on the other side of the street.

After a brief exchange in some African dialect, Ribeiro beamed. 'He say yes! Ver' big one, two day ago up th' coast.'

Renzi snapped to full alert. 'Just one? Where was it going?'

'He remember Pebane way – t' the north.'

Curious onlookers joined them, and another seamed individual broke in with excited jabber.

'He say he saw as well, four day ago but swear it were off t' the south.'

Renzi frowned. How much reliance should he place on these fishermen? A lone ship – and was it truly a big one?

'How many masts did it have?' he asked.

Both were insistent that it was three-masted and square-rigged on each. This, therefore, was not a local trader, nor yet a privateer or even an armed schooner, for it was ship-rigged in exactly the same way as a frigate or ship-of-the-line. Was it one of Maréchal's scouting frigates ranging ahead of the deadly squadron?

His heart quickened, but Kydd would need to know details. North or south – where was it headed? If he offered money to the wider community for information they would say anything they thought would please him but he did have something up his sleeve. 'Oh, Mr Owen,' he said to the purser, 'do send for my sea-bag, if you will.'

One of the boat's crew, red-faced with exertion in the heat, hurried up with a mysterious carry-all, surrounded by a noisy crowd of screeching children and their elders. Renzi took it, bowing politely to the young seaman who, taken aback, awkwardly bowed in return and for good measure touched his forelock.

Looking significantly at Ribeiro, Renzi opened it and peered

5

inside. The hubbub died to an expectant hush as others flocked to join the throng. After a pause he straightened in satisfaction, then pointedly laced it shut. 'Mr Ribeiro,' he announced importantly, 'our good King George is concerned at the hard life of the fishermen of Quelimane. He directs me to distribute these small gifts as a token of his esteem – but only to the worthy fisher-folk themselves.'

The faces around him looked doubtful, but after his words had been translated, several grinning, weatherbeaten men pushed themselves to the front. Renzi regarded them solemnly, then dipped into the bag and drew out the red uniform coat of a private of the Royal Marines. A collective gasp went up as it was presented to the oldest fisherman, who drew it on reverently.

He twirled about in his finery to universal admiration, and Renzi hid a grin at the sight of the patched and worn cast-off that had been routinely consigned to the boatswain's rag-chest. More treasures were handed out: a pair of seamen's white duck trousers with frayed bottoms, a sailor's jacket with two brass buttons still on it, half a dozen holed stockings.

Renzi allowed that he would be obliged if he could hear from any who had seen the big ship, and stood back to let the noise and jollity overflow as things were tried on, exchanged, bartered. One man detached from the rest and passed along his observation, then more came forward. Renzi carefully entered their words into his notebook until in all he had eleven firm reports.

Such men's lives depended on knowing where they were so he now had the time and position of each sighting; individually plotting them on the chart would give a clear picture of the track.

Pleased with himself, he politely withdrew, leaving them to their bounty.

'Well done, Nicholas!' Kydd said happily, wielding his dividers on the East Africa chart. 'I do hope Mr Oakley is not too discommoded by our making free with his rag-chest. Look here, I think I have it . . .'

Renzi leaned over. The neatly encircled dots marched from the south regularly until, near Pabane in the north, the last two made an irregular hook. 'He's come from around Madagascar to spy out the channel, and here in the north he's turned about and is starting to head back. We have a chance.'

'Dear chap – you're omitting one thing . . .'

'Oh?'

'These are past reports, this latest being yesterday. By now the fellow is well on.'

'Not so. See – on this track, the speed made between points is trifling. He's spending his time casting about, conducting a good search while our fisher-folk have to land their catch smartly and lose no time in returning. Nicholas, I'll wager should we rest here we'll see him topsails over, say, early tomorrow.'

Kendall, the sailing master and a man of few words, nodded in agreement and a reluctant smile surfaced. 'Sir, there's th' question o'—'

'Yes. If he's a frigate his first duty is to report to his admiral, not offer battle with a chance o' damage, so he'll bear away as soon as he sights us and we'll not discover his squadron rendezvous. We're to calm his fears in some way, I believe.'

And lure him on. There was no way Kydd could alter his ship into a lesser breed or make it appear impotent,

7

and with no handy island to conceal themselves . . . 'I shall think on it, Mr Kendall,' he said, and began pacing up and down. Nothing came of it so he went out on deck. It was pleasant under the quarterdeck awning, now permanently rigged, and by his order all officers had doffed coat and waistcoat and now felt the breeze gratefully through loose shirts.

'Sir,' acknowledged Curzon, the officer-of-the-watch, touching his hat. 'A conclusion, at all?'

'Mayhap we'll sight a scout tomorrow. We stay off and on this coast – he'll come from the north, if he does.'

'Aye aye, sir.'

Kydd looked about the bright seascape, then at the distant palm-fringed shore. It would not do to dignify these remote outposts with a visit by a full post-captain, Royal Navy, so he had never once set foot on *this* Africa, with its steaming tropical forests and all the mystery of an unknown continent, so different from the south. Perhaps one day . . .

''Scuse me, sir.' An anxious voice broke into his thoughts. It was Searle, one of the volunteers of the first class, brought on board in those dark months before Trafalgar – less than a year before, Kydd realised, with surprise.

The young lad was all but unrecognisable as the pale, terrified schoolboy who had presented himself, resolutely determined to be an admiral one day. Now he was inches taller, lithe and brown, with confidence yet still a degree of modesty about him. Here was his next midshipman.

In his inattention Kydd had nearly tripped over the bight of a circle of long-splicing that the lad was working on. He picked up the piece and squinted down its length. 'Why, that is a caution to the fo'c'slemen themselves, I'd swear.' On the gratings a blank-faced seaman sat cross-legged. A wash of warmth came at the sight of Doud, lined and tattooed, the picture of a deep-sea mariner. Long ago it had been this man who had made it possible for him, a raw landman, to climb the rigging to the main-top in the old *Royal Billy* at Spithead. Later he had ventured out on the main-yard, to the topsail yard and then—

Suddenly he had it! This thinking about masts and yards, sails – a frigate would rightly shy from another if the mission was more important, but if it came across easy meat, a contemptible little sloop, perhaps, then it could make to capture it or even ignore it. Either way it could be enticed closer until the fast-sailing *L'Aurore* had a chance of closing with it.

'Mr Oakley!' he hailed, striding back to the quarterdeck. 'I have a pretty problem in the article of rigging, and I'd be obliged if you'd attend on me.'

It took some explaining, but it brought a broad grin to the red-headed boatswain, who stumped off forward, bawling for his men. It was hard work, but by the ringing of eight bells at the beginning of the dog-watches it was done, and over supper and grog the seamen had something daring to talk about.

The morning dawned clear and bright, the weather perfect for Kydd's plans: a gentle warm breeze, a flat, calm seascape and crystal visibility to the northern horizon. It was time to prepare.

'Strike all sail, if y' please,' he said. Canvas vanished from every yard and was furled above in a tight harbour stow. *L'Aurore* slowed and then idly drifted.

'Stream the sea-anchor,' he ordered. A canvas triangle on a line was lowered over the transom. The frigate felt its gentle tug as the pressure of the south-setting Mozambique current took charge, *L'Aurore*'s bows swinging obediently to face into it – to the north.

It was time for the finale. 'Rig false sails, Mr Oakley,' Kydd demanded.

From half a hundred blocks came the squealing of sheaves as quite another suit of sails fell from the yards. 'Brace around, y' sluggards!' But this was not to catch the wind at the most effective angle – it was the opposite. Each yard was trimmed edge on to the slight breeze, the sails hanging shivering and impotent. Any with the slightest acquaintance of a full-rigged ship would have been mightily puzzled to see *L'Aurore* now. An ingenious system of tackles and beckets allowed her to set topsails where the lower course would be, topgallants from the topsail yards and royals above. In effect, setting the frigate's sail plan down by one tier.

This gave her the appearance of a small Indiaman, trying a dash inside Madagascar instead of the more direct route on the far side. Men looked up in wonder at their Lilliputian fit of sails, and overside at their total lack of motion. Kydd gave a half-smile: this was not normally the way a full-blooded frigate faced the enemy.

There was not long to wait. Within an hour there was an excited hail from the masthead. To the north, square sail! Long minutes later another cry confirmed it as a three-master. Unable to restrain himself Kydd leaped for the shrouds and joined the lookout in the bare fore-topgallant masthead. He fumbled for his pocket telescope and steadied it on the far distant blob of white. There, unmistakably, was a full-rigged ship and he waited impatiently for its hull to lift above the horizon.

Eventually, to his intense satisfaction, Kydd saw a single line of gun-ports along the length of the ship. No merchantman this: a frigate on the loose without a shadow of a doubt.

He snapped his glass shut and, with a tigerish grin at the lookout, swung down to the deck again. 'It's him. We'll soon see if we've gulled the looby.'

L'Aurore lay barely lifting with the slight sea. With no way on, only the idle rattle and bang of gear aloft intruded on the senses. It was not Kydd's plan to engage in battle: his priority was to rely on *L'Aurore*'s proven speed to keep with the ship until he was led to the squadron. There might well be additional frigates waiting to trap him between two fires but this was a chance he had to take.

'*He's seen us, an' alterin' towards!*' The lookout's hail was gleeful.

The Frenchman was hopefully seeing an Indiaman unhappily becalmed, as so often in these seas: one vessel could be in useful breezes while another lying off only a few miles could be hopelessly adrift. The sea-anchor was doing its work; with *L'Aurore*'s bow end on towards the frigate, her warlike details would remain hidden for a while longer.

By now the ship steadily heading their way could be sighted from the deck. When should Kydd throw off his disguise? It couldn't last for ever – but just as soon as he did so his quarry would instantly shy off. Or not – it might be a heavy frigate, eighteen-pounders against *L'Aurore*'s twelves, determined to crush him to preserve the secret of his squadron in the offing . . .

'Post your men, Mr Oakley,' Kydd ordered quietly. There was no way he could clear for action until the rat's nest of improvised sails and rigging had been dismantled and that had better be quick.

'Damn – he's been spooked!' spluttered Gilbey, the first lieutenant, shading his eyes against the fierce glare of sunlight on the sea.

Kydd balled his fists in frustration: the masts were

separating to show the frigate turning away. 'Get us round!' he roared. A second sea-anchor was hurled over the opposite stern-quarters and hauled on sharply, the bows being bodily rotated to maintain *L'Aurore*'s bowsprit on the other ship – but things were happening so slowly.

A few minutes later Kendall caught Kydd's eye. 'Sir, I do not think he's running. Doesn't he desire to keep a'tween us and the land – an' at the same time catch a land breeze?'

Kydd nodded. 'He thinks to prevent our escape to the shallows inshore? Not bad – but he doesn't know who we are or he wouldn't dare.'

The ship was in plain view now, heeling more to the fluky north-easterly, seeking to take a commanding situation closer to the land. How much longer could he— A warning slap of impatient canvas above answered the question, but Kydd was becoming uneasy: something about the French ship was odd.

'Be buggered!' Oakley burst out suddenly. 'That's no mong-seer frigate! It's some sort o' ship-sloop, one o' them corvettes.'

So keyed up had they been to expect a frigate that, at a distance, they had taken the corvette, a ship-rigged sloop much favoured by the French, as one. In appearance it was near to a miniature frigate, with a single gun-deck, all the sail plan and rigging identical – but much smaller. And, of course, to humble fisher-folk such a ship would appear enormous.

Now the tables were now well and truly turned.

The corvette's helm was put hard over. 'Get us under sail – now!' roared Kydd. The crazy rag-tag rigging was cast off, false sails cascading over the deck in a chaotic jumble to be frantically scooped clear while the topmen raced out on the yards to loose their real canvas.

The shock of recognition could almost be felt over

the distance, and in minutes the corvette slewed sharply and set off inshore in an attempt to shake off the bigger ship in the shallows.

'Move y'selves!' Kydd bellowed up into the tops. He had no wish at all to try conclusions among the maze of shoals offshore, for the corvette was now heading towards the land under a press of sail that suggested confidence born of sound local knowledge.

'You're going after him?'

He hadn't noticed Renzi come up from below.

'Of course! This is your foxy Maréchal, properly keeps his frigates with his squadron and sends out squiddy ship-sloops or similar. Can't be better – we can always out-sail and out-gun the villain. I'm to take him and I've a notion this captain has a tale to tell.'

'That seems a reasonable supposition, old fellow. And if you—'

'Get those men off the yard!' bawled Kydd, in exasperation. The corvette was now well in with the land, nearly lost against the contrasting vegetation and sand-hills. Until the men were off the spar the yard could not be braced round to catch the wind, but the furl had been as tight as possible to escape detection and two sailors were still scrabbling to cast off gaskets.

They finished, and crabbed frantically along the footrope inward to the top. 'Brace up roundly!' Kydd roared instantly, and the men threw themselves into it with a will, jerking the yard around to catch the wind, but the last one off the yard missed his hold and fell backwards with a shriek, cut off when he bounced off the bellying lower sail and into the sea.

'*Man oooverboooaaard!*'

Kydd hesitated only for a moment, then blurted the orders

13

to heave to and lower a boat. His features were thunderous. 'Where away?' he called to the after lookout. Obediently the man pointed – it was his duty to keep his eyes fixed on the unfortunate in the water until the boat came up with him.

The gig in the stern davits was swung out to serve as the ship's lifeboat and it kissed the water smartly, stroking strongly away at the lookout's direction and soon found the topman, who lay gasping as they hauled him over the gunwale. The boat lost no time in making it back.

'Where is that damned villain?' Kydd spluttered, vainly casting about, looking for their quarry. 'The lookouts, ahoy! How's the Frenchy bear?'

There was no answer. He realised they had glanced away to check the progress of their shipmate's rescue and neglected their duty. He had now lost sight of the chase. 'I'll see those scowbunking beggars afore me tomorrow, Mr Gilbey,' he threw at his first lieutenant angrily.

Had the corvette gone north – or south? Choose the wrong one and he would lose this precious chance of at least establishing that Maréchal was at large in the Indian Ocean and at best gaining a notion of the squadron's rendezvous position. Back to the north? That would mean a run near close-hauled in this slight wind and, as well, against the current. To the south would give a handsome quartering breeze and going with the current – but was this what the other captain wished him to conclude?

'Bear away t' the south, if you please,' Kydd decided. This was something *L'Aurore* did well, a slight wind on the quarter – there were few that could stay with her in those conditions and if the Frenchman had headed to the south he would quickly overhaul it. And on the other hand if it was not sighted within a few hours he could be certain that it was off to the north. Then any contest between one out with the ocean breezes and the other anxiously dodging the shallows would be a foregone conclusion.

Their only chart was a single small-scale one painstakingly copied from the Portuguese of nearly a century before, sketchily detailing the littoral with precious few depth soundings – and the mud-banks would surely have shifted in the years since then. Closing with the coast as near as they dared, they could be sure, however, that the brightness of the chase sails could be seen against the darker shore.

The land slid past, a dense variegation in dark green with occasional palms and small hills in otherwise unrelieved flatness. After three hours there had been no sighting.

'He's gone north. 'Bout ship, Mr Curzon,' Kydd ordered.

It was late afternoon: they had to press on to overhaul the corvette before night fell giving it cover to escape. 'Bowlines to the bridle, Mr Curzon,' Kydd said crisply, ordering the edge of the big driving sails drawn out forward for maximum speed. *L'Aurore* stretched out nobly for the horizon to the north, her wake creaming ruler-straight astern and lookouts doubled aloft.

An hour – two, more – and still there was no sign.

Perplexed, Kydd and the sailing master did their calculations. With an essentially onshore wind there was no possibility that their quarry could have made a break directly to seaward while they were away in the south, and even if they had made off as close to the wind as they could, their 'furthest on' was still firmly within the circle of visibility of *L'Aurore*'s masthead. It was a mystery.

'He's gone t' ground,' Gilbey growled.

'Aye, but where?'

There was no response.

'I rather think up a river,' Renzi suggested.

'In a ship-rigged vessel?' Gilbey said scornfully. 'Even a mongseer corvette draws more'n the depth o' water of any African river I've seen.'

'Then are you not aware that under our lee is the great Zambezi River, which for prodigious size is matched only by your Congo?'

'Nobody but a main fool would take a ship up among all th' crocodiles an' such,' Gilbey replied, but stood back as the master brought up the chart and they saw that indeed the river entered the sea close by – but with an awkward twist. Like the Nile, it ended in a delta of many mouths – four, at least.

'You're right, Nicholas,' Kydd agreed. 'But up a river? If he's there, he's trapped, but then how to get at him?'

'Sure t' be boats against broadsides,' Gilbey muttered.

'Right,' said Kydd, briskly, ignoring him. 'Which mouth's it to be, gentlemen? Four – we'll take 'em one at a time.'

Kydd did not add that, quite apart from the time it would need, there was the possibility that their prey could go inland and around, then scuttle out of one of the other mouths. They being near to forty miles apart, it would be impossible to tell from which he would emerge. 'We start with the first 'un – the Chinde River, it says here,' he said, tapping the chart.

So close in, it was an easy fix when the first Zambezi mouth was sighted. Discoloured water could be seen more than five miles out, and across their path was the white of breaking seas on a monstrous bar a mile across and extending directly out to sea for three – just one branch of a giant African river endlessly disgorging into the ocean from the vast and mysterious interior.

'I'm not taking her in,' Kydd told Renzi. 'Moor offshore, send in a boat. Go myself, I believe, reconnoitre what we're up against,' he added casually, inviting Renzi along, too. He left unspoken that it was also a chance to satisfy his curiosity and see the wonders of tropical Africa. The odds were against the corvette lying hidden in the very first river mouth they visited.

Kydd's barge was of modest draught and not designed for fighting, but they were not expecting any. With his coxswain, Poulden, at the tiller, Renzi in the sternsheets with him, four hands ready for the oars and Doud in the eyes of the boat with a hand lead, they pushed off under sail.

They passed along in the lee of the bar. A channel of some depth quickly became evident, which they used to follow into the estuary – a two-mile-wide sprawl of constantly sliding grey-green water. They then left behind the ceaseless hurry of the sea's waves and cool breezes for the lowering heat and humidity, the echoing quiet and rich stink of the dark continent.

The sailors looked about, fascinated. On either bank was the uniform low tangle of mangroves from which a miasma of decay drifted out as uncountable numbers of birds beat their way into the air at their intrusion. Bursts of harsh sounds from hidden creatures came on the air and insects swarmed annoyingly.

Doud urgently hailed aft: "Ware rocks!'

Ahead were three or four bare brown humps – but as they watched one disappeared and others turned to offer gaping mouths. 'Hippos!' Renzi said, and others turned to watch, exclaiming excitedly.

'Eyes in the boat!' Kydd growled. The age-old call to boat discipline seemed out of keeping on a frigate's barge in an

African river and a sense of unreality crept in. Naval service had taken him to many exotic places in the world but this promised to be the strangest.

Where the estuary narrowed, the mangroves gave way to low grassy banks and open woodland. At the water's edge were four of the largest crocodiles Kydd had ever seen, basking in the late-afternoon sun. The boat glided past them in silence, every man thinking of the consequences of pitching overboard.

Somewhere far upstream the wet season was sending down vast quantities of water, swelling the river and bringing brown silt, tearing clumps of earth from the bank and with it masses of vegetation, occasionally even floating islands of light woodland.

The river took a sharp left turn, Kydd straining for any sign of the French ship. He didn't need Doud's patient soundings to know that there was more than enough water for even a ship-sloop.

Or a frigate? Kydd dismissed the thought quickly. There would be sufficient depth but these sharp bends were beyond a square-rigger to negotiate. If the corvette was up one of these river mouths it would be because it had been towed up by its boats against the current; out of the question with *L'Aurore*. 'Keep to the outer side o' the bends,' Kydd told Poulden. 'It'll be deepest there.'

Obediently the tiller went over but as they neared the opposite bank a well-trodden open area came into view with a family of elephants drinking and splashing. They looked up in surprise: indignant, one made to rush at them but stopped and lifted its trunk, trumpeting angrily. A screeching bird flapped overhead.

The loop opened up but only to reveal another bend

winding out of sight. The evening was drawing in, bringing with it clouds of midges. The warm, breathy breeze was dropping: much less and it would be 'out oars' and a hard pull. By now they were near a dozen miles inland and no sign of any Frenchman.

It was time to return. 'That's enough, Poulden, we're going back,' Kydd said, twisting to see what Renzi was pointing at.

'Is that not . . . or am I sun-touched?' A piece of floating debris, caught on the bank at the sharpest point of the bend, had a regular shape that seemed to owe nothing to nature.

'Take us near,' Kydd ordered. As they drew closer his interest quickened.

'Brail up!' he snapped. When the boat lost way he motioned it into the muddy bank where it softly nudged in next to the half-buried object.

'Haul it in, Doud,' he called. The seaman wiggled it free of the mud and pulled inboard a stout round object, familiar to any seaman. The provision cask was passed down the boat to Kydd. Burned into the staves was the barely decipherable legend: '*Marie Galante*' and underneath roman numerals, then 'Rochefort' with a date.

'Ha! He's here, an' just broached his supper,' Kydd grunted, smelling the interior disdainfully. Not only had they the name of the corvette but Rochefort was the port from which Maréchal had sailed. 'Bear off, and haul out back up the river.'

Under way once more the feeling of unreality increased. Evening was setting in, livid orange inland under a long violet cloud-line with shadows advancing, yet here they were, closing with the enemy.

They swept around the left-hand bend and still another lay ahead to the right. Then, sharp black in the evening sky, above

19

the growth of the intervening bend, they saw the upperworks of a full-rigged ship.

'Easy!' Kydd snapped. 'Down sail, out oars. Now, Poulden, take us close in. Then I want you to quant us around slowly so I can take a peek without disturbing 'em at their supper.'

Using an upturned oar, the barge was poled along, nosing slowly around until Kydd, leaning over the bow, suddenly hissed, 'Avast! Keep us there.'

The bend opened into a lengthy reach nearly a half-mile long – and at its further end was their chase. Kydd fumbled for his spy-glass and trained it on the vessel. He looked intently to see how it was defended.

'The cunning beggar,' he murmured, with reluctant admiration. 'As he's made himself as snug as a duck in a ditch!'

The ship was securely moored by bow and stern to the side of the bank at the far end of the reach where her captain could have maximum warning of a cutting-out attack by boats. This also gave an excellent field of fire for, with the guns levered around, it would be an impossibly bloody affair if they approached in boats to storm it.

Kydd lifted the glass again and carefully quartered the riverbank alongside the ship. Men were slashing down the vegetation to create an open space; covered by their opposite broadside, an assault by land would be just as murderous. That left an attack after dark – but a captain so canny would have a boat out to row night guard; illuminations would follow any intrusion and the result would be the same.

He lowered the glass and slid it shut. He couldn't ask his men to take on such odds even with the stakes of intelligence to be won. The *Marie Galante* was perfectly safe: they could stay for as long as patience held out, for water and a supply of meat were on hand and it would need only occasional boat trips to tell them when *L'Aurore* had given up and sailed away. It was galling but it had to be accepted: the Frenchman had prevailed.

There was now no other course than to sail back to Cape Town, bearing the tantalising news that Maréchal appeared to be at large but where or when and with what force was anybody's guess.

'Return,' he told Poulden, and made his way back to the sternsheets with Renzi.

His coxswain waited for a sizeable mat of vegetation to be carried past by the current before poling out, then told his crew to hoist sail. The boat curved around, carefully avoiding the relic of torn riverbank that had come down from far up the mysterious Zambezi. Kydd's thoughts, however, were on what he could do to retrieve something from the situation. At least they didn't have to search up the remaining three mouths and—

A preposterous idea entered his mind that teased him with its possibilities. He twisted round to glance back whence they'd come. Yes – it could work if . . .

'Poulden. Lay us alongside the floating greenery, if y' please.'

The coxswain gave him a puzzled glance but did as requested. Close to, it was a substantial piece of densely matted vegetation, grass of quite another kind from that growing on nearby banks, tall, thick and wreathed with tangling creepers. On one side there were even young saplings and a sprawling bush.

'Seize on,' Kydd called to the bowman, who gingerly felt with his boat-hook. The boat swung closer with the current – and Kydd stepped on to the little island, taking care to keep a hold on the boat's gunwale. It gave a little under his weight and he dared to stand upright. Something near his foot hissed and slithered rapidly away, while a large clumsy bird with a fleshy beak burst out of the bush, cawing.

Kydd trod further into the thick undergrowth. It felt surprisingly substantial and he called to two of the seamen to join him. One caught an ankle and fell prostrate with a frightened oath. The island swayed a little but seemed not to object. They had a chance.

After dinner, Kydd called a council of war aboard *L'Aurore*.

'Gentlemen, the corvette rightly assumes our only means of attack is by boat and he's taking every precaution to defend against it. In the main he's lying at the head of a straight passage of the river and knows he's a line of sight that will warn him in plenty of time of an assault. Of a certainty he has his guns trained downriver to slaughter any in attacking boats.' In quick, bold pencil strokes, he sketched out the situation on a sheet of paper.

He paused and looked up. 'We will be going in, however.' Troubled glances were exchanged. 'But not from the direction he expects. We'll be coming from upstream.'

'Ah,' Curzon said instantly. 'How are we first going to get our boats past him? Even under cover of dark we'll be—'

'We don't!'

'Sir?'

'The boats will be advancing upstream – but not until we've boarded him.'

'I – I don't follow you, sir.'

Kydd explained about the floating islands. 'Six boarders concealed in one to signal down the reach when they're in sight so we'll know which island they're aboard. This tells the boats to come into view and begin their attack, drawing the attention of the French entirely to what they've been expecting.

22

'When abreast the bowsprit of the corvette, the island will be brought alongside and our men will swarm aboard from nowhere to spread alarm and confusion. At this point from concealed positions inland Lieutenant Clinton will order his marines to open a hot fire, which will dismay the defenders, they not knowing his force or what they face.

'Caught between three lines of attack, he'll be in a sad moil and that's when we strike home. Questions?'

After several minutes' digesting the details of this unconventional cutting-out action, Curzon broke the silence: 'Just the one, sir. Any signal hoisted on the, er, island will necessarily be seen by even the most dim-witted o' the French. How, then, are we to preserve our surprise?'

Renzi came in: 'The ancients got there before us, of course, gentlemen. You will recollect that, at Thermopylae, news of the advance of the Persian host under Xerxes was relayed across the plains to King Leonidas of Sparta by—'

'Be s' kind as t' spare us your history, Mr Renzi, we've a war to figure.'

Gilbey's sarcasm brought a frown from Kydd. 'Do fill and stand on, Renzi, old chap. We're all listening.'

'—by polished shields flashing in the sunlight. I rather thought a mirror in our case,' he added.

'Just so,' Kydd said, with satisfaction. Renzi had on more than one occasion retrieved a situation by recourse to his classical education. 'Taking care to shield it from being spied by the corvette, naturally.'

'Um, er—'

'Mr Bowden?' He acknowledged the third lieutenant.

'This floating island, sir. If it's to be brought alongside the Frenchy – er, how does it steer, as we might say?'

'A boat grapnel. The corvette is moored on the inside of

the bend. The grapnel is cast overside when still out of sight and paid out until we are near abreast. Hauling taut on the line will cause the island to swing into the bank.'

There was a ripple of approval. It was shaping up.

'It'll in course be m'self commanding on the island,' Gilbey pronounced.

'As first lieutenant your duty is the main attack, not the diversion,' Kydd said shortly. 'I shall take care of that.'

'What will be our force in its entirety, pray?' Curzon asked.

'Every boat that swims, all the Royals with our idlers as their loaders. And all volunteers, mark you. You shall be second to Mr Gilbey and Mr Bowden will taste command of a frigate for the first time.'

Bowden jerked upright. 'Sir, I must protest! This is—'

'You object to a frigate command at your age, sir? Fie on you!' Kydd chuckled. 'No, younker, I need to know *L'Aurore* is in safe hands while we're away. Can you think of a better? Oh, and you shall have Mr Renzi for company,' he added firmly.

'This'll do,' Kydd muttered quietly. Poulden brought the barge to the riverbank safely, lower down the river from the corvette, and the 'island party' sprang ashore: gunner's mate Stirk, who would not be denied his place; boatswain Oakley, who had sworn that only himself could be relied upon with the grapnel; boatswain's mate Cumby, who had demanded by right to be at his side; Pearse, the raw-boned master's mate, with a yen to have something to boast of when he returned home; and Wong Hay Chee, former circus strongman and inseparable friend of Stirk.

Nearby, the launch and both cutters began setting the Royal Marines ashore with their number twos – the idlers, those such as the sailmaker's crew, and stewards who did not stand a watch at sea but could be relied on for the mechanical task of reloading muskets.

There was a three-quarter moon riding high and Kydd cursed under his breath. The assembling men were in plain view, and even if they were doing their best to stay quiet, the clink and leather slap of equipment seemed so loud in the night air. 'L'tenant Clinton,' he whispered hoarsely, to the Royal Marines' officer, 'do you prove your men's weapons. If any fires accidentally, I'll personally slit his gizzard and after that I'll court-martial the villain. Is that clear?' Of all things, a musket shot would be best calculated to arouse the enemy instantly.

Clinton smiled and offered him a bag that clicked as he passed it over. 'I've taken precautions, sir. These are their flints without which their muskets will not fire.' Mollified, Kydd nodded.

A mile or so downstream from the corvette, they would travel in a straight line over the knee-bend in the river to arrive at a point upstream and out of sight from the French, on the way leaving the marines to take position. The boats would retire and wait until full daylight before coming up. Then all would depend on the island party.

They set out. The low, undulating land was mainly open scrub with thicker areas of bushes. The moonlight was not enough to locate the corvette but Kydd had a small pocket compass that allowed him to set a course to intersect the river above the vessel and led off in that direction.

At night the African bush was a petrifying experience: every little sound seemed loaded with menace, and although there were more than fifty men with Kydd, they were strung out behind. His imagination conjured up all manner of dangers.

If a lion sprang out on him . . . or one of those beasts with a horn on its nose? If it took a rage against him at the head of the column, then well before the others could . . .

'Keep closed up,' he snarled at the marines behind him, drawing his cutlass to slash at an inoffensive bush, then keeping it out at point. He had left his fighting sword aboard ship – in the bloody hacking of a boarding, its fine qualities would not be essential, and if it was lost in a swamp somewhere he would never forgive himself.

'Sir!' Clinton pointed into the silvery distance on the left. The upper spars of the *Marie Galante* were visible about a mile away.

'Very good,' Kydd said, stopping. 'You know your orders. Keep the men at a distance until daybreak, then close up to your positions when you hear firing begin.'

'Yes, sir.'

'It's of the first importance that you are not seen before—'

'I understand, sir,' the young officer said stiffly.

'Of course you do. Farewell and good luck.'

Kydd strode ahead with nervous energy. They reached the river unexpectedly, its glittering expanse suddenly in view.

'Down!' he hissed. The others in his little group lowered themselves gingerly to the ground, its earthy odour pungent, while Kydd checked forward. On his left was the tight bend that, according to his reckoning, opened to the long reach – and the French corvette.

Bent double, he skirted some bushes but before he reached the end he froze: a playful night breeze had brought with it a wafting hint of tobacco smoke. And, by its pungency, not the honest Virginian issued aboard *L'Aurore*. Parting the bush infinitely slowly, he swallowed. Not more than a dozen yards away two sentries stood in the moonlight, the occasional glow of their pipes startlingly red. They were conversing with each other in low tones, their muskets slung over their shoulders.

Kydd withdrew with the utmost care. The sentinels posted upstream spoke of a thoroughly professional opponent: were there more at the far end of the reach? This would make it near impossible for the boats to assemble unseen – but doing so would draw all attention downstream, as he wanted.

'Sentries!' he whispered to his party, when he reached them. 'We'll go a little further upstream.'

Another hundred yards brought them to the next curve of the river and a convenient slope to the water. It would do.

'Er, how about them crocodiles, sir?' Pearse asked edgily, quite out of character for the brash youth on the quarterdeck.

'Take no mind o' them,' Kydd said confidently. 'They're all asleep.' They were cold-blooded so it stood to reason, didn't it?

They settled in the bushes to wait for the night to end. Then the moon vanished and blackness enfolded them. Continuous rustles and scurries came from all directions. From not far away they heard a blood-freezing roar and the piercing death squeal of some animal being taken. And as they crouched together every man sensed a massive presence out in the darkness, close, moving.

Filled with dread, they gripped their puny weapons. A cutlass against one of Renzi's hippos? Whatever it was, there was no betraying sound and it wasn't until long minutes had passed that they realised it had moved on.

At last the first rosy lightening of the sky spread from the east and, with tropical swiftness, it was day. A precautionary look around gave no reason for alarm.

The river was wreathed with rising mist, shot through with the luminous pearly light of morning, insects darting about prettily.

Kydd got to his feet. 'Mr Oakley, you've the grapnel?'

'Aye, sir.'

'Then let's find ourselves an island.'

They went to the water's edge, the boatswain testing his swing and Kydd watching upstream, but none of the right size hove into view; any number of pieces of floating debris appeared out of the mist but none to match the stout pad Kydd had tested only the day before.

With impatience giving way to anxiety, Kydd continued to watch for their island. The light grew and strengthened. They couldn't delay much longer. When a rather lopsided but more substantial piece emerged from the white haze, clearly clumped about a central strong sapling, he ordered, 'There, Mr Oakley, we'll try him.'

It was more than thirty yards away but Oakley's cast was unerring and soon it was pulled into the bank.

'Get aboard, Stirk – see if you like it.'

Obediently the gunner's mate waded out to where it was nudging the shallows and hauled himself on. It swayed but seemed to hold firm as Stirk cast about in the tall grass. 'It'll fadge, sir, I shouldn't wonder,' he finally called back.

The harsh grass looked an excellent hiding place. 'Right, all aboard!' Kydd said briskly, ensuring that their weapons were passed first to Stirk. Cutlasses, a brace of pistols apiece – pitifully little to stand against a broadside of guns.

'Yo-ho, an' it's all a-taunt in the tight little *Pollywobble*,' clowned Pearse, once he was safely on.

'Stow it, y' idiot,' grunted Stirk, helping the barrel-shaped Wong to clamber aboard.

'I'll be forrard,' Kydd said, 'Mr Oakley at the stern with the grapnel. The rest of you hunker down amidships.' The characterless mass of undergrowth was hardly a ship but order had to be brought to an utterly unseamanlike situation, and it seemed to be accepted without question by the 'crew'.

'Cast off!'

Oakley released his hold on the bank and the island floated free. Another cast of the grapnel enabled him to haul out to mid-stream and they were on their way. Kydd took a last look about to make sure all was concealed and, with his shaving mirror to hand, Oakley aft with the grapnel watching him expectantly, they drifted languorously up to the last bend.

Concentrating furiously on the tightening ripples, Kydd judged the moment right and nodded to Oakley, who let the grapnel plunge to the riverbed while he paid out the line. Kydd lay full length among the rich-smelling vegetation, carefully parting the grasses to see ahead. Behind him there was muffled conversation and nervous laughter, which was brought to a sudden stop by the boatswain's sharp growl.

In company with scattered other oddments of flotsam the island slowly cleared the bend – and not two hundred yards ahead lay their target. A fleeting panic washed over Kydd: a lump of floating grass going head to head with a corvette of the French Navy! He fought the feeling down and took up the mirror. Glancing up at the low sun to get the angle just right and shielding it carefully he gave the signal – three times three.

Would they respond?

The corvette seemed utterly unconcerned, a few men idly standing on the bank, a wisp of smoke issuing from the galley funnel forward, the colours not yet hoisted. His gaze flicked back to the end of the reach. No boats!

Apprehension gripped him – had they not seen the signal or was it that they had been intercepted? The island was inexorably being carried down past the moored vessel. Should he go ahead with the boarding or cravenly stay hidden and drift on to safety? Then it would—

The distant thump of a swivel gun sounded and there – gloriously – was Gilbey's launch, closely followed by Curzon's cutter and then the others, spreading out across the river to make a broad approach. The frantic baying of a trumpet sounded aboard the corvette, with harsh, urging shouts. Men boiled up from below, scattering to take position at the guns.

Now the island's languid drift was maddeningly slow – it would take for ever to reach *Marie Galante*, which lay with its elegant bowsprit towards them but was still some way off. However, Kydd did see not a single flash of faces looking back; it was working entirely to plan.

Gilbey had a quarter-mile of relative safety before the guns of the corvette, levered around to bear aft as far as they could, were in a position to open fire. He used the time well, pausing to get off a good aimed shot from his bow-mounted eighteen-pounder carronade. The other boats did likewise and the corvette suffered two hits, both of which brought shrieks and cries.

The boats, pulling like madmen, were not far from the point of no return where the guns could smash in their deadly grape-shot and canister. Feverishly Kydd willed on their own ungainly craft, only fifty yards or so but—

'Sir!' It was Stirk, pulling at his ankle. 'Sir – the barky's sinkin'!'

Kydd's attention jerked back to their island and he twisted round to see. One edge of the island was drooping, bright water among the grass. 'Clear that side – and keep the damned pistols dry!' he hissed. He took his own out and laid them on a tussock. A minute later, an entire slab tore away and slowly sank, leaving what remained noticeably lower in the water.

The Zambezi lapped inches from Kydd's nose and he felt the coolness of water seeping under his body. There was now every reason to suppose it could tip to one side or even break up, throwing them all to the crocodiles. Should he tell Oakley to pull into the bank now or—

Kydd's mind snapped to a ferocious icy calm. If the island sank, that was something he could do nothing about, but if it remained afloat there was work to do. 'Stand by, the grapnel!' he said levelly. The order was relayed by Stirk behind him.

Only yards away the corvette loomed larger and larger but not a soul was visible, all out of sight at the guns on the main-deck. Where should he bring in his crazy craft? The bowsprit reared up from a neat beakhead, revealing a small half-deck within it and a dainty figurehead at its apex. Perfect. They would come in under the shadow of the bow, swing up on the stout boomkin over the headrails to the half-deck, pass up the weapons, then appear on the fo'c'sle deck above the guns.

There was a sudden lurch and a muffled cry, and the island rotated as it rid itself of another clump. The crackle and sputter of musketry above meant that the boats were close – the guns would very shortly be opening fire to cause slaughter in those who had so gamely trusted him. He must not fail after all this . . . The bowsprit was nearing . . .

'Haul taut!' he gasped at last.

The effect was almost instant and Kydd craned round. The boatswain had turns around the sapling and was controlling it in just the same way as a hawser around capstan whelps, his fierce grin a joy to see. The island wallowed and swayed but obediently crabbed sidewise in the current, coming closer and closer – and then, incredibly, they were under the trim bow and among the martingale and bobstays. Kydd thrust up for the boomkin and walked his feet over the carved headrails and rolled on to the half-deck gratings.

With the tumult above, there was little need for quiet. 'Pass up the weapons,' he hissed, leaning down to grab them. Stirk heaved himself up to the opposite side to do likewise. The men scrambled up thankfully and their near waterlogged craft was abandoned to drift away. A quick muster showed all present – seconds counted now – and Kydd hauled himself up and over the fife-rail on to the fo'c'sle deck.

In a flash he took in the scene: the sweep aft of the open deck below with its guns manned and at the far end the raised quarterdeck, muskets over the taffrail pouring in fire at the boats, figures standing apart, who had to be officers – and all with their attention fixed on their attackers. He took in other things, too: the neat order about the ship that spoke of care and professionalism, the shininess of the ropes from aloft that betrayed their long service at sea and the fact that the guns were manned on one side only: the crew was short-handed, probably for the same reason.

Stirk appeared beside him, then the others, in each hand boarding pistols and a cutlass to the side. With a lopsided grin, Kydd acknowledged the absurdity of reaching an enemy deck in a boarding and having the luxury of a steadying deep breath before the fight. 'Ready, gentlemen?'

Savage growls answered and, stalking to the after edge of the deck, he howled, 'King George and the *Billy Roarer*!' then plunged down to the main-deck, making for the nearest gun.

The crew wheeled round, gaping. He levelled one pistol

and shot the gun-captain, who dropped instantly. The other he fired directly at a large seaman who had reared up, snarling. The man fell back and dropped to his knees, clutching his face with both hands, blood running through his fingers. Two of the crew fled but another two stood irresolute. Kydd flung a heavy pistol at the head of one, which sent him spinning down to be jolted violently by a hurtling body from behind.

Pistols banged about him, men were shrieking, but other gun-crews were recovering and making a rush for them. Kydd wrestled his cutlass free and got inside a red-faced gunner whirling a ramrod, neatly spitting him. Yanking the blade out as the man fell, he was in time to parry a maniacal swing from a boarding axe and in return opened the man's face in a spurting line of blood. He felt a savage blow to his side and whipped around to see a small cat-like seaman raise an iron gun-crow for a second strike – but he fell as if poleaxed when Pearse, yelling like a banshee, brought his cutlass down with a violent slash and, without stopping, ran on into the mad whirl of fighting.

Kydd found himself in combat with a dark-complexioned Arab, wielding a curved blade with two hands, the man making almost a ballet of his twisting and slashing, unnerving Kydd. Then his opponent tripped forward and impaled himself on his blade.

Kydd swivelled around and saw Oakley's body on the deck, the red hair unmistakable, blood issuing under him from some wound. Above him, the boatswain's mate was roaring in helpless anger as he swung and clashed with two murderous assailants. On the other side of the deck, Kydd caught sight of Pearse going down under a crowd of maddened gunners.

A terrible bull-like roar came from behind him. It was

Wong, armed with nothing but a capstan bar, insanely whirling it about his head as he lumbered into the fray, the heavy timber crushing, wounding, breaking and bringing the rush to a halt. It was magnificent, but couldn't last.

Then, from inland, an invisible army opened fire on the enemy end of the deck, dropping men, the savage whip of bullets creating disorder and panic. Volley after volley came – and any Frenchman who could do so swung in dismay to face the onslaught.

It was enough. Cheering wildly, the boats made it inside the arc of guns, and seamen were swarming aboard to fall on the defenders.

It was over very quickly: Frenchmen threw down their weapons and stood sullenly.

Panting and nursing his bruised side, Kydd stood to survey the carnage, then strode aft. 'Well done, Mr Gilbey,' he said, shaking his first lieutenant's hand. 'See to our men forward, will you?'

'*Qui est le capitaine?*' Kydd demanded of the group of disconsolate officers.

'He lies wounded below,' one replied sulkily.

'Then know that as of this moment your ship is in the possession of His Britannic Majesty.' Kydd's heart was still pounding from the heat of combat.

One of the officers offered his sword. He brushed it aside. 'The honours of war must wait for another time. Be so good as to muster your men aft.'

It was the well-tried routine of taking over a captured ship – but with a twist. Very conveniently he could empty the vessel of the enemy to assemble them under guard on the open ground of the riverbank while he sent Curzon and a party of men to perform the usual rapid search below decks.

The second lieutenant reported that *Marie Galante* was essentially undamaged and ready for sea – no mean prize.

Gilbey returned from forward. 'I'm truly sorry t' say Mr Pearse is no more, and Mr Oakley has been skelped – which is t' say, he's taken a whiffler to the head, but I've a notion he'll live,' he added hastily.

'Very good. Secure the ship – I want a talk with the captain.'

Kydd found the commander in a cot below in the sick-bay, his intelligent brown eyes reflecting a sea of pain. His lower body was soaked in blood from a broken-off splinter, dark and vicious, protruding from eviscerated flesh in his lower thigh.

Kydd felt for the man. He'd been unlucky enough to be caught by the carronade fire at the very outset of the engagement and the surgeon had not yet seen to him.

'*Mes félicitations, le capitaine,*' he gasped. 'A boat from upstream, masterly! Together with your overwhelming army. Of course, we stood no chance.' He was an older man, greying early, no doubt with the strain of keeping the seas for long months in fearful conditions. His gaze almost pleaded for understanding.

'Your dispositions were most intelligent, sir, as gave us much difficulty.' Kydd would not be the one to disillusion him on the details, and went on, 'I'm quite certain Admiral Maréchal will be the first to honour you for your gallant defence under such odds.'

Instantly the wounded man's expression stiffened, the pain kept ruthlessly at bay. 'You are no doubt from a frigate, Captain?'

Kydd caught himself. The question was both astute and pointed: this officer had foreseen the possibility that *L'Aurore* might well be a scout from a powerful British squadron looking to bring Maréchal to battle and would welcome any indication of his whereabouts. He would get nothing from this defeated captain.

More wounded men were being brought down and, at the appearance of the surly French surgeon, Kydd made his excuses and left.

Curzon was 'entertaining' the other officers in their own quarters. The second lieutenant, who spoke fluent French, was attempting to bring off a *risqué* story concerning Piccadilly and a lady of the town but it was being received in an icy silence by the two Frenchmen. At Kydd's interrogative glance he shook his head mutely.

He had the vessel but it was not yielding the information he craved. Frustrated, Kydd moved on to the captain's cabin. The master looked up from the working chart he had found. 'Nary a thing, sir,' he said, swivelling it round so Kydd could see. No squadron line of rendezvous – which could mean just as easily that there wasn't one as that it was being kept private. 'An' while m' French is nothing s' special, I didn't see a mention in his log.'

Kydd scanned the neat writing, noting the regular scientific observations that this captain was in the habit of making, but nowhere was there mention of the innumerable signals and irritations of life under the eye of an admiral. On the other hand it would be in keeping with the French character to separate the two, one being confidential. So, short of bringing pressure to bear on the French seamen . . .

He returned to the upper deck and saw them being herded into a square guarded by marines and seamen. Out in the open it was remarkable how many it took to man a ship – and, conversely, how such a large number could fit within the confines of a ship. And then he had an idea.

'Collas!' he called, to one of the carpenter's mates on a hasty survey with Legge, the carpenter.

The man loped aft.

'You're relieved of work. Go down and report to Mr Clinton that you've orders from me to guard the noisiest prisoners.'

'Sir?' Collas said, bewildered.

'You're a Guernseyman, know the French?' Channel Islanders lived within sight of the French coast, and even if their own patois had diverged considerably, they had a trading relationship of centuries standing.

'Aye, sir.'

'I want you to listen carefully for any mention of their Admiral Maréchal. Anything at all that bears on where he is now. Be sure to let 'em think you're a regular-going Jack Tar as is ignorant of the French lingo but keep your ears at full stretch. The minute you hear something, let me know. Understood?'

'Aye aye, sir,' Collas replied, knuckling his forehead.

Kydd's mind then turned to the task of getting *Marie Galante* downriver to the open sea. There was only one way for a square-rigger: boats. It was too much to expect the French to man the oars and, besides, it would cost too many men in the guarding. Fortunately, few would be necessary where they were at present in the open space ashore.

Then there were the technical requirements: any seaman knew that it was much harder to bring a vessel downriver for motion was deceptive: moving at speed relative to the shore might well mean that the ship, brought along by the current, was barely moving relative to the water itself and therefore the rudder could not bite. The ultimate indignity was to lose control and end broadside to the river, stuck immovably bow and stern. In a swift-flowing and massive river such as this, the consequences could be serious.

'Three boats ahead, one on the stern,' he decided. 'Her cable on the bitts and out through the hawse, then the three tows from one bridle.' This would ensure all towing effort would be from one position, rather than from several points on the structure, which might fight each other. The boat astern was there to correct any yawing. All depended on the boats pulling hard and keeping it going: only by moving through the water would the rudder be effective.

All except the wounded were landed and every man jack available was put to the oars. Kydd himself cast off the last line tethering *Marie Galante* to the bank after she had been swung around and headed downstream. The men stretched out like heroes. This was not simply their duty but the much more rewarding task of preserving their prize.

The long reach was useful in getting the feel of the craft under tow and, standing next to Poulden at the wheel, Kydd felt increasing confidence. The first bend arrived. Taking a wide and careful sweep, the boats hauled ahead manfully and they were around. The next came almost immediately. 'Pull, you lubbers!' roared Gilbey, from the fo'c'sle. 'Put y' backs into it!'

Kydd looked over the side. A noticeable ripple was forming a bow-wave: they were making way through the water and therefore under control. Taking the deeper outer curve they were well on their way. Poulden nodded as *Marie Galante* was obediently nudged into a deeper channel. Just another bend . . . The corvette emerging to the open sea with English colours would be a sight indeed from *L'Aurore*.

'Heave out, lay into it!' Gilbey's voice cracked with the effort. At this last bend before the estuary and the bar it was crucial to keep way on through the single deep cleft channel through to the blessed depths of the Indian Ocean.

Kydd watched in satisfaction. On return to *L'Aurore*, he would personally see that the men at the oars spliced the mainbrace – an extra grog ration, even if here it was Stellenbosch wine rather than rum—

There was a sudden thud that was more felt through the deck than heard. Seconds later there were baffled shouts from forward and Gilbey turned to bawl disbelievingly, 'The tow's parted!'

It was impossible. Kydd pounded up to see. This was why a bridle was in place at the end of the thick anchor cable: if any one boat-tow parted the rest would be preserved. It could only imply that the massive anchor cable itself had given way.

At the fo'c'sle he looked ahead: the boats were at all angles, men retrieving oars where they had lost them when the heavy tension had suddenly released, sending them headlong into the bottom of the boat. He looked down over the cathead to the hawse, expecting to see the catenary of the big cable curve away into the water – but it had vanished.

Kydd then realised it could mean just one thing: that it had parted inside the hawse after it had left the riding bitts where it was belayed. But this had no meaning! Bellowing an order to Poulden to keep his heading, he flew down the fo'c'sle ladder to the deck below. Then, wheeling round, he ran to the riding bitts – where things became all too clear. Sprawled on deck under the frayed strands of the cable was the blood-soaked body of the captain, a fire-axe flung nearby.

In great pain the man must have crawled up from the sick-bay and severed the cable, bringing about the destruction of his own ship. With a crushing sense of finality, Kydd ran aft and up the ladder to the quarterdeck.

'Not answering th' helm, sir,' Poulden said. In his hands the wheel was spinning uselessly.

They were now drifting; there was far too little time to rouse out another cable and all it needed was for a counter-flaw in the current at one end of the ship . . . and there it was. Her head fell off and she began a slewing across the river that got rapidly faster. With the softest of sensations her bow caught in the muddy bank. The colossal mass of water from up-country began taking the ship broadside, an irresistible force, which sent the other end immovably into the opposite bank.

Instantly the water piled up on the upstream side in an unstoppable flood – the deck canted over and racking timber groans from deep within sounded as death throes.

Gilbey came aft, raving impotently at the situation. Kydd cut him short: 'All boats alongside. Get the wounded out, then see what movables we can take.' He gave a wintry smile. 'And don't delay, we've not got long.'

Chapter 2

Kydd squinted down the deck to where the fo'c'sle party, in streaming oilskins, were preparing the bower anchor for their mooring, a wet and perilous exercise in the filthy weather from the north-west. Another ponderous roll of thunder echoed back from Table Mountain and, ahead, ships jibbed nervously under the bluster of autumn wind and grey, fretful seas.

From the fo'c'sle Curzon's arm shot up and Kydd acknowledged. They were ready to take their place and let slip the anchor past the throng of merchant shipping among the naval squadron at the outer part of the Table Bay anchorage. And the captain of *L'Aurore*'s first duty was to pay his respects to Commodore Popham, the senior naval officer, Cape Colony.

Although he had lost the corvette he had returned with something much more precious. 'You have the deck, Mr Curzon. I'm going below to shift rig before I report.' It was a straightforward moor in the open roadstead, and Gilbey was on hand, but his second lieutenant glowed at the trust.

It was a bucketing, bruising pull to *Diadem*, the flagship, even in the launch that Kydd had called upon in place of his slighter-built barge. Walls of rain sluiced across, and despite boat-cloak and oilskins, he was soaked and chilled when he finally stepped into the commodore's cabin.

Popham regarded him without enthusiasm, saying testily, 'Kydd, do contrive to drip somewhere else, won't you?'

'My apologies, sir,' he said, handing his cocked hat to a servant. 'I do have news that I'm sanguine will interest you.'

'Oh?' Popham said coldly.

Kydd outlined his voyage succinctly, ending with his chase and capture of *Marie Galante* and her later loss by stranding.

'Can't be helped, I suppose,' Popham said, with feeling. It was well known that in his career at sea he had never been lucky in prize money. 'Butcher's bill?'

'We lost a master's mate, with two wounded in the boarding, and one killed and three hurt in the boats by musketry, sir. The French suffered eight dead and eleven wounded, including their captain, who bled to death after his deed.'

'Hmm. A small price for us, I'm bound to say. You have prisoners?'

'I have all the officers and skilled hands in *L'Aurore*, and I beg you will give instructions that will see a transport call at Quelimane, where I landed the common *matelots* for want of accommodation.'

'The next India-bound supply vessel will answer, I should think. Now, I don't suppose this corvette was with Maréchal at all?' Popham asked hopefully.

Kydd savoured the moment. 'No, sir, most definitely not.'

'Oh? You've questioned the officers, of course?'

'I did, but the intelligence I have for you came from quite another source.'

'Yes? What is that, pray?'

There was an impatient edge to his tone so Kydd went on quickly: 'I arranged for a Channel Islander to be in the guard over the prisoners. He overheard 'em say something that'll surely gratify. It seemed they were bemoaning the fate that sees them in chains in Cape Town while Maréchal and his squadron must be halfway home to Rochefort by now . . .'

'Ah! So! Excellent news! This could mean—'

'Their charts have no workings on it to suggest a fleet operation, their logs make no mention of a rendezvous and their last port o' call was Réunion. Confronted with it, their first lieutenant admitted it was so, that they were merely out on a cruise of depredation against our commerce.'

'Capital! Then we may take it that Maréchal has abandoned his venture and is returning. The last squadron of threat to Cape Town is gone. This is splendid news, Captain, splendid.'

He seemed to brighten by the minute. 'My dear fellow, I'm forgetting my manners. May I offer you a restorative negus perhaps?'

The prospect of a piping hot toddy was compelling and Kydd accepted gratefully. He could understand the relief Popham must be feeling. Rather than the negative news from his scouting frigates that the French were not to be found in this area or that, here was a positive indication that the menace was now safely on its way out of Cape waters.

'I really feel this news is worthy of celebration! You'll stay and sup with me, Kydd?'

It was an odd dinner for, with the blow from the South Atlantic kicking up respectable-sized rollers, there was no possibility of boats coming out from the shore. The company was restricted to themselves, with *Diadem*'s first lieutenant, Davis, and a bemused passenger, one Scholes, doctor of theology, whose store of amusing anecdotes petered out in the strongly masculine naval company.

'Sir, do tell of your cutting out o' this Frenchy corvette. I'll wager it's to be my dinner-table yarn for years t' come,' Davis said, his voice tinged in equal measure with admiration and envy.

While the darkness of evening fell outside and the bluster of the north-westerly rattled the old-fashioned stern-windows of the sixty-four, Kydd told of the adventure, a modest, straight account with full acknowledgement to those who had contributed.

'A capital operation indeed,' Popham declared, 'in the best traditions and so forth. I for one am honoured to drink your health, sir.'

Glowing, Kydd accepted the compliment and nodded graciously when Scholes observed, 'I, too, must add my measure of amazement at your remarkable courage. To go forward on your enterprise in the stark knowledge of Africa's perils and hazards . . .'

Kydd flinched at the memory of the sinking island and that night in the African bush, but Popham was in no doubt. 'Ah, yes, Doctor, but for the greater prize our good captain is never to be dismayed by the wonders of nature. Is that not so, Kydd?'

The talk fell away and the dinner ended quietly. Davis made his excuses and left, and Scholes found it necessary to retire to attend to his work, leaving them alone to do justice to the fine cognac.

'I do believe this to be our first chance to take our ease together, Kydd,' Popham said, after they had settled in the armchairs by the stern-lights.

'Sir.'

'You've done well for yourself since we first met, I see.'

'Er, yes, sir.'

'Mere commander of a brig-sloop to post-captain of a frigate – come, come, that's no mean achievement. Could it in any wise be connected with your stout action off Ushant?'

'Um, I think more that Lord Nelson was in sore need of frigates,' Kydd said uncomfortably. That Nelson himself had called for him when a captured frigate had become available was something he'd clutch to his heart for ever, but now did not seem the right time to mention it.

Popham chuckled. 'You're too damn modest for your own good, you know that, Kydd? You'll never get ahead without you make a commotion about it.'

'Yes, sir.'

Leaning forward to top up Kydd's glass, Popham then sat back and looked at him quizzically. 'Do loosen, old chap – I may be commodore for the nonce but this, of course, is but a temporary post while subduing Cape Town. I'll be reverting back once their lordships deem our task is done and then I'll be the same as you – post-captain, even if the senior.'

It was singular, but it was true. They were of equal substantive rank and, in terms of shore protocol at least, would then be accorded an equal deference.

'Do you remember – not so long ago – that little affair with the American Fulton and his submersible? We worked together on it . . .'

'And you frowned on his submarine boat,' Kydd said.

'I was right, was I not?'

'It has to be said.'

'Should you want to know what happened to the fellow?' Popham said idly, twirling his glass.

'His torpedoes?'

'Yes. We made some gestures towards Boulogne but with paltry result. Boney himself had the hide to say we were breaking the windows of the good citizens of Boulogne with guineas! Then we made a heroic effort and put on a show for Pitt and the Admiralty off Deal. Tethered an innocent little brig – what was her name? *Dorothea*, that's it – and sent in the torpedoes.'

He guffawed at the recollection. 'You should have seen the looks on their faces, Kydd. Not a jot of warning and the brig's exploded to fragments! St Vincent turned quite grey and Pitt felt ill. A terrific demonstration!'

'So . . .'

'So nothing! Just a fortnight later, you and Our Nel clear the seas of the French fleet, so what's the use o' these toys when there's no more invasion to be feared? They paid him off and sent him packing back to the United States.'

'Pity – a strange cove, but I liked him,' Kydd said.

'Well, we'll hear no more of his plunging boats, I believe. We've a war to fight and only the finest seamanship and gunnery will win that . . .'

'You were at Trafalgar, then?' Popham asked, somewhat defensively.

'In a small way of things, o' course. I have to say, your telegraphic signals were well received by the fleet,' Kydd said, and then, more strongly, 'Especially after Nelson made use of 'em to entertain us before the engagement. "England expects that—"'

'Quite so. I did hear of it.' A shadow passed across his features. Kydd had been present at both the Nile and Trafalgar, the defining battles of the age, but through ill luck Popham had never seen a grand fleet action. 'And now . . . here we are,' he concluded softly.

'I'm sorry, sir?'

'I meant to say that we're safe here in Cape Colony, are we not? But lacking the one thing that a naval officer craves above all else . . .'

'A chance for distinction?'

'Just so. We're both in like state – you've a fine start to your career but unless something happens you'll moulder away your best years here at the Cape. And I – well, shall we say that unless I can distinguish myself while I still have my mighty fleet then I shall join you in sliding from the consciousness of their lordships?'

'Will we not soon be recalled?'

'Why so? We're doing a sterling job, holding the Cape for King George. Why disturb it? We'll put down the occasional privateer or even a loose frigate but nothing to stand against the exploits of others who are adding to our empire by the month.'

That gave Kydd pause: it made disturbing sense – yet . . .

'We're at a strategic position here, sir. Who's to say the French may wish soon to dispute these seas in force?'

'They won't now, m' friend. Their squadrons are scattered, defeated and gone home. The Channel Fleet blockade will take care of their sorties in the future. No, we're to remain at rest foreseeably, I fear.'

'Is there nothing . . . ?'

'I'm giving it some high thought,' Popham replied mysteriously, 'as may yet yield a possibility.' He stared out into the wild darkness with a strange expression, then resumed briskly, 'Meanwhile, do stand down your ship for a week or two. You've deserved it. We'll share a dinner on another occasion.'

* * *

47

'Quite set me aback, Nicholas.' Kydd laughed, shaking out his wet clothing. 'Here we have the commodore confiding he's bored, to me, a junior frigate captain – a prickly gullion in the past, as I remember. You don't suppose he's a reason for it?' he added awkwardly, noticing Renzi wore an odd, hunted look.

His friend brightened a little. 'The reigning flag officer? I'd rather think he's more pleased at your success that rids him of a pressing anxiety.'

'Well, whatever, he's given us leave to stand down for a brace of weeks. Do you fancy a time of it ashore?'

'Er, not at this time, Tom.'

Kydd was not to be dissuaded. Only a short while before, his friend had been the colonial secretary of Cape Colony with hopes of tenure before being unexpectedly replaced by a civil-service appointee sent out from England. Now he was staying aboard, unable to face the imagined stares of the townsfolk. 'I have to say it'll be quite necessary, I'm afraid, dear chap. I'm resolved this ship is to be fumigated and sweetened while she lies idle and no man may stay on board.'

With the urgency of the situation there had been little opportunity since leaving England the previous year for attending to the needs of his ship. And she had now been through a tropic summer – and, besides, Kydd had ideas about her appearance. 'I'll be staying at my club for the duration, the Africa on the Heerengracht,' he said, with relish. 'Capital roast game, wines a supernaculum. I'd be honoured to have you as my guest, dear fellow.'

'That's civil in you, right enough . . . On a point of some delicacy,' Renzi murmured, 'would it be impertinent of me to enquire in what manner you'll introduce me?'

Kydd snorted. 'Why, this is a gentlemen's club. Should I

introduce you as my friend then that is all that need be said, old trout.'

'Then perhaps I will accept your kind offer.'

The news of a fumigation was well received by *L'Aurore*'s company, with its prospect of enforced shore leave, and even more so when it became known that a contractor would be engaged for the unpleasant business.

Next day the bad weather seemed to have blown itself out and, almost apologetically, the sun began spreading its warmth and good feeling about the anchorage. *L'Aurore* went to two anchors and secured fore and aft in preparation for the fumigation. Early in the afternoon a towed lighter approached and, gleefully, the ship's company made ready for their liberty.

'Cap'n Kydd, sir,' a large Dutchman said, raising his shapeless hat as he came over the bulwark. 'Piet Geens. Are ye prepared a'tall?'

'We are.' Kydd was used to the routine with his long service in the Navy.

Geens walked back and shouted something down to the men in the lighter and returned. 'Well, we'm ready to start, Kapitein.'

In high spirits the liberty-men were sent on their way, leaving *L'Aurore* echoing and empty, the only ones left aboard being Kydd, a small party of men on deck to assist – and keep an eye on proceedings – and Renzi.

A row-guard provided by *Diadem* slowly circled as the Dutchman and Kydd went below to spy out the task. 'What's your method, Mr Geens?' Kydd asked.

'Why, the only one as truly answers, Mijnheer. An' recommended by y'r Transport Board itself for th' use of India troopships. In short, fumes o' vitriol. Kills rats 'n' mice, weevil an' cockroach. All that creeps an' crawls ends the same.'

This was the deepest form of fumigation possible but the ship had to be sealed for greatest effect. The platform timbers above the hold had been removed and the men's belongings taken to the upper deck; gear was becketed back out of the way, gratings covered with tarpaulins and hatchways closed with laced canvas flaps. 'Ver' good, Kapitein. We begin. In twenty-four hours you have y'r ship back, sweet as a nut.'

An alarming number of casks and sacks were piled on deck. Curious, Kydd went across and peered into one. It was filled with crude yellow cakes. 'That's y'r common flowers o' sulphur,' Geens said.

'And this?' Kydd held up a sack of dirty white crystals.

'Is best nitre. Sulphur don't burn s' well, we give it nitre – one part to every eight o' the yellow cake. Then we get plenty o' them vitriolic acid fumes. Want t' see?'

'Er, no, I'll leave it all to you, Mr Geens,' Kydd said. 'Carry on, please.'

Tin pans were charged with a small coil of quick-match in the coarse-ground mixture and distributed below. Men with pails of mud moved about, completing the seal and shortly afterwards the first acrid whiffs could be detected.

'Time we weren't here, Nicholas.'

The Africa Club welcomed Kydd warmly. Word of the little action in East Africa had got about, and in a dark-polished room ornamented with game trophies and shields with crossed assegais, those waiting for a full accounting of it had assembled.

'Have t' hand it to ye, Kydd, 'twas a grand stroke!' The red-faced and moustachioed ivory trader, Ditler, chortled, beckoning him to an adjacent leather chair. 'A peg o' whisky for y' tale.'

Others drew up their chairs companionably but Kydd remained standing. 'And this is my particular friend, Nicholas Renzi,' he said pointedly.

'Of course he is,' soothed the cocoa planter Richardson, 'as will have a whisky too, eh, Renzi? Hey?'

'Thank you, no,' Renzi said politely. 'Although anything out of Stellenbosch would gratify, if it does not inconvenience.' If any knew him as other than Captain Kydd's friend, it could not be detected in their expressions.

Kydd found himself in the seat of honour in the centre and awaited his libation.

Despite what Popham had said, a lengthy stay in Cape waters had its compensations, he had to admit. Who would have thought, in those impossibly remote days in the musty Guildford wig shop, that he would later find himself in a splendid gold-laced uniform in these exotic surroundings?

'Thank you, Cuthbert,' he said, accepting his whisky – a single malt, he was pleased to note. After his experience with the Highlanders at Blaauwberg nothing less would serve.

Cradling the drink he found himself further reflecting on his conversation with Popham.

'Ahem!'

'Ah, yes, *Marie Galante*.' Kydd was not a born story-teller and in his own ears the account sounded matter-of-fact and predestined. He'd omitted his doubts and worries as they'd gone into action, the need to rise above his own fears and terror of the unknown to order men into those same hazards, yet the simple telling was received with something like reverence, and he ended the tale pink-faced.

'Good God, man! Y' sit there so cool an' tell us you spent

your night on the riverbank? Never heard o' such blazin' courage!' Ditler's admiration was clear.

'Er, what—'

'Well, the crocs f'r one!'

'Oh?'

'Surely y' know they stalk abroad at night, wanting t' devour sleeping prey. They snap their jaws shut on ye, there's no hope for it – all over!' He threw up his arms in an expressive gesture.

'And y'r hippos too, Kydd,' came the gravelly tones of the white-haired, sun-touched Baker. 'They's on land an', it being their river, should y' get a-tween them an' it, why, at four ton coming at ye faster than y' can run . . .' He shook his head, speechless.

'Not forgetting it's lion country,' Richardson brought in, with relish, raising his glass to Kydd. 'Go around in hunting bands at night, they do. Take a terrible lot o' kaffirs, poor devils.' Kydd remembered the massive presence they'd sensed passing by in the inky darkness and shivered.

Ditler put in strongly, 'And y' talked on sailing a floatin' island downriver? B' glory, and ye're a mile an' a half braver than I,' he said, in awestruck tones.

'The water-snakes?' Baker wondered.

'Not merely,' was the reply. 'I was thinking more o' your frightsome bull shark o' the Zambezi, as is not content wi' what's in the sea but must range miles up into the river.'

'Even into freshwater?' Kydd swallowed.

'Right up t' the shallows o' the headwaters. Nasty, vicious brutes, c'n take a man out of a canoe, even,' he declared. 'Not t' be beat in the article of killing. Even the crocs do step lightly around 'em, and—'

Kydd decided to change the subject. 'Thank you, Mr Ditler,

and I'll bear 'em in mind the next time we move on the enemy. You gentlemen have ventured up the coast? I'd welcome a steer on what's to be found in those parts after what I saw there.'

The talk brightened into trade prospects at the fringe of the Arab world, barely touched by events outside. Then came well-polished stories of the white man in Africa, as warm and entertaining as the yarns to be heard over any wardroom dinner at sea.

Content, Kydd winked at Renzi, then settled back and let the talk wash over him.

'It's done, Cap'n,' Geens said importantly, holding out the requisite papers to sign.

'I'll see below first, if I may,' Kydd replied, and set off purposefully. The gun-ports and gratings had been open all morning but there was still a sour, biting odour about the ship.

They went down to the main-deck where the pungency caught him at the back of the throat, making him gag. There, a half a dozen men with sacks were scooping up a carpet of vermin, some of which still writhed and contorted: dead cockroaches, grubs and other insects, all driven by the fumes from their hiding places to expire in the open.

On the mess-deck, around the dark cavity of the hold, rat carcasses lay in horrifying abundance. While *L'Aurore* had seen first Trafalgar and then Blaauwberg, these were the hidden passengers who had been lurking in the nether regions, oblivious to events and with only the ship's precious sea provisions in mind. Geens used wooden tongs to lift up a still feebly moving rat for Kydd's inspection. 'See? Does for 'em all in the end. Gaspin' for air, comes out but it's no good, he's blind, o' course. Vitriolic acid eats out his eyes, the plaguey villain.' He sniffed, dropping the rat into the sack.

Kydd felt duty-bound to stay aboard as the men reluctantly made their way back to their ship, suffering with them until the vessel was habitable again. He had split the ship's company in two to share the duties, and the first on board were set to sweeten the vessel – from stem to stern a mighty scrubbing with vinegar and lime, the deckhead beams liberally anointed with a powerful concoction of Geen's own devising. The cable tiers were lime whitewashed, and twice, two feet of seawater was let in to flood the bilges, the reeking water then pumped over the side until it ran clear.

After their heroic efforts this party happily made its way ashore to its favoured waterfront punch-house to wash away the taste with Cape brandy while the other watch came on board for the even more taxing job of painting ship.

Boatswain Oakley, his head bandaged and in pain, took charge. Preparation was thorough: wood painstakingly scraped back before the paint was carefully mixed. The pigment, oil and litharge was poured into an old fish-kettle in proportions to his satisfaction, and on an upper-deck charcoal fire, the mixture was boiled, then strained through a bread-bag to be laid on warm.

Kydd had his firm views on appearance: it was to stay the Nelson chequer, a smart black hull with a warlike band of yellow along the line of guns, the gun-ports menacing regular squares in black. Lower masts below the tops were well varnished; above the tops, they were painted black, as were the yards, with white tips at their extremities to aid in working aloft in the dark.

Then there was the detailing: scarlet inner bulwarks before the guns, a stout mixture of varnish and tar on the binnacle and belfry and here and there a dash of white. The flutings of the headrails and cheeks saw dark blue to set off the carved scroll-work, and their old-fashioned lion and crown figurehead claimed a handsome gilding of gold-leaf. Kydd himself found the necessary wherewithal to ensure the ornamentation shone around the quarter-galleries and stern-lights.

The men set to with a will to brighten their living quarters; it was amazing how much a frigate's below-the-waterline mess-deck could be lightened by a lime whitewash on the bulkheads and ship's side. The petty officers prettified their own messes, each separated by canvas screens decorated lavishly with mermaids and sea battles, their crockery mess-traps stowed neatly in vertical side lockers: in a frigate there was no need to clear for action on a deck with no guns.

Kydd found time to relax in his great cabin, the floor-cloth renewed and the furniture sweet-smelling from the lavender-oil-impregnated beeswax that Tysoe, his valet, had applied to overcome the odour of fumigation. The boys had been industrious in their cleaning and priddying and, at Renzi's suggestion, Kydd's intricate showcase secretaire had been picked out in gilt around its French polish and green leather.

The gunroom had come together in noble style to enrich their own sea home. In place of the utilitarian service barrel slung from the forward bulkhead, from which commensal wine was drawn, there was now a beautifully polished elliptical cask made for the purpose and bearing a silver plate with 'The gunroom, HMS *L'Aurore*, Cape Colony 1806' engraved in bold flourishes.

An elegant locker had been contrived around the rudder trunking, which now served to conceal the gunroom's stock of dog-eared newspapers and magazines. Gilbey and Curzon's time ashore had not been wasted: a pair of remarkably animated watercolours of Table Mountain and the Cape of Good Hope now adorned their quarters.

L'Aurore came alive again. The rhythm of a comfortable harbour routine set in, of hands to turn to, part of ship in the forenoon and liberty ashore in the afternoon. Kydd saw a fierce pride in his ship. In due course there would be hard-fought regattas and other competitive outlets but for now all could revel in as trim and saucy a frigate as any that swam.

'You've, um, not received anything from Cecilia, at all?' Renzi asked offhandedly, twiddling his quill as Kydd opened a packet of ship's mail from England.

Renzi's plans to invite Kydd's sister Cecilia to visit him in Cape Town and offer his hand in marriage had been dashed when his position as acting colonial secretary had not been ratified. Previously he had written her a letter pouring out his most tender admiration and love for her but delayed sending it until things were fully settled. When the blow came, he'd torn the letter up. Cecilia had known of his *tendre* for her for some time but the latest communication she'd had from him was a stiff letter of release he'd sent before Trafalgar, citing his lack of prospects. Who knew what her feelings towards him were now?

Kydd pushed his papers to one side. 'No, Nicholas, and you shall be the first to know of it should I get a letter from her,' he said impatiently. 'This Cape enterprise being in the nature of a secret expedition, I can well see it will have any letter chasing all over the ocean till it catches up with us – which it will, in course.'

'Yes, no doubt you are correct,' Renzi said, with a troubled look.

Kydd sighed. 'You know you now stand in a fair way of losing the woman?'

'What do you mean?'

'There's every prospect that, having conquered and held the place, the Admiralty will see fit to keep us here indefinitely, we doing such a sterling job.'

Renzi's expression turned bleak. He had sworn to Kydd he would go down on his knees and seek Cecilia's hand the same day that they reached the shores of England. That time now distant, would she still be free?

'I'd suggest you write to her this hour, m' friend.'

'Believe me, I've tried, but—'

'Then I'd think it wise to consider your position, old horse.'

A half-smile appeared. Kydd knew the signs and waited for his friend to speak.

'Dear brother, in logic, as I see it, there are three alternatives. The one, that she is already taken by another, which at the moment I cannot know; the second, that she is not, but will nevertheless decline my suit; and the third that . . . that she will listen favourably to that which I shall propose.'

After a moment's reflection he said, 'So it seems my course is clear. No dilemma, no equivocation or foolish agonising.'

'Oh?'

'On the one, I am helpless to alter the dictates of Fortune, likewise the second, neither requiring either action or decision. As to the third – this must presuppose I should prepare for the day. Now, in the absence of intelligence to the contrary, each condition bears an equal probability of being the outcome, the odds of one in three. I accept those odds, but you see it makes no difference – in the event of the first two, no prior intervention will affect matters while for the third it will. Therefore, irrespective, I am obliged to assume the last . . . that I am to marry.'

'Well done, old trout!' Kydd applauded. 'Therefore, for both your sakes *write to her now*! There's a mail to close tomorrow on *Bombay Castle*.'

'It's impossible. I cannot trust that I could write without betraying my true feelings and I abhor pity. Therefore I ask a boon – that you write to her as a brother and enquire of her personal circumstances.'

Kydd frowned, then nodded reluctantly.

'Meanwhile, in this far region there is one, and one only, contribution to my future with Cecilia left open to me.'

Kydd waited. It would come out logically, as it always did.

Renzi took a deep breath, looked skyward, then slammed both fists on the table and choked, 'That novel! I'm going to write my novel – for Cecilia's sake!'

To see Renzi so taken with emotion shook Kydd. 'Er, why, to be sure – I know you'll do it, Nicholas,' he said, with concern. It was clear his friend's so recent cruel fall from fortune and prospects for marriage had affected him more than he had revealed.

Renzi took control, then said evenly, 'I shall dedicate my heart and soul to *Portrait of an Adventurer*, Tom. Never doubt it for one minute.'

'Yes, Nicholas.'

Writing a novel had been Kydd's idea, a suggestion to which, until now, Kydd had never given much more thought, but he knew that it was probably the only thing Renzi could do that had any promise for the future. The public seemed to crave such works, and Renzi had had a number of adventures around the world that might inspire such a book. But, most importantly, it would keep his friend occupied until they returned and he could resolve matters with Kydd's sister.

'Damme – whatever it takes out of me, this is the only thing I can positively do for the both of us,' Renzi said defiantly.

'I quite understand, m'friend.'

'Not forgetting, mark you, what I said about Cecilia.'

Kydd smiled: a natural philosopher turned writer of novels? Of course she should never hear of it! He clapped his hand on the desk and gave a mock frown. 'So, what do you know of novels, ever?'

'Ah. Not much – I confess I've yet to read one, my father railing against them so vehemently. I've taken some first steps, however, which persuade me that it may not be as plain-sailing a task as first I'd conceived.'

'You'll do it, Nicholas, never fear.'

'I enquired in our worthy gunroom if there was by chance a reader of novels who might lend me a volume, but it seems there was not. Yet mysteriously by evening a pair lay on my cot. Such noble fellows!'

He fumbled in his pocket and drew out two well-used pocket editions and passed them across. Curious, Kydd opened one. *The Castle on the Rhine; or; The Fatal Warning* was its title, and lower down it went on breathlessly to declare that it was the harrowing tale of the fate of Reginald de Vere, who dared pierce the deathly walls of a deserted castle in pursuit of a ghostly love.

'Um, you've experience of ghosts at all, Nicholas?' Kydd asked doubtfully.

'We have an ancestral phantom but I've never met it,' Renzi said apologetically, 'and never a spirit, of the ghostly sort that is, have I seen at sea.'

Kydd turned to the second book. 'Then this other one, "*Quentin Dandy*, being an account of the peregrinations of a scoundrel and his dreadful end", in five volumes – but this is the third only, damn it.'

'It must serve, I fear. We need all the research matter we can lay hands on.'

'*We?*'

'My dear fellow! You don't imagine I shall exclude my most particular friend from this literary adventure, surely.'

'But I'm a sea officer, fit only to write a log or beg favour of my admiral, Nicholas. What do I know of romance and plotting?'

'Tom, dear fellow, you have a crucial role, one suited only to a clear and strong mind as will not be swayed by fashion and sorcery. In fine, dear friend, you shall be my audience.'

'Oh. To make critical remarks, review your meaning and similar?'

'Er, yes.'

'Then shall I be telling the truth or will I be losing a friend?' Kydd asked slyly.

'I've yet to write a word,' Renzi said stiffly. 'There's a mort of work before then.'

Gravely, the commodore paced slowly along the assembled divisions, asking a question here, commending an appearance there. Kydd followed: *L'Aurore* was at her best and he could vouch for her fighting spirit. Some senior officers insisted on a faultless appearance, others fell back on pedantry in the matter of ceremonials, but he knew Popham prized intelligence and audacity above all else – and who on this station had shown more than *L'Aurore*?

Concluding his tour, Popham stood genially on

the quarterdeck and addressed Kydd loudly: 'A splendid turn-out, Captain! And as fine a King's Ship as any I've seen. You shall have my order that the mainbrace be spliced this afternoon.'

'Thank you, sir,' Kydd replied courteously.

'That is, if you're able to satisfy me in one last particular.'

'Sir?'

Popham wheeled about and strode purposefully to the spotless after end of the quarterdeck beyond the mizzen-mast. 'I desire you should make to *Diadem* the following signal.'

Saxton, the signals master's mate, hastily took out his notebook.

'"Report the Christian name of the captain of your main-top."'

That would be quite impossible to send with the current Admiralty signal book.

'Telegraph,' muttered Saxton, instantly, to his petty officer, who lost no time in having the telegraph code flag bent on while Saxton composed the signal. It drew an approving nod from the commodore when 'Christian' was not found in the book and Saxton muttered, 'Um, that is, "fore, forward, bows" and then "name" will do'. He rapidly found the numbers.

The hoist soared up, to be answered with a spelled-out reply from all three masts of *Diadem*. 'Cholmondeley,' Saxton reported, wooden-faced.

'Very good,' Popham said graciously. 'You may stand down your ship's company, Captain.'

When this had been done, Kydd asked politely, 'And may I offer you refreshments, sir?'

Once in Kydd's great cabin, hats and swords were put off and Popham eased himself into one of the armchairs by the stern-lights, stretching luxuriously and loosening his neck-cloth. 'A thoroughly good-spirited ship, Kydd. Count yourself blessed you're her commander.'

Tysoe arrived with glasses on a tray. 'To *L'Aurore*,' Popham toasted. 'Long may you reign in her.'

He put down his glass, adding, 'As you won't always serve in such a thoroughbred. Enjoy her while you can, old fellow, for the time will come when you'll know only the lumbering tedium of a ship-o'-the-line.'

'I will, you may be sure of it,' Kydd said, with feeling, then realised too late that this must apply to Popham himself at the moment. 'Which is to say—'

'Of course. And you and she will grow old together on this station.'

Kydd paused. Popham must be restless if he was bringing this up again. 'There's a chance we'll be superseded and sent home, surely.'

'I rather think not. A pair of old sixty-fours and a couple of frigates is a small enough levy on our fleet – why go to the bother and expense of exchanging ships over such a distance?'

'Perhaps so,' Kydd said. 'I suppose we must rest content – it is our purpose and duty, is it not?'

Unexpectedly, Popham sighed. 'You're in the right of it, old fellow. We shouldn't complain.' He stared moodily out of the pretty windows at the vast, white-specked ocean expanse. 'Even when I know for want of communication a priceless opportunity for strategic intervention is slipping by.'

'Sir?'

'Well, in this morning's mail I received word from my friend Miranda that he is beginning an enterprise of the utmost significance.' He saw Kydd's mystification and explained, 'A gentleman of mixed Spanish ancestry known to me since the year 'ninety-eight. Went to France to learn to be a revolutionary for he ardently desires to rid the Spanish colonies in the south of America of their masters. The French being lukewarm in the matter he then secretly approached the Foreign Office.'

'And?'

'He was disappointed in his hopes and came to see me with his intentions. As a newly elected Member of Parliament I took an interest, his proposal possessing certain compelling advantages to the Crown. His plan was to raise widespread rebellion in South America while the attention of the Spanish and French was on the invasion of Great Britain. The benefits to us I need hardly point out. An immediate cessation of the treasure fleet filling Boney's coffers would provide an intolerable distraction to Spain, caught between two fires, as will probably see it sue for peace, and, of course, an immeasurable increase in trade opportunities once the continent is thrown open to England's merchants.'

He had Kydd's complete attention. Strategy and chance were coinciding for truly global stakes.

Popham continued: 'At some length I argued Miranda's case in a secret memorandum to Billy Pitt, who took it seriously and even told the Admiralty to work up an expedition to assist – this was about the time of Fulton's torpedoes, so if I appeared a little distracted at the time, I do apologise.'

'Not as ever I noticed,' Kydd replied carefully.

'Then Villeneuve sailed and the Trafalgar campaign began. We were stripped of ships and unable to sail, and when we did – well, it was to the more direct goal, Cape Town, and, successful, here we remain.'

'So, no expedition.'

'Unhappily, no. And do be discreet in what you say, old fellow. The Spanish suspect there is some villainy afoot but can't fathom from where.'

Kydd nodded. 'But surely, with both the Spanish and French driven from the seas and not to be counted on to interfere, now is the best time to move.'

'Quite.'

'So, Miranda . . .'

Popham shook his head. 'A shameful thing, I must own. Despairing that we will ever get another expedition together, he is proceeding on his own. His letter coldly informs me that he is shortly to descend on Caracas, the chief town in the north of the continent, there to raise the flag of revolution and independence for all the peoples of South America.'

'And we do nothing?'

'The plan called for us to move simultaneously against the viceroyalty of the River Plate in the south, Montevideo or wherever but . . .'

'This is hard to take,' Kydd growled. 'Such a blow as will ring out around the world! Does not Whitehall see this? Have you had any kind of word?'

Popham gave a tired smile. 'Pitt was not well when we sailed on this Cape venture. Conceivably he's distracted by the news of Austerlitz.'

'We don't know that.' Kydd had only recently heard of it: a land battle in some benighted place to the east, where Bonaparte had crushed the armies of both the Austrian and Russian emperors in a titanic battle. Most opinion had it that the Third Coalition, an alliance including Austria, Prussia, England, Russia and Sweden, was as good as destroyed.

Popham downed the rest of his wine. 'If there are any designs to move against the River Plate we should be the first to know of it – we are the closest and the forces we employed on this expedition can only be said to be in idleness.'

'But you've had no word?'

Popham shook his head.

The next afternoon Kydd insisted Renzi dine at his club and they went ashore together. As they left the old jetty for the noisome waterfront, Renzi stopped. 'Er, there's someone I'd rather not meet,' he muttered, and turned about.

'Wha—?' At the end of the lane a distinguished-looking man was directing others in some sort of inventory, then Kydd recognised him. 'It's only your old fiscal, Ryneveld,' he chided, knowing, however, that while Renzi had been colonial secretary this man had been his immediate subordinate. Now he was at an impossibly lofty eminence in government.

'You can't avoid him for ever, Nicholas,' he said, and hailed the man. 'Mr Fiscal, ahoy!'

Ryneveld came hurrying over. 'Why, the Jonkheer Renzi,' he said, with disarming warmth. 'Since leaving your position you've been so engaged in your studies you've been neglecting your friends, sir.'

Renzi gave a stiff bow. 'I stand accused and can only plead guilty, Schildknaap Ryneveld.'

'Well, that's a matter that can easily be remedied. Let me see . . . As it happens, my wife Barbetjie – whom you know, of course – is taking the girls up to the top of Table Mountain for an artistic expedition while the weather allows. Should you feel inclined, you two gentlemen would be very welcome to partake of our little picnic and perhaps to instruct them in their daubing.'

'That's very kind in you,' Kydd said quickly. 'We'd be honoured to attend.'

'Splendid. Er, your ethnical work is proceeding satisfactorily, Mr Renzi? I cannot conceive how you might concentrate with all the martial excitement about your ears.'

'It, er, progresses well, sir. And . . . and the government of Cape Colony, your distinguished new secretary?'

'Ah, me,' Ryneveld, said with a sigh. 'Those heroic days, when together we snatched order from the chaos that threatened – I'm afraid these are long past, Mr Renzi. Now it's work more fitting for the administrator and accountant, with Secretary Barnard still unwell from his long voyage.'

They walked on in silence for a space. Passing a well-weathered *wijnhuis*, they heard a manly bass booming out a jolly ballad:

> *'Aan de Kaap hoord en wilt verstaan*
> *Daar de meisjes dagelyks verkeeren*
> *Al in het huys De Blaauwe Haan,*
> *Daar wyze dagelyks converzeren!'*

'Ah,' Renzi said politely. 'A folk song of the colony, no doubt hallowed by age. Do share with me what they are singing about, sir.'

'You are right,' Ryneveld said drily. 'This is from the early days of our settlement, sung by returning sailors of the Dutch East India Company. But the words are not for ears such as yours, Jonkheer Renzi.'

Kydd hid a smile. 'Nonetheless Mr Renzi, I'm sure, is interested in its ethnical, er, origins, Mr Ryneveld.'

'Are you sure?'

'Why, yes,' Renzi said.

'Then it goes:

66

> "*At the Cape, one hears you'll understand,*
> *There maidens daily do play court*
> *At the house of the Blue Cock . . .*'"

The rhyme and rhythm were quite lost in translation but the sentiment was clear.

'You wish me to continue, sir?'

'Please.'

The unknown rich bass rolled on:

> '*Een frische roemer Kaapsche wyn*
> *Zai hem, die geld heeft, smaaklyk zijn*
> *Zo proeft men reeds op d'eersten stond*
> *De vruchten van de Kaapschen grond.*'

'And I'll translate freely this last, touching as it does on our mariner's delight in finding himself once more in Cape Town.'

> '*A cool rummer of Cape wine*
> *Is zest indeed for he with money,*
> *To taste from that first moment*
> *The fruits of the good Cape earth.*'

'Thank you, sir. Most informative,' Renzi said cheerfully, now convinced there was no longer any need to hide his face when ashore.

'And where shall we meet for your diverting expedition, pray?' he added.

They were fortunate: the autumn weather was kind and a warm sun beamed down on the little party marvelling at the precipitous edge of Table Mountain and the spectacular panorama sprawled in meticulous miniature detail below.

They were not alone: other small groups were there, taking advantage of the benevolent conditions, and cheery greetings were exchanged by all who had made the vertiginous final ascent.

It had been carriages to the lower slopes of the giant mountain, followed by a panting scramble up past a waterfall shaded by myrtle. Then had come an arduous zigzag for some hours in the warm sunshine, until in the very shadow of the final vertical shafting of the vast monolith a cool chasm had opened. This was the Platteklip Gorge, their pass to the summit, and pausing to drink at a crystal spring, they emerged at last at the top.

There were no trees, only some wistfully beautiful tiny flowers and heath with moss and lichen, and for the rest a bare grey ruler-straight flatness stretching away for what seemed miles, one of nature's truly impressive vistas. Exclaiming at the sight, the girls claimed their vantage-points, and the party joined in a tasty repast of cold meats and Cape wine.

After the picnic had been cleared away, Kydd found a spot and set up his easel, Renzi on his right. The breeze fluttered at the paper, which he clipped down firmly. After he had industriously sharpened his best Cumberland pencil, he set to.

Like most naval officers he had learned to take the likeness of a coastline and he had found he was in possession of an artistic talent. Looking out now at a prospect worthy of the greatest artists, he felt inspired: he was on the rim of the world and, in the blue-misty distance, could see the rumpled pair of mountains at the far end of the curve of coast that was

Blaauwberg where, not so very long ago, two armies had vied for dominion of the Cape. Nearer, many ships were anchored offshore – Cape Town was clearly prospering by the opening of trade with the world. With a surge of pride he picked out *L'Aurore* among the bigger naval vessels in their more northerly anchorage, yards meticulously square, a perfect toy at this distance.

As he sketched in the outlines in deft strokes, he pondered over what Popham had confided. There was sense in what he had said about their situation being out of sight, out of mind: he had seen it once before – as a new officer on the quiet North America station in Halifax, Nova Scotia. There he had met men who had been in ships that had been sent out at the beginning of the war and were still there with no foreseeable prospect of either engaging in some momentous fleet action or returning home.

He had welcomed the relative tranquillity for the space it gave him to learn his profession, but it was a different matter here. Now he was a young captain at the outset of his career. If he failed to make his mark soon, others would overtake him, gaining the plum promotions, the more powerful frigates – and be the ones to go on with the great admirals to who knew what glorious actions?

And there was another element to be considered. He was now a very eligible bachelor, by most standards, and it was on the cards that he would fall in love and want to marry. While he had command of a far-ranging frigate, it was essential to make the going in amassing prize-money now for, as Popham could testify, there was little to be had in the larger ships. While he still had a respectable sum from his privateering days, it was not enough to buy and run a country estate.

Then again, Bonaparte had triumphed on land, but how long could a war be relied on to last now that the tyrant was locked up in Europe with nowhere to go? Peacetime would see an instant freezing of promotions and certainly no opportunity for fattening the purse.

If there was a time to become active, it was now.

The outline of his scene was complete. He hooked up the box of watercolours to the base of the easel and sighed. It was not in his power to summon the French to a desperate battle. With few casualties and the unfortunate loss of the corvette, the recent action on the Zambezi would hardly raise eyebrows. If only Whitehall had seen fit for a grand assault against Spanish South America. The British had proved their amphibious skills at Blaauwberg, and such a mission could well be a repeat of that.

Suddenly restless, he glanced sideways at the girls, gossiping blithely as they worked on their landscapes. Seized by an odd feeling, he dabbed in a fearsome ox-eye, the dreadful storm portent he had seen off East Africa before a particularly violent tempest. It was colourful and vivid but didn't fit the scene. He realised he'd spoiled the painting, laid down his brush in vexation and decided to take a stroll.

Kydd had worked fast and the others in the party hadn't yet exchanged their pencils for brushes. Over to the right he noticed a dark-haired rather shabby figure rapidly executing his landscape. Unusually for a watercolour he was using a full-sized maulstick and worked with quick, economic movements. Kydd wandered over and stood behind him. Clearly this was no amateur: his field easel was well used and he was building his scene over a luminous cerulean wash that gave a shimmering quality to the foreground elements, which gained animation as a result.

'A lively piece,' Kydd offered, leaning closer.

The man, a young, intense individual with sun-touched Iberian features, turned, nodded brusquely and returned to his work. Kydd looked closer at the landscape, realising he'd seen the style before. That was it: the gunroom had bought two of his paintings.

'You paint professionally, then?' Kydd asked.

Hooking his maulstick in a little finger, the man felt in his waistcoat, drew out a card and handed it over, then resumed his rapid brush-strokes with unsettling concentration. The card read: 'Vicente Serrano, Painter in Oils, Watercolour and Gouache. Portraits and Landscapes to the Discerning by Arrangement. 150 Buitengracht Street.'

'You're Spanish, then?' Kydd asked, puzzled.

This time he got full attention. 'No, sir!' Serrano spat. 'I am not! A *porteño* of Buenos Aires, which is in South America.' He glared at Kydd, then resumed his work.

'Oh – I didn't wish to pry, Mr Serrano. It's just that the gunroom in my ship is an admirer of your work. There's now two pieces hanging there to ornament their mess-place.'

There was a pause and a flashed glance back. 'So sorry. I leave Buenos Aires because the Spanish they come for me when I speak what they don' like. I cannot return. Now I paint the picture for my bread. *Por favor, Señor . . .*' He recharged his brush and continued on the landscape.

Kydd went back to his easel and began another view. This time it was with a calm grey-blue wash, like the one he had just seen, and he wanted to make a good job of it. Perhaps he would send it home to his mother.

Stretching, he looked across at Renzi, who had gone to one of the girls and was leaning over her in conversation. He was by no means as accomplished as Kydd, proficient but with a light style that lacked individuality. Should he go over and set them both straight on the finer points?

He got up, but when he looked again he was astonished to see the girl blush deeply, glance around and then go with Renzi out of sight over the edge of the broad top of the mountain.

Renzi? Near betrothed to his sister? Scandalised, he considered whether to follow but realised that whatever he did would be misunderstood so he waited awkwardly at the girl's easel, ignoring flashed glances from the others. After an age the two appeared again. When the girl saw Kydd, her eyes widened and her hand flew guiltily to her mouth.

'Um, er – this is Miss Felicity,' Renzi said awkwardly. 'Captain Kydd of *L'Aurore*, my dear.'

At a loss, Kydd merely bowed and looked at Renzi.

'Oh, er, Miss Felicity wishes my opinion of her *veduta*. What is your taking, at all?'

It was a fine, intricate and painstaking work. With not an ounce of life in it. However, Kydd mumbled something anodyne, then added in a significant tone, 'And I would be obliged for your opinion on mine, Nicholas.'

At his easel Kydd turned on Renzi. 'Sir, might I make so bold as to enquire—'

Renzi cut him off: 'In a private way of things Miss Felicity was of some assistance to me,' he said bitingly, 'in the article of what a lady might see in a novel. In peril of her reputation she made free of her feelings in the matter. Shall we join the others?'

Popham laid down his pointer and looked at his captains apologetically. 'So, that's the situation this month, gentlemen. More of the same – the sixty-fours to remain here, the frigates to cruise occasionally. I'm sorry not to have more entertainment but, as you can see, the French have not been obliging in this.'

Byng of *Belliqueux*'s bass rumble came in: 'It has to be said, though, that life on this station does have its compensations.' He had reason to be satisfied: he had been comfortably in command of the ageing sixty-four for five years now and his wife had recently arrived to join him, as had Downman's in *Diadem*. With the pretty wife of *Leda*'s Honyman, there was now a close social grouping of the married men with family.

'Be that as it may, we have our duty. Which takes precedence over all else,' Popham said coldly.

'Well, I'm for a mort of play at the tables tonight. Frederick?' There was an affable response to Byng's query, and the captains made their way out, but something tugged at Kydd and he delayed.

Popham was collecting up his papers and Kydd saw the sagging shoulders, the slow movements, and felt a sudden stab of sympathy. He said impulsively, 'Er, sir, there's a French singer at my club, much cried up. Should you wish it, we could spend a pleasant enough evening there.'

The commodore looked up, his face lined and careworn, and broke into a soft smile. 'Why, so thoughtful in you, Kydd. I shall take you up on the offer, I believe.'

He looked down, saying quietly, 'And it's "Dasher" to my friends, as I hope you'll account me.'

The evening turned out as agreeable as promised and the two found themselves by the log fire, each with a fine brandy. Elsewhere the noisy conviviality continued but they sat in companionable silence, staring into the flames.

At last Popham spoke: 'Pay no mind to me today, Kydd. I'm prey to the blue devils at times – I'm unhappily possessed of a mind that's ceaselessly conjuring up quantities of stratagems and devices that have no hope ever of seeing light of day.'

'It is a disappointment, no doubt, that Mrs Popham is not joining you,' Kydd said gently. Presumably she would be the one to tame his restless spirit, if anyone could.

'Elizabeth does not take kindly to foreign climes, and we have a clutch of daughters whose education would suffer if they were parted from their school.' It was known that Popham had a wife and family, but they had never followed him and he was left, like so many other naval officers, neither bachelor nor married man. Some had taken the easy way out but he had always remained faithful.

Kydd shifted uncomfortably, aware he was talking to the one who had surveyed in the Red Sea, conceived of the Sea Fencibles, had devised the near-invisible catamaran torpedo launchers and a radical new signal system used by Nelson himself, originated the secret Miranda memorandum and was no less than a full fellow of the Royal Society. What possible diversions were to be found in Cape Colony for this fecund brain?

'In my lower moments I feel driven to strike my flag and return to England, away from this exile.' He took a deep pull of his brandy. 'That would be the end of my sea service, of course, but . . .'

Aghast, Kydd tried to find something to say in brotherly sympathy but could think of nothing that did not sound weak.

'And at other times I damn the eyes of the sluggards in London who couldn't see a strategical opportunity if it bit them in the ankle. For two pins I'd sail against Montevideo with what I have, rather than wait for their interminable approval until it's too late.'

Kydd caught a betraying flash of the eyes and, with a tightening of the stomach, realised what it meant. He was being sounded out: the commodore was up to something and needed to know where he stood.

A wash of apprehension was quickly replaced by a surge of understanding and loyalty. Popham was driven by his own need for action but it was in direct accord with his higher duty to his country and the more basic requirement they both shared to achieve something of distinction. Did he really mean it?

'As well you might, Dasher,' Kydd said warmly. 'It would try the patience of a saint.'

He allowed some moments to pass then added casually, 'And a move against the Dons in South America could well knock them out of the war, I'm persuaded.'

'You are? It would discommode them to a degree, that much is certain. And the treasure there – I'd rather it were in English hands than Boney's, don't you think?'

The eyes were now steadily on Kydd and he returned the gaze confidently. Nothing had been said that was either the truth or what he truly felt.

'I do. But then all this is to no purpose – there's nothing can be done without there is approval from Whitehall.'

'Um,' Popham said, his gaze not wavering. 'This must be so, but . . . purely out of curiosity, if I were to be so rash as to make a motion against South America, would you follow, old chap?'

So that was it. A strike against Montevideo!

His mind raced. The question, of course, was hypothetical: if Popham ordered it, Kydd must obey. What was really being asked was: would he join with a whole heart in the enterprise or hang back with carping objections, as some might do in the absence of formal orders from above? If Popham really contemplated the move he must tread very carefully indeed, for if it was later disallowed by the Admiralty then, from this point on, anything Kydd did that smacked of collusion was meat for a court-martial.

There was one overriding objection to any talk of a pre-emptive assault and Kydd knew it had to be brought up immediately: 'Well, I have to say it, Dasher, it's a bold enough stroke – but wouldn't this leave you open to the charge of quitting your station without leave?' It was axiomatic to faraway Admiralty planning that the strength and whereabouts of its assets around the world were reliably known in the grand chess game that was central to political strategy, and an admiral who was absent from his post was a dangerous liability.

Almost as soon as he had spoken, Kydd found an answer to his own question. 'Then again, I'd have to confess before you that I followed Nelson when he left his Mediterranean station to chase Villeneuve across the Atlantic, and where would we all be if his courage to leave had failed him then?'

'Just so,' said Popham, imperceptibly relaxing. 'Would that all my captains were of such stout heart.'

Kydd made play of fixing on the light of the fire through his brandy. 'But then all this is idle talk. The Navy might desire it but the Army must achieve it. How would they be persuaded?'

'This is true enough, but if you'd heard the talk after mess dinner in the castle enough times, as I have, you'd not be in doubt. They, poor wights, are in far worse case than we. At least we've the passing prospect of a privateer or cruiser to look forward to. They've nothing but idleness each and every day and pray for any kind of alarum that might test their mettle. To dangle a chance before them to share in such an adventure, why, we'd be trampled underfoot by eager military not desiring to be overlooked.'

Kydd joined in the comradely chuckle but knew the discussion was becoming pointed. 'Um, yes. But at the same time if ever we'd think to make a descent it must take an expedition of size . . . of cost. Where would—'

'I should think that question easily answered. If our doughty governor, himself of some record as a military strategist, should be taken by the idea, then he has the power and resources to mount such a one. As to equipment, surely that which served in an opposed landing in Blaauwberg would serve us in an identical campaign elsewhere.'

There was no question but that Popham was seriously considering a full-scale move against Spanish South America and all that that implied. The only question now was where Kydd himself stood. With him . . . or against him?

Chapter 3

'He what?' gasped Renzi, choking on his breakfast. 'You seriously mean to tell me—'

Kydd nodded.

'This cannot be! He's implying that there's going to be an assault on Spanish America with – if he strips Cape Colony of its entire sea defences – a pair of old sixty-fours, two or three frigates and a brig-sloop? Ha! Either you misheard our noble commander or I'm compelled to believe this southern moon must have powers to induce lunacy beyond the ordinary.'

Kydd paused. In the cold light of day it did seem more of a dream than a possibility, but then he returned strongly: 'Think of it, Nicholas! Not only will it tear away their main source of income from the Spanish but we deny Bonaparte his tribute and means to wage war. And with such a market opened up to us, our factories and merchants'll swell in riches past all counting. It's . . . it's a chance that, for the sake of England, can't be missed.'

Recovering, Renzi said, with an irritating air, 'Tom, have

you any conception how vast is the continent of South America? How many leagues of mountains and deserts, hills of silver, towns and cities? I'll grant it's a worthy aspiration – but conquest?' He broke off in snorts of laughter.

Nettled, Kydd waited for him to subside. 'You don't know the whole of it, Nicholas. He's in confidential communication with a cove called Miranda, who's said South America is ripe and ready for rebellion. And he does know about things – Billy Pitt himself asked him personally to write a secret memorandum on the subject.'

'That's as may be. It doesn't take anything away from the utter hare-brained idiocy of it all. Even supposing he gets an expedition from England prodigious enough in size to land an army, what then? He wins a first battle – and where will he go next? When it takes a year to march to the other side, how does he prevail upon the Spanish to wait for him there?'

Kydd reddened. 'So this is how you treat commanders of spirit and enterprise? At least Popham's not falling asleep on a quiet station – he's looking to find ways to annoy the enemy in the best way he can, and if he's considering ways for an assault, I, for one, honour him for it,' he snapped, then helped himself to the last of the precious English marmalade in silence.

'Humph. Leave us trust he'll come to his senses. Now, I've had some thoughts about *Portrait*. If you'd be so kind as to hear these out . . . ?'

'Well, if you think they're important. I've a busy day, Nicholas.'

Renzi pushed his plate to one side. 'Then this. What do you think is the best measure of the scale of the task that awaits?'

'I've no idea.'

'The simple exercise of multiplying the words on a page, by the number of pages in a book, gives the result of no less than *one hundred thousand words*!'

He went on in awe, 'Scratching away at, say, a brisk two or three words a second – why, it'll be months continuous for me just to cast it in words.'

'Very well. To first things first, Nicholas. What shall be the meat of your piece? That is to say, you've shown me two books which are novels and each is different from the other. Yours will be like . . . ?'

'Mr John Murray, a most estimable publisher whom I consulted before, I seem to remember did mention that the female fancy is not to be neglected and that a travel work would answer. Should I combine the two it may well prove fruitful.'

'And shall it be a biography?'

'It will be built upon the events of my life to be sure but, good heavens, none must suspect it.'

'Nicholas, you're aware a novel is a work of fiction? You may write what you will, providing it satisfies.'

'Ah – there you have it! What will please a reader? An extensive treatment of the customs and economy of the local polity, as observed on my travels? Or is it to be a detailed account of events, whether uplifting or tragic?'

Kydd sighed. 'I'd be happy with a rousing good tale of your wenching in Venice with your poetic friend on that Grand Tour you never want to talk about.'

Renzi coloured. 'That is never a subject worthy of literary endeavour, as well you know. Recollect, brother, this has to be fit for a gentlewoman's eyes.'

'Then I'd say that you're at a stand, old chap. Until you know what your readers desire, your words are all puff and vapour.'

'I'll think on it,' Renzi muttered, with a hurt expression.

An apologetic knock on the door announced the mate-of-the-watch with a note. 'Sent from the commodore, sir. His boat's still alongside,' he added.

Brief and polite, the message had obviously been written in haste: 'If you can spare the time, there's someone I'd wish you to meet.'

Kydd folded the note and put it into his waistcoat. 'We'll talk novels again later, Nicholas.'

There was no indication of the rank of the person, and Kydd compromised by omitting his sword. This was not like Popham: he was generally considerate to his subordinates in the matter of timing. It must be a matter of importance.

The commodore was waiting for him at the rail of *Diadem* beside a chubby figure with a florid face, dressed in comfortable merchant seaman's rig. 'This is Captain Waine, Kydd. He's master of the trader *Elizabeth*, yonder.' Popham indicated a plain-featured brig at the edge of the anchorage.

The man touched his old-fashioned tricorne respectfully. 'Cap'n,' he said carefully, with a slight American accent.

'Captain Waine has some interesting things to tell us, Kydd. Shall we go to my cabin?'

Dismissing the sentry, Popham offered wine, then turned to Kydd. 'This gentleman has been talking to me about his recent experiences in the viceroyalty of the River Plate, which I thought you'd wish to hear.'

'My pleasure, Admiral,' Waine responded.

'Among the things he's imparted is that at the moment there are no Spanish ships of war in the whole River Plate – none. They've left to sail north to contest a rumoured landing at Caracas.' He winked at Kydd, and went on

81

smoothly, 'And it seems the inhabitants are restless and bitter, concerning the state of trade obtaining there. The Spanish, being at war with England, have been sorely affected, their relations with their colonies all but severed by our blockade.'

'Ain't none been seen this two-month!'

'And what is worse to the situation is that commerce with any other nation is forbidden under the direst penalties. It's true there's a species of smuggling of contraband into the main metropolitan centres, but none may legally trade without leave from the viceroy.'

'From Viceroy Sobremonte hisself!' Waine picked up a newspaper, which he identified as the *Telégrafo Mercantil* of Buenos Aires and waved it at Kydd. 'There it's at, less'n a couple o' months old.'

He spread it out, a blunt forefinger running down the columns of type to find a passage. 'There!'

In Spanish, it meant nothing to Kydd, but Waine translated. 'A *porteño*, man o' property an' standing in the city,' Kydd remembered this was how the painter on Table Mountain had described himself, 'gets mad at the viceroy, sayin' the city's going t' ruin over trade being cut off and demands he goes over t' free trade.' He jabbed at the text in several spots where the words '*libre comercio*' were prominent. 'Didn't do him no good, though. He's slammed in chokey f'r his cheek.'

'And you say there's unrest against Spanish rule?' Popham asked innocently.

'Unrest? Why, I'd say a stronger word'n that. Them as is born there, they's called *criollos* and, no matter how high 'n' mighty, they has to bow down to any as comes from Spain an' takes all the top positions in trade an' gover'ment, no mind how low they's been born in the home country. No, sir, *unrest* is too kind a word.'

'Can you tell us anything of the military? What forces do the Spanish have?'

Waine winked slyly, tapping his nose. 'Why, you're not thinkin' to do mischief there while there's no men-o'-war doing the guardin', b' any chance?'

Popham assumed an appalled look, leaving Kydd to ask awkwardly, 'I was more concerned with how the Spanish might put down any pother at all . . .'

'Well, reg'lars at Montevideo an' a whole lot o' militia in Buenos Aires. A sorry bunch an' nothin' to worry on.'

'Er, I'll not detain you further, Captain,' Popham said, taking his empty glass. 'I know you've cargo to clear. My thanks for your information and we may well talk again.'

After Waine had left, Popham sat down, his brow furrowing. 'You heard that. From one who has nothing to gain by concealing the truth. This sharpens the urgency considerably.'

With Renzi's words and sarcasm still ringing in his ears, Kydd asked, 'Dasher, you can't *really* be thinking to invade South America?'

Popham looked up with a lopsided smile. 'Invade? Of course not. But here's a thought: the Dons have left an open door to seaward while they deal with Miranda in the north, and the population is simmering with revolt. Should a British squadron appear, offering liberation from the oppressors and at the same time throwing open the entire port at last to free trade – which is precisely what we did with such success here in Cape Town – then wouldn't you, as a South American, feel just a little bit inclined to side with us?'

'I'd think so, but the size o' the continent! How can we—'

83

'No, no, *not* an invasion. We haven't the resources and that was never in my thinking. While we can, we seize Montevideo and neutralise the Spanish military. The people rise up and we ride in triumph into the capital. By the time Spain hears of it, for them it's too late. They've lost their seat of power in the south and Miranda is raising the standard of revolt in the north. A mighty empire of three centuries standing – brought down by us!'

It was nothing short of mind-shattering. To go from humble overlooked naval squadron to empire toppling? There had to be a reason why not.

'Er, we'll need an army of quite some size, I'd warrant,' Kydd said, trying to keep his voice steady, 'as can be transported in what vessels we have to command. The guns? And horses, o' course.' He was flailing about now, trying to find solid ground under his feet.

'Leave that to me,' Popham said, with a seraphic smile. 'As soon as our Mr Waine can give me details on their barracks and forces, we'll know how to proceed. I'm sanguine a regiment of Highlanders is worth three of the Spanish. And guns – do remember that there's been no threat to South America since the days of Francis Drake, and never to the River Plate. Even a brace of our paltry field guns will send 'em packing the first time they smell powder.'

'You really *are* going after the Spanish!' Kydd said in awe. This was a breathtaking display of moral courage, not only in the conceiving but the firm self-reliance in initiating and planning the entire matter.

'I am! Should I be satisfied in the odds and what we have to face them, that is.'

Kydd looked at him for a long moment. 'Then, Dasher, you have m' full support. Is there anything I can do?'

84

'Why, thank you. I suppose there is, old fellow. This is no small matter. I'd be obliged to you if we could get our heads together in the planning. With so many strands coinciding in our favour at this time, there's not a moment to lose. Say, at four?'

Renzi arrived late for breakfast, tousled and bleary-eyed.

'Why, you wicked dog! You've been up carousing half the night!'

'Your jest is ill-timed, brother. In truth I've been wrestling with chapters and endings and . . . things, and nothing will answer that would satisfy. How can a character be a feckless rake, yet take our sympathy at one and the same time? It's just not logically possible,' he said bitterly.

He flopped into a chair, picked up a new local newspaper, the *Cape Town Gazette*, and distractedly leafed through it.

'Himself in a taking over *L'Aurore*? I shouldn't have thought it,' he murmured, when Kydd said he was going to the flag-ship shortly.

'Oh, just an enquiry,' Kydd said casually. With Renzi's attitude to Popham, he could see no reason that his friend should know of what was afoot until it was at a more mature stage of planning.

'Then you'll have time for a small discussion of *Portrait*, brother?' Renzi said hopefully, closing the newspaper.

'Not now, Nicholas,' Kydd said absently, looking for his leather dispatch case. He found it and tested its lock with his fob key. 'I have to, er, keep Mr Popham abreast o' things, I find.'

Renzi's eyebrows lifted at the sight of the dispatch case, normally used for the transfer of confidential materials, but he refrained from comment.

* * *

'Right. To the first. How do we proceed from here?' Popham said briskly, pulling out papers and looking encouragingly at Kydd. 'I've questioned our American friend at some length and have discovered that for us things are looking better and better. It seems that not only are there few and poor military but their equipment and fortifications are in dolorous order. I'm content that what we are possessed of here will be sufficient to achieve the goal.'

He passed across some lists. 'I don't have to remind you, I consider this discussion and materials in perfect confidence between us. Surprise is everything.'

'Of course.'

'No one shall know until we have our full dispositions in the matter.'

'You have my word.'

'Not even that secretary chap of yours – what's his name again?'

Kydd paused. 'It's Renzi. You've never really taken to him, have you, Dasher?'

'Well, no,' Popham said, straightening his cuff. 'A little too much of the dark side about him. As one might say, he's the air of a fox, too cunning by half. I'm actually intrigued as to why you have the fellow about you all the time.'

'We've known each other for years. I'd trust him with my life,' Kydd said steadily.

'Quite. But not with planning confidences.'

'As you wish,' Kydd said, 'but if I might make just one observation, Dasher?'

'Fire away.'

'Shall it be you who commands the expedition? Your experience in the military line is . . .'

86

'It will be in the character of a joint venture, naval and military, as was the case with Cape Town.'

'You're not expecting General Baird to leave his governorship here to take command of a South American army?'

'Sir David? No, not at all. But I have a special mission for you, my friend, the honour of co-opting our future general-in-command.'

'I – I don't understand you.'

'You're in the right of it. I'm a military tyro, no acquaintance to speak of in the planning of an army action. We've need of a field officer to advise, to render assistance in the promoting of the operation and so forth. It would appear . . . self-aggrandising if it were I who approached the man. It were better that you broach the possibilities, don't you think?'

'Very well. Whom do you have in mind?'

'There's only one I'd feel has both reason and desire for the position.'

'Beresford?'

'Just so. An ambitious brigadier general, twice thwarted of glory in Cape Town – at Saldanha and with Janssens's hasty surrender – and destined to rot unless he can find himself some other adventure.'

Tall and commanding, Beresford's figure was always prominent in social events at the castle. He still basked in the reputation he had won in a forced march across the desert with Baird from the Red Sea to the Nile, which had resulted in the defeat of the French Army abandoned by Napoleon. And in which the unknown sloop commander, Kydd, had played his small part.

Was this sufficient grounds to strike up an acquaintance with the general, become comradely enough to impart confidences of such giddy import? He felt a jet of nervousness at the thought, for social manoeuvring did not come easily to him. 'I'll, um, see what I can do,' he said cautiously.

'No need to make an immediate approach,' Popham said pleasantly, 'as the initial objective has first to succeed.'

'Being?'

'I think it proper that my captains should be made acquainted with what we plan at the outset. We carry them with us, and our approach to Sir David will be that much the easier, particularly since by your golden words his colleague General Beresford will stand persuaded of the necessity of a descent at this time.'

Kydd was beginning to feel out of his depth, but he also knew that in a post-captain such skills were requisite if he was going to progress in his profession. 'They'll need some convincing,' he said, as heartily as he could, 'evidence of our military resources as will have them satisfied in every particular of the enterprise.'

'Exactly. So – to work. These papers list our assets and an appreciation of what we face across the Atlantic. You shall be a captain and I shall rehearse on you what will be presented. Then I beg you will say whether or no you are decided.'

'Well, I'm ready for you, Dasher.'

Popham leaned forward. 'This is no triviality I'll have you know, my dear Kydd,' he said gravely. 'If you are not agreeable in any wise, for any reason, I shall not proceed. That is, the whole venture to be called off – abandoned. I will not risk men's lives unless there is good prospect of success. You understand?'

It was unfair: he was being put in a position where his word would be enough to destroy a daring and far-sighted stroke against the enemy – or to send men to their deaths.

But then again, wasn't Popham being scrupulous in his planning, getting a second opinion such that if it went against him the world would never hear of it again?

'I do. Be certain you'll hear from me should I feel to the contrary.'

'Stout fellow! Then shall we begin?'

Popham had pleaded ignorance of military affairs but, if this was the case, it didn't show to Kydd. Perhaps it was his experience of the Cape Town expedition or even the previous Red Sea joint operation but he certainly seemed perfectly at home dealing with forage for horses, biscuits and rum for the troops and second-run stores for the follow-up, as well as the joint administrative structures to be set up.

Numbers were demonstrably inferior, but Kydd had seen the Highlanders in action. And when Popham produced his trump card, he found it hard not to applaud. It was to formalise what had worked so well at Blaauwberg: that the invading ships would each contribute a proportion of their seamen and marines to form a sea battalion that would increase their effectives by a considerable margin.

'Considering we have only to make a show against the Spanish, and the natives will flock to our banners, it should suffice,' Popham said.

'I hope you've something more interesting for us than last time, old bean,' complained Donnelly of *Narcissus*. 'I've an important appointment ashore, an' she won't wait.'

Popham ignored the gibe from the senior frigate captain and waited for the meeting to settle. At the other end of the elegant table in the flagship's great cabin sat Kydd, studiously blank-faced, along with the men commanding the other ships of consequence, in all the totality of the rated vessels in his fleet.

'I've called you here for one purpose only. That is to seek your advice.'

This brought immediate attention, for not only was Popham not given to asking what to do but in a flag-officer it was unprecedented.

'Whatever we can do, sir,' Downman said loyally. The others kept a wary silence.

'Then it is in this matter.' Glancing at each man individually, his manner confiding, persuasive and convincing, he spoke slowly: 'I've recently had an extraordinary intelligence that reveals the Spanish have left their province at the River Plate completely unguarded, sailing as they have done to quell unrest in the north of the country and leaving contemptible forces only to guard Montevideo. Understanding that the French squadrons are now no longer threatening, that Trafalgar has robbed the Spanish of any means to contest us at sea and that we still retain most of the same fleet that succeeded so nobly here at Cape Town – then how absurd would it be to consider a sudden descent on the viceroyalty to achieve a famous victory, one that could well knock the Spanish out of the war?'

There was a stupefied silence, then a sudden eruption of astonished talk.

'Gentlemen, gentlemen! One at a time, please!' Like a kindly vicar smiling benevolently on his flock, he allowed the excitement to subside, then calmly said, 'Captain Donnelly?'

'This is madness!' he spluttered. 'Are you proposing an invasion of South America? To attack—'

'No, sir, I am not proposing anything. I'm merely asking your advice, your views, if you will. And never an invasion. If anything, conceivably the suggestion of some species of move against Montevideo, perhaps to hold it for a space until reinforcements arrive. You see, there is an opportunity – a rare conjunction of conditions – that make it feasible to consider the detaching of the Spanish colonies simply by encouraging rebellion among the indigenes. As you may apprehend, they will never hold their possessions against revolt from within while attacked from without.'

'I see,' Byng said, in dawning realisation. 'This is by way of a gesture against the Spanish, giving heart to the natives to throw off the yoke and so forth. I like it. A lot gained for little risked.'

'And what precisely will this adventure secure to the advantage of the Crown?' Donnelly sniffed. 'If this has any chance of being set afoot, that should be known to us in advance.'

'Don't be an ass, Richard,' Byng said scornfully. 'Think it to be a hundred – a thousand times bigger than Cape Colony! Under our enlightened rule we show free trade, encourage the market and there we go – a river of gold from selling our manufactures into the place and another from trading, er, whatever they grow to the rest of the world.' He blinked. 'Sure to be something or other . . .'

'So we're to acquire another continent for our empire? We lost the last American one by grievously underestimating the costs of such, and foisting them on the colonists, who then loudly objected and threw us out,' Donnelly said contemptuously.

Downman came in quickly: 'As you've no imagination, Richard. Aren't you overlooking one thing? The Spanish have been shipping out millions in silver every year since they made conquest. I dare to say that in our hands it will see the administration well served in the article of costs.'

'And, o' course, at this moment that silver goes into Boney's coffers to pay for his war,' Kydd said enthusiastically. 'We have a chance to put an end to it.' There were slow nods around the table as the implications of both sank in.

Popham resumed: 'Supposing us to be interested, I've drawn up some simple lists as will show the relative military strengths, which, I'm obliged to observe, do favour us in the details.' He passed them around.

'It says here but four guns! Against an army?'

'Let me be clearer,' Popham said patiently. 'Any descent will obviously be in the nature of a complete surprise. Although the enemy has numbers, these are untrained native militia who've never seen a single day of action. Do you truly believe them capable of standing against our formidable Highland troops? No, I thought not. The guns are there merely to provide a whiff of smoke at the right time.' He smiled grimly.

'And, again, this is a limited objective only – the reduction of a single stronghold until reinforcements arrive. With undisputed command of the seas, do you doubt our forces can be supplied?'

He allowed an air of weariness to show, then said, 'For a little enterprise much is to be gained – which must result, with such a bold stroke, in honour and distinction to those involved. In our quiet little station I would have thought the prospect of such would be enough to set the blood astir. Is there none of spirit here willing to take the Dons by the ears and at the same time earn notice before the world?'

'Dammit, I'm for it,' Byng burst out. 'Better'n lying eternally at anchor all winter.'

'And me,' Kydd said forcefully. 'I'd think it no less than our duty to annoy the enemy in any way we can contrive, and I've not heard a better.'

'Hold hard, Mr Fire-eater Kydd!' Donnelly said impatiently.

'We're not voting in some council-of-war, we're giving our views, and what I need to hear is the position of their lordships in the matter, they giving the order and providing the expedition. It's not for us to come up with some wild plan and expect them to fall in with it.'

'Well, that's easily answered,' Popham said, a confident smile playing. 'A year or two ago, after my investigation of the patriot Miranda and secret memorandum to the prime minister himself, plans were set in train to implement an assault on Montevideo, but then the Trafalgar campaign took precedence. Therefore this may be seen simply as the resumption of an existing expedition.'

'A resumption?' Donnelly said, exasperated. 'Then why the devil are we confabulating about it at all? We follow orders as received.'

'Ah, it's not quite so simple. Our conquest of the Cape was rapid and complete, taking days only, and no doubt fresh orders for our deploying are being drafted as soon as they may. However, time and tide wait for no man and so forth, and so it is in our case. The whole River Plate is open while their forces are called away, and additionally the French squadrons have been destroyed or have retired to regroup, and at this season in the south there is little mischief to be expected locally. This is a precious opportunity that may not recur for a long time.'

'Pardon me for being so slow in stays,' said Donnelly, barely hiding his incredulity, 'but isn't this saying you've intentions of sailing *without* orders, mounting your own expedition, starting your own war? Why, it's – it's—'

Popham's easy manner fell away, his eyes suddenly steely. 'I have your views, sir. And I say we can't wait – do you propose remaining in idleness while the opportunities pass us by until such time as orders can reach us from six thousand miles away? I do not! I'm minded to reconstitute the Cape Town expedition as the Montevideo expedition and, on sailing, to send word directly to Mr Pitt that the previous plan is now going forward. I shall request that the agreed reinforcements do meet us in the River Plate, by which time I'm utterly confident we shall have made a first foothold on the continent.'

There were surprised but approving murmurs around the table. Bold, decisive moves were wanted in this war, which was on a global scale like no other.

Honyman had not yet spoken but now pronounced, 'And Billy Pitt will see his chance and send out an army. It's a capital idea, Dasher.'

'Liberators of South America! Ha! The world will hear of us then.' Byng chuckled. 'I'm not doubting it'll mean parades in London, kneeling before His Nibs in the Palace, a medal or two . . .'

Suddenly the prospect became not impossible. 'Show us those figures again,' Honyman said, animated. 'I've a notion we should do it.'

Kydd caught the sudden gleam in Popham's eyes. The magic word 'we' had now been been uttered.

Discussion became general. Popham played it very carefully, allowing suggestions to take root, following objections and taking notes. The sentiment of the meeting was rapidly moving towards an urging of Popham to take action with a full-blooded acclamation of the possibilities. Within the hour he had what he wanted.

'Very well,' Popham declared expansively. 'I shall take our conclusions to the governor and I'm sanguine he'll approve an immediate call to arms. I'll suspend this meeting in the trust that the next shall be in the nature of a full-scale planning for our Spanish Surprise.'

As they rose he called down the table, 'Er, Mr Kydd – if you'd be so good as to remain? I'll need some assistance in the readying of a presentation to Sir David, and as you're junior present . . . ?'

It was neatly done. Kydd's regular presence at the flagship would not now be remarked on.

As the last captain filed out of the cabin, Popham turned and, with an audible sigh, collapsed into his armchair by the window. 'Such a hard beat to windward,' he murmured, 'you'd think it a forlorn hope I'm contemplating. Donnelly has the spirit I'd expect in a town beadle, and some of the others . . . Still, I do believe they're with me – don't you?'

'They are, as so they should.'

'If General Beresford shows willing, he'll make sure Baird comes in. So I suppose I must possess myself in patience until you've made your play. Have you any idea how you'll do it?'

'Renzi, old fellow, are you not well?' Kydd said in surprise, seeing him crouched by the stern-lights. There was no movement and Kydd crossed to him in concern. 'Are you all right, Nicholas?'

There was a muffled groan. 'I just can't get started,' Renzi mouthed. He heaved himself up and into a chair. 'Tom,' he croaked, 'it doesn't fadge – nothing works, it's coming out too . . . too wooden, if you catch my meaning.'

'You mean your novel?'

Renzi gave him a withering stare. 'And what else, pray?'

Kydd sat down. 'That is, your hero is not, as who should say, a satisfying enough cove.'

'No, not just that,' Renzi said wearily. 'It's that . . . Well, you'd never understand.'

'As I've not the headpiece of an author?' Kydd said tartly. 'Look, m' friend – you're going to have to face it. It may be . . .'

'May be what?' Renzi said, with unease at Kydd's tailing off.

'It could be . . . that you have to be born to the craft, the same as prime seamen, brought up in it from a younker.'

'It could be that authors have it inside them all the while, awaiting release.'

'And you all this time at it and no headway?' Kydd said sadly. 'I don't think so, Nicholas.'

Renzi said nothing, but his frustration was pitiful to see. Kydd softened. 'Look, why don't you think again? It's about a well-born chap who has all these adventures. Isn't that you? Why don't you write about yourself directly? If you'd care to, o' course.'

'No, no. I can't do it. To write is to expose yourself to the world, to let everyone see into your . . . well, all of you. I could never allow that.'

He pulled out a crumpled sheet. 'Just listen to this, though. "I walked into the salon, the duchess looked at me and I had to think of something to say but I couldn't!" How can you get a novel from that?'

'Well, I'm not the one to ask it, but have you thought about Curzon? He mingles with the nobs, possibly knows an author.'

Renzi bristled. 'No one is to find out what I'm writing!'

'No, of course not. I'm sorry to say I'm at a loss, Nicholas. You might have to admit—'

'Thank you, Tom, you've made your point.'

'Well, I have to go. There's divisions at eleven.'

Renzi shifted uncomfortably in his chair. Kydd's talk of authors being born to it was a worrying bar; if anyone could be such, why wasn't the world filled with authors? It was not a pleasant conclusion. He'd worked damned hard, and he was no further forward than he had been at the beginning. The plot was logically perfect, the hero's name and character replete with fascinating and subtle classical nuance, the factual material impeccable. Why then did it read so heavily, so . . . so dull to the eyes?

It was lacking something. He was no stranger to words but they were simply not playing out as he so ardently wished they would. Was Kydd right in suggesting he write about himself? No! Putting aside the embarrassment of exposing his inner self before the public, this was to be a work of fiction and his own experiences had no right to appear.

Wearily he got up and went down to his cabin to put the day's work in order. The balled-up paper, the scribbled sheets, the endless crossed-out notes – he just didn't have the heart. He sat down and let his eyes roam over the tightly packed bookshelf above his tiny desk. They were the work of authors, of course, the blessed, the favoured, the felicitous. Would he *never* join their august band?

As ever, his eye softened at the row of poetry volumes. The tight crafting of precise and numinous meaning from shining words had always given him satisfaction and comfort and he reached for the first and oldest, from the time of Francis Drake, a work by Sir Philip Sidney, that turbulent and gifted Elizabethan. He opened it at random.

And the words leaped out at him:

Thus, great with childe to speak, and helplesse in my throwes,
Biting my trewand pen, beating myselfe for spite,
Fool, said my Muse to me, looke in thy heart – and write!

He blinked and held his breath. A rising feeling of giddiness overwhelmed him, for that was exactly the problem and the solution! In a heightened state of mind, he felt a supernatural thrill – that down the centuries this man was speaking to him, giving of himself to deliver a fellow scribe from the thrall of stasis.

His mind cleared. He had treated the whole thing too logically, too much in the abstract. Was it possible to look into a man's heart from a distance? To generate sympathy at arm's length? No. But the solution was there as well.

He must look into his own heart and write about what caused pain to *him*, gave joy and grief, stirred his deepest emotions, caused his darker, detestable self to reign – and he could do it, for it would be a release. He could at last speak of those years of blind, youthful extravagance and meaningless existence, which had ended with the epiphany in Venice that had sent him back to confront the moral imperative which had changed his life utterly.

Yes! He'd do it! And he could see how – both passionately and as a detached observer: simply tell the tale from the outside, knowing the inside. He snatched a sheet and his hand flew over the paper.

In his regimental dress, the pipe major looked both barbaric and splendid in the massed candlelight as he passed slowly between the tables. No allowance was made for the modest enclosed space of the Castle of Good Hope's banqueting hall and the volume of sound was visceral. Kydd revelled in it, however, for there was nothing like this sense-numbing martial wail to be found in a man-o'-war's wardroom.

With the utmost dignity, the piper concluded his processing at the head of the table next to the mess president, General Sir David Baird, and duty done, stared fixedly ahead.

The moment hung in a heady whisky fragrance, the gold and scarlet of regimentals in rows interspersed here and there with the rich dark blue and gold of the Navy as both services joined in the tribal ritual of the loyal toast. Baird rose solemnly; with a massed scraping of chairs every officer got to his feet likewise, his glass, charged with a golden glow, held before him.

'Gentlemen – the King.'

'The King,' murmured half a hundred men, some with an added, 'God bless him.' It produced a powerful sense of union with the country that had given them birth, now on the other side of the world but to which each and every one was bound by this common tie of allegiance.

With a rustle and occasional clink of ceremonial accoutrements, the assembly resumed their seats and conversations continued in a lively hum.

'Your jolly good health, sir!' It was the adjutant of the 93rd, sitting down from Kydd and the more senior officers.

'And to yours, sir!' Kydd called in return, raising his glass. He enjoyed attending army mess dinners with their different ways and effortless banter, not to mention the fine victuals to be had in a garrison town and, of course, their well-found cellar.

Tonight was no exception: a regimental occasion with the 71st as hosts and the rest of the military as guests in a splendid affair – but for Kydd there was a purpose and he prepared to make his move.

Next to him was the red-faced and happy Lieutenant Colonel Geoffrey McDonald, Lord of the Isles, and further towards the head of the table the firebrand Colonel Pack held forth, but for Kydd there was only one of notice that night: the brigadier general and second-in-command of the Cape Colony military, William Carr Beresford, sat some places up.

The dinner was over, the toasts made and cloths drawn, and amiable converse became general. Now was the time.

'A right noble dinner, General Beresford, sir,' he called genially. 'I've not had better this age, I declare.'

Beresford had a reputation for stiffness, a liking for the forms, but he turned politely to Kydd and replied, 'The victor of the Zambezi does us honour in the attending, Captain. As it happens I've just sent for a bottle of Malmsey of the old sort. Would you care to join me?'

As was usual at this time, a number of officers had taken the opportunity to perform what the Navy delicately alluded to as 'easing springs' and by their absence the hardier remaining were able to choose a more convenient seating. Kydd left his and, after a polite bow to Sir David, took the chair opposite Beresford.

'This is most civil in you, sir,' he said, as his glass was filled. 'I've quite forgotten the taste of such after so long on this station.'

After murmured appreciations it was established that the distinguished captain in the Royal Navy by the same name was indeed Beresford's brother John, who had been active and enterprising in the war against the French in the Caribbean, and had, as who might say, been fortunate indeed in the matter of prizes and notice.

Kydd confided that his own family was quite undistinguished, living as they did in the country near Guildford, and changed the subject – not so much out of concern that his humble origins would be discovered but more in the knowledge that this was the eldest son of the Marquess of Waterford, but one who had not succeeded to the title for he was acknowledged illegitimate.

Beresford was surprised by and professed delight to learn of Kydd's role in the Abercromby action in Egypt and, unbending at last, detailed his own legendary dash across the desert to take the French in the rear, illustrating the route with cruet marshes and a decanter range of mountains, not forgetting a perilous defile between two forks that left no doubt as to the hazards bravely faced.

After another mutual toast, Kydd set down his glass with a sigh. 'I do confess it, I'm taken with the entertainments commanded by your most celebrated 71st Regiment. I do wish it were in my power to conjure a like in return, but my ship – trim and graceful as she is – cannot possibly stand with a castle in the article of convenience in entertaining.'

He allowed his head to drop. Then he looked up again brightly. 'I have an idea! Yes – it's possible! My duty as captain must surely be to make certain those rascals of a crew do not wither in idleness while long at anchor. I've a mind to put to sea and exercise 'em. Sir, how would you welcome a day's cruise in a saucy frigate whose sailors are set to every task in sea life before you? Racing up the rigging, bringing in sail high aloft, a few rounds with the great guns, boatwork . . .

'Sir, I can promise entertainments and edification a landlubber may never be witness to in a lifetime.'

'Oh. Er, I would not want to put those splendid fellows to overmuch trouble, Captain.'

'Nonsense. You shall be my guest and see how the Navy conducts its manoeuvres, and be damned to their feelings. Shall you wish to see a flogging with the cat o' nine tails at all?' Kydd asked innocently.

'No, no, that will not be necessary. The spectacle of a grand ship working its sails and, er, things will be diversion enough. That's most kind in you, sir, and I mean to take you up on the offer.'

'Splendid!' Kydd exclaimed. 'And I'm sure your staff might be accommodated if they can bear to be escorted by midshipmen. Shall we say on Thursday, then? My first lieutenant will call upon you at two bells of the forenoon, as we do call nine o' clock.'

'All in hand, sir,' Gilbey said, touching his hat to Kydd on the quarterdeck. 'Stand fast that th' officers' cook is in a fret that he can't find artichokes an' he's heard the general is partial to 'em.'

'Never mind, I'm sure he'll manage. Take away my barge and coxswain and be sure to warn the boat's crew to feather and don't wet the general.'

There was widespread anticipation at the news that there would be a high-ranking redcoat general aboard to experience for himself how the Navy did things. Even the gunroom found time to priddy their abode with the most tasteful decoration to be found, and after Kydd had indicated that the general would be visiting the mess-decks to see the sailors at home, an astonishing level of industry had produced quaint and intricately wrought ropework ornamentation to adorn the mess-trap racks and table corners.

On deck every conceivable rope's end that could be spied from the quarterdeck had been inspected, and if not pointed, a seaman was set to the painstaking task of working it thus – fashioning a pleasing taper to the end of the rope and finishing with a lengthy whipping.

Guns were treated with a mixture of lamp black and copperas, then polished well with a linseed-oil woollen cloth, the result being favourably compared to ebony. Kydd knew, however, that this was a fighting general and personally ensured that every fire channel between pan and vent was clear and bright: there had been cases when zealous blacking had resulted in a perfect appearance but a blocked touch-hole had rendered the gun useless in action.

Decks had a snowy lustre where holystone and bear had been plied with salt water, and on all sides, if a touch of colour might bring a fitment to more pleasing prominence, paint was produced and the more artistic seamen set to wielding a brush.

The visit was a perfect excuse to break the monotony of harbour service and to build on the pristine condition of the recently cleansed ship to produce a state of perfection not normally possible. For the rest of the commission, they would have a standard by which to judge themselves.

'Boat approaching!' called the mate-of-the-watch, importantly.

'Side-party!' growled Curzon. A line of white-gloved midshipmen and lieutenants assembled at the side-steps by the hances, each with a grave expression, Kydd taking position at the inboard end.

The barge curved about and hooked on at the main-chains with a showy display of seamanship. Hidden from view, it was not possible to see what was keeping the general, and the boatswain continued to lick the mouthpiece of his call nervously. Finally, Kydd peered over the side and saw a red-faced general awkwardly trying to fasten his sword-belt and fending off Poulden's well-meaning assistance. Ashore, army officers scorned the loose-fitting naval arrangement for a tight, soldierly fit but this was quite impossible to wear in boats as the general was now finding.

Kydd jerked back and rearranged the side-party, placing the boatswain's mate and a brawny seaman by the ship's side. 'See the general doesn't kiss our deck – compree?' he hissed.

At last the general's plumed hat and solemn face appeared as he mounted the side-steps. Twisting his highly polished boots awkwardly over the bulwark and catching sight of the ceremonial line, he made to raise his hat – and the inevitable happened. His sword caught behind him and he toppled forward. In a flash the two seamen had him firmly by the arms, while his cocked hat was caught by a quick-thinking midshipman who clapped it back on his head before scurrying to his place in the line.

While General Beresford recovered his composure, the boatswain's call pealed out and he advanced down the line of blank-faced sidesmen to be greeted by *L'Aurore*'s captain, who of course had not seen anything of the general's discomfiture.

'You're most welcome aboard, sir. Might I present my officers . . .'

In the captain's cabin a restorative taste of naval-issue rum had Beresford in good humour and ready for his day.

'Shall we venture on to the upper deck? There you'll see our sturdy tars at as hard work as ever you'll see them,' Kydd invited.

The capstan, situated in *L'Aurore* between the mainmast and the wheel, was already pinned and swifted; grinning at being under such an august eye, the seamen and marines spat on their hands and clutched the bar upwards to their chests in readiness.

'Carry on, Mr Curzon!' Kydd ordered. A fife and drum struck up a jaunty tune and the men stretched out with a will. Beresford was shown the cable ranged along the main-deck below coming in dripping, hauled from forward by the messenger line before it fed down into the cable tiers amidships. It tautened and the pace slowed; men strained and heaved until the boatswain, with his foot on the cable coming in the hawse, roared, 'Anchor's aweigh!'

'Ah. Then I have to inform you, sir, that the anchor is won clear and this ship is now legally at sea.'

'Lay out and loose!' The waiting topmen raced out on the yards and sail magically blossomed. Braces were manned and, with a graceful sway of acknowledgement to Neptune, the frigate took up on the larboard tack, the familiar swash and creak of a ship under way growing in volume as Beresford found his sea legs on the slightly canting deck.

Kydd was soon explaining to his intelligent and attentive guest the relative forces between the sails and their resulting course through the sea, the strains to be expected aloft and the options for trimming.

'Course nor'-west, Mr Curzon.'

Beresford then took in the work on deck necessary to bring the canvas aloft to a proper accommodation to this new direction and the helmsman's interplay between binnacle compass and set of the sails that ensured the course was maintained. He and Kydd paced the deck together, speaking of the functions of lines and spars, blocks and tackles, until Kydd ordered the ship close-hauled, by the wind as close as she could lie.

The different motion was immediately apparent, much as

a horse changes gait when moving from a canter to a gallop, with seas taken on the bow resulting in a spirited pitching and spray carrying aft in exhilarating bursts. Kydd's intention, though, was to show the limitation of a square-rigger, that she could come up no closer than six points to the wind's eye.

They made fine speed, and when the land was sunk, all but the far distant blue-grey flat rectangle of Table Mountain, the frigate shortened sail and took up a more sedate pace for the next show: the great guns at drill.

To Kydd, a fine sailing ship was a thing of majesty but what decided battles were the guns, and every man aboard *L'Aurore* knew his views. The starboard and windward side twelve-pounder main armament was manned and cleared away, fob-watches significantly flourished, and gun-captains with dark expressions mustered their crews.

Beresford took a keen interest in the guns: while they were the lightest frigate main armament in the Navy they were twice the calibre of the largest field gun his army possessed. And quite different: a more compact carriage than horse-drawn artillery, they were on trucks, small wooden wheels, and were tethered to the ship's side by thick breeching ropes with tackles each side to run them out.

When all gun-crews were closed up, Kydd went to a gun-captain and told him to show the general his equipment – slung powder horn and a pouch with spare flints, cartridge pricker, quill tubes and the rest. Each gun number was told to prove his gear: worm, rammer, sponge and crow, a powder monkey proudly holding out his salt-box for carrying the charge.

'Slow time, Mr Gilbey.'

His first lieutenant clapped on his hat. 'Fire! Gun has fired!' he roared.

The exercise had begun. Tackle falls were eased and the guns rumbled back down the canted deck. The gun-crew got to work – sponge and rammer, invisible wad and shot, the gun-captain showily bruising his priming and slamming the gun-lock down before the gun was run out once more.

Then it was quick time: the fearful muscle-bulging round of heaving the gun in and out in a synchronised choreography, four men furiously serving their iron beast each side, nimbly sharing the limited seven feet of space between each gun with an adjacent crew. After ten minutes of frantic activity, Kydd called a halt.

'We'll have three rounds apiece from numbers three and five guns, Mr Gilbey, and to make it interesting we'll stream a mark.'

The float was found, and on its mast a red flag was fixed, its nine feet square looking enormous on the frigate's deck.

'A trifle large, wouldn't you think?' Beresford murmured.

Kydd gave a tight smile but said nothing as it was heaved over the side, sliding rapidly astern. While *L'Aurore* went about to clear the range, the guns were loaded, grey cartridge and iron-black shot, quill tube inserted and gun-lock cocked.

At three hundred yards the jaunty bobbing of the flag was in clear view on the grey-green sea but Kydd took Beresford to the first gun. 'Do see if you feel the gun is rightly pointed, if you will, sir.'

Gingerly, the general bent to look. 'There's no sights!' he said, astonished. Only a bare barrel looked out into the broad expanse of sea. 'How do you lay the weapon?'

Kydd pointed out the quoin under the breech for elevation and the handspike to lever the gun bodily from side to side. 'The gun-captain must lay the gun to his own satisfaction.' Obligingly, the man did so, with hand signals to his crew.

'There, sir.'

Once more Beresford bent down, squinted along the barrel to the muzzle, then rose ruefully. 'As I fail to even see your target, Captain.'

It was a common mistake for first-time gunners. The trick was to locate the target first and draw the muzzle to it, rather than the other way round. After explanations, Beresford picked up on the flag, now a tiny thing set against the sighting along the gun barrel, which unreasonably reared and fell each side randomly with the pitch and heave of the seas.

'Do say, sir, when you, as gun-captain, will fire your piece.'

Beresford wouldn't be drawn. 'It's quite impossible. The damn thing won't stay still.' Kydd hid a smile: unlike the rock-still conditions on land, the sea was a moving, live thing that altered everything, from the footing of the gunners to the eventual flight of the ball.

'Stand by, gun-crews! Over here, sir, if you please.'

They stood back at a respectful distance, but before Gilbey could give the orders Beresford called out imperiously, 'And it's five guineas to one, Mr Kydd, that not a one shall strike within fifty yards!' The gun-crews turned to look back incredulously.

Kydd, keeping a straight face, nodded in agreement. 'Carry on, Mr Gilbey.'

'Number three gun! Fire when you bear.'

The gun-captain crouched, staring along the barrel, giving large then smaller signals, the gun-lanyard in his hand until he went rigid for a few seconds. Then, in one fluid motion, he jerked on the lanyard, swivelled to one side and arched his body, as the gun, with a brutal slam of sound and moment-arily hidden in smoke, hurtled back in recoil.

The smoke cleared quickly in the brisk breeze and, after a

second or two, a white plume arose gracefully – not twenty yards to one side and fair for elevation.

'If that were another frigate, he'd be looking to a hit a-twixt wind and water,' Kydd commented smugly.

'Number five!'

Eager to do better, the gun-captain took his time and was rewarded with a strike in line but beyond. Beresford had the grace to look rueful. 'Your guinea is safe, sir. These gunners are in the character of magicians, I believe.'

Kydd relented and explained how it was done. A field gun in the Army was fired with port-fire and linstock, bringing a glowing match to the touch-hole, a practice that was long gone in the Navy. Aboard ship, a gun was fired with a gun-lock, a larger version of that to be found on a musket, and the lag between yanking the lanyard and the gun going off was a manageable small fraction of a second.

And Kydd, like others who were gunnery-wise, made a practice of rating only top seamen gun-captain, those who had long experience on the helm, who could 'read' a sea, anticipate their ship's behaviour in any conditions. This made all the difference when it came to judging the exact moment to fire during the roll of the ship when the muzzle of the gun swept down over the target.

He would leave it to another time to make the point that most gunnery was conducted at the range of a cricket pitch when, in the blood and chaos, only the fastest and steadiest gun-crews would be left standing.

'Good practice indeed,' Beresford acknowledged, when the three rounds had been expended. While they had not blown the target out of the water, all that was wanted had been achieved: that in the invisible profile of an enemy ship around the float, every shot would have told.

'Sir, stand down the people for dinner?' Gilbey asked respectfully.

Kydd nodded.

Gear was secured and the welcome blast of 'Up spirits' was piped by the boatswain's mate. A happy line of mess-men was soon lining up by the tub in the waist where the grog was mixed in the open air, under the strict supervision of the master-at-arms and the mate-of-the-watch.

The general wanted to visit the mess-decks during their noon meal. Kydd knew it would be an eye-opening experience for him. Army other-ranks were in truth the lowest forms of humanity, from ignorant farmhands and factory workers down to thieves and murderers, their training little more than musket drill and marching. Aboard ship there was no room for these untrained masses: the skills and teamwork in bringing in madly flogging sails on the yardarm or serving the great guns in a no-quarter fighting match were vital and essential.

As well, daily life at sea within the confines of a man-o'-war had its own demands. The committing to test courage on a daily basis put side by side with the human need to relate to one's shipmates brought out character and strength in the relationships that shaped them. These men were individuals, formed in a crucible of ordeals, ranging from personal combat to the howling menace of a gale, and over time they drew together in a mutual interdependence and regard that was at the very core of what it was to be a member of the company of a fine ship.

The general, with his hat under his arm and therefore deemed invisible, passed between the tables, hearing yarns and ditties, laughter and concerns, feeling the temper of a prime frigate at her best. Afterwards he visited the galley, with its large, purpose-built Brodie stove. The cook in his kingdom ruled his mates and skinkers with an iron fist, lordly checking the metal tallies on the nets of fresh meat doled out from the huge copper vats to the mess-cooks and quick to see that the slush rising on the seething surface was diligently skimmed for his later profitable disposal.

Of course, changes would come after only days into a sea voyage, away from a friendly harbour source of fresh victuals. No more fresh meat but salt beef and pork from the cask, bread replaced by the hard tack that the Navy insisted go under the same name, and in place of greens, preserved stuff such as sauerkraut and trundlers, dried peas.

In the afternoon, those off-watch went to their accustomed leisure on the fo'c'sle while the watch-on-deck took grave glee in exercising their sea skills – stropping a block, invisibly joining two ropes with a long-splice, or rattling down the shrouds on the leeward side. Intricate knots were worked, thick canvas was sewn with palm and needle, and impossibly complex tackles and purchases were devised to move an inoffensive mess-tub. The general took in that these were but a small part of what an able seaman was expected to do for his ship.

'Four bells, sir,' Gilbey reported.

'Very well. Make it so.'

This was a signal for the last act. 'Hands t' take stations f'r lowering.'

The launch at sea was stowed on the upper-deck waist, the pinnace nested inside. To ensure its ton weight safely afloat was no trivial feat, demanding the rigging of heavy tackles from the fore-yard and main-yard, connected together with stay tackles and masthead top-burtons to ease the weight. The entire operation, from rest on the chocks to a lively boat in the sea alongside, was conducted in silence, the only sound the harsh piercing of the boatswain's call.

It was a telling illustration of the skills and training necessary for even the most straightforward of tasks at sea. By contrast, the gig on davits over *L'Aurore*'s quarter descended to the water in a squeal of sheaves, the boat's crew making light of scrambling along the driver boom to the jacob's ladder at its end to tumble handily into it.

Beresford's attention was drawn back to the launch, which was stroking away to the frigate's beam, and he was startled at the light-hearted cry from the main-top lookout. '*Deck ahooooy! I spy pirates! Pirates on the st'b'd beam!*'

The launch had rounded to and boated oars but up the stumpy mast rose the dread banner of the skull and crossbones. From their hidden positions in the bottom of the boat a dozen pirates appeared. Fearsome in red bandannas and eye patches, they screeched curses and brandished cutlasses. Then the launch was joined by the gig, and the two, manning their oars, swept round and headed straight for *L'Aurore*.

'Repel boarders, Mr Gilbey,' Kydd ordered crisply.

The first lieutenant wore a sour expression at the sight of the men disporting themselves, but he had his orders. 'Stand t' your fore!' he snarled.

The pirates came on in fine style, swarming up the sides and spilling on to the deck in a tidal wave of action. The brave defenders did what they could but were hard pressed and fell back, hewing and slashing, pistols banging. Casualties mounted on all sides until, with a dreadful roar that startled even Kydd, the awe-inspiring figure of Stirk appeared at the main hatchway, bringing a wave of reinforcements for an attack from behind.

It was quickly over, the last pirates alive preferring a watery grave overside to the wrath of the King's men.

'Well done, well done!' Beresford laughed. 'His Majesty's jolly tars triumph again!'

But Kydd had not finished. As the panting men stood down, he called over a pikeman.

'On guard!' he ordered. Obediently the man stood firmly, legs astride, the butt of the long pike wedged on deck in the ball of his foot, its forged iron tip questing outward at eye level for the first over the bulwark. 'Sir, you see here a formidable weapon awaiting a boarder. But it has a fatal flaw.'

He took a cutlass from another and made to strike at the pikeman, who instantly responded, the deadly point turning unwavering on Kydd's eyes. In a flash Kydd had dropped to one knee in the classic fencing pose for a lunge, but with his cutlass diagonally above his head. Then his blade swung up with a clash on the pike, preventing it lowering, and at the same time he rose, forcing the blade along the pike in a lethal slither – inside the man's defences.

'This man is now at my mercy, which does not exist in a boarding.'

Beresford acknowledged with a slow nod. 'Pistols?'

'One shot only,' Kydd replied shortly, 'into the face, then it's aught but a club.'

'Knives?'

'Worse than useless.'

'Tomahawks?' He remembered some boarders had carried these.

'Never carried by defenders as not for fighting – their use is to cut away defensive ropery when rigged.'

'Then—'

'Far better to stop 'em boarding in the first place – canister or grape from carronades, the marines and such with muskets seen to be waiting, and swivels on the breast-rail or in the tops. In harbour there's boarding nettings spread from below the gun-ports, which can stop even the most vicious assault. We've naught to fear except in close battle with a larger.'

'Oh. So your little show is nothing but a confection.'

'No, sir. It has a purpose.' Kydd waited until he had full attention, then went on quietly, 'In all my professional life at sea, I've only been boarded by the enemy once, yet I've taken my men to the enemy three, four, five times. This is the reality: that the Royal Navy is more active, enterprising and resolute than the enemy.

'I ask you, General, now to reverse the situation here and consider that each time you read of a valiant boarding or cutting-out *we* are the attackers who must overcome any or all of these defences which the enemy can be relied on to throw out.' He had the attention he wanted.

'Therefore, sir, think on the quality of the men that I have the honour to command, that I lead in perfect confidence that none will shrink, that all will follow me whatever the day brings.'

Beresford stood for a moment, pursing his lips and watching *L'Aurore*'s men cheerfully disperse. 'Captain Kydd. I've never before given you an order, but I'm minded to, should it be in my power to issue it. Sir – and forgive if the form is wanting – do you *splice the mainbrace!*'

The gunroom dinner went off to the greatest satisfaction. Kydd yielded his customary position at the head of the table, when guest of the wardroom, to Beresford, who was unanimously voted Mr Vice by an awed mess. *L'Aurore*, under easy sail, daintily dipped and heaved, the gimballed lights setting uniforms a-glitter and casting constantly moving shadows, the feeling so beguilingly that of a living being that, for the thousandth time, Kydd wondered at how shore folk could be content with the inert deadness of the land.

After the cloth was drawn, Mr Vice was prompted for the loyal toast, restrained from rising in the Army way, and, suffused with good humour, did the honours most graciously.

Talk then became general, with anecdotes of service in all the seas of the world coming out.

Renzi, gently teased for his performance the previous year as a Russian to seize enemy documents, set the gunroom in a roar with his tale of a Lieutenant Kydd furiously signalling to an invading fleet in Minorca with a pair of red undergarments. Lieutenant Bowden added to the glee by detailing the forlorn state of Kydd's first command in Malta when they had nevertheless formally commissioned HM brig-sloop *Teazer* with only themselves as both crew and witness.

Beresford responded with reminiscences of his adventures as a young captain at the fraught siege of Toulon in the first year of the war, when the royalist insurgency had been destroyed single-handed by the actions of an equally young French captain of artillery, one Napoleon Bonaparte.

A most agreeable evening concluded with the appearance of a midshipman to report the lights of Cape Town in sight.

'A cognac in my cabin, General, while these gentlemen go about their duties?' Kydd suggested.

This was what the entire day had been leading up to, uninterrupted access to the one who was seen as most likely to take the bait as military commander of the expedition – and he was the chief conspirator.

Tysoe served their drinks and silently withdrew. Kydd summoned his wits: this sly politicking was foreign to his nature but he knew it would not be the last occasion he would need to deploy it.

Beresford raised his glass. 'I don't mind telling you, Kydd, I'm impressed. In my twenty years in the Army I've learned to be a judge of men, and you have the best. I honour and envy you for it.'

'Thank you, General,' Kydd said, flattered, then, seeing his chance, added, 'As they'll no doubt be needed only too soon.'

'Oh?' said Beresford, with a puzzled frown.

'The expedition, sir?' Kydd glanced up with a guarded expression.

'What expedition?'

Kydd looked hastily over his shoulder at the door, then leaned forward. 'Sir, the one that has us all a-buzz. You know, to the River Plate.'

'River Plate? I know nothing of this.'

Allowing a touch of anxiety to show, Kydd said, 'I'd be grieved to hear it's not been taken up, sir.'

'An expedition to the Spanish Americas? I've never heard of it!' There was, however, a telling gleam of interest in Beresford's eyes.

'Oh? I do apologise. I'd thought it dependable you would have heard it from Sir David or the commodore, it being a matter at the highest level.'

'No, sir, I have not. Pray tell, who did you get this from?'

Kydd replied, in some embarrassment, 'Well, it's in the nature of a common rumour among the naval commanders, Commodore Popham letting slip once that he was privy to Mr Pitt's designs on Montevideo and as how it was such a pity to let the opportunity go now that conditions are favourable.'

He briefly outlined the audacious plan with its breathtaking consequences, ending, 'And it would seem only reasonable that the governor, having higher duties, must require one other to lead the Army ashore. If it seems that another has been chosen then I do apologise again for making mention of the subject . . .'

The fuse had been lit.

'Time's not on our side, Kydd,' Popham said, with a sigh, when Kydd reported. 'Every hour we delay a move, the more likely it is the Spanish will return to their station. Recollect, friend Waine has been some weeks on the voyage here and Miranda will be deeply engaged in his invading, but not for ever. I'd have thought you better advised to speak directly instead of spending days on your little circus.'

Kydd flushed. 'Beresford is now trusting in the Navy and he has much to think on. I'd feel it the surer course, Dasher.'

'We'll see. If there's no movement on this in the next three days I'm going to—'

A flustered officer-of-the-day appeared at the door. 'From the castle, sir,' he said, proffering a slip of paper. 'And needing immediate reply.'

Popham read, and a broad grin appeared. 'Why, by this it seems you've done splendidly, old chap.' He handed it to Kydd.

It was a personal note scrawled by Baird himself. '. . . *and the fellow's raving something about a descent on the Spanish Americas! He says you know all about it and so I'd be most obliged if you'd tell me, Dasher!*'

'No reply,' Popham told the waiting officer. 'Captain Kydd and I will attend on the governor this hour.'

* * *

117

Baird was waiting with ill-concealed impatience. 'Well, Dasher? Why am I always the last to hear of high things in my own kingdom? A conspiracy, what?'

'As it's in the nature of wry talk, is all, David.'

Baird looked suspiciously at Kydd. 'Am I to be told why he's here?'

'Of his own concern only, sir. He wishes to hear from you directly why the River Plate enterprise is quite impossible at this time, and won't be denied.'

'Damn it, Dasher!' Baird exploded. 'All this tomfoolery talk about the Americas! Won't someone tell me what it's all about?'

'I am probably in fault for the whole thing, but it's nothing to speak of, David. Simply said, Mr Pitt commissioned a scheme by me for laying the Spanish by the tail in their own colonies, which was interrupted by Trafalgar. Now, as it happens, it seems conditions are unusually opportune to resume the enterprise, and officers of spirit in my command are clamouring to be let loose on it.'

Popham outlined his dealings with Miranda, the development of plans to provoke an uprising against the Spanish, with its consequences for the wider war and, quite incidentally, the probable fame of any who would be concerned in the shattering of centuries of empire.

'And now this fellow Waine sails in direct from Buenos Aires with the news that the viceroyalty is clear – quite clear – of any defending warships, leaving it wide open to any descent of ours. Captain Kydd here is of the opinion that, with the retirement of all the French marauding squadrons, there is a shining opportunity to execute the plan – if only we move instantly.'

Baird looked at Kydd keenly. 'And where do you hope an

army of invasion might be found at this instant, young feller?'

Popham came in smoothly, 'It needs but a comparable force to that which we employed to reduce Cape Town, David, for its purpose is only to hold a strong point, such as Montevideo, until reinforcements and garrison troops arrive.'

'Then if that's so why isn't this plan being put in train?' demanded Baird, loudly. 'Be damned, when the stakes are so high, why not, man?'

Popham shook his head ruefully. 'It not being the province of a sailorman, I'm reluctant to judge, but the situation as I see it is that without orders we are at a loss. London has hardly had time to receive the glad news of Blaauwberg, let alone conjure plans for wider gains. And they're hardly in a position to know the strategics of what is happening on the other side of the world, so they'll not be in haste to complete our orders.'

Baird threw him a piercing glance, then began pacing about the room. 'What you're telling me is that, if you received orders to do so, you'd sail against the Spanish.'

'With pleasure.'

'To resume what was planned and prepared by Whitehall before?'

'Just so.'

Baird's pace accelerated and furrows of concentration deepened on his brow. Suddenly he stopped, wheeled around and confronted Popham. 'I'm governor and ruling panjandrum in these parts. If I get together a picked army, a few guns and a supply train, would you then sail?'

'I could be held culpable of quitting my station,' Popham replied carefully, 'as not having Admiralty orders.'

'This is something you'll have to square with them later,'

Baird retorted. 'I've no authority in that line, as well you know. And I've my own worries. Detaching forces when so pinched, and justifying all the expenditures, well . . .'

'I'd do my part, David.'

'Yes, of course you will. Dasher, we'd be in this together, dear fellow, but think what a noise about the world we'd make! I'm sanguine their lordships will overlook the details when this great stroke be known. After all, we're but antici-pating orders, is all.'

'So you think—'

'Give me your plans. We'll work something out together and be damned to the rules!'

'Seize the hour!' Popham murmured.

'Time and tide!'

Chapter 4

Renzi tucked into the lamb silently. Kydd was getting used to it, the faraway look, the air of distraction, the sudden scribbling in a pocket notebook; it was not the Renzi he knew. Gone was the languid observer, the courteous gentleman, in his place a man oblivious to the world.

'Nicholas,' Kydd began carefully, 'the master-at-arms is complaining that he sees light in your cabin in the silent hours contrary to ship's standing orders and must beg you put it out time and again.'

'Oh, er, yes. Pray understand, dear fellow, that the muse is not to be commanded by mere mortals. There are times when—'

'You put him in a hard situation, he not being of a mind to make a charge against you, but he has his duty by me and the other officers. If—'

'Yes, yes – very well, I'll try to remember.' He bolted some bread and made to rise.

'Do stay, Nicholas, and tell me how it's all going, this writing o' yours.'

With a sigh Renzi took his seat again. 'There's not much to say. I've reached the point where Il Giramondo has left home for he's fatally taken by Jenny, a pretty milkmaid.'

'Il Giramondo?'

'My hero, if you'll remember,' Renzi said acidly. 'I rather think I should be getting back to work. This talking is to no end.' He stood abruptly.

Outside the voices of passing seamen at their work came to them. 'I bin t' Monty-wi'-dayo, cuffin. Rare time there, be good t' see them Spanish biddies again.'

Renzi froze.

'Aye, but we's having t' fight afore we gets t' see 'em this time.'

The voices faded.

Renzi turned on Kydd: 'You're making that attempt at South America! And it needs a common sailor to tell me!'

'Well, I was going to brief the officers later,' he said weakly, 'but Jack Tar already seems to have it from somewhere.'

Renzi sat down slowly. 'Do you mean that at this very moment there's an expedition afoot to raid the Spanish Americas?'

'To make a landing in the River Plate, yes.'

'And am I right in thinking that the projector is Commodore Popham?'

'As being the only one of spirit and dash who puts attacking the enemy before all else.'

Renzi bit his lip. 'What does Baird think of this?' His voice was steel-edged.

'In course he's persuaded that the conditions are right for the assault and is providing troops and supplies for the expedition.'

'Good God,' Renzi said slowly. 'He's going to do it!'

Kydd frowned. 'Nicholas. I don't want to say it, but this is really none of your business. You go back to your writing – I'm sanguine we'll be sailing within a week. There's nothing more to discuss.'

'Yes, there is,' Renzi said intensely. 'Depend upon it!'

'This is a military expedition, my friend, and in case you've overlooked it, you have no part in it and therefore have no cause to fret,' Kydd said irritably.

'You can't see it, but the man's a popinjay, a slippery toad and a damned cunning fellow.'

'Hold your tongue, sir!' Kydd barked. 'This is our commander you're referring to. Anyone else, they'd be in bilboes this instant for those words.'

'They are not only my words,' Renzi came back. 'I could add others, but I will not.'

'You'll keep your opinions to yourself or I'll swear I'll have you removed from this vessel.'

'As is your prerogative, but I'll not keep silent at this mountebank's contumacious—'

'Sentry!' Kydd roared.

The marine posted at his outer door entered quickly. 'Sir?'

Renzi, his face pale and set, looked at Kydd. 'I think it better for us both should you allow me a little time to explain myself,' he said quietly.

'Wait outside,' Kydd snapped at the sentry.

He turned to Renzi. 'Ten minutes, and damme, you'd better find good reasons, or . . .'

'For reasons not unconnected to the duty of *politesse* in a gentleman – '

'Belay that catblash! I want an explanation o' your conduct, sir.'

' – until now I've refrained from mentioning certain facts, not necessarily to the credit of your commodore.'

'Which are?'

'Understand that I tell you with the utmost reluctance, it not being the act of a gentleman to delate upon another, still less in an atmosphere of blind loyalty.'

'This had better be good,' Kydd said dangerously.

'Then this is the substance. While you were closely engaged with him on the American's submarine boat I had occasion to visit Count Rumford in London. Both he and Fulton being American, both being fellows of the Royal Society, I pressed the count as to Popham's character and he laid before me this: that in fashionable society he presents as a money-getter, a restless man of insinuating manners and too sharp by half – an excess of cleverality, as I remember the term.'

'This is worthless! Society gossip and jabberknowl! You'll need to do better than this, sir.'

'I did not accept this alone. I determined to investigate for myself. And confirmed that unhappily there were good reasons for this view. A hydrographer of the first rank, inventor of the first telegraphic signal code and other matters – how do you believe he'd be received at the Admiralty?'

'Honoured for it, o' course.'

'I found the first lord, St Vincent, in utter loathing of the man. The same with his secretary. Why? It seems that by personal manipulations he went from being a lieutenant on half pay through to commander and then to full post-captain – without once commanding a naval vessel, let alone a ship-of-the-line in battle.'

'Be damned to it, that's because he was too busy with his inventions and things. I heard he was the only man who could persuade the Russians to come in with us in Flanders – knew

Tsar Paul himself. No mystery there. And manipulations? How can he—'

'He has himself elected to a rotten borough in the Tory cause so he has the ear of the highest, Pitt himself. This he's used on many occasions – the most favourable description I've heard of him is "incurably plausible" in his schemes. Are you aware that he's deep in litigation with the Admiralty Court in respect of a personal venture, a ship whose master was none other than himself, trading under the Tuscan flag illegally with Bengal? He was caught by a British frigate trying to land smuggled goods in Ostend and his *Etrusco* seized as a prize of war.'

'Any naval officer on half pay may with Admiralty permission trade to his own account,' Kydd said hotly.

Renzi smiled thinly. 'His first and only command before his present, *Romney*, was caught in a monsoon and needed repairs. Instead of consigning this to the naval dockyard at Calcutta he mysteriously had it completed at a minor commercial yard in Bombay.'

'So?'

'On his return a committee of inquiry in Chatham found that he'd overstated the real costs by many thousands. Proceedings against him are even now under way. And you'll find there's every kind of pamphlet in public circulation that accuses him of other defalcations and defects of moral character that would make you stare.'

'Jealousy! And I've never heard any o' this before – why should I believe it now?'

Renzi went on, 'You might this hour determine the truth of it all, merely by interrogating Curzon closely. His family is tolerably well placed to know the matter.'

'He's not—'

'I've spoken to him sharply in private that this is not a matter for public debate in the gunroom, which he's honoured since.'

Kydd glowered but said nothing.

'Dear fellow,' Renzi said, 'why do you think I should risk our friendship by this talk?'

'You tell me, Nicholas – why?'

'For the sake of your future. The man is in debt to his eyebrows, no prize money for him, of course, and no prospects of it on this remote station. He sees the immense fortunes won by captains who've seized the Spanish treasure ships and has a cunning idea. Why not make a descent on the source of the wealth itself – in effect, to sack the River Plate and carry off the silver?'

'You're out of your mind!'

'I don't think so. Why the haste to move on the Spaniards unless it's to preserve a position of commanding authority that will ensure his direction of events and ultimately the greater share in the plunder? Any proper expedition from England will, of course, displace him as commander and no doubt change its object entirely.'

'And you tell me all this for my sake?' Kydd snorted. 'Guesswork and envy! Why should I—'

'I cannot stand by and watch you destroy your career when the world believes that you've put yourself in league with such a one. Can't you see? The expedition will end in disaster and a vengeful government will want to find villains to put to the stake and you'll be up there with him. He's quitting station without leave – that's a certain court-martial for a start, let alone—'

Kydd cut him short: 'Yes, yes. I hear what you're saying, for God's sake.'

'It's – it's only my regard for you, brother, that makes me speak in this way.'

'So I'm to be beholden to you for your concern?'

Renzi remained silent as familiar shipboard sounds slowly asserted a degree of calm on the charged atmosphere.

Kydd finally spoke again: 'I've much to think on, I believe.' He stared blankly out of the stern windows. Then his expression softened. 'I spoke hastily and out of order to my friend, and I'm truly sorry for it, Nicholas.'

He rose, went to the side cabinet and found glasses, poured a generous measure into each and handed one to Renzi. 'Thank you for your candour, but there's one thing you must accept in me: whatever you think his motives, a higher purpose is being served. I still honour him for his vision of seeing the Spanish humbled and His Majesty's arms glorious, and while he leads I will think it my duty to follow.'

'In hazard of your reputation?'

'If so be it.'

Renzi nodded gravely. 'Very well. Then although I must beg to differ in my views, I shall say no more.'

'Handsomely, y' bastards!' The boatswain's ire was directed to the party swaying aboard stores, who had good reason for their impatience – hazing from the first lieutenant and their knowledge that at last *L'Aurore* would be at sea, on her native element, once more, and their penniless liberty would be transformed into an active sea life.

Kydd watched the loading for some moments. Preparation for the expedition had raced ahead and Cape Town seethed with rumours, but with the Navy as one behind Popham and with the military in high feather at the expectation of a strategic master-stroke there was no stopping the momentum. But what if—

He forced the thought away but it kept returning. What if he and all the others had been gulled into supporting a private dash for plunder? What if he was unwittingly being used in adding his name to a scheme to give it credibility?

And Renzi's prediction of disaster? Success was based on one central belief: that the inhabitants were so disaffected by Spanish rule that at the appearance of the expedition they could be relied on to rise in rebellion and together they would prevail. A dangerously simple presumption – and the only word they had to back it was that of Popham's shadowy Miranda, and Waine, the American trader.

Were they sailing to catastrophe? The more he considered the possibility the more uneasy he became. How, a world away from the South American continent, would it be possible to gauge the mood of that population? It had to be a risk that—

A thought came to him. The artist up on Table Mountain. What was his name? Serrano, yes. He was some sort of recent exile from the region and no doubt he could tell him the truth of how the people felt.

'I'm stepping ashore for a space, Mr Gilbey. Call away my barge, if you will.'

In the autumn greyness there was no likelihood that the artist would be up Table Mountain but he had the man's card. 'Vicente Serrano' at '150 Buitengracht' – not a smart address: he seemed to remember it was the area at the edge of the old part of the town.

The artist's place of work was a shop with a powerful odour of pigment and oils, dust and canvas and a diverting array of finished works around the walls. 'Mr Serrano?'

He appeared from behind an easel, wiping a brush. '*El capitán!*' he greeted Kydd, when he had recognised him. 'My honour! Can I do you service, sir?'

'I've a need for ornament in my cabin, Mr Serrano. I was thinking of, say, Table Mountain from another view. From Blaauwberg strand, perhaps? A capital sight indeed!'

'Would thees be in nature of commission, sir, or th' ready found?' Serrano's deep-set dark eyes were unsettling in their intensity.

'Why, if you have something ready, of this size, perhaps.' Kydd indicated a modest landscape.

The artist crossed the room and selected a painting. Kydd noted the short, stabbing strokes that contrasted with extravagant sweeps across the scene to arresting effect. 'Er, yes, this will do. What is your price?'

In rixdollars it was little enough. 'Um, do you enjoy to live in Cape Town, Mr Serrano, you coming from so far?'

'Ees home to me, now.' He wrapped the painting, drawing the string around it and cutting it off.

'And here we are, both in the southern hemisphere – it must be autumn as well in Montevideo. Is it so cool and windy there?'

'The same,' he answered, without further comment. 'Your painting.'

Kydd tried another tack: 'You said before that the Spanish are making trouble for you. Does this mean you will never return to South America?'

His gaze piercing, Serrano replied slowly, 'Not never. One day . . .'

'Yes? Do you mean to say that if the Spanish are . . . overthrown in some way you will be able to return?'

'How they be overthrown? By we? *No es posible.*'

'Tell me – are there many as you, who would take joy should the Spanish be replaced by . . . others?'

'Many – many! An unspeakable herd from all the town, all the country will give praise for thees! Old, young, ever'one – if they's *porteño*, they want! Any give to them, they bless for ever and ever!'

'Then it will not take much to start a rebellion to throw out the Spanish, I'm thinking.'

But Kydd saw that Serrano had retreated into himself. He turned to go, just catching as he left, a ferocious whisper: 'One day – one day, these peegs will taste the people's justice. Only then we be free.'

Kydd walked slowly back to the boat. There was no doubting the passion of the man. It seemed it would take little to spark a revolt, and in a town the size of Montevideo or Buenos Aires even a small proportion supporting a rebellion would start something near impossible to stop.

But there was still the question of Popham's motives.

Was it credible that he was manipulating others for his own venal cupidity? In effect employing His Majesty's armed forces for personal gain, to make a grab at the fabulous source of the Spanish silver before retiring with fame and wealth? All Kydd's dealings with the man to date made him rebel at the thought – and as well, why was Popham taking such trouble to attend to the securing of a strong foothold and the opening of trading links? This didn't sound like the action of a free-booter on a quick raid.

Yet Renzi had painted a very different picture, one of a man who took chances, was comfortable at the boundaries of moral conduct and dangerously plausible. Popham was intelligent and clever to a degree – were these merely tales told by lesser men against the gifted?

No: there was no going back – he would be loyal and supporting to the commodore until and unless he saw with his own eyes that Popham was unworthy of such. Resolved in his decision, he came aboard *L'Aurore* and energetically set about completing preparations.

When the expedition sailed, the sulky autumn wind had settled to a low, hard blow, keen and cold and directly from out of the west. It kicked up white caps that rode and seethed on a long swell that had made taking aboard last-minute stores and water a wearying and dangerous effort. Kydd's experience in the region told him that there was every likelihood it would get worse before it got better.

There had been no question of riding it out until it improved. Apart from the risk of losing their opportunity, every hour they lay at anchor the troops would be consuming vital provisions and water. These would be needed in the thousands of extra miles occasioned by the northerly arc that their course demanded to fall in with the big driving winds of the open ocean.

'Shorten sail when two miles to wind'd,' Kydd ordered, feeling the lengthening restlessness of the deep Atlantic coming in. Detailed off as shepherd to keep a wary eye open, he took in the magnificent panorama under leaden skies of the audacious little force setting out on its voyage to destiny.

There were the two sixty-fours – the flagship *Diadem* with *Raisonable* and then the fifty-gun *Diomede* recently joined in line and forming the core of the fleet, with the cockle-shell *Encounter* gun-brig falling in astern. The transports sailed loosely on either side – only five compared to the many that had accompanied the Cape Town expedition but aboard were the doughty Highlanders of the 71st Regiment, who had made such a name for themselves at Blaauwberg. The frigate *Leda* was hull-down out to sea on distant watch, and *Narcissus* was manoeuvring to take up the rear when the fleet had properly formed up. Their own station would be to range far ahead and fall back the instant any enemy were sighted.

It was a magnificent undertaking – or insanity: a tiny force to set against the vastness of a whole continent, smaller by far even than the one that had so narrowly seized the Cape. But the circumstances were very different, Kydd reminded himself. Here they would be welcomed as liberators, the catalyst that would set Montevideo aflame with rebellion and end Spanish rule for ever.

That they had left before formal orders had been received was of concern, of course, but once word of their bold stroke reached Pitt, the prime minister who had steered England successfully through the worst that Bonaparte could do and who had originally agreed to the expedition, then it would be quickly made up with the Admiralty.

This was precisely what the exercise of sea-power was all about. Kydd's heart lifted. 'Sheet in – we're off to war, Mr Kendall.'

L'Aurore responded with a will, and as the others came round ponderously to their course of north-west by north he went below to deal with the inevitable paperwork that the purser had laid out for him.

During the morning the wind had hardened and backed more to the south, the sure sign of a blow in these parts. After his customary turn around the decks at dawn Kydd stopped to peer out at the distant sails of the fleet. All were down to topsails and making heavy weather of it, tiny bursts of white appearing continually and the ships spread well apart. He felt a pricking of sympathy at what the soldiers must be

enduring packed below, and then remembered they themselves had forty-five redcoats and a dour lieutenant squeezed
on to their single mess-deck. But there was nothing he could
do; they would all have to live with it.

He went to his cabin for breakfast. Renzi was at the stern
windows, braced in a chair and reading the last newspaper
obtained in Cape Town.

He looked up and offered, '*Buenos días, Señor.*'

'Er, I didn't quite catch that, Nicholas.'

'Oh – um, *cómo es el clima. Vamos a tomar el desayuno?*'

'You're vexing me with your classical lingo, you dog!'

'Not at all. I'm learning the Castilian of Cervantes and
Mendoza, that noble language of far Hesperia.'

'As I said.'

Renzi sighed. 'It is the Spanish, dear fellow, which you will
have cause to require before long, I'd hazard.'

'I suppose so – the prisoners, of course.'

'Or worse.'

Kydd lifted his chin defiantly. 'If you're not to be warm
in the cause then I'd thank you kindly to keep your opinions
to yourself.' He caught himself and then asked, 'Er, but
why . . . ?'

Renzi adopted a pained expression. 'In all conscience there's
little enough I can offer to my friend at this time.' Before
Kydd could reply he added, 'And then again, the acquiring
of another Romance language is always to be applauded.'

This brought a grin from Kydd. 'I thank you for the thought,
m' friend. It could be damned useful at the capitulation.'

'Er, yes. So now you are safely to sea on this . . . crusade,
shall you wish to know the latter adventures of Il Giramondo?
I rather fancy I'm in a flow of sorts and am quite exercised
to know if others do see it as I.'

'Why, er, I'm rather pressed at the moment, old chap. I will when I can, never fear.'

The day wore on, the unremitting wind bringing a dirge-like drone in the rigging and reefs in the topsails, with an uncomfortable corkscrew sea on the quarter demanding rolling tackles to the yards and an eye to nearby handholds. A pall of blackness lay out to the south-west with startlingly vivid white rain squalls hanging before it as it drifted towards them. Prudent measures were put in train to meet the unpleasantness, for although Kydd was confident that they had won their offing there was no sense in taking risks.

Sail was shortened in conformity with the blow, which was now flat and hard, its whistling moan rising in pitch as spindrift torn from wave-crests filled the air with the tang of salt. Kydd glanced across at the flagship. *Diadem* was a wet ship, a fluke of design seeing her bows buried in the rollers for much of the time, then reluctantly rising to shed the seas each side like a waterfall. Working headsails in her would be dangerous; it was not for nothing that sailors often called the bowsprit 'the widowmaker'.

There was no signal from the commodore, however, no order to lie-to or scud; Popham was anxious to avoid loss of time and the little fleet kept on course, the winds nearly abeam. In a way this was merciful for while they were still under sail the force of the blast was dampening the roll, but things could change quickly.

And not only for the worse: it was just as conceivable that they might be crabbing across the worst of the gale to emerge to calmer conditions the other side.

'Life-lines,' Kydd ordered, before leaving the deck to Curzon.

It was a customary Atlantic gale of this time of the year

but the knowledge didn't lessen the hours of moving from hand to hand, the muscle-bunching brace against the deep heaving and the endless vigilance against a violent squall coming out of the blackness of night or a wild wave rearing up to smash, surge aboard and snatch the lives of any whose attention had grown careless.

Morning brought a seascape of white – long combers, spray lazily curling from their crests, the air alive with driven spume and the near horizon a broad blur of white. But it was becoming clear the bluster was easing.

As the forenoon wore on the horizon moved out, and from the mist a light-grey phantom hardened – another ship, one of the transports gamely heading on course with them.

It became possible to allow their soldier passengers on deck, solitary figures dragging themselves to the ship's side, draped hopelessly as they 'cast their accounts at the court of King Neptune', soon joined by others. They were tended with rough kindness by the watch-on-deck but by nightfall there were substantial numbers needing to be shooed below.

There was always the cheerful time after every storm when the galley fire could safely be lit and the first hot victuals issued. Ravenous after days of hard tack and cheese, the seamen wolfed theirs, their captain no less appreciative as his was served after the men had eaten. 'Rousin' good scran,' Kydd mumbled to Renzi. 'Never thought I'd lust after a hand o' mutton so.'

His friend dabbed his mouth with his napkin. 'The very pinnacle of the art,' he murmured in satisfaction. 'As it—'

A tentative knock broke in: it was the master-at-arms, his usually impassive features creased in bafflement. 'Sir, we's got a bit of a puzzler. See, there's a man bin found as we don't know who 'e is, like.'

'You're not being clear, Master.'

'Why, when th' watch went below, an' took them who was seasick t' put 'em in their hammick, there's one who couldn't say where he slings it. He bein' sick, like, we got no sense outa him. We asks about, an' no one pipes up t' claim him.'

'Where's he now?'

'On the uppers still. Won't let go an' get his swede down, so I left him wi' the bosun's mate, sir.'

'You did right to inform me. Ask the officer-of-the-watch to look into it and report, if you please.'

Gilbey was down in minutes. 'An' I stand well flammed, sir. It's our artist cove, the one in Cape Town we commissioned our ornament pictures off.'

Serrano! 'When he's of a condition to talk, bring him here.'

Kydd guessed their destination was an open secret and assumed that Serrano had wanted to be at the scene of action when the hated Spanish were humbled. He had gone about it intelligently, insinuating himself aboard, then insisting he was of the other when questioned by either a sailor or the military. It had only gone wrong when he had been laid low by seasickness.

Or was he a spy, ready to slip ashore the moment they arrived to ingratiate himself with the Spanish? It didn't seem likely, though, not with the depth of feeling Kydd had personally heard.

The weather eased and a wan sun had given heart to the sufferers when the artist was brought before Kydd in the coach.

Shooing out the midshipmen at their workings, their estimates of the ship's position by calculations, he demanded, 'Now then, sir. Your actions are both foolish and unlawful. I've to decide what's to be done with you. What have you got to say?'

Serrano was in rumpled, soiled clothes, his eyes empty and

slack. Kydd felt there was little prospect of getting much out of him. Inevitably, it meant that he must be held prisoner, fastened with leg irons in the bilboes outside the gunroom, like a common malefactor, until things were resolved.

But there was a defiant stirring, his eyes trying to focus while he croaked, 'This is heestory. I be there, I see my home free. *Libertad para el pueblo . . .*' The words trailed off weakly but there was stubbornness and pleading in the ravaged expression.

'I understand, Mr Serrano, and you have my sympathy, but this is a ship of war and may bear no civilian passengers. My proper course is to keep you confined until we touch at St Helena and then land you in custody.'

'No! I mus' be there! Meester Kydd, you must understand, sir!'

Kydd softened. 'There is a way. If you shall enlist to serve under English colours I can promise you'll be there.'

'I – my family, they are *patricios*, sir. I cannot.'

'Then . . . ?'

'Er, may I not be your interpreter, your man of trust as will talk with *los españoles*, can treat wi' the patriots, what they want?'

Kydd could see times when delicacies of conduct would be needed in dealing with proud revolutionaries and the like, and Serrano would presumably know them.

'And, sir, while the ship guns do roar an' your army storms the citadels, as witness I will paint for you such a scene as your gran'children will for ever admire!'

'Why, that would be well appreciated, Mr Serrano. Let me see . . . you shall be assistant to Mr Renzi, who is my secretary, to perform such duties as he bids you to do.' This would place him in Kydd's personal retinue, rather than on the books of the Navy, and therefore answerable to him alone. It would also keep him under eye.

'You will berth in steerage and mess with the gunroom. Your wages will, um, be decided.' He went on more sternly, 'Do mark what I say, Mr Serrano – by so doing you place yourself under ship's discipline, to obey all lawful commands of myself and my officers. Do you so agree?'

Kydd took a muffled groan as an assent and shortly told a curious Renzi, 'You may use him how you will, old trout, but he's mine when we raise the River Plate.'

Soon Renzi's assistant was another being. Taken in hand by the gunroom steward, he had been instructed in the art of slinging a hammock and his little bundle of possessions had been safely stowed in Renzi's cabin. His appearance at table provoked good-natured curiosity but he kept to himself, saying little, remaining polite but watchful.

For Renzi his presence was gratifying. At any time he chose he had on hand a Spanish tutor and linguist sparring partner, who was both interesting and challenging to the intellect.

Of a noteworthy family, it seemed, he had been a student in philosophy and letters at the National University in Buenos Aires and, having been less than discreet in his writings, had been imprisoned twice before his expulsion. In the simmering atmosphere of discontent the Spanish had been merciless and he had fled for his life having been caught up in a hot-headed street rising.

'You are not acquainted with the sainted Locke? Then, *mi compadre*, for the sake of your soul you will cast in the purest Castilian the paragraphs I will mark out in his *An Essay Concerning Human Understanding*.'

'*Sí, maestro, lo haré con encantado.*'

Chapter 5

St Helena lifted above the horizon, a rumpled grey shape set against deep blue seas with eager white horses as far as the eye could see. A vast azure heaven was populated with gambolling fluffy clouds, the warmth of the sun grateful to the skin. After their time of testing, the ships of the fleet had found one another and now proceeded in proper formation.

However, of the five transports there were now only four. Somewhere out in the howling chaos *Ocean* had disappeared. It was possible that she would suddenly appear but the frigates quartering far out after the storm to gather in the scattered band had seen no sign of her, and three days had passed. There was the outside chance that she was already at St Helena, the appointed rendezvous, and waiting for them, but Kydd doubted the lumbering merchantman could have overhauled them all.

The probability was that at some time during the night she had not proved equal to the stress of tempest: her shattered wreck had finally yielded and sunk, taking with her to a watery grave not only captain and crew but several hundred officers and soldiers, a significant part of the expedition. Kydd grieved at their fate.

An improbable dot in the immensity of ocean, St Helena was at the near geographic centre of the South Atlantic. North to south, east to west, it could be no further from land, to which the majestic height of the rollers close to the coast attested. As they rounded the last point, the haven of James Bay opened up and telescopes were quickly searching – but *Ocean* was not there.

Popham was not about to waste time. Even as anchors plunged, a precautionary single flag whipped up *Diadem*'s mainmast head: the blue square pierced with white, which was the Blue Peter, the signal for 'prepare to sail within twenty-four hours'. Soon afterwards, 'all captains' was hung out: it was the order for them to join Popham in going ashore to meet the governor. But there would be no solemn gun salutes: this governor had been appointed privately by the East India Company to rule over this vital rendezvous for the India convoys and therefore was not entitled to such.

The soaring crags and cloud-wreathed peaks were all of two thousand feet in altitude, and the narrow valley that led up to Plantation House was steep and spectacular, requiring the services of a government *calesa*. Governor Patton was waiting for them on the front lawn of his residence under the myrtles and mimosa.

'Welcome, gentlemen, whatever your occasion.' He had met most of the captains before during the Cape campaign and clearly suspected something was afoot.

White-gloved footmen circulated with wine. In the sun and pleasant oceanic breezes, most of the captains found they had a yarn or two to tell of recent stormy experiences. All too soon the sky greyed, a rain squall threatening, and the group was ushered inside to a reception room.

Popham was in striking form, in the finery of a flag officer attended by his lieutenant and with an air of serene authority. Patton approached him. 'Tell me, Commodore, would it be altogether too presumptuous of me to ask your mission? I rather thought the French squadrons had been scattered – or is this some new adventure?'

Popham smiled, then confided, 'As it promises to be the greatest stroke this age, Robert. Not for the ear of the common herd, of course, but this little armada is on its way to set South America ablaze.'

'Good God!' said Patton, faintly.

'Indeed. It seems the natives are ripe for rebellion, and since Trafalgar, the Spanish being powerless to defend their interests, our fleet is able to sail in the character of liberator.'

'Why, that would mean . . .'

'Yes. Detach their empire and source of wealth and the Spanish must treat for peace, despite any bluster Bonaparte may put up.'

'Trade! That's where the real excitement is. Be damned to their colonial laws – this would open the whole of the continent to us. And that's to be reckoned in the millions, tens of millions the least of it. Damme, but this is blood-stirring stuff.'

Beresford joined the group, in the red and gold regimentals of a general a splendid match for Popham. Patton asked him, 'A military challenge of sorts, I'd think it, William. The Dons have all those irregulars and must keep a sizeable garrison in Montevideo.'

'Our information is that these are not as formidable as

rumoured,' Beresford began cautiously. 'However, it's vital we secure a quick and visible victory to encourage the rising or we're lost, and with few enough men . . .'

Popham came back quickly: 'And to all involved a capital opportunity for distinction, I'd believe. Especially one that's set fair to make fortunes.'

'I do envy you fellows,' Patton said, with feeling. 'It's to be a grand occasion, I'm persuaded – but is the East India Company not to be invited to a change of empires? It's too bad, really too bad.'

There was good-natured laughter, then Popham rubbed his chin thoughtfully. 'Ah, as to that, Robert, it does cross my mind that in the recent storm we somehow mislaid *Ocean* transport, which leaves us short of artillery and, er, it would not be without precedent for John Company to lend support to His Majesty's arms when requested. A trifle of field pieces, amounting to, say, a hundred men in all, and there you would have your invitation.'

Patton immediately cooled. 'You're seriously asking that I authorise a detaching of our St Helena garrison, with their guns, for service with you?'

'Only a suggestion, Robert. And simply for the term of the initial showing before the Spanish. Naturally your outgoings would be compensated by the Crown, and other fees I'll leave with the fiscals, but this would certainly ensure your appearance in the annals of the expedition.'

'Then, pray, what do your orders say precisely concerning an involvement of the Company?' Patton challenged.

'I can most definitely assure you that I have no orders whatsoever forbidding your assistance,' Popham replied earnestly. 'And when I last spoke with Mr Pitt on the matter he was most insistent that all local resources be employed.'

'Mr Pitt?' Patton said, impressed. 'You've discussed—'

'This entire expedition is merely the resuming of a venture planned and agreed upon by myself and His Majesty's government, lately interrupted by Trafalgar.'

'Oh, well, I can see—'

'Be that as it may, Robert, most would see it to your advantage to be first to plant a mercantile interest in the new lands, to secure a preferential trading position before the City hears of our coup.'

'Quite so. Um, it would seem a reasonable request you are making, m' friend. And considering an early success is much to be desired by us both, then perhaps the artillery detachment might profitably be accompanied by, perhaps, two or three hundred of our infantry. You could make use of them?'

'That's handsome in you, dear fellow, and I'm sanguine we'll be able to exercise 'em for you in the field.'

'Their transport?'

'We'll see they're well taken care of, Robert, never fear.'

Beaming, the commodore turned to the circle of his officers. 'Gentlemen! The gods of war are smiling upon us. We sail just as soon as your green stuff and water are complete. You'll want to return to your ships – no liberty for the hands, of course, and not a moment to be lost.'

In the general stir, he called, 'Captain Kydd, if you'd kindly wait on me – details of the St Helena reinforcements to be dealt with.' The other captains, taking the hint, quickly made to leave.

'I'll wish you well of your mission, sir,' Patton said warmly, shaking Popham's hand, then lifting his arm in salute. 'As enterprising a piece of work as ever I've heard.'

'Thank you, Robert,' Popham said, and made for the door,

but stopped at a small marble side table where some news-papers were neatly piled.

'Oh, papers from home, new arrived. Haven't had time to read 'em – do help yourself, old chap.'

Popham reached for one, then paused. Without looking round he hurriedly stuffed it into his waistcoat. 'Er, you'll have my earliest word, of course. Goodbye.'

They joined the others in a waiting *calesa*, which ground off down the steep road. Cheerful conversations started up, but Kydd was disturbed to see Popham's set face and to note his unusual quiet. At the seafront the captains took boat for their commands but Kydd was ushered into *Diadem*'s barge, Popham still serious and thoughtful.

Kydd kept his silence until they were alone in the great cabin, then said, 'A good day's work, if I might remark it. But *Ocean* is "mislaid"?'

'Never mind *Ocean*, we've more pressing concerns, damn it.'

This was not like Popham. Hardly believing his ears, Kydd blurted, 'Lost at sea, three hundred souls! How can you possibly—'

'I said forget it. There's a pretty moil we must deal with right at this time.'

'Forget it? How, in God's name, can you—'

'*Ocean*'s safe,' Popham snapped irritably. 'I told Audley to take her direct to the River Plate. Now let's—'

'Safe? You knew all the time?'

'What better can you think of to prise troops from Patton?'

'A trick – a ploy!'

Popham sighed. 'Dear fellow, we've secured four hundred more troops in the assault. Nearly a third of our force. Don't you think it worth the harmless subterfuge? The higher cause

144

is our expedition, and for that I'm prepared to use anything that presents itself as a means. Wouldn't you?'

Kydd was unable to reply. There was no illegality, no moral issue at stake – but was this the action of a noble commander?

'I'm sure you would if you'd given it thought. Now, down to more serious business. Much more serious – and I don't mind confessing that the services of a friend would be of infinite value to me at this time.'

Kydd stiffened awkwardly, still unsure.

'A friend. As will hear me and test my words,' Popham pressed, his features tight with worry.

Kydd made up his mind and replied stoutly, 'As I can help, Dasher.'

Popham hesitated, then brought out the newspaper. 'Pitt's dead,' he said simply.

Kydd reeled. This was the prime minister who'd been at the helm of state since the very first day of the war, when Kydd had still been a perruquier of Guildford. The man who'd scorned the slaughter of the French Revolution while Spain and most of Europe had allied against him. And until now had been locked in a lethal struggle with Napoleon Bonaparte, who stood astride his conquests like a colossus.

'There's a new government – Grenville,' Popham added.

Kydd remembered dimly that he was a statesman of the Whig Party, implying an administration radically different from Pitt's Tory government. Then he understood. Popham's expedition was a resumption of a plan agreed with Pitt and his ministers, especially the first lord of the Admiralty, Melville, and then Barham. These now being out of office, he could count on no supporters in high places, and conceivably there would be those who might see it in their political interest to oppose any Pitt-inspired operation.

'Of all times to choose to leave this world . . .' Popham said bitterly.

'We'll have to turn back, of course.'

Popham looked up sharply. 'That is not in my thinking.'

'The Grenville government might act differently about the strategics, Dasher. We must wait for new orders.'

'I'd have thought you of stronger mettle, Kydd.' He forced a smile. 'I didn't mean it to come out like that, but you must agree that nothing has changed. Not a single iota. The Spanish are occupied in the north, their navy is reeling in defeat after Trafalgar, we still have surprise – and our armada is gathered and ready. If we turn back now, all this is wasted. Any new orders will only confirm the preparations, but we will have lost our moment.'

Kydd was torn. All that Popham had said was true, but where did their higher duty really lie? A change of political alignment to be allowed to destroy a daring initiative that could alter the entire direction of the war, or the prudent awaiting of instructions before proceeding any further?

Damn it, here was a man who was willing to risk everything for the sake of his country's future. 'For what it's worth, Dasher, this is what I feel. As a patriot and an Englishman, I can think of no greater cause before me at this moment than South America. But as a professional naval officer I find that we're sailing a mort close to the wind, at peril of disobedience to the wishes of their lordships.

'As a man – why, with all there is to be gained, I'd a hundred times be hanged for doing something as doing nothing at all.'

'Bravo, my friend!' Popham cried, the worry melting away. 'As I'd hoped you'd say! It's my decision – and it's to go forward with the enterprise.'

Kydd grinned. 'And we'll see those politicking trimmers in

Parliament change tack at the run, once they see what we've achieved for 'em.'

'Damn them all for a parcel o' rogues. They'll see their way clear to consolidating us once we've done the initial hard work, of course. Now, there's much we've to do, the chief of which is to find berths for our reinforcements.' There was not a prayer of cramming any more men into their ships but it would be doubly ironic if they and their guns had to be left behind for lack of room.

'It's by way of a puzzler, Dasher,' Kydd said cautiously.

'Yes. But I'm leaving it entirely to you, old chap. I'm bound up for the next few hours in working up dispatches as will persuade the Admiralty that it's to be their first duty to get those consolidating reinforcements to us as soon as they may. It has to go off before we sail.'

Kydd gave a rueful grin. 'So it's my own good self who must conjure a way to get four hundred more men to Montevideo, it seems.'

'As you can. And, by the way, we'll keep it to ourselves, Mr Pitt's untimely demise. Morale, of course.'

'From the officers as well?'

'I would think so.'

Four hundred men. Close to double the number of a frigate's entire complement. And their guns and impedimenta. It simply couldn't be done – the ships had already been loaded to safe limits and, with every conceivable space taken up, they would be hard pressed to fight in such crowded conditions if confronted by an enemy.

No – there was only one possible course: to find another ship. There were no naval vessels available but a co-opted merchant ship – if any could be found – would demand hire as a transport to compensate for lack of a commercial cargo, which would necessarily be at considerable cost as there was an empty return voyage to include. And where was the ready cash to come from? And what would they do with her existing cargo?

There was no question of the Crown taking over a merchantman for the task. While the law looked on impassively as ships were stripped of their crews by a press gang, if a ship itself were taken it would be deemed nothing less than an act of piracy. In fact, in these matters there was an entire Board of Transport department of the Admiralty to deal with the intricate details. That the Board was hopelessly distant was no excuse.

It was one of those unwritten naval laws: at the end of everything, and even to the end of time, there was always to be a due accounting.

No ship, no precious troops. In despair Kydd looked about the James Bay roadstead. There was shipping a-plenty but only one of size. What were the chances that it was going to South America? Or could be persuaded to render a loyal service to its country? There was only one way to find out and time was crucial.

In the boat out there were only himself and the purser, Owen, with Curzon as a counter-signatory if they achieved a miracle. As to Kydd's exact authority to incur expenditure, whether as ship's captain or proxy for the commodore, the purser was hard put to establish a clear line and had wrung his hands in dismay: without the requisite form or written order from above there was no source of credit against which to issue a note.

Kydd noticed that the ship was high in the water, then spotted a lighter leaving from the opposite side. Transshipping cargo – was that a good or bad sign? But she was a sturdy, ship-rigged vessel that would not need nursing in the ocean crossing.

'Go about her stern,' he ordered. He saw that *Justina* was of British registry, a considerable advantage.

The three boarded amidships by the wooden-runged pilot ladder. The hold was open, displaying a nearly empty cavern, and they were quickly confronted by a suspicious individual with a deeply lined face. 'Hardiman, master,' he growled.

Conscious of eyes on them and the need for privacy, Kydd introduced himself in a friendly manner, adding, 'Not the press, sir, but I'd be obliged for five minutes of your time, if you would.'

The master gave him a piercing look, then grunted and took them aft to his cabin.

'Could I ask where you're bound?' Kydd began.

'Cape Town for orders.'

'Not so profitable therefore. Captain, I've a proposition to make to you, as will be to your advantage.' Nothing could be learned from the man's stony expression so he pressed on.

'We have need to ship a parcel of soldiers to South America and were wondering if you—'

'Not possible. M' papers say we're cleared for Cape Town and be sure that's where we're going.'

'A cash profit on a straightforward voyage? I'm surprised you refuse even to hear me.'

'South America – you're off t' some war or other. No.'

'Not even if you'll render a great service to your country, sir?'

Hardiman gave a cynical grunt, then got to his feet abruptly. 'I'll see you off.'

Kydd felt a rising anger. 'Be so good as to ask your

supercargo to join us, Captain,' he said, with a touch of steel. His single voyage as master in the merchant service had taught him many useful wrinkles. A supercargo was there to look after the interests of the freighting party against that of the ship.

'He won't—'

'*Please.*'

The master gave him a foul look but leaned out of the door and bellowed orders to send for a Mr Maycock. After some delay a flustered little man came in. 'This'n wants t' talk with ye,' Hardiman said coldly.

'Ah, Mr Maycock, Captain Kydd. Sorry to have interrupted you, but I have a proposition for your principals. Should I offer you a cargo this very day for a quick voyage to the River Plate, as will be a bareboat charter party, would you be willing to talk?' If it was taken up, the master would most surely find himself overruled.

There was an unmistakable gleam of interest. 'Cargo?'

'Soldiers is all.'

'A transport.'

'Of sorts. We must move very quickly on this, Mr Maycock.'

'Ah. With a return voyage empty, I'd think a sum of . . . let me see . . .'

Kydd had only one card to play, and he gave it all he had. 'Before we discuss rates, there's a little proposal I'm authorised to make.' This was not quite true for he had only just thought of it, but he knew Popham would back him.

'I can say to you in confidence that we are on an expedition to Montevideo to join with rebels in overthrowing Spanish rule in the viceroyalty, which we have every confidence will be achieved rapidly. If you feel able to assist us, then the leader of the expedition states that, when the port of Buenos Aires is thrown open to free trade, this ship will be given the status of preferred vessel. This means that with the merchants there starved of export, all other shipping present must nonetheless first wait for you to take your pick of any cargo you desire, bound for anywhere to your best profit.'

It was irregular, if not downright illegal, but was within Popham's power to carry out simply by forewarning *Justina* of dates and times ahead of any declaration. The pickings to be had would be princely, vastly outweighing any considerations of delay in reporting to Cape Town for orders.

He was rewarded with a quick intake of breath. 'I understand you, Captain. We accept your offer.' He rose, offering his hand. Kydd took it, suppressing a surge of elation.

The act was revealing: Maycock was not expecting anything written down that could later be used against either of them.

'Be damned to it, an' you can't do that, mister!' Hardiman snapped triumphantly. '*Justina*'s voyage insurance is t' Cape Town only.'

Kydd hadn't thought of this. It was no trivial point: the value of a well-found merchantman this size must amount to something like his annual salary for fifty years or more; even if the premium could be renegotiated it would certainly not cover an act of war.

Maycock looked at him pointedly and waited.

'Very well. She'll sail uninsured.'

Maycock kept a polite silence.

'You'll have my note of hand to say you'll be reimbursed for her loss if the worst happens,' Kydd said. There was no help for it. The risk was all his – the Navy would never agree to what he was proposing, and if the vessel was wrecked or captured, they would wash their hands of him.

He ignored Curzon's look of appalled bewilderment and hoped his winning smile was convincing. 'Excellent. We have an arrangement. An officer of the St Helena's Infantry will be aboard directly to supervise your fitting for troop accommodation. Good day, gentlemen.'

The expedition sailed in two days with Kydd worried. Popham had approved of his move but had carefully ignored the mention of personal risk. The estuary of the River Plate was notorious for shoals and reefs, and when they sailed, *Justina* was not with them. She was still frantically being outfitted and stored and would follow when she could, easy prey to anything hostile, Spanish or French.

Popham had not felt able to deplete his main force to offer escort, and the thought of the vulnerable merchantman thrashing along alone in their wake was hard for Kydd to bear. Despite his nature he grew surly and snappish, swearing when Oakley's bawling out of the afterguard on the open deck above broke into his dark thoughts.

The next land raised would be the enemy coast and the climax of the expedition, when they would be entirely alone and their best-laid dispositions would be tested to the full. Would they be good enough? Their knowledge of the viceroyalty was sketchy at best, the charts commercial ones of a previous age and by no means to the technical standard he was used to. Furthermore, details of the military deployments to be faced were based on rumour only.

When he and Popham had prepared the operation orders, he had been dismayed by the generalisations and assumptions they had been compelled to employ to cover for lack of intelligence. Before Blaauwberg they had been equipped by ships that had regularly touched at the Cape with vital knowledge of the terrain and enemy strongholds. Here the Spanish had kept away all but their own ships and smugglers, who were not about to make free with their information.

And with barely a quarter of the troops and a handful of guns. In the cold light of day it was beginning to seem more an ill-conceived impertinence than a decisive military assault. His disquiet about the entire conception and its implementation was growing.

L'Aurore, with her relatively shallow draught, would no doubt be the one ordered to conduct an early reconnaissance and he felt the responsibility keenly. Poor charts and hostile waters were by no means unknown to the Navy – feats of seamanship were performed regularly by the heroes on blockade off the French coast with never a complaint. He recalled Captain Hurd, an officer, like himself, from before the mast. In a humble sloop in fearful conditions he had conducted a secret hydrographic survey of Brest under the very noses of the enemy.

He couldn't let the Navy down. Besides which—

'If I'm intruding, I'll come back later, brother.' He hadn't noticed Renzi hovering.

'No, no, m' friend. You've every right.'

'Well, I . . .'

Kydd looked up and saw that Renzi was carrying a sheaf of papers.

'You're sore pressed, I know, but you did say you'd take a look. Do give me your opinion of its worth – as a regular-going reader, in course. I'm now half done, you know.'

'I did say that, but I have m' worries, Nicholas, as are taking attention. It might not be a fair judgement, is all,' he finished lamely.

Renzi's face fell and Kydd held out his hand. 'Let me have 'em and I'll tell you when I've read through.'

'Things aren't going so well for you?'

'Just your usual mullygrubs afore an action, nothing to worry on.'

He had not told Renzi about Pitt's death and his increasing unease that they were sailing without Admiralty orders. By now the gunroom would be agog with the tale from Curzon of how their captain had cozened passage for the reinforcements and there would be considerable speculation as to why it had been necessary to go to such lengths.

Renzi hesitated, as though he was about to say something, then left quietly.

Kydd put down the sheaf of paper. Damn it all to blazes! This was the final act of what should be an historic occasion and it was turning into a nightmare. And if anything happened to *Justina*, most surely he'd be ruined financially – would he then be expected still to play his full part?

Mind full of worry, he picked up Renzi's manuscript. Anything was better than being left alone with his thoughts. The paper was well used, crossings-out and tiny insertions everywhere, but in Renzi's strong, educated hand it was easy to read. He focused on the first page, remembering with a sigh the awkward delivery the first time he had read it. He determined, however, to persevere for at least an hour.

Within minutes he was gripped. It was so *different*! The first scene was not the father's study, it was the milking shed. And without any elaborate setting out, the action opened quickly with the hero, Jeremy, tiptoeing into the dark, playfully whispering for Jenny, the milkmaid, who finally emerged pouting from the shadows. It went on from there in startling detail until the closing act of the chapter when the doors were flung wide and they were discovered.

It was extraordinary! The flow was quite different as well – instead of a modest first-person telling it was now a confident invisible observer drily chronicling the vigorous adventurings of a young man learning about life. Kydd read on; the succeeding chapter in which Jeremy was rusticated to a country academy was unexpectedly pathetic and noble by turns, Renzi's device of standing outside the character yet at the same time in intimate connection with thoughts and desires nothing short of masterly.

Kydd found himself a whisky, then settled back in anticipation. The passage of young Jeremy's staunch defence of a younger in the face of bullying by a master had all the hallmarks of Renzi himself but his ultimate expulsion for whoring in town was not. Or was it? Just how much was this his friend and how much fiction?

'Sir?' It was the first lieutenant, leaning through the door.

'Er, yes?'

'The master-at-arms reports all lights out, an' we're full an' bye on the larboard tack, course sou'-sou'-west, commodore in sight.' Kydd realised that he'd not been up to take his accustomed turn about the upper deck before retiring, which must be puzzling the watch-on-deck.

'Oh – er, thank you, Mr Gilbey,' he said pleasantly, 'and, um, goodnight to you.'

He turned back to the tale, spellbound.

The wasted years following, spent in idleness at the grand family estate under the eye of his noble and irascible father, were set out in unaffected detail; the growing emotional crisis resulting from their differences was temporarily resolved by his unexpected friendship with a certain other-worldly young man, a poet, whose wild and romantic leanings seemed to give so much point to existence.

The writing darkened, though, as it went on to describe how they set off together on a tour of the continent, vowing to live life to its fullest. The first scenes of debauchery and carnal excess were forthright and clear – Kydd could hardly believe what he was reading, still flowing as it did in the strong hand he knew so well.

Bemused, then astounded, Kydd read on until, with a pang, he realised that what he had of the manuscript had come to an end. He considered going to Renzi and waking him up, but of course he couldn't. Instead he leaned back in admiration. Either this would be the wonder of the season or it would be howled off the streets for its wickedness.

He chortled, hearing the marine sentry outside the door stir uneasily.

Before a spanking north-east trade wind the little armada made good speed across the South Atlantic, the weather remaining kind if steadily dropping in temperature into the southern late autumn. The continental influence far to starboard was of a quite different quality from Africa at the same latitude. At five hundred miles off, *Leda* and *L'Aurore* were detached to range on ahead.

Kydd complied unhappily, for *Justina* had still not hauled into sight. His mind shied from the implication and took refuge in his duty, the satisfaction of shaking out sail and quitting the slow progress of the rest of the force.

They criss-crossed the sullen grey wastes for days without incident until they reached the parallel of the great estuary at which their instructions were to make rendezvous with *Narcissus*, sent on before to reconnoitre. Shaping course due west, the pair ran down the latitude of the River Plate until, astonishingly, even at seventy-five miles to seaward, discolouring of the monotonous grey-green seas became noticeable, strengthening until the entire character of the sea was changed.

By nightfall they were within the loom of the land but prudently lay to until morning for there was every possibility that *Narcissus* would have news of the return of the Spanish warships. At first light they resumed their course, and when a rumpled grey-blue rising on the starboard bow announced their landfall on South America, with it was the distant pale blur of sails – *Narcissus* on her beat across the wide estuary mouth.

The three ships lay together in the cross-swell and exchanged news. The captain of *Narcissus* blared out from his speaking trumpet that, to his knowledge, the Spanish Navy had not yet returned, that all was quiet but that navigation in the estuary was the very devil due to its uncertain and shifting shoals, mud-banks and terrifying squalls.

Kydd hailed back that the fleet was on its way and that all was well, while Honyman in *Leda* wanted to know if *Ocean* had been sighted.

Narcissus then spread sail for the open sea to find the commodore. She was replaced on station by *Leda* while Kydd, with the shallowest draught, was dispatched to penetrate deeper into the River Plate to make sure of the reconnaissance.

It was a fearful task: at nearly 150 miles across at the mouth to a mile or two at its inner end hundreds of miles away, every rutter, pilot and guide they could muster was unanimous in its warnings. The chief peril was the shallow and treacherous trending of the river, which made impossible any approach into the estuary by a sea-going vessel unless by the deeper channels, which wove among the notoriously shifting hard-packed banks. It was said a thousand ships had laid their bones in this bleak place.

The other threat was the weather. The southern bank of the River Plate was in effect the edge of the endless flat plains of the Pampas across which the wind could blast without check. The notorious pampero could become so strong as to kick up a sea potent enough to stop the river in its flow – one from the south-east was sufficient, incredibly, even to reverse the tide – and a hard blow coming from the north-west could virtually dry out the estuary.

Kydd and the master pored over the charts. The funnel-shaped estuary had on the north side the outlying port of Maldonado, with Montevideo fifty miles further in at the true entry to the River Plate. The river narrowed there from sixty miles to thirty, at which point the past Portuguese settlement of Colonia lay opposite Buenos Aires. Twenty miles further on, it ended abruptly in a maze of marshes.

The south side had, except for the capital, no settlements of note and was very low-lying, with cloying mud-flats that stretched for miles. And in the river there were two main sandbanks: the long Ortiz Bank in the middle, and the sinuous length of the Chico closer inshore towards Buenos Aires. Beyond there was nothing but un-navigable shallows.

In hostile waters, without local knowledge or a pilot, they stood in as grave danger as anywhere Kydd had known before. Their stowaway, Serrano, was apologetic: he knew nothing of the sea so their track was entirely their own decision.

'We stand towards Montevideo, then keep in with the north,' Kydd finally decided.

Narcissus, a heavy frigate with a draught to match, had been unable to look into this port, the most likely to harbour defending Spanish men-o'-war. It was an essential first step, of course, for this was the designated assault point for the expedition.

With Maldonado safely out of sight, well to the northward, *L'Aurore* set her prow to the west with doubled lookouts. The lowering grey skies were menacing and the captain and ship's company were sombre. As they headed in, it was hard to believe they were sailing up a river for there was no land in sight and none expected: it was as if they were in the open ocean, but for the shorter wave-shape and tainted sea.

The master studied intently his *Remarks*, a printed booklet produced by a merchant captain of half a century before that persuasively gave sailing instructions for safe entry into the port of Montevideo. 'Bear west b' north until we raise the isle o' Flores,' Kendall intoned.

L'Aurore progressed under cautious sail. A shout came from one of the seamen looking over the side: the water had now turned a repellent mud-brown, solid and impenetrable – the great effluvium of a continental river.

'Leadsmen!' Kydd snapped.

A monotonous chant began from the forechains. 'No bottom wi' this line!' It would be a wet and cold job but it would last for as long as they were within the estuary.

Then they reached soundings. 'By the mark – fifteen!' So far from land and only ninety feet . . .

Barely half an hour later it was by the deep twelve and then eight, shoaling fast – they must be reaching the vast extrusion of sediment extending seaward. At six fathoms Kydd put another man in the opposite forechain to call out of sequence with the first.

'*Laaand hooo!*'

Kydd could not see it from the deck. Then came the hail that it was a long, rambling island – Isla de Flores. Montevideo was just fifteen miles further on.

'The island – no nearer'n three mile, sir.'

They bore away and almost immediately anxious shouts came from the leadsmen. 'I've five fathom! B' the mark five!'

It was incredible but with no land in sight they had less than twelve feet of water under their keel. Any rise or knoll in the invisible seabed and they would touch.

'Heave us to, Mr Kendall,' Kydd ordered, and turned to the boatswain. 'I want three boats in the water ahead with a hand lead in each.'

Spread in a line across their bows, they would give indication of the best passage. 'Says here, sir, if you brings up mud, you're in the channel, black sand and ye've strayed either side.' Now the leadsmen would be looking to the base of their leads, smeared with tallow to bring up an indication of the nature of the sea bottom.

It was agonisingly slow work. The fitful wind fluttered the sides of the sails; it had been mercifully constant until now but if it veered from its south-westerly direction they would be headed, and the reconnaissance would be over.

After a little more than an hour, the mainland of South America was raised at the masthead: Punta Brava at the outer point of the Bay of Montevideo.

When the land could be seen from the quarterdeck it was flat and uninteresting, scrub, occasional sand dunes and then the last point before the bay. Would they see a tell-tale forest of masts, a swarm of angry gunboats emerging?

The water shallowed further and Kydd kept the frigate well offshore as they made the final low headland and the bay opened up. Instantly telescopes trained and searched – and there was no fleet at anchor.

They were still five miles or more off so Kydd swung into the shrouds and mounted to the tops, taking out his pocket telescope. He could see deep within the bay, nothing hidden from this vantage-point.

On the right he saw the untidy low sprawl of a large town, which must be Montevideo, and on the left of the bay a conical hill about four hundred feet high, no doubt the 'mountain' that could be seen from across the bay and gave the city its name. There were vessels within but not one that answered the description of a man-o'-war.

In a rush of relief Kydd descended. 'Nothing,' he told the group on the quarterdeck.

'Where now, sir?' Kendall enquired anxiously.

They had news that would gladden Popham – but would he be satisfied with just that? There had to be deeper channels, perhaps dredged, that would allow large vessels to enter, but these would be known only to pilots and local captains. At the same time this would imply that other channels were available that led deeper into the River Plate. It was his duty therefore to attempt further penetration.

'We stand on.'

With the boats still leading they hardened in and, close-hauled, stood away. Before they had made more than a few miles the wind failed. Kydd was too much the seaman not to know that this was usually the precursor of a shift in direction and there was only one action that could be contemplated.

'Get the boats in. We're going back.'

But in the time it took to heave to, hoist aboard their boats and put about, everything had changed.

In these strange climes, it seemed, it was not to be a simple change of wind direction: from the south-west spread a wide, glistening white fluffiness, a sea-fog. It reached and enveloped them in a clammy embrace until they were swallowed in its soundless immensity.

L'Aurore glided on in the eerie whiteness, the only thing to be heard the subdued chuckle of water at her forefoot and the mournful chant of the leadsmen. If this were an English Channel pea-souper they would be surrounded by a bedlam of horns, gongs and drumbeats, Kydd remembered.

It would be reasonably safe to return to the open sea simply by reversing the plot of compass courses, the wind conveniently on the beam, but he wouldn't feel secure until—

From the tops came an agitated, breathy hail: '*Deck hoooo!*'

Kydd looked up.

'*Sail – jus' a pistol shot t' loo'ard! I see tops'ls of a schooner!*'

'Silence fore 'n' aft!' Kydd ordered savagely, in a low voice. This could only be the enemy – at that size never a threat but if they could question the crew . . .

'Where headed?' he threw to the lookout.

'*'Cross our bows.*'

Their priceless advantage was that in a fore-and-aft-rigged vessel like a schooner there could be no lookout positions aloft, but their own, high up, had been able to see the betraying upper sails of the ship above the fog-bank.

'Get men below. On my order, just open all gun-ports to larboard,' Kydd hissed at Curzon.

Gently rippling along, there was ample time to prepare. 'M' compliments to Mr Renzi and would he step up here.'

Judging his moment well, precisely as the grey shape of the other craft materialised out of the fog, he swung *L'Aurore* parallel and roared out the order for the gun-ports to open while trumpets blared and marine drummers beat out a terri-fying tattoo.

In the schooner it must have been the stuff of nightmares, a towering enemy frigate appearing like magic out of the mists, apparently about to blast them to splinters. The hapless vessel was grappled and boarded before even her colours had been jerked down in terrified surrender.

'Nicholas,' Kydd said, gratified that Renzi's coming on deck had coincided with the sudden commotion of the appearance and taking of an enemy, 'would you kindly accompany Mr Gilbey aboard and invite the captain to join us?'

When Renzi returned it was not merely with a Spanish captain but a distinctly unamused gentleman of imperious manner and fine dress. 'Sir, I have the honour to present His Excellency the Governor of Truxillo.' Bows were exchanged but the smouldering dark eyes barely concealed thunder and the desire for vengeance.

Kydd nodded to Renzi. It was impressive, the suavity his friend was managing with his new-found Spanish. 'I shall look forward to entertaining His Excellency in my cabin shortly. As soon as we have concluded our business here.'

The schooner was a fine one, trim-lined and well appointed, her crew standing disconsolately along the deck. An *aviso*? If so, this was an official vessel and quite likely to be charged with dispatches. The speed of her capture meant almost certainly that these were still aboard. Gilbey could be trusted to intercept any attempt to get rid of them.

The governor was surly and abrupt, and nothing could be learned from courtly questioning except that their pres-ence had been utterly unexpected. No matter: the commodore would follow through with his own interrogation.

The small crew was another matter. When under way once

more, the schooner under prize crew and demurely in the frigate's wake, he had her company examined one by one.

Renzi came up to see Kydd in his cabin. 'I think you'll find one man an interesting fellow,' he said mysteriously. 'I've had Serrano concealed nearby and he swears he's an Englishman.'

The man was under guard in the gunroom, a large, somewhat florid individual in the plain dress of a warrant officer of sorts.

'This is Crujido, sir.'

'And what is his rank?'

'*¿Cuál es su rango, señor?*' There was a flow of mumbled Spanish in reply.

'He's being evasive about it, sir.'

'Tell him that unless he's more truthful, he'll be sent back to Cape Town in irons as a suspected deserter.'

The nervous start he gave before it was translated was all the evidence Kydd needed. 'So we understand each other?'

'Aye, Captain. Jed Russell it is, an' I been here since before the Frenchies started. Emigrated, a new life I has now.'

'Then you've sworn allegiance to the Spanish Crown?'

'Had to, o' course.'

'And now we're at war with the Spanish – with you,' Kydd said mildly. 'What do you say to that?'

There was a reluctant silence. Then, 'What do ye here, if I c'n ask it?'

Kydd gave the man a shrewd look.

'I'm thinking ye're here to do a mischief agin the Spaniards in Montevideo. Are ye a fleet?'

Kydd said nothing, letting Russell make the running.

'Aye, well, if ye are, then there's many o' these here who'll relish 'em being humbled. What say I give help? What'll ye do for me?'

'Give help? What's your situation, sir?'

A satisfied smile emerged. 'Why, an' I'm a senior pilot for the Río de la Plata under the viceroyalty, is all.'

Kydd couldn't suppress an answering grin. 'Then, Mr Russell, you shall be satisfied in all particulars should you choose service with us. Is there anything else you'd be wanting?'

'There is.'

'And what is that, pray?'

'It's been all o' these fifteen years an' I've never tasted a right true drop. If ye can see y'r way clear . . .'

'What do you mean, the man's indisposed?' Popham snapped. 'I want him here. It's imperative I get answers, and this instant!'

Kydd sighed. 'That is to say, he's been taken with barrel fever, it being the first grog he's faced this age. I thought it necessary if we have to use him.'

'For God's sake, are the Spanish going to—'

'Dasher, the substance of what he told me is this, and it's the first direct intelligence we've had, damn it. He says the people would look kindly on being made free, as we know, and as of this moment it's a prime time to attack. They've no idea we're here or why. There are no Spanish men-o'-war as they're all in the north still, engaged with Miranda. In Montevideo the fortress is manned but by a smallish number of regulars and a sad parcel o' militia who won't stand against real troops such as ours. In particular, in a few days it'll be the feast of Corpus Christi in which all will join in drunken riot for a week, a fine time to move against 'em.'

'That's more like it,' Popham grunted, in much satisfaction.

'Oh, and he says there's a considerable treasure in Buenos Aires waiting for want of escort to Spain.'

'Is there, by heaven?' Popham said slowly, his eyes widening.

'There's more – I have a man aboard, a native of these parts with strong sympathy towards a rebellion. He stowed away to be in at the kill so I signed him on as translator. If he can make his number with the rebels ashore . . . ?'

'Yes, yes – see what you can do,' Popham said, distracted. 'I need to think.'

Kydd took his leave and returned to *L'Aurore* in high spirits: when he had emerged from the fog to rendezvous with the fleet off Maldonado, he'd seen the unmistakable outlines of *Justina* primly at anchor in the middle of the little group, her voyage and contract now fulfilled, and beyond her, the welcome sight of *Ocean*, at last come to join.

Renzi stood forward, in conversation with Serrano, who was looking fixedly at the Maldonado shore.

'So – this is your South America, Vicente,' Renzi murmured, seeing the rapt expression on his Spanish friend's face.

'*Sí!* Is very beautiful, no?'

The distant shoreline, dry, flat and a study in ochrous brown, looked anything but inviting.

'Most attractive,' Renzi agreed hastily. 'Are you looking forward to setting foot on shore?'

'When the Spanish have left, not ever before.'

'And then?'

'Ah. The first – it to be *mi cariño*, the girl who wait. I finish my study, we are married. Maybe business. The silver, it will finish, the Pampas our true riches, I think. The – how you say? – skin of cow, these the whole world always want. Our meats, grain – with *libre comercio* we sell, all profit will stay wi' us, we be rich.'

'Just so, m' friend. As soon as you're independent.'

Serrano looked pensive then asked abruptly, 'You English – why you're helping wi' us?'

'It's to our advantage should the Spanish lose their colonies.'

He looked sideways at Renzi's set face with a slight smile. 'Why quiet? You're not agreeable wi' this?'

Renzi hesitated, then admitted, 'The governance of a country is its own business. Even in war I cannot see we have any right to interfere in its sovereign affairs. If the people rise against their rulers, then that is for them and only them to resolve.'

'Your chief not think like that – he will attack, soon.'

'As I understand it.'

'Good. I will paint a grand battle, your soldiers with ours fighting to beat the Spanish. A *magnífico* drama like as Señor Shakespeare write!'

'Er, possibly. Do enjoy this prospect, my friend. I must return to my writing, I find.'

'Ah, Mr Serrano,' Kydd said, rising in welcome as the artist was escorted into his day cabin. 'There is a matter I wish to discuss.'

'At your service, Captain.'

'I will not hide it from you – an assault on Montevideo will begin shortly. Our commodore is desirous that all who wish to throw off the Spanish yoke may join with us to share in the glory of this occasion.'

'Of history!' Serrano breathed, his face glowing.

'Er, yes. To enable this to happen, it will be necessary to join forces, to talk together of where we shall strike first, where supplies are to be found.'

'Yes, sir.'

'So we must speak with the leaders of the, um, movement for freedom.'

'*Los patriotas!* The patriots, Captain.'

'Do you know them?'

'These I know an' hold close to my heart, sir.'

'Very well. We would be much obliged should you go and inform them that the British leader desires a parley.'

Serrano's eyes shone. 'Is dangerous, but for freedom I do it.'

Kydd remembered that the man was wanted by the authorities and hesitated. 'Not if it places you in hazard at all.'

'I want to landing at Puerto del Inglés, Captain. At darkness.'

It seemed only fair to send for Renzi at this point. 'Nicholas, your friend is assisting us by contacting the rebel band. Shall you want to supervise his arrangements at all?'

'Vicente,' Renzi said, with concern, '*mi amigo*, you are only to find the leader of the band and bring him to us. There's no need to play the *temerario* in this.' The young painter was so intense, so bound up with his place in the destiny of his country. Would he, like Wordsworth, be caught up in the roaring chaos of a nation in revolt and then be disillusioned with its price in blood and terror?

'Is my duty, Nicholas. I playing my part.'

The exaltation had passed and there was now seriousness – and resolve. 'But not so easy. *Los patriotas* they are many, but many leaders also. They quarrel, fight each other. I will tell them for the sake of freedom they must join in one.'

'Then – would you wish it that we go together?' In Renzi's past he had seen his share of naïvety and treachery and feared for his young friend.

'*No es posible*. Here is no place for the English gentleman. The country is raw and wicked, the people as untamed animals. No, is my duty, my glory.'

'Then I honour you for it, Vicente. So, Puerto del Inglés, where is it at all?'

'Ah, Maldonado, to the west twenty miles. Is where you English take on shore your smuggled goods to trade. A lagoon of seven mile protect and it have a pretty beach.'

'Captain Kydd wishes to make contact as quickly as possible. You should be prepared to land in the darkness tonight. Are you ready?'

A knapsack of rations and a canteen of water was all he would accept, together with a stout boat-cloak and scarf, insisting he go entirely unarmed. It was Renzi who quietly pointed out that any documentation of authenticity provided by the commodore would be a death sentence if he was taken up by the authorities.

In the evening, *L'Aurore* ghosted into the bay. A boat was put in the water with Renzi and Serrano as passengers and they warily made for the point at the northern end of the beach, passing inshore fishermen in their curious flat boats, ignoring them as they worked. In the gathering gloom the boat doused sail and, under oars, hissed into the sand.

Serrano stood in the boat and hesitated, staring into the anonymous countryside with its wafting odour of dryness and cattle.

'If you'd rather wait . . . ?' Renzi offered.

He shook his head, made his way clumsily down the boat and dropped on to the beach, remembering to turn and lift a hand in farewell.

'*Vaya con Dios, mi amigo*,' called Renzi, in a low voice. He watched the man trudge up the beach and into the thickets.

Chapter 6

'Flag, sir. All captains.' It was Calloway, now holding a temporary warrant from the commodore as master's mate after the death of Pearse. With a vacancy on the quarterdeck for a midshipman, the earnest Searle had been elevated, seeming young and vulnerable in the inherited uniform that hung about him.

'Thank you,' said Kydd. The summons was expected: at this critical point Popham had decided on a proper council-of-war, which had full legal standing – no mere gathering of opinion but the coming to a course of action that they would all agree upon. Then if there was a calamity, no one could claim they had known it all along and not been heard.

Diadem's great cabin was soon packed. At one end of the table athwart was the commodore, at the other Beresford, general officer in command of land forces. The naval captains were along one side, the army on the other.

'Thank you for your attendance, gentlemen,' Popham opened, with a broad smile. 'This council-of-war now begins.' One of his lieutenants sat to his right, taking note of the proceedings, a subaltern next to General Beresford doing the same.

'Prospects for our success remain excellent, I'm happy to say. The strength of the enemy is as we heard before and there appears no reinforcement contemplated. Should we make our stroke with boldness and speed, we shall be able to avoid a protracted campaign.'

Beresford coughed discreetly. 'That is all very well, sir, but may we be told where such information has come from? Do you have sources of intelligence among the Dons that can be trusted to reveal all to us?'

Popham looked pained. 'Sir, as in most expeditions of my experience, the usual fishermen, merchants and others are well capable of providing a picture of their circumstances, which, taken in the round, can establish the situation better even than a lone spy or traitor. They have nothing to gain by giving false information, which will be discovered later, and everything to gain when it is over and we are in power.'

The general harrumphed but offered no further question.

'I'm interested to know how your revolt is to be managed,' rumbled Honyman. 'Are they to play in our show? When will we know they're of a mind to rise up and such?'

'I've an envoy passed ashore to speak with the chief of the rebels, and another courtesy of Captain Kydd. Their task is to bring them to a meeting with ourselves with the object of co-ordinating our attack with their rising. Their instructions are to proceed with the utmost celerity.'

'Have you communication from them?'

'I expect it hourly, General.'

'So, no word yet after three days. We cannot delay matters for them,' Beresford came in sharply, 'and, further, it's my opinion that no reliance whatsoever be placed on the services of irregular troops, whatever their dedication. Are they to be under my express command? If not, then they cannot appear in my order of battle.'

'Neither do we expect to see them there, sir,' Popham replied smoothly. 'Any accession to strength from these irregulars is to be welcomed but not relied upon. Our expectation is that any revolt will be more in the character of a general and spontaneous uprising in the population as a whole, following the example of our assault, which will go on to overwhelm the Spanish forces.'

'Hmph,' glowered Beresford. 'Let us now consider the reduction of the Montevideo fortress. We've little enough in the way of siege engines and such, and you admitted before, did you not, that this is the chief stronghold for the entire River Plate?' He looked about him significantly.

'I'm not saying we've no chance of success, merely that our planning has to be meticulous. Therefore this is what I propose. We land well to the east, marching rapidly for a hooked advance from the interior instead of—'

Popham held up his hand. 'Thank you, General. Before we discuss these details I wish to advise that in the light of recent intelligence I've been looking at quite another strategy as it offers itself.'

'Recent intelligence?' the general growled. 'Should we not be told of this?'

'All will become clear in a moment, sir,' Popham said patiently. 'The intelligence comes from an unimpeachable source – the chief pilot of the viceroyalty, lately taken. He may be considered the first major figure coming over to us. He's laid before me the defensive situation of the Spanish, and this is that all their regular troops have been moved to

Montevideo on the assumption that that city will be our objective.'

'Any fool knows this.'

'He further specifies that, as a consequence, the city of Buenos Aires is defenceless, a paltry militia battalion only.'

'Are you seriously suggesting—'

'It crosses my mind that as this is the chief city and seat of power, its loss will, at a blow, paralyse the Spanish and give heart to the people in their rising.'

'This is a foolish notion that flies in the face of military science. To leave an enemy position of strength in the rear of one's advance is of the first rank of idiocy and I cannot countenance such an act.'

'Umm. Not only this, General, but you may not be aware that in the city treasury lie untold millions in silver that cannot be freighted to Spain for want of ships . . .'

There was an immediate stir of interest. 'Purely out of curiosity, dear fellow, but should this be confiscated, for the Navy . . . will it be put forward as in the nature of, er, prize money?' Captain Byng asked.

'There is precedent, George. I rather feel that Droits of the Crown will not be asserted in this case,' Popham murmured.

Another voice came in: 'Ah. Then—'

'Shall we get back to the matter in hand?' Beresford broke in heavily. 'Montevideo will not easily be taken by storm with the forces I have to command. Therefore we will—'

'General. I have shown how a successful assault on the Spanish might be contemplated. Should we not consider this before going into operational details of any one stratagem?'

Beresford looked at him in amazement. 'You really desire

us to make a direct assault on the capital? With less than a thousand and a half under arms? Ridiculous! A city of what, thirty or forty thousand, a central fortress and an unknown number of defenders under the command of the viceroy himself? Preposterous!'

Popham leaned forward and spoke forcefully. 'It's effectively an open city for we've heard that it is drained of their best troops, who have gone to Montevideo. As well, it's the last thing the Spanish expect, a rapid and direct move on their capital – and you've not considered the effect on the population of a confident and well-conducted thrust against their military. Recollect, sir, there has in history never yet been a full-scale field engagement on the soil of South America. Consequently their troops must be accounted quite untried and will certainly flee when confronted by soldiers of the quality of your Highlanders.'

'A single bold stroke straight to the heart of the Spanish. I confess I do like it, sir.'

'Thank you, Captain Honyman,' Popham said modestly, and shifted his gaze to the captain of *L'Aurore*.

The talk of silver had disturbed Kydd. Renzi's words about venal motives still echoed in his ears, but the attraction of a daring thrust straight for the centre over a methodical reduction in the usual way was undeniable. 'I, er, agree,' Kydd said, adding, 'particularly as we haven't the resources for a lengthy engagement.'

'Quite!' barked Beresford. 'I would have thought it elementary that we first take Montevideo – if we can – before embarking on any other adventure.'

'Few resources, yes,' Popham said, with equal energy, 'then how much better it would be to use these in going straight for Buenos Aires and leave Montevideo to wither alone.'

Colonel Pack was the first to speak up from the Army side. 'Damn me if there isn't some sense in what he says, sir. If we're to be short o' men, throw 'em at the main objective and be buggered to hanging back waiting.'

Beresford winced and looked about for support. Seeing none, he stiffened. 'For the record of proceedings I want it known that my counsel is to take Montevideo and, defending same, to send dispatches to England advising reinforcement for a later assault on Buenos Aires.'

Kydd knew this was a course Popham would never take. The initiative would be lost and command would be passed to an Admiralty nominee who would succeed to the honour of taking the city, let alone the certainty of losing the opportunity while the Spanish warships were absent.

Popham gave a curt nod. 'Thank you, sir. Your position is abundantly clear. However, also for the record, I'd be interested to know of the officers here how many would consider a direct assault on Buenos Aires preferable to a more . . . circumspect approach.'

Looks were exchanged around the table and hands went up hesitantly. Besides Kydd, all the Navy captains, save Donnelly of *Narcissus*, indicated support, with Pack leading more than half of the Army.

'I see.' Popham kept his tone level. 'Then it appears this council-of-war has a majority agreement on the way forward for the operation. Gentlemen, there's much to be covered in preparing for this assault and I propose that it be accomplished by forming two planning groups, one naval, for landing and support, and one army, for operations ashore. I shall head the naval. Might I ask General Beresford to head the army?'

* * *

Renzi was neither in the gunroom nor his cabin. Kydd hid his irritation and went on deck looking for him; he couldn't set messengers to finding him because a captain's summons would be relayed in the strongest terms – which was not what he wanted with his friend in the mood he had been under these past days.

After several blank looks at his enquiries he remembered that when the vessel was at anchor Renzi sometimes secured solitude, that prize above all things in a small ship, in one favoured place. Kydd made his way forward and swung up into the fore-ratlines, climbing up and over the futtock shrouds into the fore-top.

Renzi was there, his back to the mast and with a book. He looked up coldly. 'Do I inconvenience at all?'

Kydd sat next to him. With all sails in, no men aloft and lookouts absent, it felt strangely bare and deserted, the maze of rigging thrumming softly in the quiet with the far-off sad keening of a sea-bird carrying across the water.

'You're not at your scribbling, then.'

'No.'

'Er, it would oblige if you could favour me with your presence at this time.'

'If that is your order.'

'Time presses, Nicholas. We make our move on the Spaniards very shortly but there's a mort o' planning to be done first. This is not work for the captain's clerk and I'd appreciate it if—'

'I'd hoped to have escaped an embroilment in this absurdity.'

Kydd's voice hardened. 'And could I remind you that you're aboard this ship courtesy of a position which carries duties. If you're not of a mind . . .'

'Very well, I shall come, if such is necessary.'

'Damn it, Nicholas!' Kydd burst out. 'What more have you got against the man?'

'Since you ask it,' Renzi replied coolly, 'I shall point out to you how this whole business must look to the world.

'Here we have a flag-officer who quits his station for the other side of the ocean – and for what? Not only is it for the fantastical notion of invading a continent but now it appears he has persuaded his command that they abandon the reduction of the enemy's fortress stronghold for an attack on the seat of the viceroyalty itself. Why? Well, in the meantime he has learned of a king's ransom in silver in the city's vaults, and— '

'This is not the way it is, Nicholas,' Kydd said thickly, 'and unworthy of you!'

' —therefore most would be hard pressed to find a real difference between this and Drake's raids on the Spanish Main two centuries past. No strategics but gain and plunder.'

'You've the opening of trade and—'

'Do spare me the recitation, old fellow. I've said I'll come,' Renzi said wearily, and got up. 'Shall we get on with it?'

The first draft of planning brought back from Popham was a sobering document. Shifting the objective had brought with it some near insuperable problems, the worst of which was Russell's emphatic statement – confirmed by boat – that the depth of water was such that not only were the sixty-fours unable to penetrate much further into the River Plate but neither were the frigates.

This was a severe blow for it meant that their landing far up the river would go in without heavy gunfire support of any kind, the boats at the mercy of any artillery brought to bear from the shore as well as being under the merciless lash of musketry as they tried to group on the landing beach, with no chance to reply.

Actual forces defending were unknown: the viceroy could be counted on to garrison a battalion or two, but what if a much larger militia force had been mobilised? Perhaps an army in the interior was on forced march to the coast even as they delayed.

Their own force was frighteningly slight. Eight hundred or so officers and men of the 71st and a handful of light dragoons, together with the reinforcements from St Helena, bringing the total to something over a thousand all told. Against a city of so many tens of thousands.

'If you are determined upon it, then there's only one rational course,' Renzi pronounced.

'What, pray?'

'Suspend your immediate ambitions and wait patiently for reinforcements.'

Kydd gave a grim smile. 'There's another.'

'Oh?'

'Our ships are obliged to lie at anchor, idle – if we make levy of every marine and seaman who can carry a musket we'll have half as many troops again. Remember the sea battalion at Blaauwberg? And we've a mighty ally that'll count for a whole army.'

'I'm intrigued to know what.'

'Surprise! No one will believe we really intend to fall on Buenos Aires with what few we have.'

'True indeed,' Renzi agreed fervently.

'We tide up in one of these damn fogs and set ashore as close as we can to the city, then go straight in. I've heard there's a pitiful harbour there and now I know why, but we'll be coming ashore south o' the city.'

'And the Good Lord have mercy on us all,' murmured Renzi.

'Damn it all, Nicholas,' Kydd blazed. 'If ye can't think of else to say, clew up y'r jawing tackle an' stand mumchance f'r once.'

Renzi started at the return of Kydd's fo'c'sle lingo. He shuffled awkwardly at the sudden realisation of the depth of his friend's feelings. 'My apologies. If there's aught . . . ?'

Kydd subsided, but growled, 'Then what's to do with your painting friend? A general rising an' natives flocking to our colours would be prime at this time, I'd believe.'

Renzi's face shadowed. 'There's been no signal from Puerto del Inglés these five days. I'm sanguine Vicente will be doing what he can, so it has to be assumed there's to be no immediate action on the part of the rebels. Whether this is due to him not being able to find or communicate with the leaders, or that he hasn't been able to secure their agreement to meet us, I've no idea.'

'Or he's been taken by the Spanish before he's spoken with 'em.'

'Er, just so.'

The next morning Kydd arrived back from consultations on the flagship with a wry grin. 'He's already thought of my idea about landing seamen and takes my bringing it to him as a mark of enthusiasm. Be damned to it, and I'm therefore made chief of the Marine Battalion.'

'My earnest felicitations, brother.'

'I've two days to bring 'em up to snuff. So let's begin – an order on all captains for a return of men trained in muskets, the ship's company set to stitching up some sort of red coat for each one. We'll have – let me see – a field mark on the left arm of a stripe o' white cloth. No harm in taking precautions. Then we have to know what they'll need in their knapsacks and such.'

He snorted. 'But this is all lobsterback territory. I'm to send for our l'tenant o' marines, I believe.'

Clinton heard Kydd out gravely and promised to bring his recommendations within the hour.

'Now we've only to find seats for a thousand and a half men in craft as will swim among the shoals.'

'And more for the running in of stores and ammunition,' Renzi added.

'And the field guns,' agreed Kydd. 'And we've horses to get landed. So let's be moving on it.'

'It's a miracle, I agree, Mr Gilbey,' Kydd said, waiting for the boat to take him to *Encounter*, the little craft that was to have the honour of leading the expedition in its thrust into the heart of the enemy. Hollow-eyed and weary beyond feeling, he surveyed the scatter of humble vessels that was now the invasion fleet. Small transports, captured coasters, the largest ship's boats – anything that could carry men was now crowded with soldiery, on time and ready to sail.

And, praise be, one of the cold fogs had rolled in right on cue. This was the chance they needed to slip past Montevideo and achieve some measure of surprise, but at the cost of all landmarks obliterated as they closed with their objective among the fearful shallows and reefs. It would take seamanship of the highest order to get through without casualty.

'You'll take care of her for me,' Kydd said to Gilbey, as *Encounter*'s boat approached.

'Sir, I will,' his first lieutenant replied gravely. 'An' good fortune in what must come.' Kydd shook his hand before he was piped over the side.

Twisting around he took a last sight of *L'Aurore* – her trim beauty wrenched at him for he had no illusions about what lay ahead. Service ashore had been inevitable after his experiences with the Army, particularly in the recent capture of Cape Town with these same soldiers, but . . . A premonition lay on him, one that welled up with memories of his time as a young seaman involved in a royalist rising in Brittany those many years ago when all hopes had dissolved into chaos and blood.

He tried to shake off the ghosts and looked back again at his lovely frigate, those divinely inspired lines, the rightness of the curves and proud elegance of the lofty spars – and there was Renzi's white face at the open stern window, his arm lifted in a sad farewell. Unaccountably a lump formed in his throat and he turned resolutely forward.

Encounter was a gun-brig, one of the plain, stout workhorses of the Navy. That this little inshore gunboat had been expected without hesitation to cross oceans with the fleet was yet another reason why Bonaparte could never prevail against such a navy. But were they now expecting too much of timber and sinew, daring and resolve? Where were the limits?

He shook off the morbid thoughts as he heaved himself over the modest bulwarks to see Godwin, the youthful lieutenant-in-command, waiting for him. 'Welcome aboard, sir. It's said as where Captain Kydd is, there's always sport to be had,' he added.

Kydd couldn't help an answering grin. '*L'Aurore* will have to bide her time – I've a fancy *Encounter* is to have all the entertainment to herself.'

'Er, my cabin for refreshments, sir?'

'No time,' Kydd said briskly. 'And I desire you hang out the "preparative" as soon as you may.'

The breeze was light but steady, the fog-bank a dank, impenetrable screen of dull white. There was nothing to be gained in waiting longer. 'The "proceed" Mr Godwin,' Kydd ordered.

Three boats closed with *Encounter*, their task to sound ahead. A white or red warning flag would fly from each; a row-guard of pinnaces armed with swivels accompanied them – a pitiful defence if the Spanish had hidden sea forces further in.

Kydd glanced back at the ghostly grey of the anchored sixty-fours. They looked so insubstantial but he knew Popham was watching their little expedition leave to be quickly swallowed up by the fog with the entire fate of the expedition in their hands. An indistinct but elaborate signal hoist was up in the flagship – there was nothing that could be done now so without a doubt it was a deeply meant farewell.

Their anchor won and the soldiers crowded on deck, trying to keep to one side, the little ship got under way. The enterprise had begun.

His heart beat a little faster as he glanced back at the rest following. The broad-beamed *Melantho* was a reassuring bulk, a light in her bows steady to confirm that her own next astern was safely in sight. And then came *Triton*, the transport containing General Beresford and elements of the 71st with their two guns.

There was little Kydd could do to occupy himself. He was aboard in the leading ship under sufferance to make decisions should there be trouble and to be among the first to land. While Godwin was amiable and attentive, he had his responsibilities. The quarterdeck was ludicrously small, with no room for pacing about, and before long Kydd found himself picking his way forward through the redcoats on deck.

Initially they stiffened as he approached but soon Kydd was able to pass among them without fuss, overhearing the age-old military banter of fighting men about to go into battle. He made his way back down the other side to find a chair waiting for him on the quarterdeck.

Time passed. At a speed of something like three knots it would take several days to cover the hundred and thirty miles to their landing zone. Painstaking work with the hand lead in the boats was needed to establish a safe channel and Russell's muddled directions were confusing – somehow he had found more drink and now, surly or riotous by turns, he was under personal guard by a relay of midshipmen.

They had agonised over the conflicting charts and finally settled on Punta Quilmes, a dozen or so miles south of the city, the furthest point where the depth of water was anything like adequate, but first there was the fraught passage to negotiate between the notorious Ortiz and Chico banks.

The fog held as they left Montevideo invisibly to starboard, the muddy water gurgling, over-loud, in the pale closeness, their ceaseless motion ever onward into the anonymous reaches of the languid river. When the darkness closed in there was no option but to anchor. Rations and grog were distributed to the troops.

The officers shared the stuffy confines of Godwin's cabin for their evening meal, humorously making light of their conditions, but as soon as he could, Kydd made his way back to the upper deck. The soldiers lay all about, drawing their blankets around them. 'They'll see far worse in the field, believe me,' a subaltern confided. 'A few days there and they'll be yearning for a nice comfortable plank to sleep on.'

Godwin had offered Kydd his cabin, but at his insistence they had compromised on a hammock aloft and alow in the old way and he tumbled into the ''mick' comfortably, like the foremast jack he had been so long ago.

He slept little. The sounds of the ship, the anonymous creaks, rumbles and distant slithers as it swung with the current, were foreign, and his thoughts were chaotic and anxious. It felt quite different from the nervous exhilaration before the Cape Town landings: he could not throw off the feeling of foreboding that was clamping in on him.

The morning dawned with a thinning fog and visibility out to nearly half a mile. As soon as the boats could be seen reliably they were under way once more and, as the day progressed, the fog finally dissolved to reveal a grey desolation of empty sea.

They had made it past Montevideo, the secret of their departure still safe, and Kydd's spirits rose.

Towards evening they were near the tail of the twin banks, allegedly buoyed, but Russell had warned that mud-scouring would continually shift their moorings and they could not be relied on. A few distant sails were sighted, flat fishing craft that ignored them – and always the drab grey-brown water sliding monotonously past.

As Kydd deliberated about anchoring for the night, *Melantho* slewed and stopped, nearly bringing *Ocean* into collision with her. The forced delaying of the fleet settled the question – but had the vessel touched on mud or an outlier of the hard-packed sand of the Chico bank?

In the last of the light it was established that it had been mud – there would be no damage, but freeing the deep-laden transport from the thick, glutinous ooze would not be easy. Her crew would have a hard night of it, lightening ship and hauling off.

But Kydd's mind was on the next day. In a matter of hours

they would be in sight of the enemy. Given the general's strong opposition to their alteration of plans, would he be looking for an excuse to call it off? Kydd knew if that happened he would be caught up in the inevitable bitterness to follow. He must take care to do nothing that could be flourished at a later court-martial.

Full of dark thoughts he finally drifted off. He awoke early to a cold and cheerless day, rain threatening, a serious matter if they had to land with damp muskets in the teeth of heavy fire. Kydd felt unable to finish his breakfast.

They got under way as soon as possible, and before midday, a low, monotonously flat coastline was raised to larboard. It continued on as scattered buildings came into sight, and then from the masthead a hail, the city itself.

After signalling the fleet to heave to, Kydd joined the lookout and took out his pocket glass. At this moment the entire expedition was in his hands: if he overlooked any threat, failed to see an enemy column, mistook a distant feature and then set the assault in motion . . .

He quartered the terrain with care, cursing at the thrum and judder of the rigging as he braced on it, but could see nothing remotely like a threat. The closer shore was low and featureless, open scrub and flat heath, as far as he could tell, while further to the right there was a modest river, set about with thickets of small trees and with a slight rise on the far side.

And some miles beyond, at the limit of vision, he saw the spires and domes of a city – Buenos Aires.

After taking one last sweep of the nearest coastline he returned to the deck.

'I see nothing of the enemy,' he told the expectant faces. It seemed astonishing, but the Spanish were simply not there.

He boarded *Encounter*'s tiny jolly-boat and was taken to *Triton* to report to the general.

Beresford greeted him impatiently. 'Well, now, and what can you tell us, sir?' Significantly he was wearing his sword, and officers began hurrying up to hear the conversation. At deck level only an anonymous low coastline was in sight.

'From the masthead I could see no sign of the enemy,' Kydd said carefully.

'Nothing?' Beresford said incredulously. 'No camp, no lines being thrown up, troops on column of march?'

'The terrain is flat and open, sir. I should have seen them.' He spoke firmly, 'Therefore I counsel the landing takes place.'

'Ah!'

'We're some two miles south of Punta Quilmes, with the city a dozen miles north.' Kydd did not add that this was only if the river they had sighted was indeed the Ria Chuelo – the featureless landscape and sketchy maps made an exact fix impossible.

Beresford beamed at his officers. 'I rather think Dame Fortune is smiling upon us today, by Jove.'

The actual landing had demanded meticulous planning. The order of the troops first ashore and their support required pinpoint timing, with the men in different ships around the fleet coming together, the few horses and guns essential to be landed with them marshalled at the same time before all moved in together. Because of the hours this would take before they could meet the enemy in a protected formation, a dawn assault was expected. 'Then we move at first light, sir?' a dragoon officer enquired.

'No offence to our gracious hosts, but the sooner we're on dry land the better I'd like it,' Beresford said grimly. 'And while we've an unopposed descent, I'm to dispense with the order of assault.'

He paused for effect. 'Gentlemen – we go in today. Now! Just get the men ashore and form 'em up. We'll take it on from there.'

A wash of relief swept over Kydd. Despite his worst imaginings, for some reason they were to be granted a landing without fire from the shore. Beresford was a general who was not afraid to take decisions.

But how long were they to be given before the Spanish woke up to what was happening?

'I'll get it under way, then, sir,' the dragoon officer responded smartly.

It would not take long to send boats around the waiting fleet to order the transports to get their men landed as soon as they had kitted up. Kydd would take the first boat heading inshore.

Back in *Encounter* he watched the sudden surge in activity in the ships following the dispatch boat's visit. They were positioned some three to four miles safely to seaward of the mud shallows; the boats had far to pull, but even the smallest ships could get no nearer in safety in these treacherous waters.

The sky overhead was louring and dull grey, the dark-ruffled sea fretful and alien. Washed by a fever-pitch of anxiety, Kydd watched as the assault boats began assembling, among them *Diadem*'s launch.

'Take me to it,' he demanded quickly. The jolly-boat pulled over strongly and Kydd was heaved into the crowded launch after a disgruntled infantryman had to be exchanged out of it to make room.

'Sir?' The lieutenant in charge of the boat looked at a loss.

'Never mind me,' Kydd snapped. 'Get this boat under way.'

The men at the oars heaved and grunted; the boat was jammed with soldiers, crammed along the centreline, wedged under thwarts and hunched together in the sternsheets. Nursing their muskets carefully, they gazed on the silent shore.

Other boats fell in astern and the first wave was on its way. Kydd was distracted by the passing thought that he was seeing history unfolding but it was quickly overtaken with worries for the present.

Should he set up a signalling station when they were ashore? No, there weren't any trained naval signalmen in these hired transports to receive and decipher the messages and, in any case, to what purpose? These weren't warships with covering gunfire support to manoeuvre or superior commanders to advise; once established ashore the only communications from the Army would be by boat to *Encounter* and then the long haul out to the anchored ships-of-the-line and the commodore.

Effectively, therefore, he was the naval commander on the spot and carried every responsibility for operations afloat.

Other anxieties crowded in but he beat them back with the thought that everything had gone well so far, there was no opposition, and when all were landed he could hand over the whole to General Beresford. In fact he—

The boat suddenly lurched and stopped dead in the water, sending men down in a tangle. Kydd glared over the side at the roiling discolour. There was no escaping the fact that, quite simply, they had insufficient depth to make it in. They were left on the mud a quarter-mile short of the tide-line.

Was Fate returning to deal them a cynical counter-blow? Containing his anger at the unfairness, Kydd knew that to retreat would cost them their precious surprise. He grabbed the gunwale and jumped into the sea. Feeling the soft embrace of the mud he steadied himself; the sea was above his groin but this was the only way they could go forward.

'Toss y'r oars!' he snapped. Obediently the rowers smacked down on the looms of their oars, bringing them vertical and allowing Kydd to wade along outside the boat. The mud tugged and resisted, sending him staggering, but he gradually made progress to beyond its bow.

'All out!' he bellowed.

With muttered comments, the soldiers followed him into the water, splashing and cursing. 'Port your weapon, y' fool!' he rasped at one, who had allowed his musket to dip into the water. The others raised their firearms above their heads as they stumbled along.

Soon there was a line of men behind Kydd in the long squelch and wrench that was now their strike ashore. Other boats followed suit and the foreshore became filled with redcoats straggling in.

Muscles burning, Kydd heaved himself forwards again and again. The coastline ahead seemed so far. Gradually it took on detail and character, flat scrub and occasional hard-green tree-clumps alternating with bare gaps in the low skyline. Nearer, with the water-level below the knees, it became a faster splashing progress. A hoarse cry from a soldier behind caught his attention: the man was pointing away to the right.

At the edge of the sea a young boy in a rough cloak was gaping at them. Someone waved – the boy's hand flew to his mouth and he ran off yelling.

Reaching the tide-line Kydd squelched up the stinking mud-packed foreshore to a sparse grass clearing. He passed through the scrub to the more open plain beyond. Nothing. Not even a flock of sheep, or whatever passed for stock animals here. They had made it – they had achieved a landing.

They were standing on the mainland of South America . . .

Turning quickly, he strode back to the soldiers stumbling ashore and beckoned a sergeant, who panted up, unfurled and raised a standard. Men started to move towards the banner.

An officer arrived, shedding muddy water with a grimace. Kydd gave a broad smile. 'The day is ours, sir. Do form up, if y' please, Lieutenant.'

The man barked orders to another sergeant, who bawled incomprehensibly up and down the shoreline. Answering calls came from elsewhere, and before long, recognisable groups were coalescing and Kydd, feeling oddly unwanted, stepped out of the way.

A piper began a stirring wail with several drums rattling out in accompaniment. Screams of orders echoed, the springy turf muffling the stamp of boots.

After an hour or so *L'Aurore*'s lieutenant of marines, Clinton, strode purposefully towards him. Throwing a magnificent salute, he announced, 'Marine battalion ready for inspection, *sah*.'

Twirling and stamping faultlessly under the eyes of the Army, he led off smartly to where the lines of Kydd's marine brigade were drawn up. Their impromptu uniform was a pleasing mix of blue or red jacket, white trousers and gaiters, and surmounted by an ingenious black cap and feathers. They shouldered arms and came to the present like veterans.

Kydd started to inspect them gravely, accompanied by Clinton, with drawn sword, but was interrupted by a horseman who dashed up and saluted. 'Respects, Cap'n Kydd, and the general requests your attendance.'

An outstretched arm indicated the direction to take but Kydd first concluded his ceremony with all proper salutes.

Before he left he drew Clinton aside. 'Your first duty is to their weapons. We may have warm work before long and I'll not be caught unprepared – their rations and stores will follow directly.'

He stamped off, aware that there were precious few horses and none to spare for sailors ashore. Beresford and a knot of officers cantered towards him.

'Ahoy there, is it not, Captain?' the general hailed him, with a salute. He was obviously pleased by the day so far.

'Sir.'

'Just to make claim of my new colonel of the marine brigade. How are your numbers?'

'Um, over four hundred of foot – three hundred and fifty marines and near a hundred seamen.' He wondered briefly whether a battalion was bigger than a brigade and settled on the general's term. 'Marine brigade mustered and ready, sir.'

'Yes, I saw 'em. A stout body o' men. I shall call them my "Royal Blues", I believe.'

'Aye aye, sir.' So, from commander of a fleet he was now a colonel of foot-soldiers.

'As will be used where and when the circumstance dictates.'

So they would not find a place in the line . . . Kydd saluted, then tried to wheel about in military fashion and march off with dignity.

Clinton had the men on the foreshore unloading stores from the boats and piling them where directed by a distracted army quartermaster. In one place the St Helena artillerymen were assembling their field-pieces: six-pounders and a pair of howitzers. Later, no doubt, the Royal Blues would be asked to tail on and haul these guns.

Kydd found himself once more getting in the way and rued the fate that had him playing the soldier.

The afternoon wore on, then a rustle of expectation spread: the enemy had at last been sighted ahead. Kydd made his way through the encampment to an open area where the general was looking north intently. 'Ah, Mr Kydd. You understand, old fellow, that you should stay by me until I send you away on a service,' he said.

'Yes, sir.'

An aide dismounted expertly and handed him his reins. 'Sir, you have use of my mount until, er, we have need of it.'

Gratefully Kydd heaved himself aboard.

'There you may see them, the villains!' Beresford said dramatically, and pointed across to a slight rise about two miles ahead. Spreading out along the skyline was a vast horde, many on horseback, the wan glitter of steel clearly visible.

'Sir, they're in front of a village of sorts. Called "Reduction", it says here,' an officer with a map offered.

Beresford ignored him and said crisply, 'I'll have a forward line of Highlanders thrown out ahead, the six-pounders if they're ready, but I have m' doubts they'll attack this day.' He pursed his lips. 'We'll be waiting for 'em in the morning. See the men are well fed.'

As night fell, the last of the stores and horses were brought ashore, miraculously in good order, and the expeditionary force was complete.

Kydd's apprehensions returned. It couldn't be possible, not against a city – a continent! The odds were ridiculous – he needed to hear again just how few they were going into battle with.

'What's our count now?' he asked a nearby officer.

The major consulted his notebook. 'Let me see. There's eight hundred of the 71st disembarked and with your marine brigade of four hundred and fifty that puts us at a bit over the thousand. Add in the odds and sods of the St Helena's Infantry and Artillery and we're at something like sixteen hundred officers and men – and that's not forgetting our good general and his field staff of seven.'

'Guns?'

'Why, here we have four six-pounders in all, our heavy artillery,' he said, with a sniff, 'and not to mention a pair of small howitzers with the St Helena volunteers. As to horses, at last count three go to the general's staff, the rest to dispatches and artillery. No more'n a dozen in all, I'd say.'

Little more than a thousand and a half to go up against . . .

In the distance a twinkling of fires started among the enemy until more and more were strung out along the rise.

During the night, light rain drifted down, a cold, dispiriting and endless misery. With few tents most soldiers hunched under their capes and huddled together to endure. Kydd shared an improvised tent with the major but the ground became sodden, and icy wet insinuated itself from under his blanket until he awoke, shivering.

The morning broke with leaden skies and a piercing wind from across the plains, but Beresford was in no mood to linger. As soon as it was light, trumpets sounded and, after a hasty breakfast, camp was struck.

Mercifully the rain was holding off and Kydd joined the small group around the general, all of them drooping with wet and odorous with the smell of damp uniform and horses. 'Good morning, gentlemen,' Beresford said briskly. 'I should think about three thousand of the beggars. We've sighted eight guns among 'em, positioned on top of the rise.'

He gave his first orders, which were for a defensive line with a six-pounder on the flanks and the howitzers in the centre. It was the Highlanders who would take the brunt of the attack but close behind them the marine brigade was ready to move to where the battle was hottest.

Together a thousand men were a mass; spread out over a battlefield they were pitifully few, and when the guns of the enemy opened up and the opposing infantry began to march down the rise against them in a flourish of tinny trumpet calls it seemed certain the whole adventure could finish that morning.

Kydd felt for the reassurance of his sword and glanced about. There was anything but concern on the faces of the officers, and the men were settled in two ranks, the first kneeling and looking steadily ahead in disciplined silence. The officers wore a look of professional interest and Beresford had out his glass, calmly scanning the advance.

By this time the Spanish guns on the hilltop were hard at work, their concussion a continuous roll but to no effect. The tearing whistle of their shot went well overhead. The gunners were apparently so raw they hadn't allowed for their superior height of eye.

'They're coming on well, but a motley crew, I'm persuaded,' Beresford murmured. 'I do believe they need livening up. Sound the advance, if you please, and we'll go and meet 'em.'

A volley of drumming was answered by the rising wail of pipes, and the entire line stepped off together in a steady tramp. The going was not easy, the scrubby plain populated with bushes and tussocks, but the seasoned men paced on stolidly, saving their strength for the hill ahead, which would inevitably have to be stormed. On either side their own guns spoke in sharp cracks but with little result at this range.

Then, quite without warning, the line faltered and milled in confusion.

'What the hell's wrong with those men?' snapped Beresford, shifting his glass from the enemy and training it on the floundering troops.

They had run into a quagmire and the advance came to a complete halt. On the other side of the marsh the Spanish drew up in ranks and began a murderous fire with their muskets while on the heights the guns were finding their range. A well-sprung trap – and the first line of defence.

Beresford bit his lip, then swung around to Kydd. 'Get your men on a brace of guns and find your way around the marsh to take 'em in the flank.'

'Aye aye, sir!' Kydd saluted, wheeled his horse around sharply and galloped off to his men.

'Clinton!' he snapped. 'Send a couple o' men out to find a way around this bog, the rest to the traces an' haul a pair o' guns.'

After crisply dispatching Sergeant Dodd and his corporal, Clinton gave Kydd a lopsided smile. 'And how did I know we'd be called on this way?' Behind him the hauling manropes were already ranged for service.

'Well done, Mr Clinton,' Kydd said. 'And as quick as you may.'

Back with Beresford, Kydd found the officers watching a display of Spanish horsemanship that had them bemused and affronted by turns. From the crest of the hill, riders in colourful and flamboyant dress were furiously pounding down to the edge of the marsh, skidding to a halt and showily dismounting, only to turn and make unmistakable gestures before racing away.

At this the Highland soldiers plunged into the morass after them, furiously staggering in the black mud-holes and stagnant pits, defying the musketry fire. Some spun and dropped but there was no stopping them, and when at last the crack and thump of field-pieces announced the arrival of their man-hauled guns out on the flank, the enemy's fire began to fall away.

The first kilted soldiers stumbled out of the other side of the swamp and, without waiting for others, roared their defiance and made straight for the Spanish. This show of raw bravery unnerved the enemy – they turned and fled back up the hill. A colour-sergeant rallied his Highlanders at the base of the rise and, with a fearsome battle-cry, they stormed up the hill in line.

The ineffective artillery at the summit fell silent. A few figures could be seen moving and then there were none at all.

'They've abandoned their guns, the villainous crew!' Beresford said, in delight. 'General advance!' He urged his horse forward into the marsh; it stumbled and splashed through. Followed by his little group of staff, he rode to the top of the rise.

Most of the guns were in fact still there: six brass cannon with their impedimenta – even the mules that drew them remained nervously tethered nearby.

'Still loaded!' cried one of the St Helena gunners.

'Well, why do you wait? Give 'em a salute!'

The guns were swung round and, to loud cheers, crashed out after the fleeing figures.

The terrain now lay in a gentle slope forward towards a distant line of trees – clearly the sinuous course of a river. 'That's the Ria Chuelo. I dare say they're to make a stand on the other bank,' mused Beresford, seeing the retreat converge on the crossing point, a wide bridge.

He snapped his glass shut. 'Let's give 'em no rest. Form line of advance!'

As an aside he muttered, 'Would that I had horses – a squadron or two of cavalry would make it a fine rout.'

The troops stepped off again, heading for the bridge, pipers to the fore and, despite their torn and mud-soaked appearance, Kydd felt a surge of pride in their resolute marching.

But as they approached the river, smoke spiralled up from the bridge, and well before they reached it the structure was ablaze. On the opposite bank enemy troops were spreading out. The second line of defence.

Brought to a reluctant standstill, there was nothing for it but to bivouac for the night. While the camp was put in hasty preparation, Beresford summoned Kydd. 'Sir. It would infinitely oblige me if . . .'

It was appalling work but the Royal Blues saw it as a point of honour to get the expedition's guns across the 'impassable' mire. With muscles tempered by years of heaving on ropes, they turned their skills to another kind of hauling. They were well into their agony in the darkness when, without warning, there was a livid flash and an ear-splitting explosion, sending every man into an instinctive crouch.

They looked round fearfully for a gigantic piece of ordnance arrayed against them. Another, even louder, crash burst on them. Then the rain came. Cold, murderous and in unbelievable torrents. The sticky mud began to soften and fast rivulets started everywhere. Soaked, numbed to the bone and blinded by the ferocity of the deluge, the men turned back to their work, now made near impossible by the slippery grip of mud and rain.

For hours they laboured, but when a freezing dawn broke there were guns at the water's edge facing the Spanish. They were safe – but their way forward was irretrievably blocked by the Ria Chuelo.

It was one of the seamen who found a way. 'Sir – there's some o' them flat fishin' boats in a puddle dock yonder. If ye c'n keep the Spaniards' heads down for 'un we'll swim across an' fetch 'em for a bridge.'

Kydd could hardly believe it. In order to retrieve their situation the man and his mates were volunteering to plunge into the icy water and swim the forty-odd yards under fire to them. 'How many?' he snapped.

'Four on us.'

'Very well. Let's have your names.' At the very least the commodore would get to know who had saved the expedition.

Beresford lost no time in accepting. 'Range the guns opposite and give fire continuously, if you please.'

When the bombardment started, the Spanish slipped back out of sight, seeing little point in enduring the near point-blank fire. The seamen stripped off and, shivering, slipped into the turbid and fast-flowing river. They struck out with frenzied strokes, every soul on the British side willing them on until they reached the boats. A boatswain's mate with a heaving line stood ready. Then, as coolly as he would on the deck of a ship, he made his cast and the line sailed across, to be seized by the men, who quickly hauled in on a heavier rope.

One by one the boats were cut free and pulled across. Each was lashed, nose to tail, to another until there was a continuous line of them and then – *mirabile dictu* – they had their bridge.

Under covering fire from the guns the Highlanders stormed across, quickly establishing themselves under the bank where the Spanish could not aim at them without exposing themselves. More and more poured over, and when they were ready, they flung themselves up and into the body of the enemy.

They had broken through! From where Kydd was he could see the panic and consternation of the enemy, who scattered under the threat of the steadily advancing Scots and disappeared into the distance. Once across the river he saw a thrilling sight – not more than three or four miles in front of them were the steeples, towers and dense mass of buildings that was Buenos Aires.

It was past believing – could it be . . . ? Then reason asserted itself. The viceroy, the Marquis of Sobremonte, would now without doubt bring all his forces to a climactic confrontation with the invaders and all would be decided that morning.

But there was no army massing ahead, no sudden opening of an artillery barrage. Only an ominous silence. Under low grey skies, the wind piercing their damp bodies, they marched on, nearer and nearer. A road firmed, leading into the suburbs and making the going much easier, and on either side there were curious flat-roofed houses, faces at the windows. Surely—

'Flag o' truce, sir!'

Six mounted soldiers under a white flag were winding their way towards them.

'Halt the advance,' Beresford ordered. 'Let's hear what they've got to say for themselves.'

The men were in splendid uniform, with gold sash and silver spurs, but there was an air of controlled ferocity about them. Stepping his mount forward, the general's Spanish-speaking aide heard them out.

'Sir,' he said to Beresford, in a perfectly even voice, gesturing towards the most richly dressed. 'This is the Virrey Diputado Quintana. He desires a parley concerning capitulation.'

'Damn it!' Beresford hissed. 'His or ours?'

'He is empowered to give up the entire city of Buenos Aires, sir.'

There was a shocked pause, then Beresford came back haughtily: 'Tell 'em I'll only discuss that with Viceroy Sobremonte himself.'

The men exchanged quick looks, their gaze dropping. His dark features contorted with shame, Quintana muttered something and looked away.

'Sir, the viceroy has fled the capital and is unavailable.'

A breathless sense of unreality stole over Kydd. That they had thought to seize Buenos Aires with a mere handful of soldiers was incredible, but that they were now conquerors of the whole Spanish empire in the south with those same few was beyond belief.

'Ah. Then, er, my terms are these. The honours of war to these stout defenders, the protection of the people and their property, and the foreseeable continuation of their justice and, er, municipal authority.'

This was the same as offered to the inhabitants of Cape Town, Kydd remembered.

'Sir, they ask two hours for deliberation.'

'Not granted. In half an hour my advance must resume and I cannot be held responsible for what my enraged Highlanders will do in the event of resistance by the city.'

The deputation withdrew, but when they returned, Quintana agreed and stiffly offered his sword. Beresford accepted it and, in accordance with his own terms, graciously returned it. 'We shall enter the city in three hours, gentlemen.'

It had happened.

Popham's audacious plan to bypass Montevideo had succeeded.

And at exactly the time specified, the British South American Expedition marched off to take possession.

In the event it was the best show that could be made – thin

rain was beginning to fall again and, apart from some pipers and drummers, there was no military band. The soldiers were ordered to march well spaced in open order and stepping short to give an impression of greater numbers.

Kydd, riding with the staff, gave the honour of leading the Royal Blues to Clinton, who went pink with pleasure. There would be much in his next letter home, no doubt.

They swung along in that same sense of unreality. The houses on either side were now filled with curious onlookers, but Kydd could see no hatred, simply a mix of foreign-looking people looking more confused than hostile. Soldiers grinned at girls on latticed balconies who were waving and smiling, some even throwing blossoms as the men marched past.

The city proper was no sprawling provincial backwater. It was laid out in regular rectangular blocks of substantial buildings, the largest of which were finished in white along fine avenues. They passed a noble twin-spired church and frowning public edifices until at last they reached a vast square facing the river.

There was a domed cathedral, spacious colonnaded buildings and at one end a long arcade with a central arch. The parade marched through, the sound of the pipes and drums echoing dramatically, until they emerged before a massive square fort, the red and yellow colours of Spain prominent on its flagstaff. On all sides and from every passage and doorway, hundreds upon hundreds watched, silent and fascinated.

The parade came to a halt; hoarse shouts from sergeant majors made a show of dressing off and stamping to attention, and then it was the final act.

Beresford dismounted, paced evenly to the disconsolate group at the gates of the fort and answered their salutes smartly. Kydd could not hear what was said but it was clear what was happening. After some polite exchanges and bows, an object was handed over which he guessed must be the keys. The gates were flung open and a small body of soldiers marched out.

Taking the keys, an aide and two soldiers entered the fort. Nobody moved for some minutes and then, abruptly, the flag of Spain jerked down. In its place the Union flag of Great Britain soared up in a breathless hush. A low murmur spread around the square but in the distance came the rumble of guns. It was *Encounter* – acknowledging the yielding of the city of Buenos Aires to His Britannic Majesty.

It had happened.

Inside the fort it was bedlam. While a distracted Beresford stood at a desk snapping orders to his harassed staff, a constant stream of messengers arrived, continually interrupting with urgent news. He thrust scribbled orders at his aide, which, hastily relayed, brought on distant shouts and commotion as they were put into effect. Other officers impatiently waited their turn for clarification and detail, every man still mud-spattered and dishevelled, direct from the field of battle.

Kydd kept apart, knowing that there was little he could do until the situation cleared. There was, of course, the tantalising prospect that, as his role ashore had been concluded, surely there was nothing to prevent him returning to the comfort and order of his ship. His pulse quickened at the thought but he took in the scene as the future of Buenos Aires was decided.

It was a titanic task: nothing less than the securing of a great city, new conquered.

In the near term, armed parties of reconnaissance would be sent forth, urgently seeking out pockets of resistance, while at the same time a nucleus of rule had to be established to centralise decisions and orders. Then there were the troops, who must be fed and sheltered, lines of supply established, at first with the fleet and later locally and after that . . .

Then it would be necessary to make public announcement of intentions – how the new masters of Buenos Aires would rule, what the position of the former great and good would be in any ruling council and, above all, how the price of victory would be exacted in taxation. With a staff in single figures and few able to speak Spanish, it was going to be a Herculean task to perform in just a very few days. But it had been done before – so recently at Cape Town.

They had achieved their triumph in a very short time – was this why there was no uprising of the disaffected? It would be of incalculable value to be able to install a rebel government, keen to preserve their standing against a Spanish counter-move, but so far none had made communication and therefore, in the sturdy tradition of the British military, they would make shift for themselves.

Seeing his chance, he moved across to Beresford. 'Sir, I'm truly sorry to intrude, but would you not say my character as a colonel of foot is now at an end?'

When the general looked up, it was with a smile. 'Ah, yes. You sailors are notoriously restless if kept from your element overlong. I do thank you for your service, sir, and bid you to be gone – but if you've no objection, I'll retain your brigade until things become more certain. You have a lieutenant who . . . ?'

'You'll be well served by Lieutenant Clinton, sir,' Kydd said, exulting inwardly.

A new disturbance sounded outside. The crash of boots and muskets – it could only be the arrival of an officer of rank.

It was Commodore Popham, who strode beaming into the room, his spotless uniform a picture of splendour against the mired soldiers. He acknowledged Kydd's presence but went straight to Beresford.

'My word, William, and what a stroke!' The din subsided a little out of respect for him. 'The conqueror of Buenos Aires! Three days and you have the city. You're much to be congratulated, you devil.'

Beresford regarded him stonily. 'The rabble I faced in the field was not an adversary worth the name, sir.'

'You prevailed. Saw them off in fine style – that's all that matters and, I'd say, gives us heart for the future.'

'Yes, to be sure. Now, there's much to occupy me, Commodore . . .' Beresford said meaningfully.

'Of course! Not the least of which must be the safe custody of so much treasure.'

'So much . . . To what do you refer, sir?'

'Why, here in the fort. You must know it's the holding point for the cargo of the Spanish treasure fleet before it ships across to Spain?'

'I had heard something.'

'Well, surely you—'

'Sir, there are other matters touching on our survival that would seem to have more claim on my time. If we are to—'

'I can only think that such a vast sum, unguarded, will quickly be a focus for every species of adventurer, to the hazard of our security. It would seem to me prudent at least to make an account of its amount and situation.'

Beresford's lips thinned. 'This is not—'

An army lieutenant intervened hastily: 'Er, gentlemen, may I interrupt? As having but this hour returned from making inventory of the armoury and similar in this fort, I can say with certainty that there is no bullion or specie held in this building beyond a trivial amount.'

The room fell silent, all turning to the young officer. He continued nervously, 'You see, Viceroy Sobremonte in fleeing into the country took care to remove the treasure to take with him. Some thirty tons of silver at the least, I was told.'

'You mean there's . . . nothing in the strong-room? At all?'

'Er, some four hundred piastres for the payment of troops is all, sir.'

Popham turned pale. 'Then – then we must go after this damned viceroy! William, if we're to—'

'We do nothing of the sort, sir. What will the world think? That we're here on a mission of depredation and plunder? No, sir, I won't have it.'

'We must!' Popham blurted. 'Let's send after him with a troop of fast-riding dragoons or some such. They'll soon come up with the wretch – that weight of silver in ox-carts will slow—'

'I will not, sir! And, in case you need reminding, I hold a commission from Governor Baird that honours me with the title of lieutenant governor of this city. All such orders will emanate from me alone.'

Popham took control of himself and replied evenly, 'Then, sir, I would beg you consider the consequences in London—'

'Pray keep silent, sir!' Beresford barked. 'I find your display at this time of difficulty an impertinence.'

'No, sir, I cannot!' Popham snapped. 'This expedition is a joint affair – we all bear responsibility for what occurs. And should it be known that, for want of due dispatch, a treasure in the amount that will pay for this expedition many times over is let go for the sake of a nicety then we shall all answer for it.'

Beresford glared at him as he went on strongly, 'And where, pray, do you expect to find monies sufficient to pay troops for an extended occupation? And reserves for works of fortification? And other? Sir, we have no choice whatsoever – we must go after it.'

The general hesitated. 'The people here will resent its seizing. We cannot.'

'The City of London will be much encouraged by its display and will hotly desire to invest in such a place, while Whitehall must perforce send reinforcements to safeguard same – the greater object is achieved.'

'Nevertheless, I haven't the troops.'

'A small detachment will suffice. The Spanish are not expecting a bold move.'

Beresford gave it thought. 'Perhaps those dragoons. Very well, they shall set out this hour,' he said coldly. 'Now, if you'll excuse me . . .'

The room resumed its clamour.

Popham mopped his brow and, recovering himself, went to Kydd. 'An entertaining time for you these last days, I don't doubt.' He surveyed Kydd's soiled uniform and winced. 'Did our marine brigade put up a reasonable show of it?'

'They did so indeed,' Kydd answered warily, unsure what construction to put on Popham's outburst.

'But you'll be happy to part with them.'

'Sir,' he said carefully.

'Good. For I've a particular service for you that is of vital importance to our existence here.'

'It'll be my pleasure to be back aboard, Dasher, that I'll confess.'

Popham smiled briefly. 'That is, I have no power to elevate you to the felicity of port admiral but I can make you port captain. A very necessary post – responsible for all ship movements in and out of the port, and for the sake of our survival here the effectiveness of our resupply and cargo handling. You will keep a weather eye open for any motions of the enemy to agitate against us, and regulate the merchantmen when they come, which they surely will when they smell the trade.'

'But—'

'*L'Aurore* is in good hands. In your absence your premier has behaved himself well – and, in any case, her tasking is simple seaward picket duty.'

'I had hoped—'

'Yes. Oh, and one more thing.' Popham leaned forward and lowered his voice. 'It would oblige me greatly should you keep me in touch with what's going on among our army colleagues. Not that I don't trust 'em, but they have odd ways and I'd rather not be surprised, if you take my meaning.'

Kydd bristled. 'In all fairness, Dasher, I think I've done my part. Can you not find another to—'

'No. You're the only one of my captains experienced with the lobsterbacks and, besides, this is but an extension of your current situation, which will last only until our reinforcements arrive in a few weeks.'

Kydd paused: it was a necessary and responsible post, certainly, but not best suited to his temperament. Yet, if looked at in the light of his career as a whole, Kydd had to concede it was a not unwelcome development. A spell ashore as port captain was often a necessary prelude to active flag rank in order to demonstrate organisational ability. Further, if *L'Aurore* was indeed to be kept criss-crossing the vast estuary, it wasn't as if he was missing any action.

It settled his mind. 'An office? Staff?'

'You shall have my written order this day. Raise what you need against it. And do remember, a healthy and profitable trade is what is most calculated to rally the people to our cause.'

He clapped Kydd on the shoulder, turned and left quickly.

The din resumed but Kydd's mind was engaged. The first priority was to register an account of every marine resource, from the total length of alongside berths to docking facilities, slipways, shipbuilding and repair. Then to establish procedures for Customs clearance, legal quays and all the apparatus of port control together with the outer services, such as pilots and surveyors. A form of coastguard and revenue service would be needed, but was that within his remit? And—

'They said this was where I'd find you.'

Kydd looked round in surprise. 'Why, Nicholas – what are you doing here?'

'Is it so strange, old fellow, to witness a confidential secretary bearing ship's papers to his captain?'

'I know you too well, Nicholas. You're curious – you want to see the ethnicals of South America.'

'And so I have,' Renzi said, with a grin. 'In my short walk here . . . Look, if we go to the roof of this stout fortress, you'll see.'

They climbed a flight of stone steps and emerged on to a flat roof, edged by parapets and populated by guns, to gaze out over the city.

'Behold!' Renzi exclaimed, throwing out his arms.

The fort itself was modest in size compared to other

buildings, one side of it facing on to the large square, with the great cathedral in one corner and all parts connected by colonnaded pathways and arcades. On the far side there was an impressive, multi-arched building, which Renzi suggested was the seat of city government, the *cabildo*.

Closer to, the high gateway they had gone through was apparently the entrance to the marketplace, already with hopeful traders bringing in their produce. But beyond the opposite wall was the river, still a limitless expanse to the horizon. A long stone mole extended out but at this state of tide no boat could reach it. Instead they came to a stop some way out and peculiar carts went to attend them. Narrow, with a pair of immense wheels that served to keep them clear of the thick mud, they were drawn by listless, pitifully thin horses.

They looked downwards on to a stretch of foreshore and saw washerwomen at grassy pits working vigorously with wooden mallets, completely oblivious to the great happenings about them. Further along sea-birds wheeled in noisy clouds, shrieking as pieces of fish offal were thrown into the water, and out in the bay dozens of small ships lay at anchor, waiting for the situation to resolve.

'A certain fragrance, don't you think?' The air was thick with competing odours: the fish, a suggestion of the grasses of the Pampas and the usual exotic cooking smells of a foreign land.

'Yes, as may be. Did you hear I'm to be port captain?'

'No, I didn't. Then we shall be deprived of your presence on our good ship?'

'The next few weeks or so until the reinforcements arrive, I'm told.'

Something passed across Renzi's face, and Kydd added, 'Nicholas, you never thought we'd do it, did you? Doubted that we'd win over such odds as we saw, that Popham's plan was nonsense – isn't that so?'

Renzi shook his head and looked at him gravely. 'Dear fellow. It's more that I have misgivings, not to say a sense of foreboding. I can't say it more precisely, but it was all too easy, so like our success at Cape Town – but this continent is strange, ominous in its differences in a way Africa never was.'

'Ha! You've grown qualmish, old trout. We've made a conquest and mean to keep it. As simple as that.'

'Just so. You haven't heard from our Mr Serrano, at all?' Renzi asked, with concern.

Chapter 7

Serrano knew it was fearfully dangerous – not to say utter madness – to return to the place he had fled, hunted by the authorities and in peril of recognition. Now, when they were alerted by the British fleet off their shores, it needed only one to betray him and . . .

He fought down his emotions and a flood of patriotism returned as he waved a proud farewell to his English friend Renzi in the boat. He was on a mission to bring about the conjoining of the forces that would result in independence for his country. It might even be that future generations would see his name emblazoned in the history books.

First things first: he must make haste into the anonymous countryside and procure a horse to take him to *los patriotas* at Las Piedras. Was the venerable and wise Don Baltasar still the leader, or was it now the fiery and impulsive deputy, Manuel Bustamente? He prayed it was so, for he'd been told of the rash actions of the man at the abortive affair at Juanico, which had led to Serrano's exile.

He had a plan. A fellow student at the university, Martín

Miguel de Güemes, as ardent as he himself for freedom, had been placed by his father as an ensign of cavalry and stationed at Montevideo. His family was respected and he was trusted by the patriots.

The next morning his confidence rose after he had successfully bargained for a horse for himself from an *estancia*. It was a rangy cob, which he soon had galloping towards the garrison town. He was familiar with the place and took modest lodgings not far from the fort. A passing soldier knew Güemes and promised to deliver a note to him.

That evening he heard a discreet knock at the door. There was a whispered exchange and then, after all that had happened, he was looking at the finely drawn features of his friend.

'Come in, *mi querido amigo*. It's been so long!' The door was shut quickly and they embraced.

'What are you doing here, Vicente? If they catch you again . . .'

'Not now, Martín. There's more at stake this night than you can possibly conceive.'

'How is this, old friend?' Güemes asked.

'We must say my life is in your hands from this moment. I'm on a mission that is of the gravest importance to our future. Tell me – does Don Baltasar still lead?'

'I believe he does,' Güemes said guardedly.

'The Blessed Virgin's name be praised. I have a chance!'

'Vicente?'

'Do you swear to keep what I say in your heart and tell no one?'

'This is to do with the *armada inglesa*, is it not?'

'It may be.'

'They are here to do a mischief to the viceroyalty, that's

plain, and all are in a fever to know what they intend. Your presence here at the same time is no coincidence, I'd wager.'

'It is not! I return from exile by their hand . . . but, Martín, I have wonderful and terrible news!' he burst out. 'The English are preparing an invasion. They wish to set free the South American colonies as part of their grand war on Spain and invite all those who desire liberation to join with them.'

Güemes stood still, emotion working on his features.

'I've been chosen to make contact with *los patriotas* to open communications. I'm to bring Don Baltasar to their councils so that a rising might be timed to coincide with their descent on Montevideo, such that nothing the viceroy can do will stop us.'

At first, Güemes did not speak. Then, huskily, he said, 'You want me to take you to him?'

'Of course! Who else, *amigo*?'

Güemes slowly turned away. 'You don't know what you're asking, Vicente.'

'Yes, that—'

'Things have changed. You must understand. I'm no longer a student, I'm an officer in the cavalry – I've sworn my life to the King. The enemy is massing at the gate and therefore my duty is clear. If the patriots march against His Majesty it is my burden and honour to fight them.'

Serrano caught his breath. 'Then the oaths we swore in our youth count as nothing. Even as we pledged to do all in our power to bring down the Spanish overlords and raise up a great nation, this is now to be cast aside as inconvenient? That moment of destiny is now upon us. How will history judge *you* that at this time you hang back, reluctant to seek glory in the tide of war about to break that brings us our liberation?' he said, with contempt.

Neither spoke. Then Güemes turned back and faced him. 'I will have no part in any rising.' He held up his hand at Serrano's protest. 'Yet to keep faith with the cause I will take you to Baltasar. But not to join, for I will then return to my post.'

'To fight the liberator.'

'To fight the enemy.' He gave a twisted grin. 'Which I fancy will not be so arduous. I'm no veteran but five transports speak of no more than one or two thousand under arms – against our five. And more in the capital. It would take a madman to think to challenge El Virreinato del Río de la Plata with such contemptible force.'

He surveyed Serrano briefly, then said briskly, 'So. You have a horse? Good. You will not wish to lose a moment so we'll ride hard through the night. Are you ready?'

Tired and sore but elated, in the early hours of the morning Serrano found himself in the barely furnished room of a country *finca*, as far as he knew somewhere to the north-east in Paraguay province. Güemes told him to remain there and rode off once more.

Serrano lay on the floor, pulled a small, smelly rug around him for warmth and slept fitfully. He was awakened by the thud of horses, then the massed jingle of harness as they came to a halt. A little later the door was flung open. The larger than life figure of a gaucho stood there with a wicked grin – not the shabby imitations seen on the streets of Buenos Aires but a free spirit of the open Pampas, his moustachioed face burned dark by the sun, a wide flamboyant hat strung around his neck and large rowels on his boots.

'*En pié, compadre,*' he rasped.

Serrano obeyed quickly, scrambling to his feet. A gaucho

was not to be crossed – a large knife, the *facón*, tucked famil-
iarly in the sash was his only eating instrument but was just
as easily the means of settling personal differences.

The man crossed to him, spun him around and blindfolded
him with a red bandanna.

'*¡Muévase!*' He was jerked forward, led stumbling to a horse
and helped into the saddle. They cantered off, the horse
picking its way. The ground seemed to get rough, its
stride interrupted more than once. At one point it jibbed and
he lost his grip, sliding down one side and painfully into a
cactus. Harsh laughter broke out at his predicament and he
was left to remount by himself.

At length Serrano smelt cooking fires and heard voices.
They slowed to a halt.

'*¡Desmontad!*'

He dismounted and the bandanna was removed. He saw
he was in a straggling camp of many horsemen; an imposing
figure was coming towards him.

Drawing himself up Serrano asked gravely, 'Sir, do I find
myself addressing Don Baltasar, Hidalgo de Terrada?'

'You do, sir, and you are?'

'Vicente Ignacio Serrano de Santiago Vazquez y Colón, at
your service.'

'I don't know you.'

'I was a messenger in the Legión de Voluntarios Patricios
at Juanico,' Serrano replied.

'And Martín Miguel de Güemes has spoken to me on your
behalf. You have my ear, sir. Now, what matter is so pressing
that I must hear you?'

He became aware that behind Baltasar a thick-set man with
a chest-length black beard and extravagant ornamentation
had appeared. Bustamente.

'Sir. I've been in exile in South Africa since Juanico and—'

'Why are you here, then, if Africa is more to your fancy?' Bustamente snapped, difficult to understand in his hoarse voice.

Serrano tried to ignore him. 'And a meeting by chance—'

The big man lunged forward, caught him by his shirt and lifted him bodily. 'I asked a question, *cerdito*,' he snarled.

'Leave him, Manuel. Let's hear what he has to say,' Baltasar said.

Serrano patted himself down and continued: 'I became friends with an English officer and learned they planned a strike against the Spanish. I took passage as an interpreter and, once here, I saw my chance.'

'To act the spy?' croaked Bustamente, with an evil glint.

'No, sir.' He took a deep breath. 'To offer to them my services to bring the chief of *los patriotas* himself to a council of war to join an army of liberation.'

The two men stared at him – then Bustamente roared with laughter, holding his sides. Suddenly he stopped and fixed Serrano with a cruel expression. 'So! You are a high delegate from the English fleet.' He thrust himself into Serrano's face. 'There's only one trouble with that, little man – we already have one.'

He laughed again, then turned and bellowed, 'Bring Barreda!'

A tall individual, dressed in black breeches and in a plain naval cocked hat, was brought forward.

Baltasar held up a restraining hand at Bustamente and asked quietly, 'Señor Barreda, do you know this man?'

Looking at Serrano distrustfully, he said, 'I cannot recollect ever having seen this individual. No, sir.'

Turning back Bustamente said silkily, 'This gentleman is

from your ship-of-the-flag *Diadem*, sent by Comodoro Popham, and he does not know you.'

A cold wash of fear came over Serrano. It was the last thing he had expected, and he knew that if his credentials were doubted, they would assume he was a spy for the hated Spanish authorities. 'That is because I come from another ship, the *L'Aurore* of Captain Kydd. You may send for confirmation, naturally.'

'That won't be necessary,' Baltasar said easily. 'Just be so good as to show us your papers. You have some, of course?'

The cold inside turned into a knot of terror.

'Do show this gentleman yours, if you please,' Baltasar told Barreda.

The papers were handed across. They were undoubtedly genuine, from the naval cipher to Popham's signature.

He had possibly five seconds to save his life.

A way out suggested itself: his very being revolted at the act, but in the longer term, what was the fate of one man against the cause?

He pretended to peruse them, then looked up. 'Why, these are perfect,' he declared. 'So close to the genuine as would fool the commodore himself.'

Barreda goggled at him as Baltasar snapped, 'Explain!'

'Very simple. No military commander would put his delegate at risk by having him carry papers on his person – and, even worse, would never compromise his own position to the extent of personally signing an admission of subversion.' He sighed and handed the papers back to the thunderstruck Barreda, avoiding his eye.

'And he must explain also why he had the complete confidence to pass through Spanish-held territory so easily, unless . . .'

Baltasar eased into a tight smile. '*You* are vouched for by Güemes, *this* – by clever papers.'

The smile vanished. 'Take him away!' he rapped at Bustamente. 'And find out what he knows.'

Serrano fought back a tremor as Baltasar asked softly, 'Now, sir, what is it that you have to tell me?'

A tearing shriek came from the corral, then another. 'Well?'

'Sir, the British fleet lies at anchor off Maldonado. It will shortly set sail to fall on Montevideo.' His voice had become unsteady at the inhuman sounds coming from the corral.

'This we know.'

'Er, they are anxious that *los patriotas* are not denied their just share of glory in the wresting of this country from the Spanish.'

'You mean, they want us to assist them.'

'They are saying that the Spanish cannot withstand a simultaneous assault by land and sea.' There was a last ragged squeal from the corral and then silence. 'They do respectfully request a council-of-war with yourself.'

Baltasar eyed Serrano thoughtfully. 'The idea has merit, but there's much to be settled. First, what guarantee have I that this is not a trap?'

'Sir, I signal with my red flag from the shore and a boat will be sent to convey you to the commodore. You will see this and there can be no Spanish trap aboard a Royal Navy ship.'

The older man gave a tight smile. 'You have much to learn in wars of the people, Señorito Vicente. For instance, who is to command? What is to stop the *inglés* general placing our glorious cavalry before his to take the casualties in place of his own? And if we suffer reverses and the campaign is long, who will supply us, pay the fighters, arm our men?'

'These things you may discuss with the commodore, sir.'

'Not so fast, young man. When we face the English it will be with our demands clear, our decisions made. For instance, what is the status of prisoners taken? If this is a war of liberation then they will be in a very different situation from your usual prisoner-of-war. Do you not wish to be avenged on them for your exile?'

'Sir, time is short. I heard the officers on board the ship complaining that supplies are limited and the sooner they are landed the better.'

'Quite. But there are other matters to settle, which, because they bear on the whole, can be agreed upon only by the full council of the Sociedad Patriótica. Be tranquil, *compadre*, I shall summon a meeting.'

A conclave met that very night. From far and near men of legend were called to bring their wisdom and authority to the congress, riding in with wild speed and *élan* as the true gauchos they were. They sat together around the fire, tales of derring-do echoing into the night, until at last they could be prevailed on to debate the matters in hand. They exuberantly entered into discussion – which then turned to argument.

Beside himself with despair, Serrano could only wait for the interminable to-and-fro to end.

There was much to talk about: to ally themselves with an almost unknown foreign power would need careful consideration and they were not about to rush into this. The arguments raged on through the night, into the next day – and the next night. Then, as a cold morning broke, came the grand spectacle of half a thousand gaucho warriors on the move, riding to the sea.

For the fiftieth time, Serrano felt for his red flag. Pray God that the boat was quick.

Then it was the last rise before Puerto del Inglés and the sea.

At the summit he looked out over the glittering sea but with something approaching terror he saw that it was quite empty: there was not a ship to be seen.

Chapter 8

G eneral Beresford raised his glass. 'Gentlemen, do join me if you will. To *audacity* and its just rewards!'

The toast was noisily acclaimed and bibulous shouts rose above the hubbub from the assembled officers. 'Stand up! A speech!'

At the other end of the hastily improvised table, Popham took his cue and rose to a storm of applause. 'Gentlemen – my fellow warriors! I can confidently say that in the long history of our nation there are few deeds of military daring that can stand with what we have accomplished so rapidly and so efficiently.'

He paused to let the exuberant shouts of agreement subside. 'We have achieved nothing less than the taking of Buenos Aires in a lightning thrust that has sent the Spanish viceroy fleeing and which has turned over this great city to His Majesty's protection. A city, which I may remind you, of some forty thousand – and if you count the province of which it is the capital as a whole, then some six million, more than the entire people of England!

'It is at the end of the silver trail from the Potosí mines, and has a prodigious population hungering for the products of English mills, ready to pay for them with the bounty of this immense region.'

A hush descended as the enormity of the achievement sank in. Kydd, flushed with wine, could only shake his head in wonder at the whole thing. Where was history leading now? What lay in their future?

Popham continued, in full flow, 'And let me speak plain – this is our doing, and ours alone. Sixteen hundred to achieve what takes Napoleon two hundred thousand! And with Britain an impossible seven and a half thousand nautical miles distant, there's been none to help in the planning, the support, the execution. We've seized the moment and been proved right. All we have to do now is stay where we are, keeping our position secure for another few weeks while we await the reinforcements, and then return to our loved ones, victorious and fêted by a grateful nation.'

There was an ovation, but now strangely restrained, as if each man was struck in awe of the occasion – or troubled by their sudden elevation from puny expedition to masters of the land.

Beresford's face had turned sober and grave and Kydd felt for him, the lieutenant governor of a piece of empire that no one knew existed and without a single order or authority to stand behind any of his decrees.

In the morning the wonder of their achievement was still with Kydd, but there was work to do. He was found an office on the upper floor of the fort, small but well situated near the steps that led down to the main floor and, importantly, up to the roof, for he had plans to erect a small signal mast there.

Outside at ten there was much saluting and crashing of arms as a deputation arrived. Kydd peered down from his window and saw a religious procession wending its way towards the high-arched entrance below. He was able to keep to his office while Beresford dealt with them but later there was no escaping the *cabildo*, the governing council of the city. These were dignified Spaniards of another age, richly dressed in ruffled shirts and elaborately groomed, rigid with formality and barely concealed hostility.

They filed into the biggest room Beresford could find, one that his new interpreter revealed was the *real audiencia* where the viceroy would receive his petitioners.

The harassed general listened courteously to their long-winded address, and when it became clear they wanted assurances on the future, he patiently outlined a programme of peace, the upholding of local authority and, above all, a new era of *libre comercio* – the blessings of free trade. This caused the first stirring among them, and Beresford went on to affirm the undoubted advantages and profit to be gained from their city being flung open to commerce with the rest of the world.

For some reason it caused mutters and frowns. A little baffled, Beresford asked the port captain to set out some of the working details for them.

Kydd picked up on his request: these men wanted to know how the system was to be run, whether it would be truly open or an elaborate front behind which arrangements were to be made.

It was not so difficult to explain for he had seen that the methods that had proved so successful in Cape Town could be applied here: the waterfront, with its freely accessible warehousing inward and outward – this, of course, with the necessary side advantage that all was visible to his officials, no enemy contraband possible – and duties a mere pittance, but at the same time rigidly enforced to cover harbour maintenance, with no other charges incurred in order to be cleared for the open sea. A recipe for commercial success if ever there was one.

There was grudging acknowledgement and they left among a flurry of stiff bowing.

'A sour lot,' Beresford ruminated, 'but they'll get over it in time.'

Towards evening there was a much more agreeable prospect. Instead of army campaign beds in the fort, the officers were to be billeted close by. 'You're with a Señor Rodriguez,' Kydd was informed by the adjutant, 'a merchant of means, who speaks English.'

The man was waiting for him on the steps of a very fine stone house in the grand San Benito Street. 'Ah, Capitán Keed. You are expected, sir. Do enter – your baggage, it follows?'

The house had a balcony with ornate lattice-work; inside, Kydd noted the heavy, dark furniture and curious rugs of some kind of animal skin. 'This is my wife, Doña Corazón.' A petite, dark-eyed woman in silk with a profusion of lace and long black hair curtsied shyly to Kydd. Accompanied by an Indian maid in formal attire, she showed him to his room and then led him back to the sitting room.

'*Jerez*?' enquired his host.

'Er, yes, thank you, sir.' Kydd guessed that he had been offered sherry.

'We favour manzanillas from around the port of Sanlúcar de Barrameda. Would you . . . ?'

Kydd picked up on the casual name-dropping, realised that any wine from far-off Spain would cost a great deal and therefore allowed himself well impressed. When it arrived he was surprised to discover it had a light and fresh yet almost saline quality. He would surprise Renzi with it one day.

'Most acceptable, Mr Rodriguez,' he said warmly.

After a short interval, dinner was declared, Rodriguez apologetic that evening meals were much lighter than at midday; tonight it would be *cabrito*.

As the roast kid was expertly carved by his host and a platter of *papas al horno*, golden potatoes, arrived, Kydd felt at a loss: how could he make conversation with a man whose country his own had so recently conquered? But on the other hand, he realised, he would not have been taken in to lodge unless there were certain sympathies.

'How goes your business, sir?' he asked mildly.

'As you would expect in the circumstances.'

'We do intend to make Buenos Aires a free port.'

'Thees we hear.' Oddly there was no gushing enthusiasm.

'And you will take advantage of it?' Kydd encouraged.

'Possibly.'

Baffled, Kydd decided to leave it for the moment.

'Do you find Buenos Aires very different from Spain?' he ventured shortly, tucking into the delicious dessert, *dulce de leche*, that Rodriguez had described as 'milk jam'.

'I was born here, as my father and his father before. A *criollo*, I am he.' He added, 'My advice, Capitán, the people here are not as in England, one race, one speaking. There are so many . . .'

By the end of the evening Kydd had the picture.

The local born *criollos* were despised by the Spanish-born *peninsulares*, who dominated the upper reaches of society and government, and in return were restive under a rule that gave them little power even though they were the economic driving

225

force. Then there were the *arribeños,* those born in the vast interior with little understanding of the world outside, and Indians, both native and of mixed race, together with a bewildering spectrum of others. There were slaves, country gauchos, peons and any number of foreigners who had decided to make this their home.

And cutting across all was a divide: on one side the loyalists, who stood with Spain and the old ways, and on the other the patriots, who strove to free themselves to achieve independence.

'And will they succeed, do you think?' Kydd asked carefully.

'Only a little, a very little, and the city will explode. Then – God help us all!' Rodriguez said fervently.

Over the next few days the city settled to a strained quiet. Beresford's proclamations were received without murmur, the first a restating that the supremacy of the Roman Catholic Church would remain unchallenged and untouched, closely followed by a state opening of the *cabildo* and the installing of the previous *alcalde de primer voto* to officiate from his same chair.

Bull-fighting at the Retiro would continue; currency reform and the judiciary could wait. The most vital matter was the opening of the port to free trade. Kydd found his time taken up with explaining over and over that this was no Byzantine ploy to entrap traders into incurring punitive fees later, but when a few nervous shippers began loading and sailing others started to come forward.

Passing vessels with no knowledge that the port had changed hands were agreeably surprised to be welcomed in, and from the roof of the fort Kydd could take satisfaction in looking out at a fair number of sails moored in the River Plate, goods being lightered to and fro, and the sight, unique in his experience of a major port, of the strange high-wheeled carts wending their way out across the mud-flats to the flat boats.

Renzi, his curiosity satisfied, preferred to stay with the ship, no doubt in a fever of creativity with his novel, but from time to time various L'Aurores were sent as relief.

Kydd was in a conference when a subaltern of the light dragoons galloped into the square and demanded to be taken instantly to General Beresford.

'Sir!' the young man declared, as he was shown into the room. 'Captain Arbuthnot is in need of escort.'

'Why so?'

'Sir, on account we caught up with the viceroy's treasure, and having relieved 'em of it the captain's on his way back. He's now encumbered with fourteen mule-carts of bullion.'

The meeting broke up in a buzz of astonishment. Beresford snapped orders detaching part of the garrison, then growled, 'And now we'll have every gold-crazy lunatic in Buenos Aires about our ears until we're rid of it.'

It made an incredible sight, winding into the square: an endless file of carts accompanied on each side by troops of soldiers. A gathering crowd was held at bay while the treasure was transferred into the fort's strong-room.

In the evening word came through: a first count had the amount in the sum of an incredible half-million pieces of eight, as well as gold and silver bars, more than a score boxes of doubloons and at least a hundred pouches of coins, three thousand clinking in each.

Together with what had also been discovered hidden in

the city treasury they were now in possession of considerably more than a million Spanish dollars. The dragoons, royally entertained that evening, told of how Viceroy Sobramonte, disbelieving that the British would chase him so far into the interior, had panicked. Dropping everything, he had fled towards distant Córdoba, leaving his party to throw the treasure down wells. It had been a tense day or two in the recovery, for roving bands had come down to dispute it, but discipline and haste had won the day.

Needing to report, Kydd went to see Popham in his flagship off Maldonado.

'A prime catch,' the commodore purred, 'as will warm the cockles of every man in the fleet.'

'If it's not deemed Droits of the Crown,' Kydd said, uneasy at what others might see as naked plunder.

'It won't be.'

'We did main well in the article of guns, Dasher. Eighty-six pieces of artillery and five hundred-odd barrels of powder found in the arsenal, not to mention some hundred or so stand of muskets.'

'Very good indeed. I would like to think that at last things are going our way.'

He extracted a sheet from out of a neat stack of papers before him. 'Do look at this, old fellow, and tell me your opinion.'

Kydd read:

To the Mayor and Corporation of Manchester, . . . I consider it a duty to the commercial interest of Great Britain . . . that the conquest of this place opens an extensive channel for your manufactures . . . Hitherto, the trade of this country has been cramped beyond belief, and

the manufactures could only find their way to this rich province by
neutral bottoms and contraband intrigues . . . from this moment its
trade will be thrown open . . .

'If that doesn't set them in a tizzy of speculation as to
who's to be here first, then I'm a Dutchman!' Popham added.

Kydd was impressed: it was a direct call to the northern
industries that a market of immense size was suddenly open
to them with premium prices going to the first to satisfy the
hunger for manufactured goods. The River Plate should very
soon be thronged with enterprising merchantmen.

'And our reinforcements?' It was critical that these were
not delayed for it would not be long before the Spanish in
the north heard about the catastrophe and, stretched as the
British were, there could be only one result.

'In St Helena I sent dispatches to England with our intentions, and now by fast frigate I shall tell them of our victory
against the odds. This news will be accompanied by freight
to the value of a million silver dollars to delight the crowd.
Do you not think then that the Admiralty would wish to
safeguard the nation's hope?'

Kydd came to the alert instantly. Any frigate captain fortunate enough to return with news of a famous victory and
treasure to prove it would be the talk of the hour, not to
mention the considerable fee he would earn by right for
carrying specie. 'Er, have you given thought to who—'

'Oh, well, it will have to depart very soon, of course,'
Popham said airily. 'I've dispatches to complete and General
Beresford pleads for much in the way of army stores and
supplies – I'd think *Narcissus* would answer, she being new-
victualled for sea.'

Kydd kept his thoughts to himself: was Popham taking the

opportunity to rid himself of Donnelly, a senior captain and outspoken critic of his handling of the expedition?

'And, of course, as a heavy frigate she's of limited value in these shoal waters,' Popham finished.

Smiling briefly, he enquired, 'So. How is our port captain taking to his responsibilities? Does all march well on the waterfront?'

'No, sir.' His adjutant was polite but firm and Beresford had no choice but to hear him out. 'Since your proclamation went out six days ago, there have been but sixty-five citizens sworn.'

'So few?' the general said incredulously.

'Sir.'

This was perplexing: of the tens of thousands of inhabitants only a tiny handful had come to pledge allegiance to the Crown. Did this suggest that the people had no sense of relief at having thrown off the yoke of Spanish rule, or had it deeper significance to do with the King of Great Britain also being Defender of the Faith but not the old one?

'Should we perhaps follow it up with some form of coercion, loss of citizen's rights, that sort of thing, do you think?'

The officer spoke carefully: 'Sir, your words to the deputation of *patricios* were, I'm persuaded, not best calculated to settle their fears. They asked for an undertaking that we would defend them against a Spanish counter-attack and you—'

'I know what I said, damn it! They wanted me to guarantee their security against all and every motion of the enemy. This is militarily impossible and I cannot sacrifice my honour to a false promise, sir.'

'Yes, sir,' the officer said patiently. 'But it were better you didn't say so in so many words. The implication now is that, if it suits us tactically to withdraw from the city before the

Spanish return in force, they will be subject to reprisal for collaborating with us, and your Spaniard is well known to be cruel in vengeance.'

'I'm not pledging my word to an absurdity. Besides, any undertaking assumed by the Crown is a grave responsibility, which is always to be taken seriously. I cannot possibly bind any future military commander to such terms.'

'I understand, sir.'

'Now, we must buckle down to the matter in hand. Supplies. We're settled in and need to find our own forage instead of relying on the ships. This is always a necessary business and I want it in hand as soon as possible. Who knows what the future might bring, hey?'

'Yes, sir. To another matter, we have our fifteenth desertion reported by Colonel Pack and—'

'More?'

'It does seem to be the same class of man, sir. Irish – they find the same religion, and opportunities here not to be countenanced in Ireland, and we suspect they're being lured away by the Spanish women.'

'Deserters will meet the same penalty as they would on home station. Harder – this is in the face of the enemy.'

'Enemy, sir?' the officer asked innocently.

Chapter 9

With rising emotion Serrano paused in the darkness of the doorway, exhausted and famished. '*Mi flor – mi bella flor!*' he called out.

Rafaela opened the door and squealed with delight. Throwing her arms around his neck, she kissed him with a passion that melted his terror and confusion. '*Alma mia, mi corazón,*' she sobbed, caressing his matted hair.

Once inside, she held him at arm's length; then her hands dropped and she slapped his face. '*Hijo de perra* – where did you go that you left me with no word of what you were going to do? I worried that the *partidarios leales* had betrayed you and I lied to everyone that—'

Serrano shook his head and pulled her close, breathing her fragrance. 'Rafaela – *mi ángel.*'

Then he stood back and declared, 'I was *betrayed.*'

'*Cariño,* who . . . ?'

'Not by the loyalists or the patriots, but by the British.'

'The British?' she said incredulously. 'What have you to do with them?'

'In my exile in Cape Town I heard from their officers that they were to fall on the Spanish here, and I hid in one of their boats . . .'

It all came tumbling out, and hot tears of anger pricked as he told of the cunning and all-too-believable secretary who had wormed his way into his confidences by pretending to learn Spanish, before setting him up to lead the patriots away from Montevideo, probably to distract the Spanish eastwards while they made their move on Buenos Aires.

'They told me it was a mission of glory, to bring the forces of Great Britain and *los patriotas* to a triumphal destiny of liberation. Instead I was used as a common *tonto* to deceive and blind.'

In a rush of feeling he described his devastation at Don Baltasar's side when they had looked out over an empty sea. Only by quick thinking – saying that the British would be returning to look for his signal – did he escape being branded a spy leading them all to destruction.

'That night I fled for my life, feeling the hounds of hell at my back. Now I have both sides after my skin,' he said bitterly.

'You're a fool, Vicente, and I love you. Can you not see? By running you have confirmed their suspicions. And the Spanish have proof of your sympathies with the *independentistas*. You're in deep trouble, my little cabbage.'

She bit her lip. 'Does anyone know you're here? Did they see you enter this house?'

'Do you think I'm stupid? How do you think I made it this far? No. It's dark. I kept close to the wall and watched carefully until it was quiet.'

'Good. We must think what to do.'

Her brow furrowed – then suddenly she tensed. 'Did you hear anything? It sounded like—'

The door flew open with a crash, revealing a tall man with a cynical smile, others behind him.

Rafaela moved protectively in front of Serrano. 'Who are you? Why do you enter my home like this?'

The man gave a languid bow. 'Doña Rafaela Callejo? A thousand apologies for the inconvenience but our business is with your friend.' He closed the door.

In the low candlelight the man's face was lined and cruel, the black eyes piercing. He circled them slowly, his hand loosely on his poniard. Stopping, he addressed Serrano in a voice barely above a whisper, 'It is entirely my decision whether you leave this room alive or no. Do you understand?'

'I demand to know who you are,' Serrano said shakily.

'For you that is of no concern.' The poniard leaped into his hand and he inspected its gleaming edge. 'I come from Don Baltasar to clear up a few points that still vex him.'

'I didn't betray him. It was British treachery – they *said* they wanted to join with us, overthrow the villainous Spanish and – and—'

'He never doubted that for one moment, my little chicken.'

'Then . . .'

'He knows you to be young and impulsive and foolish in the ways of the world. What he wants to know is how ardent in the cause you still are.'

'Liberty? Freedom? On my soul, I put them first in my life. He must believe me.'

'And what of your friends, the British?'

'I hate them!'

'I see. You will be interested to know that the council has met and decided that, in the furtherance of independence, we must throw our entire force at the main enemy.'

234

'Yes – Spain!'

The tip of the poniard flicked out and came to rest at Serrano's throat.

'Not at all,' the man said silkily. 'They are not the main enemy. It is the one who tries to lure us into joining them to make conquest of the viceroyalty, only to turn on us as it seeks to add this country to its swollen empire.'

'The British!'

'Just so. There will be no independence for us, only a change of masters.'

'Why do we not make use of them to throw out the Spanish and then—'

'Fool!' His lips curled in contempt. 'By trickery, and the unforgivable craven flight of Viceroy Sobramonte they were enabled to take a great city. It is done! They hold our capital and will never give it to us. Therefore we must take it.'

'Against their mighty force?'

'In this emergency it has been decreed that nothing is too sacred to be sacrificed to this end. *Los patriotas* will join as brothers with the royalists, the *blandengues* will be summoned and the gauchos armed – all in the great cause to drive *los imperialistas* into the sea whence they came.'

Serrano caught his breath. The *blandengues* were a centuries-old militia with roots deep in the frontier, and gauchos as cavalry would be glorious – but would it be enough? This was either catastrophic folly or inspired.

'Who will be leader?' he asked carefully. If Baltasar—

'Don Santiago de Liniers.' At Serrano's incomprehension he added, 'At Montevideo he commands our only regular troops and is experienced in war. It is he whom we allow to issue the orders.'

Serrano drew himself erect. With rising exultation, he knew now which was the true cause. 'I wish to serve.'

The poniard slid back into its sheath. 'That is what Don Baltasar wants to hear. Very well, you shall, for there is a service that will silence your enemies for ever.'

'Oh?' said Serrano, in sudden apprehension.

'You shall return to your British friends with a tale. Then you will pass us all we want to know of the vermin.'

'A spy!'

The man smiled.

'Captain Kydd?' The aide looked distracted. 'General Beresford is calling an urgent meeting, sir.'

With relief, Kydd put down the tortured wording of a Customs regulation, then felt a stab of concern. Beresford was a good administrator and not one to disrupt his staff unduly with idle meetings.

They assembled in the usual room but Beresford was not there. Minutes passed and they began to talk uneasily among themselves. As far as anyone knew, no Spanish armies were massing, no fleets sighted. The summoning of all his commanders to meet together at this time was disturbing.

Beresford strode into the room as if he was eager to plan a campaign but his expression was grave. 'Right, gentlemen. Are we all here? We have our uprising well enough but, I'm sorry to say, not in our support as expected.'

'A Spanish counter-attack?'

'I rather think not. Our informant tells us—'

'Our spies.'

'The employment of spies and similar is beneath my honour, sir, and will not find service with me. You will find in this city, however, parties who are quite without scruple in delating upon their countrymen.

'Now, what I have learned this day is unsettling, if not alarming. Where before we looked to the rebels to rise up with us against the Spanish in the hope of independence, now they have completely reversed their allegiance and are in amicable alliance with their old foes to go against us.'

'Good God! They stand to lose so much by going back to the old ways – why is it, with the golden prospect of free trade, that they turn their backs on us?'

'Ah. The free trade we've all been trusting will be our shining gift. I believe Captain Kydd has discovered something that throws a quite different light on our assumptions. Sir?'

Kydd nodded. 'I'm billeted with a merchant and have the full griff. What I've found out is that our talk of free trade is meaningless to them – the merchants, that is. It's true that, before, they were liable for the *quinta real*, a royal tax of twenty per cent on all landed cargoes, and that all freights must under penalty be carried in Spanish bottoms. Naturally we assumed they'd jump at the chance of open trade under our protection, particularly as all Spanish ships were swept from the seas after Trafalgar.

'What we didn't count on was what they did in response to their situation. The colony had great need o' modern manufactures and such, and as well the people were loud in their demands for foreign and luxury goods. So much so that the government took fright and settled with the big merchant houses. For a fat sum in bribery they promised not to notice discreet arrivals of shipping in a quiet bay set aside for it. This grew into quite a sizeable arrangement, with even foreign commercial agents invited to encourage their ships to call.'

He chuckled. 'Who would have thought it? A government setting up a smuggling operation against itself!'

'Quite. And the result?' prompted Beresford.

'Why, our notion of free trade is upsetting to a degree. The grand businesses having paid big sums for the privilege of landing cargo are not to be welcoming a system that places them at an equal standing to any johnny-come-lately, and as well upsets their cosy relations with the nobs in Government House. No, sir, nothing would suit them more than that the Spanish come back tomorrow.'

Beresford let it sink in around the table, then said, 'This means we've lost the support of most of the middling sort, who cannot now be relied upon. And the common people are being stirred up by hotheads who claim that the only way to wipe away the shame of forty thousand capitulating to two is by a grand rising against us, but with what success I cannot say.'

'Then what is the threat, sir?'

Beresford looked up with a grim smile. 'We chose to bypass Montevideo to assault directly. Now we must pay for it. A leader there has stood up and declared that, with regular troops there being reinforced by irregulars in considerable numbers, he will march on Buenos Aires.'

There were shocked looks around the table. After so little time, an enemy had now become visible, a menace that could only continue to grow and threaten.

'I don't have to tell you that our choices are few indeed. Our prayer is, of course, that our expected reinforcements do arrive without delay. Therefore I've decided that, to this end, my strategy must be to keep the enemy confined to the north shore of the River Plate, which they term the Banda Oriental. As of this moment Captain Kydd is relieved of all duties to attend to it.'

The northern shore where the troops were concentrating was separated from the southern at the head where it joined a forty-mile width of impassable marshes through which six tributary water-courses meandered slowly to become the River Plate. It was an effective enough impediment: the only way the enemy could reach Buenos Aires was by sea and that was where they must be stopped.

To clear his head Kydd mounted the stone steps to the parapets and open sky. He looked out over the foreshore to the fretful grey-brown expanse of sea. All big ships and even the frigates were unable to sail up to administer a thundering barrage because of the impassable mud-flats but, more to the point, he had not a ship of any kind that was his to command.

The foreshore was in its usual rowdy disorder, sailors staggering out of grog shops, others fighting, and wafting above it all, the odour of mud, horses and putrid fish offal. It was a foreign land in quite a different sense from Cape Town and he would be glad when he was free to sail away in his dear *L'Aurore*. But he had been given a duty to perform and he would do all he could to discharge it.

But it was a damn near impossible thing to ask: to stop an entire army in its tracks? How in heaven's name could a sea officer accomplish such a feat? He balled his fists helplessly.

What would Nelson have done?

He would not have been disheartened! Find an enterprising action – anything, as long as it was positive.

After a few moments' concentration he had the solution. A *miniature* navy! If the muddy shallows would defeat a proper one he'd lay hands on everything under sail that could take the conditions and, with them, throw a blockade against the other shore.

Resolved, he clattered down the steps and bellowed for the duty master's mate to bring the charts.

It was possible. At no point was the distance between the two shores narrower than thirty miles: any sally by a heavily laden enemy would be spotted in time and he could quickly bring up his forces to dispute the crossing. He gave a wry smile. In many ways it was a small-scale version of the invasion threat to England the year before. Would there be a miniature Trafalgar as well?

Beresford approved the plan and detailed an adjutant to assist him, for which he was grateful. As a young lieutenant Kydd's first thought would have been to move fast to sweep the harbour clear of the right vessels and send them out immediately to face the enemy. As a somewhat wiser post-captain he was only too aware of the devil behind the details.

There was no question: the Navy did not have the necessary craft and therefore these would have to be found locally. But were the citizens of Buenos Aires the enemy, meaning he could simply take them as prize? If they were of local registry, it would amount to piracy if he seized vessels under the protection of the Crown. So they would have to be paid for – but how? And, much more importantly, under whose line of account?

Then there was the problem of manning them. Enlist rebels and the disaffected? Not if they were reported to be turning on the British. And letting loose a 'press-gang' on the riff-raff idling about the port was not practical, for where a big ship could absorb the unwilling or unable, in small craft every man must be relied on to pull his weight.

It had to be their own men therefore, which brought all kinds of other problems. It was not just that it would sap the already tiny numbers available to garrison the city – in view of the seriousness of the situation the commodore would certainly authorise a manning from the big ships – but that it would throw an unknown extra number on slender supplies that could no longer be guaranteed, to the detriment of them all.

And other matters: where were they to be quartered? In ships, crews stayed aboard, there was no need for living spaces, but these vessels would be little more than boats and unfit for extended habitation. If they were to maintain lengthy patrols there was the question of clothing and victuals of a kind that could be readily stowed, a dockyard of sorts with skilled hands for timely repairs, a reliable source of water in a city that carried its own about in carts . . . The complications went on and on.

General Beresford was in a foul temper. 'God rot his soul!'

'Er, who is that, sir?' his aide enquired.

'Why, this Liniers in Montevideo, in course! Sent to me that he begs to attend his sick family here in Buenos Aires. I grant him a passport and he spends his time creeping about, noting down our strength and positions.'

'Liniers, sir?'

'An officer lost to honour and civilised conduct – yes, this is the scoundrel who's leading the insurrection out of Montevideo. A cunning fox, I'm told – and a Frenchman. Been in the Spanish service for twenty years but he fought us in the American war and knows his onions. We'll need to keep good guard, I'm persuaded.'

Colonel Pack glowered from the other end of the table. 'What sticks in m' craw is those priests o' yours. You give 'em leave t' range as they will and next thing the damn papists are topping it the spy.'

'I had little choice in the matter, Dennis. They claim it their religion to take their ministration to the people and will not be denied. Should I forbid their free movement it'll anger the populace, and that is something neither you nor I wish.'

'So we—'

'I have a plan that should give you heart. The people are restless and inquisitive of our small numbers. I now propose to free the slaves on the grounds that as slavery is not countenanced in England neither is it here. This will result in many thousands of grateful men who, at the same time, are unemployed. You will offer the more able-bodied service in the Army – at the very least it will double, if not triple, our strength.'

'Ah. Now that's a capital idea! I've taken t' dressing as a soldier any common servant on his rounds, the odd sailor an' such, just t' have 'em march about the place to impress. When will I have 'em?'

'I'm to tell the *cabildo* tonight. Now, I'm getting reports that up-country horsemen are massing against us from this side, to the north-west. Gauchos, who are apparently splendid light cavalry. As we have next to none it's of grave importance that they are prevented from joining up with Liniers. I've pickets out on that side of the city but I don't fear any assault – unless Liniers gets to 'em.'

For a moment his eyes glazed and he muttered, 'These damned reinforcements cannot come fast enough for me.'

Then he stiffened and snapped, 'Captain – how are our sea defences proceeding?'

Kydd tried to give a confident smile. 'Sir, should you come with me up to the lookout you'll get a sight of our progress.'

'Then I shall! Gentlemen, let us remove to the upper regions.'

The same prospect of muddy grey sea looked increasingly morose under a threatening low winter sky. Small clusters of merchant ships were moored together further out, and at the far distant dark grey horizon two specks of white, spaced far apart. 'I've named 'em *Staunch* and *Protector*,' Kydd enthused, 'on patrol already at the far side of the Ortiz Bank. And here—' he indicated the mole below the fort where four other craft were in varying stages of fitting out '—there are more. In all, seven armed vessels.'

'They look very small, Captain,' Beresford said doubtfully, eyeing the half-decked, two-masted craft and the men swarming over them.

'Sixty feet long, sir. This is accounted sizeable in these waters – any bigger and they'd take the mud, and we need 'em to go into every creek and bay without fear.' This was the local *sumaca*, nearly flat-bottomed and with a gaff main, square sail on the fore, and headsails aplenty, often to be seen about the province carrying local cargo.

'How are they armed?'

'Carronades,' Kydd answered immediately. This gave them a great advantage in fire-power but only if they could close with the enemy – and these were boat carronades only, not the formidable weapons of a frigate. In the close-quarter scuffles to be expected in lonely bays, it would be cutlasses and pistols that must settle the day.

'And how deployed?'

'General Liniers will not want to take boat from Montevideo as this is a long voyage and leaves him exposed to our cruisers. He'll stay on that side and march to the only other port o' consequence, Colonia, which is opposite us thirty miles, and wait his opportunity to cross, which in course we'll deny him.'

'I asked how deployed.'

'Two on watch off Colonia, two at large off the coast. One on passage to relieve, two under replenishment and repair.'

'Umm. So they'll live on board.'

'Yes, sir.' There was no need for details: it would be the hardest of conditions but these were all volunteers and he'd been insistent on extra foul-weather clothing, a double rum ration and pre-cooked meat, the best he could do for them. Jack Tar's jaunty spirit had known worse.

'And your captains, are you confident that—'

'They're selected by me personally, General, and bear my complete confidence.' There had been no shortage of bored junior officers in the larger ships who were eager for action, and Popham had had to decide whether or not he should weaken their sea defences against a return of the Spanish Navy from the north.

'Very well. I'll be sleeping a little better for your efforts, Captain. Thank you.'

Back in his office, Kydd held his head in his hands. So much depended on him. One thought hammered in: was there anything else that could be done? The strategics were straightforward, but stopping Liniers crossing now had added urgency with the reports of gauchos gathering on this side. If they managed to join together, it would be a short time only before they must be overwhelmed or sent running like rabbits from their new-won piece of empire.

Where were their damned reinforcements?

Then there was the threat of winter weather. If a dreaded pampero struck it would decimate his little fleet, the only comfort being that the enemy would suffer likewise. Yet there was no alternative. They had to keep the sea, whatever the cost.

He picked up a half-completed provisioning list, irritated by the task. Despite the increasing threat, it seemed he had to find time to attend to pettifogging details like this. The Army was given forage money if not supplied in the field. The Navy received no such allowance because it was assumed that the men would be properly victualled in their ship. The contrived solution was complicated: the seamen would be borne on the garrison books but the army quartermaster would be reimbursed by individual pursers, even though the ships' muster rolls would show the men present on board, obliging the purser to seek compensation from the Admiralty directly.

He ground his teeth and set to, authorising the insanity.

'Sir?' The master's mate approached hesitantly.

'Well?' Kydd gave an ill-natured grunt.

'L'tenant Garrick, *Dolores*, sir. He's below, wishes to report – there's two sizeable enemy men-o'-war just been sighted opposite.'

Chapter 10

Kydd was out of his chair and down to the entrance room in a flash. Garrick scrambled to his feet and took off his hat. 'Sir. Er, pursuant to your—'

'Be damned to it, what did you see?' he demanded.

'Two ship-sloops enter Colonia.'

This changed everything: three masted square-riggers, often termed minor frigates, were a dismaying menace to his little navy and obviously brought up for the job of securing the vital crossing. Where they'd come from and how they were handling the shoal water was another matter. For now . . .

He snatched up his boat-cloak from behind the door. 'I'm going to take a look,' he threw at the duty master's mate, then turned on Garrick. 'Let's be having you, sir!'

The two hurried down to the mole where *Dolores* lay alongside, rotated to face seaward. Kydd grabbed a stay and leaped lightly on to its humble deck, closely followed by Garrick, who quickly gave orders to cast off.

'I do apologise, sir,' he said, as sailors in pairs got to work with long quant poles in the mud, heaving off the ungainly flat-bottomed vessel. Their departure would obviously not be in crisp naval fashion. Only after reaching open water could they set the gaff main and headsails and later a square fore to begin a workmanlike clawing to seaward in the rattling easterly.

Standing out of the way on the small after-deck, Kydd glanced back at the receding coastline, utterly flat as far as the eye could see, the buildings of the city the only objects in a vertical dimension, not a single mountain or cliff to relieve the monotonous level.

However, with the wind in his teeth and the willing surge of motion Kydd's heart swelled. He was at sea once more.

Dolores picked up speed. Kydd could see why this workhorse with her exaggerated beam and generous sail area was relied on to ply these waters, but squinting astern at a mark, he noted the dismaying amount of leeway she was making with the wind abeam.

The seaman at the long tiller, which was comfortably wedged into his thigh, chewed contentedly on his quid of tobacco with the customary glassy stare forward of his tribe when under the gaze of an officer.

Suddenly restless, Kydd snapped, 'Put us about quickly, Mr Garrick. I need to see how she handles before we go in.'

The sails, heavy and tanned ochre with a peculiarly rancid-smelling mixture, were difficult to handle but he could appreciate that they would take substantial squalls without fear. They went about without fuss but there would be no sharp manoeuvring in *Dolores*: the tiller had needed two men to throw against the pressure of the turn but the tacks and sheets were easily handled by the other three.

Kydd gave orders to take up on the original course and

waited until they had settled to speed, then went across and relieved the startled seaman at his tiller. He adopted the same pose, leaning against it, feeling the thrum and life as they foamed along. It was correctly balanced a little to weather, and he brought the vessel more by the wind, feeling its direction with his cheeks as he experimentally luffed and touched, much as he had as quartermaster in *Seaflower* long years ago in the Caribbean.

Kydd found *Dolores* surprisingly agreeable to close-hauling, probably due to the big headsails, he reasoned. Satisfied, he gave up the tiller and paced forward, an anxious Garrick close behind.

Her armament, a twelve-pounder carronade on the foredeck and swivels each side of the after-deck, was enough to dominate in an action between equals but near hopeless if they were ranged against ship-sloops, which could muster a full broadside of six-pounders.

It was a measure of how close Colonia del Sacramento was that they raised the opposite shore soon after midday. The sharp-eyed Garrick spotted *Staunch* further in with the coast. 'We'll join her, if you please,' Kydd said.

His thoughts raced. If these did prove to be sloops, what the devil was he to do? Even concentrating his entire force of seven he could not be expected to prevail against them, but sending to Popham for heavier metal would take time and risk stranding his vessels in this damnable maze of shoals that was the Río de la Plata.

Leaving the sloops alone was not in question for in the crossing they had only to lay off each side of the transports to crush with broadsides any foolish enough to contest their passage.

What was puzzling was that vessels of such size were sailing with impunity among the banks and shoals. It was a mystery demanding close reconnaissance.

They reached *Staunch*, which jauntily dipped her ensign on seeing Kydd. 'We're taking a look at your ship-sloops,' he hailed.

'The water's very shoal hereabouts,' Selby, her captain, came back anxiously. 'Must be certain of the channels – those devils damn well know what they're about.'

Kydd had made plenty of allowance for leeway in coming over and they were upwind of Colonia by some miles, having only to bear away before the wind and past a few headlands to reach the hooked point that was the port's shelter. The chart – little more than a crude sketch in Spanish – gave scant help, scrupulous in showing the positions of churches inland and giving names to every one of the scatter of offshore islands but not mentioning the presence of sub-sea reefs or deep-water channels.

The hook in the coastline gave Kydd his clue. In its lee was Colonia but, more importantly, it then trended sharply away northward. There would be tidal scour around it as the waters scurried past to make the wider bay, and where there was scour there would be deeper water. He looked up. 'We'll take it close as we can. Bear away, if you please.'

With *Staunch* in their wake they closed with the land. It resolved into a partly wooded area with long strips of pale beach and little sign of habitation but he had been right: the seaman forward with the hand lead was reporting steadily deeper soundings. This was how the pair had reached Colonia.

The town was ahead. Kydd had little information to go on other than that it was yet another ancient Portuguese colony that had passed into Spanish hands. He had no idea how formidable it was, still less of their likely reception so close.

After more curving beaches and nondescript woods, the first signs of settlement appeared. Caught to seaward of them, wary fishermen stood motionless in their punts while they passed. *Dolores* was fast coming up to the last foreland before Colonia. Pale buildings and the incongruous end of an avenue were spotted but then came the thud of a gun, and smoke driven downwind from an unnoticed little fort at the water's edge. Another. The alarm had now been given. Were they small enough targets?

They barrelled along the last few hundred yards and passed the point. There – two ships at anchor off the small harbour, the red and yellow of Spanish climbing to the mastheads. Their design took after the French corvettes that were causing mayhem in the Channel; these vessels were smaller, but he could see the menacing line of six-pounder gun-ports on each side. A swarm of little craft encircled them.

Kydd quickly took in other details. An exaggerated beam and turn of bilge meant shallower draught; bald-headed with sail only to topsails, they would not be speedy on a wind but, with low top-hamper, were well suited to these conditions. He looked more sharply at the further one, closer inshore. It had no sails bent on the yards and had a definite heel – it was resting on the mud. Careening: he could see the tell-tale gleam of white among the weed on the hull, the same preservative used in the Royal Navy before the use of copper had become widespread.

With these two as the nucleus of a crossing force it was all too clear he hadn't a chance. His ambition for a classic blockade, leaving Liniers and his growing army impotent at the shore, was now in ruins and they could cross with impunity when they were ready.

Where the *devil* had they come from? How had they got past Popham's patrols?

And what was he proposing to do about it?

He felt Garrick's eyes on him while he tried to think. They were completely outclassed, and the reasonable conclusion was that it would be nothing but a waste of lives to throw his little fleet at them. Yet to give up without trying, to run from the scene, was intolerable. If only *L'Aurore* were here to set about them like a terrier after rats.

It was a stalemate. The best he could do—

Sail dropped from the fore-yard in the nearer sloop, then jibs and courses blossomed. It was putting to sea and its quarry had to be the insolent *sumacas* flaunting the British ensign.

Kydd hesitated. He'd seen what he'd needed to see and the sensible thing was to return and confess this grave turn of events to General Beresford. Over on the sloop, its fo'c'sle party finished, the anchor cable was buoyed and slipped, and the yards were bracing round for a lunge to sea.

He hailed *Staunch* through cupped hands. 'Return to Buenos Aires independently.'

'We go back,' he told Garrick. Their passage had taken them well past Colonia and on into the bay beyond. Beating back against the easterly the way they had come was unwise under chase in these waters. Over to larboard, a mile or so off, lay one of the islands, low and thickly wooded. 'Take us around it and then direct home,' Kydd ordered. As an after-thought he added, 'Post a couple of men in the bows for I mean to make it uncomfortable for our friend to follow.'

After his service around Guernsey he knew what to look for in shoal waters, the arrowed ripples, out of synchrony wavelets, the dark of seaweed beneath the surface. As well, he posted two men to lie flat on deck in the eyes of the craft, staring down into the water for the ghostly shadow of reefs or banks looming.

He shielded his gaze to take in the lie of the island. It was often possible to note a backbone of rock stretching out into the sea that would later be a jagged underwater spine extending out – and indeed there was one, pointing like an accusing finger back at Colonia. 'Two points to starboard, leave it well clear.' He glanced back at the sloop. It was making remarkably good sailing before the wind, its plain, broad sail-plan working well in this north-easterly. North? The wind was backing – what did this mean in these unholy waters? A faster return certainly, and once around the island they'd take advantage of their fore-and-aft rig to cosy up to the wind and leave the ship-sloop standing.

It would almost certainly be satisfied with seeing them off and let them go. For the moment it was half a mile or so in their wake, but when they began passing the island it gave no sign of breaking off the chase. It made no difference because—

The double yell from forward came too late. With a sharp wooden thump and squeal of outraged timbers, the *sumaca* reared up and ceased forward motion. Sent sprawling, Kydd picked himself up. 'Get sail off her – move yourselves!' he bellowed hoarsely.

The craft had mercifully slewed round, spilling the wind; if it had gone the other way they would have been a dismasted wreck by now. Kydd looked over the side – in the turbid water he saw the line of a ledge below the surface, at right-angles and as abrupt as if it had been built that way. No wonder the sloop had let them crowd on sail.

Garrick scrabbled up the canted deck, nursing an arm. 'Tide's on the make, sir. If we could . . .'

Kydd looked sourly at the oncoming enemy. 'There's no time. If you've any signals, papers, get 'em ditched now.'

Their nemesis hove to well clear and quickly had two boats in the water, pulling strongly towards them. When they found that not only had they a prize but also made prisoner a senior officer of the Royal Navy, there would be no end to the crowing. It was hard to take.

'Be damned to it! I'm not f'r a Spanish chokey!' one of the seamen shouted, and leaped into the sea forward, quickly followed by another. It was foolish for they would soon be picked up by the boats and—

Then Kydd saw they had found firm ground under them and were now standing in water no more than chest deep. Kydd looked at Garrick. 'To the island, I think!'

They scrambled for the bow and lowered themselves in. Trying to ignore the cold and wet, Kydd waved them forward. 'To the island!'

He thrust ahead, feeling iron-hard sand beneath, powering towards the island a good three hundred yards off. The others followed in a straggling line. Snatching a glance behind, he saw both boats making straight for them and redoubled his efforts, panting hard, stumbling at occasional hidden rocks.

The seabed began rising and the last hundred yards were done in a stumbling run. Suddenly they were among a scatter of light-grey rocks in the sand and then into low woods, spiky branches whipping across their faces until they stood gulping and wheezing together in a clearing.

'They's more interested in the *Dollars*,' one seaman said. Originally the sailors had called *Nuestra Señora de Dolores* 'Our Lady of the Dollars', but the Spanish now swarming over her would find little to plunder. And then they would come after her crew.

'I c'n see *Staunch*!' a sailor shouted, pointing through a gap in the trees to the sea the other side of the island. Spontaneously they broke into a stumbling run, crashing through the undergrowth and low branches until they emerged on to a rock-studded beach where they waved and shouted.

She sailed on and their hopes faded. 'They're not keepin' a lookout, the shonky bastards!' But then the two masts started to come together as she began to put back – they were returning to pick them up.

'God bless 'em, every one!'

'See if the Dons are after us yet,' Kydd told a seaman, pointing back the way they'd come.

The man loped off, but returned quickly. 'Boat on its way,' he panted. 'Too many on 'em.'

They were completely unarmed and must surrender to any with a weapon. And *Staunch* was still some way off.

'Into the water!' Kydd barked urgently, and waded into the sea. On the weather side the waves were several feet high, slamming and jostling against him. The seabed under his feet was much less even, with rocks and crevices that twice nearly had him sprawling full-length. From the splashes and cursing behind him he knew it was slowing the others, too.

The sea bottom grew steeper and before they had gone out a hundred yards the water was to his armpits and he was being carried off his feet by the surging waves. They could go no further. Ahead, *Staunch* was cautiously slowing, but she was way out of reach.

Suddenly, to the right, there was the smack and plume of a bullet. Another whipped over to strike between Kydd and *Staunch*. He swung around – on the beach, the Spanish were running down to take aim at the water's edge. He turned back to *Staunch* – and saw that a boat had been launched, but with only one aboard. Then he understood: they were streaming the boat downwind to them at the end of a long line.

The meaty thump of a ball in flesh and an agonised cry came from nearby as Kydd pressed on. It had been a lucky shot: it would have been impossible to take accurate aim at this distance after a fast run.

The boat was coming quicker. Nearer and nearer, and then within reach. He grabbed at the gunwale and hung there, urging others in, seeing them tumbling over each other and roughly heaving in the wounded seaman. The remaining men hung on where they could and, at his signal, the boat was hauled bodily through the water to the waiting *Staunch*.

'Well done, L'tenant,' Kydd gasped, gratefully accepting the stout oilskin pressed on him. 'A pity about *Dolores*.' He broke off as Selby bawled orders to get under way.

Then he stopped as a thought came – and stayed to blossom into a beautiful, glorious possibility.

The sloop had stopped to take possession of *Dolores*. It had men away on the island and was otherwise occupied. What if . . . ?

'L'tenant, I desire you to make best speed to the barky. Not ours – the one hove over for careening.'

A broad grin appeared on the officer's face. The sloop might be grounded but there would be depth of water for a *sumaca*. 'Er, we've only the carronade,' he said apologetically. It would take hours of bombardment to reduce a warship with it but Kydd had other ideas.

'No, not that. Fetch me all the combustibles you can find – we set her afire.'

By the time they had reached a line of sight from the first sloop they were well on their way but had minutes only to accomplish their mission. As they approached, it must have become obvious what they were about, but Kydd was leaving nothing to chance. They came in on the immovable vessel's bow where its guns could not bear, then lay off.

At the first crash from the stumpy carronade the few men left aboard emerged and hastily tumbled into boats for the shore.

'Go!' Kydd roared, himself taking position at the blunt prow of *Staunch* with two others. A quick look told him that the other sloop had spotted them and was making to return, but in her square rig she was hard up against the wind – yet it was still only minutes they had.

Skilfully the two ships were brought at an angle nose to nose and Kydd reached out to clutch the martingale, swinging a leg up and then levering himself atop the naked bowsprit to slither into the plain fore-deck. The bare decks were deserted and awkwardly canted over but he knew where to go – passing hand to hand he found the fore-hatchway and went down, casting about in the gloom.

Behind him he heard the footsteps of his men. One made salty comment on the alien smell. All ships were much the same between decks and Kydd quickly found what he was looking for: the carpenter's store-room and workshop. Inside they set to, feverishly heaping into a pile the wood shavings with the oakum and torn cotton ration bags they had brought.

Flint and steel were nervously produced. Kydd took them and ordered the room cleared before upending glue-pots, jars of spirit and anything else he could find over the mess. He struck some sparks but they went out before they could catch the flammables – he had to get nearer to the dangerous mixture. An eddy of the sharp stink of fumes hung in the air, and when he struck again they caught in a *whoomf* of searing flame. He staggered back, temporarily blinded, but felt the hands of a man behind plucking him out and steering him for the hatchway.

His eyes cleared in the open to see the other sloop plunging vengefully towards them but *Staunch* was there, hauled under the bowsprit, and Kydd thankfully dropped to its deck. Now for the crowning moment – if it came off.

'Back down our track,' he snapped, when he reached the wheel. It caused frowns – it was the course home, but would take them past the returning sloop, which would not hesitate to salute them with a broadside.

The two vessels closed. 'Bear away to leeward, if you please,' Kydd said tightly, his eyes on the Spanish. This would take them downwind of the bigger ship – which was precisely what he wanted. 'A trifle more, I think.' It would not do to appear too brazen.

It was not long before they met: a fleeing mosquito of a craft, trying to make the open sea in time, and a righteous avenger. And the temptation was too much – with no flames from their work yet outwardly visible on the other sloop the Spaniard put over his helm and lunged for them, probably relishing Kydd's mistake: at this point of sailing it was going to be the square-rigged ship that had the advantage.

Kydd watched the sloop gradually close, and set his trap. 'A little to larboard – that will do.'

Now it was all down to the cupidity of the Spanish captain, so eager to cap his day by taking both craft. They were passing the end of the island, where the long finger of a point entered the water. And Kydd now remembered the significance of the wind backing northerly: in this vast funnel of sea an easterly blowing in would have a heaping effect on the mass of water, resulting in a greater depth. With this backing to the north, it would be released and—

The effect of several hundred tons of ship striking at speed on the underwater spine of rocks was dramatic. Instantly the ship slewed and the fore-mast, bowed forward under press of sail, fell majestically, quickly followed by the main, transforming a fine creature of the sea to a ruin.

Disbelieving yells of triumph went up and the young captain turned to Kydd with such admiration that he felt a blush rising. 'Sir – you knew he'd follow.'

'Then let it be a lesson to you, sir,' he said modestly.

Flames were now shooting up from the fore-deck of the grounded sloop and the boats coming out from the shore were hanging back – as Kydd had intended: the fore magazine was not far from where they had started the fire.

Selby looked over at the distant figures clambering disconsolately over the wreckage of the other. 'Sir, shall we . . . ?'

'No, my friend, we'll leave 'em to it.' There was no point in finishing it – both sloops put down was a quite acceptable result. In any case, there was still something he had to do.

When they arrived, *Dolores* was still aground but now quite deserted and ready to be restored to the British flag.

'Mr Garrick – do you desire to take up your command again?'

There was little damage aboard for it appeared the Spanish had been more concerned with searching for booty and keeping their prize in good condition. All it took was a modicum of skilful seamanship to have her towed off the bank.

Kydd swelled with satisfaction. Even in the face of his little fleet there was no chance Liniers would risk a crossing now. Let the Army strut and parade: it was the Navy that had held the line.

* * *

When they arrived back at the mole Kydd could feel an oppressive, uneasy atmosphere. As he reached the waterfront he caught averted glances, lowered voices, the sudden stilling of laughter. Things were changing fast.

He went to his billet. It was the same there, a stiff disinclination in the ladies of the house for conversation, the children running off, and Rodriguez formidably polite but of few words. Kydd left quickly.

At the fort, Beresford was still out on inspection and Kydd wearily made his way to the officers' mess to take a meal and seek company.

On seeing his Royal Marines lieutenant he called over, 'Ah – Mr Clinton. Might I sup with you?'

'I'd be honoured, sir.'

'We've just heard of your success on the other shore and we'll all rest the better for it.'

'Thank you. A diverting occasion for a clerking warrior, I'm bound to say.' Kydd turned his attention to the food – a hot breakfast would be a welcome change, but the egg that was placed before him was small and discoloured with an unmistakable reek. 'Stale and off, damn it. Steward!'

Clinton looked uncomfortable 'Sir. I beg you – he's not to be blamed. The situation with victuals is getting insupportable, the city market near deserted, and we dare not go into the country to secure our own. I fancy we'll be on short canny before long.'

Kydd sat back in dismay. That it had come to this so quickly was a serious development.

Clinton went on, 'All the transports have been stripped of provisions and been sent up and down the country to try to get more at any price, but in a hostile province I think not.'

'Has the commodore—'

'Yes, he's been informed,' the lieutenant said matter-of-factly. Naturally it was squarely the senior officer's problem. He ventured, 'Sir, should you wish to take the temper of Buenos Aires we could go for a stroll and . . .'

Kydd felt he was being invited for a reason and fell in with the suggestion. They walked out of the fort into the main square. Here again there were few people: a handful of forlorn basket traders, a couple of children running and the familiar grind of the high-wheeled water carts. For the rest there was an uncanny silence.

They passed into a minor street and heard the tramp of boots, the squeal of fife and drums. As they emerged on to a main street they saw a broad column of redcoats with a splendidly ornamented sergeant major to the fore. The few people watching stared dully or turned their backs.

Clinton snapped to attention, Kydd did the same, and they were acknowledged with screamed commands and a salute by the sergeant major. The soldiers marched stolidly along in widely spaced threes, not at all with the crisp profession-alism Kydd had come to expect from these veteran troops. As they passed he recognised, to his astonishment, *L'Aurore*'s purser's steward stepping it out in a corporal's tunic and, further on, the duty coxswain.

'Daily we rope in every idler we can find – servant, boat-boy, shore party – dress 'em up in uniforms and ask them to march about for a period. Notice how they're spaced apart. We hope it gives the locals the impression we've numbers beyond what we really have,' Clinton explained.

'I see.'

'I must allow it's a powder-keg, sir. Forty thousand kept at bay by one and a half. If they take it into their heads . . .'

Kydd nodded gravely, then asked, 'Er, by now you know Buenos Aires well enough?'

'Why, there's continuous streets and buildings all of two miles long and a half wide, and it spreads out far into the country. You'll be wondering how we keep watch and ward, I fancy. Well, as to that, the general desires that we make a presence everywhere we can, so we've posts on the roads regulating entry into here, and roving patrols and sentries at important locations. I've stood sentry-go as a private myself, just to see the lie of the land, but our biggest problem is men. Even in two watches we can't really secure a city this large.'

'Are the men in good heart?'

'They're doing their duty, sir,' Clinton said firmly.

'Do sit and take a taste of wine, Mr Kydd,' Beresford mumbled, through his food. 'I've not yet eaten today, and I'm clemmed.'

He finished his modest meal quickly and turned to Kydd. 'A capital action against the ship-sloops, sir. We're safe – for now. You've heard of our difficulties with provisioning?'

'Sir.'

'The commodore has sent the victuallers *Elizabeth* and *Mary* on a cruise to chase up supplies but I'm not sanguine we'll find any in the province. I'm persuaded they'll need to go to Rio, possibly as far as Cape Town.'

Kydd had his doubts about the Cape. There would probably be little enough to be found even at that distance, so soon after it had been taken: there hadn't been a harvest and the Capetonians were still on thin times. But what else could the defenders do?

'Rations are vital, of course, but what worries me is that

we've no line to other military stores. We're quite on our own with what we've brought with us. For instance, I've taken the precaution of buying up all the gunpowder I can lay hands on among the merchantmen lying here. What I'll do for the other I cannot say.'

'Sir, we've only to hold on for the reinforcements.'

'Ah, the reinforcements. And when do you conceive they'll be here? If I knew, we could make our dispositions – as it is, we're forced to plan for months. If you've any ideas, I'd be glad to hear them.'

Kydd said ruefully, 'St Helena?'

'We've sent *Jane* there but they're East India Company, not set up for Crown supply. No, it has to be comprehended that we're in a devilish pickle.'

'The slaves – are they to be added to our colours?'

'No. The local merchantry plead their economy will be overset should they lose their services. I've had to let them keep their slaves. A good thing, too,' he said absently. 'I couldn't feed 'em.'

Topping up the general's wine, Kydd commented, 'A sullen enough crew about town, I've noticed. I'm puzzled to know just what it is that's made them set their faces against us.'

Beresford sighed. 'Hard to say. At a guess, I'd presume it's something to do with the Dons' pride, that we've taken the place with so few. And what we're offering of prosperity and freedom does not weigh that much with them.'

'They've the chance to rid themselves of Spanish rule and they refuse it?'

'Ah, yes. This they would value above all things, but they are asking too much of me.'

'Sir?'

'There are many who would accept us, possibly the majority

of the better class, but first they desire a guarantee of protection against reprisal from the Spanish, should they return. This I cannot on my honour sign up to, as it is not within my power to defend against everything unforeseeable.' He sighed. 'Therefore that puts paid to any hope of a harmonious future. So, none will be seen to collaborate with us for fear of retribution later.'

Kydd knew what he was saying. 'Like Guadeloupe when the French returned. The streets ran red for weeks I've heard.' He had been a young seaman on the island when . . .

Beresford sniffed and added sourly, 'And those priests are a pestilential lot. They're making open offer of a place in the country and a new wife if a soldier deserts his post and takes off his hat to the pope. I'm sorry to say there's been more than one Irishman think it the better bargain, the *señoritas* being so obliging.'

Abruptly he stood up. 'Hard times, but we have our duty.'

Chapter 11

'You are quite clear, *amado mio*, what we must do?' Rafaela said, her voice breaking with intensity.

'Of course,' Serrano replied, although in his nervousness his hands were working together.

'You will wait at Los Tres Reyes and I will bring the English captain to you. Now, don't forget—'

'*Mi rosa*, you do your part and I will do mine. I shall not fail Don Baltasar.'

They walked together in a wary silence through the shabby streets, then separated towards the centre. The city was unusually quiet and had an air of tension and dread that played on Serrano's mind. He tried to tell himself that it was safer now: he was known where it counted as an agent of the patriots and need not fear them. But was it really true that they were in sacred alliance with the loyalists, whose hatred had seen him exiled?

Distant sounds of a military column marching came echoing through the streets. In a panic he hid in a side alley while the tramping feet went by – he had no idea how the

British must regard him now. It was Rafaela's job to feel for this before she brought Captain Kydd to the back room of the tavern. The column seemed endless: there must be many thousand troops in the city – and now they were his sworn enemy.

'I say, for the ears of Captain Keed only!' Rafaela snapped at the fortress guard. She stood there stubbornly until eventually an important-looking naval officer and a plainly dressed man descended.

'*¿Señorita, qué quieres con el capitán?*'

Ignoring him she addressed the officer directly. 'Doña Rafaela Callejo, an' I have *información* for you, Captain Keed.' He was a handsome man with a strong, open face that paradoxically allowed her fears to subside a little.

'How do you know my name?' he challenged.

She said nothing.

'Very well, I'll see her inside,' Kydd told the translator, and led the way to his office.

'Now, what is it you have to tell me, Miss Callejo?'

Rafaela adjusted her shawl. He looked directly at her, no play with the eyes or attempt to dominate or charm, and she felt a twinge of guilt at what she was about to do. 'Sir, you know my lover. Vicente Serrano.'

'I do,' Kydd said cautiously. 'He left my ship some time ago.'

'Yes. To reach *los patriotas*. I am to tell you he was not in time for your attack and only now has arrive in Buenos Aires.'

'I'm pleased to hear it.'

'You're not angry wi' him?'

Kydd shook his head. 'No. We had to sail quickly. These things happen in war.'

'Capitán, he wish to do more. To help King George against the Spanish so they can be throw from our country!' She smiled winningly. 'Sir, he is hiding, he frighten that someone will see him if he come to the fort.'

'I understand.'

'He know you, he trust you. Sir, will you see him at all?'

Serrano stood up when Kydd and Rafaela entered, his nervousness allayed by her smile.

'Captain Keed! I, er . . .' But all his imaginings for a suave line of questioning leading to secrets fled before the reality of facing the man he was about to betray.

'You wanted to help us against the Spanish?' Kydd prompted.

'Er, yes, sir.'

'Then I'm not at all sure what you can do unless first you tell us.'

'I – um, then what is your problem, may I ask?' Serrano blurted.

'That must be finding victuals for the soldiers – bread and spirit, provisions. We're in much need – but this is not something you can help us with, I fear, unless you know of secret stores or such,' Kydd finished hopefully.

'I will try. Thank you, sir – thank you!' he spluttered, the excitement in him building while Rafaela looked on in bafflement.

'And if you ever hear of mischief from the Spanish . . .'

'Yes, yes. Goodbye, sir, goodbye!'

Blinking, Kydd allowed himself to be escorted outside by Rafaela, who hurried back afterwards.

'What are you doing, you fool?' she blazed. 'Where are the secrets to tell Don Baltasar? You should have—'

Serrano gazed back with a saintly smile. 'I have the biggest of all, *mi bella flor*,' he said, challenging her with his eyes.

'What is this big secret then?' She pouted.

'Only that I'm to tell General Liniers to order his soldiers to rest easy. There will be no battles, no mortal struggle with the English.'

'What are you saying? This is lunatic, Vicente!'

'Tonight I shall leave in the fishing boat and at dawn I shall be speaking to the general directly,' he declared. 'You shall wait for my return.'

Colonia del Sacramento was now overwhelmed by an armed encampment that extended far out into the country. As Serrano was escorted through it he was thrilled by the sight of legendary regiments, soldiers in blue with red sashes, drilling proudly, and countless volunteers in their tall shakos, with their muskets a-slope, led by officers in magnificently plumed headgear.

Over to the right the *blandengues*, the veteran frontier militia, had their distinctive poled tents in rows, and in the distance cavalry thundered in mock charges. These *blandengues* had just completed a forced march over the ninety miles from Montevideo to Colonia but showed no sign of it.

Serrano threw out his chest: he was not in a fine uniform but he knew he had tidings for the commander in chief that would affect every last one of them.

Approaching the headquarters tent, he saw Güemes talking to an officer and waved gaily. His friend looked back at him in astonishment and Serrano felt his gaze follow him into the tent.

Several distinguished-seeming officers stood over a desk where an older man in a severe black uniform, finished in gold and scarlet, was seated, writing.

'Sir, an agent from Buenos Aires with news.'

'Wait.'

The man finished scratching away, then thrust a paper at one of the officers before looking up at the intruder.

'Don Santiago Liniers!' whispered someone behind Serrano.

'Sir. I have to report . . .'

'Well?' The voice was soft and calm.

Encouraged, Serrano went on, 'Sir, there is no need for a battle, sir.'

There were gasps and a stifled giggle.

'Go on.'

'I, personally, have interviewed the *capitán de puerto* himself and have made discovery that the treacherous English are in dire want of any kind of provisions. I put it to you, sir, that it is only a matter of a short while and they will be starved out. If we are patient, they must soon surrender to us, and without a drop of our own blood shed.'

'What do you know of military affairs?' snarled one of the officers. 'Leave us to—'

Serrano's face burned.

'No, no, Miguel, he means well. Tell me, what account of the present state of their stores can you give me? How many men are on rations? Where is it kept? Can they supply from the sea? These things I need to know for if we wait longer we must find more supply for our own army.

'And the biggest question is, when will their reinforcements arrive? If you can tell me the answer to that it would be of the greatest service. As it is, I must go forward without delay on the assault, you see.'

A tall officer bent down and whispered to Liniers, who nodded and said, 'There *is* an office you can perform for me, as it happens.'

'Anything, sir!'

'You'll no doubt be aware that our naval forces at Colonia suffered in a recent reversal at arms. This has had the unfortunate effect of frustrating our strategy to cross the Río de la Plata and join with our brothers for the grand assault on Buenos Aires. I would not have them think we are unwilling and therefore I shall write a message of encouragement and patience, which I desire you shall take to them.'

'Sir!' said Serrano, stiffening to attention.

'It will be to Colonel General Pueyrredón, commander of the Voluntarios Montados Bonaerense.'

'The gauchos?'

'Quite.'

'We'll stand on a little further, I believe,' Acting Lieutenant Hellard said evenly, watching the three craft fleeing ahead of him, each not much smaller than his own and which, together, could overcome *Stalwart*, the *sumaca*, if they chose – but they were at a crucial disadvantage: they faced the moral superiority of the famed Royal Navy that had the year before at Trafalgar crushed the best that Spain could send against it. These would never chance a confrontation.

The chill wind was getting stronger, tearing the tops from the waves – it gave speed to the more stoutly built *sumaca* but was threatening the odd assortment they were chasing: two *felucca*s whose soaring lateens could not easily be reefed and a *balandra*, a more European-styled cutter. All were clawing into the wind, the edges of their sails fluttering desperately, pale faces looking back on their implacable pursuer.

The heading could not be sustained. Up the River Plate to its end there was a maze of mud-flats and the blunt thirty-mile barrier of impenetrable marshes that separated the two shores. Sooner or later they must turn and face their fate or drive aground to be taken separately by *Stalwart*. Hellard grinned in anticipation and glanced at his crew, each with a cutlass and a brace of pistols: they didn't need to be told what was in prospect.

Abruptly the lead *felucca* put her helm down and lay over on to the other tack, followed like wheeling starlings by the other two.

'Ready about,' Hellard ordered languidly, and *Stalwart* made to follow suit. In an instant the three ahead swung back to their original course, gaining nearly a hundred yards, but the end could not be long in doubt.

It was the *balandra*, marginally larger than the other two, that took the ground first. Almost comically slowing as the muddy seabed rose to brush her undersides she stopped, still under full sail. The other two pressed on.

Hellard ordered savagely, 'Come to, a half-pistol-shot abeam.'

Then he snapped, 'Ahoy there, the swivel. One round to wake him up!'

The shot was sent low over the little half-deck aft where the crew crouched. They ducked out of sight and he ordered, 'Boarders away!'

In a well-practised move their boat was launched; with Hellard at the tiller and four men at the oars, they pulled strongly towards the *balandra*'s squared-off stern. Muskets banged from the deck-line but Hellard smiled cynically – in their inexperience they were firing much too early and the shots were going wide.

At the last minute he threw over his tiller and brought the boat in at an angle with a thump. With a roar a brawny seaman tossed his cutlass aboard and reached for a rope to heave himself in. Four crouched men rose to meet him – but Hellard's ready-aimed pistol kicked in his hand and the first went down in a gurgle of blood. A seaman's pistol behind him took the next with a bullet in the stomach and the man toppled forward, screaming, into the sea.

The third held his blade at point and retreated, pale and shaking. Hellard swung aboard and faced him with his sword, motioning for him to drop his weapon. The man was rigid with terror but kept his position, the tip of his crude cutlass wavering, his eyes black pits of fear. The lieutenant made a threatening gesture but the sailor kept up his weapon. A plunge overboard the other side was presumably the last making his escape.

It was butchery but there was no alternative: Hellard swept up his blade as though to slash down – the cutlass went up to protect and, with a sharp twist and stoop, Hellard was lunging inside, catching the man in the throat in a bloody spray. He fell to his knees, choking his life away.

Out ahead the two *felucca*s were making a broad circle, looking to an opportunity for revenge – Hellard and his party had little time.

In the cabin he found an oil lamp. He shouted down into the waist for the wreckers to stop smashing at the bottom of the vessel with broad-axe and maul, then dashed the lamp to the deck. It splintered and the oil caught in roiling flame.

As men tumbled into the boat to return to *Stalwart* the bowman leaned over and fished out a shapeless dripping black object. 'So what's this'n?'

'Get on your oar!' Hellard snarled at him in reply and they were away.

* * *

In the dim twilight, Serrano stood up to his knees in the sea, clutching his arms and shivering uncontrollably with cold and fright. It had taken hours for the blaze to be noticed from shore and a cautious fishing boat sent to investigate, but now it was coming and he would be back in blessed safety and warmth before long. It had been the worst experience he had ever had – the quick crossing abruptly interrupted by scenes of stark terror ended only by the plunge for his life over the side.

The desolate time standing in the mud was preferable to the alternative: being seized by the British and taken before their senior officer – Captain Kydd, who would quickly recognise his real position. And he could congratulate himself that even in all the horror he had thought to cast his precious dispatches overboard to prevent their capture.

The fishing boat loomed close, hands hauled him in and he was found a blanket and a mug of rough *aguardiente*.

Suddenly he realised their direction. 'Where are we going? I've to report to General Liniers himself – take us back!'

'What? We're from Las Conchas, and I can swear to you by the Holy Name we're going there.'

It was the wrong side of the river. 'But—'

'You'd rather get out and walk?'

He slumped down. Then he realised that telling Liniers he had not been able to deliver the message was neither informative nor helpful. Las Conchas was well to the north of Buenos Aires and he could safely move down to the gauchos who were secretly concentrated at the Perdriel ranch. Much better to see Pueyrredón himself and pass on the message personally.

'Las Conchas will do,' Serrano said loftily.

The old and stinking fishing village provided a measure of

compensation: a resident, impressed with his tale of escape from the clutches of desperate English pirates on the high seas, lent him a horse. In a matter of an hour or so he was cantering into the sprawling Perdriel ranch.

Juan Martín de Pueyrredón was tall, handsome and imperious, and of startling youth in his blaze of stars and epaulettes.

His piercing gaze never left Serrano as he heard his story. 'Very well, I'll accept this comes from General Liniers – your father is known to me.'

He mounted his horse with a flourish, then gestured towards the open country where great numbers of horsemen were thundering backwards and forwards in mock charge. 'How he expects me to keep these noble *caballeros* entertained while he and Baltasar dally is quite beyond me.' He sniffed. 'And, should the English dare to show their faces, I cannot be held accountable that these brave fellows insist on falling upon them without recourse to orders.'

'It was fished out of the water near the *balandra*,' Hellard said, handing over the sodden object. 'I saw there was a packet inside.'

Kydd inspected it curiously: a small leather hold-all, not military, and inside, a well-folded package secured with rawhide fastenings. Its covering was a stout oilskin preserving its contents against the seawater.

His pocket-knife soon had it open – it was a message, still quite legible but in Spanish. What was plain, however, was that, from the conspicuous Spanish royal coat of arms, this was official and of some importance. Yet why was it not in a military form? And would anyone be foolish enough to ditch valuable dispatches without the customary pair of musket-balls to weigh them down?

It had to be a deception but he was duty-bound to pass it on to the general.

'Found in the sea near a vessel taken by one of my captains,' Kydd murmured.

'A trickery, no doubt,' Beresford said immediately, but handed it to an aide. 'What does it say, Erskine?'

The man scanned it closely then looked up. 'Sir, it's a note from General Liniers to a Colonel General Pueyrredón.'

'Ah. That's our gaucho fellow, I'm told. Carry on.'

'A warm message encouraging them to hold fast until he can find some way to cross, their progress being halted at the shore by our navy, which holds the sea. Then, he says, they will join together to liberate their fair city from the invader.'

'Ha! I can't see how they believe this might constitute a misleading. We know very well that Liniers is confined to Colonia in idleness and we also know that the gauchos can't move without he crosses and joins up with them, so where's the deceit?'

He frowned, then a slow smile spread. 'Yet there is a message in this for us.'

'Sir?'

'If this is their admitted position I see no reason why we can't take advantage of it. Gentlemen, I'm to make a sally out of the city and deal with our country gaucho friends while they're thus separated. I shall not lose a moment. Send for Colonel Pack, if you please.'

In the chill dawn a column of infantry of the 71st Regiment with fifty of the St Helena Infantry and their guns tramped through the silent streets, watched by citizens awed by the warlike array of an army on the march. The general was taking more than half his strength – a grave risk, for if the future battle went against him Buenos Aires could not be held by those remaining.

They moved quickly, the guns and limbers pulled by mules and the soldiers with light packs, their marching rhythm eating up the miles until they had left the city and its suburbs well behind. With few horses, scouts could not be deployed on either flank and therefore it had to be assumed their progress was observed by Pueyrredón's outriders and the news relayed on.

The land was flat and monotonous, scrub and occasional trees bent with the wind adding to the feel of a God-forsaken landscape. A forward observer galloped back with news: ahead there were at least two thousand troops, mounted and with field guns. Near four times the British number, in their familiar country and on ground of their own choosing.

Beresford took the news calmly and the column marched on without pause.

At a little after ten they passed two ranch outbuildings, then caught sight of the enemy. They were taking advantage of a long stone wall for a defensive work, their guns at regular intervals, behind them a mass of horses and troops, the glitter of steel and the colour of pennons clearly visible.

The guns thudded into life too early with wild firing; the British continued advancing in column and the balls gouged earth well away from them.

Then Beresford gave the order to deploy, bringing his men to a halt while his guns took position.

His artillerymen opened up with devastating effect. A stone wall was the worst shelter imaginable – as the iron balls struck, they dissolved it into flying, razor-sharp splinters that carried into the packed mass behind.

'Fix bayonets! To the fore – march!' The 71st formed a double line and advanced; the St Helena's stayed with the guns.

From the enemy positions a stream of riders burst out to the left, another to the right, maddened gauchos in an impulsive charge that owed little to soldierly discipline and much to their lust for glory.

Against veteran Highlanders it was a mistake. With crisp commands the redcoats halted and formed a loose square. The gauchos were met with the concentrated fire of the first rank, which brought down men and horses in a chaos of flying bodies and squeals of terror. To the front one gaucho officer was spectacularly unhorsed, but staggered to his feet and stood defiant against the foe, the gold of his epaulettes and decorations an incongruous glint against the filth of the battlefield.

The British resumed their advance, but the officer didn't run – he snatched up a flag, which he flourished aloft, shouting heroically into the anarchy and confusion. Seemingly from nowhere a gaucho dragoon galloped wildly towards him, low in the saddle, beating his horse mercilessly. In a feat worthy of a circus spectacle the unhorsed officer vaulted into the saddle behind him and they made their escape.

Gauchos circled out of range – then a pair made a wild dash for the British lines, straight towards where the general and his staff were standing. Beresford tried to draw his sword but it jammed in its scabbard. Musket fire brought one gaucho crashing to the ground but the other, sabre at the ready, thundered in. The general's aide threw himself between them and parried the swing with his own weapon. The rider circled for another pass but was brought down with pistols.

Ahead, two Spanish guns fired but fell silent before the charging Scots. The gunners fled – all save one, who valiantly stayed by his weapon and was captured.

The 71st had taken Perdriel, the equipment and guns for no loss. There was nothing the gauchos could do but leave their dead and retreat.

'A glorious day, sir!' a young officer enthused to Beresford.

'You think so?' the general said. 'What do you see? A conquered army at my feet? No, sir. We have the field, but what are we going to do with it? We have to quit it immediately and return to Buenos Aires, having taught 'em respect, but their force still exists and we must meet them again. This only buys time.'

He called to his aide: 'Do bring that prisoner before me. The bravest fellow the Spanish had this day.'

The man was led forward. 'Tell him I shall compliment him on his conduct as his own commanding officer would. What's his name?'

There was no response from the gunner, who stood defiant and silent. 'Come, come, sir – you have nothing to be ashamed of. Tell us your name and rank,' Beresford said.

Colonel Pack stormed up, red-faced. 'The villain! I know that man, sir! He's an Irish deserter!'

The general's expression turned bleak. 'You see?' he said, to the young officer. 'Now I have to hang a good man. A glorious day? I think not.'

There were shouts of men returning – but they were Spanish. Serrano had not heard English spoken for some time. Were the British abandoning the battlefield? Fearfully, he cleared a hole from his hiding place under the mule feed to see a colourful gaucho swaggering past.

He got up to find the camp in ruins. The British had destroyed what they could and had left, taking the guns, and now there was nothing but the desolation of a battlefield and wailing women. He wandered around in shock – they had outnumbered the enemy by four to one yet had been soundly beaten. What had happened – what now of the future?

He saw Pueyrredón with his officers around him and heard him cry out, 'The glorious sacrifice of our men on the field of battle will not be in vain. We know we're children in the arts of war compared to the *imperialista* British – but we have an advantage: a mighty sword in our hand. Our cause is just.'

There was a roar of support, but impatiently he cut through it. 'And every last *bonaerense* son would flock to the colours if they could and join us in our time of glory.'

Serrano was spellbound. With leaders like this man, how could they fail to stand against the English, and then in the fullness of time march on to seize the golden crown of liberation and independence?

Pueyrredón went on, 'I have a plan that will grant them their sacred wish. We cannot prevail in the open field of battle before the forces the British can muster against us. Therefore we shall arm the people and as one we shall rise up against them in numbers they cannot withstand. By stealth and courage we will infiltrate muskets and pikes, guns, swords and powder into the city. When General Liniers crosses to join us at last, a trumpet will sound forth our freedom's call and the entire city will rise up and humble them.'

Joining in the storm of applause, Serrano pushed forward eagerly. 'I shall be first to return. I know the British – let me be the one!'

Pueyrredón looked around grandly, then fixed on Serrano. 'Very well, you shall have your wish. You shall accompany my chief lieutenant and emissary, Charcas, Hidalgo de Sarmiento, to Buenos Aires, there to raise our people's army.'

Eyes shining, Serrano snapped to attention. 'Yes, General.'

'Then go,' Pueyrredón said, looking pointedly over his shoulder.

Serrano turned round – and met the eyes of the man he had last seen in the home of his lover.

Charcas's cynical smile sliced through his elation. 'Do lead on. Be first – and I will follow,' he added grimly.

They left disguised as farm peons on a cart of donkey hay but under the load lay a dozen muskets. At the reins Serrano led off towards the city in the distance, his apprehension turning to terror as they approached the first sentry. Charcas took over, chewing a straw and spreading his hands in incomprehension. The nervous young soldier let them pass.

The cart wound its way through the meaner streets of the northern suburbs, passing into an enclosed courtyard at the back of an inn. In a dramatic gesture Charcas threw off his poncho to reveal a glittering uniform, then stood on his seat and waited haughtily, his arms folded.

A curious face appeared at a window, then a few customers stepped out to see. Charcas declined to notice them. More came, filling the little courtyard. Then, taking a long and significant look about him, he proclaimed, 'Citizens of Buenos Aires! I am here at the peril of my life to bring you hope . . .'

His words swept over them, promises of glory and sacrifice, war and patriotism until the space rang with shouts of fire and ardour.

He drew himself up and looked about impressively. 'Who will then be first to enlist in the glorious Legión de Patricios Voluntarios Urbanos de Buenos Aires? With a purse of dollars each month and freedom to elect your own officers . . .'

A thrusting crowd pressed forward with a roar, and Charcas pointed at one individual. 'What is your name, sir?'

'Ah, Manuel Galvis, as it pleases you, sir,' the man said, whipping off his cap.

'Then it is now Sergeant Galvis. You shall take the details of all who will serve their country and I will come later to enlist them.'

A priest pushed through, frowning, but was carried along by the excitement and insisted on giving heaven's blessing to the uprising.

'We thank you, Father,' Charcas said, in dignified tones, 'and crave a further service.' This was to act as trusted intermediary between various units of the people's army, the British having issued special passes to priests to go about freely in ministering to their flock.

'And now as an earnest to the future – Sar'nt Galvis!'

'Sir!'

With a flourish he swung down and went to the rear of the cart, snatching away the loose hay to reveal the muskets, gleaming and deadly. 'Take these for your good men – be certain there's many more to come.'

In the sudden hush Charcas added, 'In your hands is the destiny of our great city. *Guerra al cuchillo! Mueran los ingleses!*'

When they met up again that evening, Charcas wore the black cloak Serrano remembered all too well but Serrano himself was still in his shabby and torn clothes. They slipped through the darkened and near deserted streets until, once more, he was before Rafaela.

'Find me some clothes, *mi ángel*,' he said importantly, at her wide-eyed apprehension. 'Tonight I'm about the work of the patriots.'

Looking at the impassive Charcas, she shivered. '*Mi querido*, you know what it is that—'

'The clothes!' Serrano demanded.

She returned with them, herself arrayed in a cape and hood.

'Rafaela – you cannot possibly—'

'I can go in places denied to a man. Will you stop me playing my part?'

The three hurried down the Calle Victoria to the mansion of Martín de Álzaga where they were hastily admitted.

'Señor Charcas,' the silver-haired man said softly. 'Is it planned?'

'I have word from Don Baltasar, now in amicable alliance with the royalists. It is . . . that you should proceed as planned.'

'Ah,' breathed Álzaga, 'I shall start hiring tomorrow. And who are these?' he added carefully.

'Servants of the fatherland!' Serrano said loudly, with a bow.

'I see.'

Charcas allowed a thin smile to show. 'Señor Álzaga is a rich man but he is dedicating his fortune to the glory of his country.'

'And to his honour,' Serrano blurted.

'He is funding the construction of a secret tunnel, which will begin under the seminary of St Francis – and will end under the barrack rooms of the soldiers. Thirty-six barrels of gunpowder will put an end to them as they sleep.'

'Wait for it . . . About *turn!*' Sergeant Dodd's effortless bellow echoed across the square to the lines of Royal Marines opposite. They stamped about crisply, their dress faultless. A few passers-by stopped to watch but most ignored them.

'*Companyyyyyy . . . halt!*' Dodd strode up and inspected them before reporting to Clinton with a quivering salute. The lieutenant acknowledged and, accompanied by Dodd, went over for an officer's inspection. That complete, Dodd stood before the men while Clinton reported to Kydd, who had emerged from the fort.

He went up and down the ranks, here and there giving words of praise and encouragement. 'A splendid body of men, Lieutenant. Carry on, please.'

The men marched off, Kydd receiving a magnificent salute from Dodd. The drill had been devised to give heart to the men, solid evidence that the world, while being out of joint, was still under discipline.

'A dish of tea, William?' Kydd offered.

Kydd's room was cheerless and cold, a fire now a luxury, and the two kept their coats buttoned.

'How goes it, then?'

Clinton paused before he answered. 'I'd be to loo'ard of the truth should I say we're improving our situation. Those on sentry-go are taunted daily and some even suffer rotten food thrown at them. They're being tempted by offers of women and employment if they desert – but no chance of that with our chaps, sir.'

'It's asking much of 'em, I believe, to stand alone on those far posts in the city. If things begin to . . .'

'They'll do their duty, sir, never fear.'

'If only those damnable reinforcements . . .'

They took their tea, the leaves used twice to eke them out, in silence. So close to the foreshore the miasma of rotting fish offal was always on the air, and the harsh cawing of a soaring condor sounded above the rumble of a passing cart.

'And they're changing – the people, I mean,' Clinton said. 'They're now openly contemptuous, defiant, hard to handle as a crowd.'

The young man was maturing fast: only in his early twenties, his face was acquiring lines of care and his voice now had the practised calm of authority. He and the fine long-service Dodd were a shining credit to their service and Kydd wished he could express this – but it would never do to say it.

'How are our Royal Blues bearing their lot? The short canny, I mean.'

Clinton gave a wry smile. 'They say as how they've always held our reasty pork is to be preferred over foreign kickshaws.'

They were reduced to picking the bread – going through the last of the hard-tack for insect life – and buying up voyage-end stores from merchant ships, but in the absence of provisions from up-country there was little else. Kydd knew the older marines were making light of conditions for the sake of the younger men.

An aide interrupted: 'Captain Kydd? General Beresford desires you should attend on him at convenience, sir.'

He rose, dreading what emergency it was this time.

Beresford sat moodily at his desk, twirling a quill, and looked up with a start when Kydd entered. 'Ah, Kydd. There's trouble afoot, I'm persuaded. One of our patrols found three stand of muskets in a house not far from here. Someone's arming the mob and it has to be stopped.'

'Have we any conceiving of how they're entering, sir?'

'No. I've doubled up on checkpoints into the city where we search everything – it must be by another route.'

'By sea.'

'It seems so,' Beresford said flatly.

Kydd was at a loss to know how to prevent this with nearly

all of his vessels blockading the far shore, but he replied, 'I'll do what I can, sir.'

Beresford nodded bleakly and Kydd took his leave.

It came to him as he made his way back to his office. Some thirty miles further down the coast there was a discreet landing place, Ensenada de Barragán, where in the past dutiable goods had been smuggled into the viceroyalty by that unofficial arrangement with the authorities.

But his little navy was now stretched out along the opposite coast, bar one ship in repair, *Protector*, and Hellard's *Stalwart*, in only that morning, her captain and crew exhausted after days in action. Rather than drive them to sea once more, Kydd's impulse was to spare them and do it himself.

'I'm taking *Stalwart* away,' he announced. 'Muster the Protectors as her crew.'

They put out into driving rain from the north-west and squally, spiteful winds, which kicked up an uncomfortable short sea against the incoming tide, yet having the advantage that it was fair for Barragán.

Stalwart was plainly built with few comforts but a snug 'mess-deck' had been fashioned within the cargo hold. In the way of sailors, it had all the touches of home in a space that would be spurned in a London rookery – racks against the side for mess utensils, hooks to take the ditty bags that held each individual's ready-use gear, mirrors and small ornaments, and forward a neat rectangular bin for stowed hammocks.

In accordance with Kydd's own standing orders, they stopped on the way and boarded the larger flat-bottomed fishing boats, a form of deterrence against contraband that was proving remarkably effective.

Then, as the wan sun was lowering over the flat and bleak shore, they came up with the maze of channels and shoals that was their objective. Off the point there were four vessels – a *sumaca*, a lugger and two *falucho*s, local craft, two-masted with a lateen and jib. Even as Kydd watched sail was hoisted and they were rapidly off downwind.

'A bad conscience,' grinned Dougal, *Stalwart*'s master's mate, who'd insisted on keeping an eye on his ship.

'We'll have that gaff higher,' Kydd snapped. These could either be innocents wary of pirates or, indeed, those they were looking for, but either way he had to stop them to prove the case.

The chase was played well by the Spanish. Fairly quickly they separated, the larger *sumaca* heading for deeper water offshore and the two *falucho*s shying from *Stalwart*'s progress to each side, the smaller lugger with its three masts beating hard into the wind and away. 'The *sumaca*,' Kydd decided, and they headed after it out to sea.

It didn't take long to discover that the bigger craft was making better speed, standing away in regular bursts of white until it was obvious they had lost the race. Kydd swore and turned to see where *falucho*s were. They had vanished.

It was impossible – but there was no sign of them. Feeling foolish, he called down the deck. 'Stalwarts, ahoy! Any who saw where the *falucho*s went, sing out.'

'Saw 'em down sail an' then go in a creek or some such,' a young lad said diffidently, touching his cap.

He pointed out where it had happened. The area had once been a watering place for ships but had gradually silted, the dark grey mud now extending for miles with an offshore island entrapped in its creeping embrace. An old coastal fort was some miles inland, possibly connected through channels, but the evening was well advanced and there was nothing for it but to leave further investigation for the morning light.

Taking position off the creek the anchor went down in two fathoms, the weather easing with the onset of night, and as the darkness crept in they snugged down for the long hours until morning.

Kydd had served in the Caribbean in *Seaflower*, a tiny cutter. There, the threats had been many and diverse, and now his old instincts came back to assert themselves. While there was light to see, he had the two bow carronades loaded and primed and the arms chest of cutlasses and pistols open and handy. A pair of lookouts took position fore and aft. Satisfied, he went below – not to the rabbit hutch of a captain's cabin but to the mess-deck with the soft light of its single oil lamp. The seamen looked up in surprise, then dismay. A post-captain, even in worn and faded sea rig, was a formidable being and now their stand-down time was set fair to be an awkward trial.

'Stand fast the puffery – we're all Stalwarts here,' Kydd said easily, taking a stool at the corner of the small table. 'What's for scran, cuffin?'

Easing into a smile, Dougal slid across the bread barge, a wicker basket that held pre-broken hard tack and carefully sliced cheese. Kydd took a piece of the wood-hard and greyish cheese and helped himself to the dry biscuit, which he calmly tapped on the table. No weevils emerged and he tucked in with appreciation, feeling the disbelieving eyes of the three foremast hands on him.

'We've the Dago biltong to follow,' piped up Beekman, a South African midshipman originally brought aboard *Diomede* in Cape Town. He hesitantly offered some to Kydd.

'Thank 'ee,' he said, with a grin, and set to on the dried beef strips. These were not the spicy, toothsome morsels of Africa he'd enjoyed but they would have to do. With no galley fire in a craft so diminutive there could be no coffee or piping hot *kai* – cocoa stripped from a chocolate block – until they made port once more but there was a welcome mug of grog: Kydd had insisted that it be included in the rations.

As the evening drew on, the talk eddied back and forth over the age-old sailorly concerns of wind and weather, the quality of Buenos Aires as a step-ashore port, the prospects for action. Inevitably it turned to the immediate future, and Beekman asked, 'Sir, if you please, things are in a pretty moil, you'll agree. What will happen to us if— ?'

'Don't pay any mind to that, m'lad,' Kydd said heartily. 'We've one parcel of Spanish locked up on the north shore and we've just beaten the other. All we've to do is hold out until the reinforcements arrive.'

'When's that, then, sir?' the young man said artlessly.

'Who's to say? Tomorrow, next week? On the way here the commodore sent dispatches from St Helena requesting 'em, which I saw with my own eyes. They'll be here shortly, never fear.'

Knowing that the rest of the table were behind him, the midshipman persisted. 'If'n Mr Liniers gets across and joins with the goochies, the Army'll be hard pressed to hold 'em. And if we can't get ships in close to give fire . . . '

Kydd nodded: these were no ignorant loobies and deserved an answer. 'If things go against us, we retire,' he said flatly. 'Take the Army off and return to Cape Town. No heroic last stands. Clear?'

It seemed to satisfy and he stretched and yawned. 'Well, I'm for my 'mick. I'll take a turn about the uppers and then get my head down. Dougal, I'm to be called the instant there's a change o' weather or tide.'

'Aye aye, sir.'

'Goodnight, then,' Kydd pronounced, and left for his customary sniff at the wind before sleep.

The weather had eased even further: there was nothing but a light offshore breeze and the pale dappling of wavelets. The moon was totally hidden behind low cloud that stretched in a sullen stillness in every direction, leaving a dull, uniform luminosity just sufficient to make out the low, scrubby shoreline.

He shivered. The thought came again that the sooner he was quit of this place the better. Then he paused for a moment, something subliminal touching his senses. The scene was blameless, a bird flapping on the sea the only disturbance, and nothing but a grey desolation of mud-flats and reeds.

Hairs prickled on his neck – there was something.

'Keep a bright lookout, you men,' he called, and stood for a space, listening intently. Nothing. Then something caught his eye along the shoreline to the left – he strained to see but couldn't make out anything, then tried the old lookout's ruse of looking off to one side to trick the eye into perceiving motion.

And then he saw. somewhere among the scruffy wooded inland, a barely perceptible spider-web-thin vertical line that moved. And, close by, another. He froze, trying to make sense of it. Then he had it.

'Get below and turn up the hands!' he barked. They tumbled up, confused and blinking.

'Sir?' Dougal said, with a bewildered look.

'The Spanish. They're in the channel under oars and mean to take us.' Too long the stalker, they had not imagined themselves to be prey – Kydd mentally took off his hat to the audacious commander who had looked to turn the tables on them.

It was their masts he had seen, unavoidably above the level of the undergrowth as they made their way stealthily out to the open water. The question now was whether to open fire as soon as they were visible or keep quiet to lure them near and to destruction.

But there was a big risk. If these two had soldiers to swell their boarders the Stalwarts might easily be overwhelmed. And if they were resolutely handled they could press home their attack through *Stalwart*'s 'broadside', which consisted only of the two carronades and two swivels. After that they were defenceless, apart from their small arms.

This implied a single course of action: allow the Spanish to believe their surprise had been successful, then open up with everything that could fire in a single devastating blast of shot. In the night it might be terrifying enough to deter the onslaught or, at the very least, to gain them enough time to reload.

'Silence fore 'n' aft!' Kydd snapped, and made his dispositions, having the men keep out of sight until his order. Each had a blade weapon and a brace of pistols with four muskets lying in the chest, while the oil lamp was suspended out of sight by rope yarns, ready to be lashed to the foremast as a fighting lantern for reloading the carronades.

There was little more he could do.

Water chuckled against the vessel's side, the wind dropping yet more to a cold night zephyr bringing a stillness that carried every sound in breathless clarity. The distant betraying slither and clunk of unmuffled oars on the air became plain as the two *falucho*s emerged from the channel and came around. Kydd gave a conspiratorial grin at Dougal, lying on the deck next to him – that would never do in a professional cutting-out expedition.

It was a half-mile of hard pulling for them; they could have hoisted sail and done it in less time but the sudden pale glimmer of canvas would have been an immediate giveaway. Kydd was content to let them tire themselves, the better to dull their fighting ardour.

At two hundred yards he hissed, 'Stand by!'

In the winter gloom men gripped their weapons, loosened pistols in readiness and tensed for the order.

'Fire!' Kydd roared.

The night was split apart by multiple flashes and concussion as ball, grape and musket fire hammered into the hapless *falucho*s, shrieks and shouts accompanying the mayhem. Slewing sideways the leader canted to one side, out of the fight, but the other stretched out frantically with the obvious intention of falling on *Stalwart* before her guns were reloaded.

The fighting lantern was in place but to go through the motions with sponge, rammer and charge was asking a lot of men who were half blinded by gun-flash. Kydd felt a creeping anxiety as the enemy craft came in fast, broad on their beam. An officer was shouting encouragement and foreign-sounding cheers came floating over the water.

Kydd saw the white face of Beekman looking back at him from forward, waiting on his decision. A gentle puff of the night breeze came; they were at anchor, stemming the slight current and—

'Get that mizzen hoisted!' he bellowed, in sudden conviction.

Startled, men turned in incomprehension.

'Now! Hoist the bugger!' His voice cracked with the effort, but it lashed them into movement. Two seamen clambered aft and helped him raise the ponderous sail. It flapped twice, then bellied, and under the leverage of sail aft on the anchor

forward, *Stalwart* obediently began swinging into the wind –
bows on to the approaching enemy.

It had worked! Now the target they offered was reduced
and, most important, under oars there was no easy coming
in to board at an angle amidships; instead they must either
grapple and come in over the bow by ones and twos or crab
around to get alongside while under fire the whole time.

They chose the bows.

With three men on muskets and pistols and two reloading,
Stalwart did what she could but a grapnel came sailing in and
hauled the craft together, the other bowsprit spearing over
their fore-deck until the two were awkwardly locked side by
side. With a roar of triumph the enemy boarders crowded
forward.

Throwing aside their empty pistols the defenders drew their
cutlasses and, with bared teeth, dared them to try. The first
two ran out on the bowsprit – if *Stalwart* had had pikes they
would have been dead men – and with sword points extended
they leaped down either side, then raced for the defenders.

Kydd had four men in a line across the wider part of the
triangular fore-deck and the two closed with a vicious clash
of steel. Dougal took one and Kydd the other but, behind,
two more were jumping down and Kydd was aware of the
set-faced petty officer beside him lunging forward to meet
them, and a vague impression of their fourth giving savage
blows to one side before he was swallowed in the
confusion.

His opponent had an old-fashioned rapier, which flicked
about like a snake's tongue, searching for an opening, its
lightness giving it deadly speed while Kydd's snatched-up
cutlass seemed heavy and unresponsive.

In the flickering pool of light, the fight was brutal and

with no quarter possible – but they had to hold the line: no more enemy boarders could make it on to the crowded deck while they did so, and their attackers knew it, throwing themselves forward in a frenzy of violence, stabbing, hacking, smashing.

As he parried and slashed, a tiny part of Kydd's mind coolly told him he was right: this ferocity owed its intensity to the need to stop a secret being spilled, which could only be the point of entry of the arms smuggling.

His momentary lapse in concentration was punished by the sight of the pitiless features of his opponent as the rapier pierced his defences in a lunge to his face. He reflexively tried to avoid the blade but it hissed through his collar and he felt its hot burn along his neck. Instinctively he twisted away – it brought pressure on the rapier blade, impeding its withdrawal, and Kydd desperately brought his cutlass in a wide slash across towards the belly. The man pulled back – and tripped, falling full length, and Kydd was on him, the heavy cutlass swinging down and laying the man's body open in a welter of blood and viscera.

In a split second Kydd trampled over the body and thrust his bloody cutlass at the one bearing down on Dougal. The man swung to meet him but Dougal's blade transfixed his side – in this morbid hackery there was no space for the gallantries of the fencing code and he whirled around to meet one about to impale him from behind. His blade at parry, something made the man hesitate – Kydd pressed his advantage and his opponent stumbled backwards against the low bulwark to topple over the side.

The sound of the plunge was loud against the grunts, steel clashing and slithers that filled the air. Thinking, perhaps, that his comrades were abandoning the fight and swimming for their lives, one made the fatal mistake of looking over his shoulder and was cut down in an instant; another turned and ran, and a last leaped over the side.

There were more in the *falucho* but they hesitated. A figure bravely darted past Kydd and began sawing at the grapnel line with his midshipman's dirk. It fell free, the craft swinging clear, but with their boarders out of the line of fire there was a last vengeful burst of musketry from the enemy. In the vicious whip of bullets, Kydd's upraised blade took a ball squarely, with a numbing clang that caused him to drop it in pain but, with a sudden flash, their starboard carronade had banged out and a storm of grape tore into the men opposite, throwing them aside like bloody skittles.

It was the end of the fight: the *falucho*, out of control, drifted away, leaving the Stalwarts to count the cost.

There were two enemy dead, one seaman on his hands and knees rocking with pain, another biting off gasps as a shipmate bound his forearm – and the huddled form of Beekman still forward. Kydd hurried over but by the sputtering light of the lamp it was obvious his wound was mortal: even as the midshipman had knelt at his ship-saving task, a ball had struck in at the shoulder and raked down into his body.

The lad's consciousness was slipping, his eyes flicking from one side to the other, desperately scrabbling for life. Kydd tried to cradle the absurdly slight body while the last battle was fought, his heart wringing at the pity of it. A sudden spasm seized the boy in a paroxysm of desperation but when it had left – so had his life.

Chapter 12

The sound of Kydd's steps echoed from the stone stairs as he made his way yet again to the roof parapets of the fort. He stood and looked out to the restless grey water, with its limitless horizon, feeling for the freedom and contentment of the open sea.

With every fibre of his soul he wanted to be quit of the place, with its mood of foreboding and treachery; the monotony of the flat, endless landscape; the inescapable stink of mud and animals; the pinched rations and strained faces; the tedium of waiting and keeping his flotilla at their vital blockade until relief finally came.

He thought of brave little Beekman, who would leave his bones here, never again to see the grand sight of Cape Town's Table Mountain and the sun-splashed veld. In his sea life Kydd had seen countless tragedies and had acquired a detachment that usually kept him distant, but Beekman had got under his guard. Such a pitiable waste.

Swallowing, Kydd forced himself to concentrate as he made his usual appraisal of the weather. The glass was falling but too little to worry about, the winds gusty and sulky from the north-east, not a concern for the blockade of Colonia. Moreover, the mud-flats close by were under water, ensuring there was navigability around the Chico Bank. There was no telling, however, in these duplicitous waters: he had heard of one occasion when, with an adverse wind, the incoming tide had actually been cowed into retreating, leaving the whole River Plate a vast mud-flat, shore to shore.

He turned to go, but hesitated at what he saw developing inland to the south-west. A peculiar roll of cloud, separate from the rest, stretched for miles and had a dark, unhealthy hue. It put him in mind of the Southerly Buster, a phenomenon he had once been caught up in some years ago off Australia: it had the vicious trick of advancing with high winds from one direction, then whipping round to attack an unfortunate ship from the opposite direction.

When he wandered back up just before noon to check, it was considerably nearer, a peculiar uniform long tube of brown-grey, slowly and ominously rolling forward. Under its baneful influence the winds before it faded, bringing an oppressive humidity and the feral apprehension that always came before a storm.

Kydd thought of his little band of vessels on their ceaseless patrol against the far shore. At the sight of this kind of weather he himself would be taking full storm precautions, no matter how big his vessel. Should he call off the blockade and bring them all safely back to port? If this was a harmless local phenomenon he would be risking all, for Liniers with his superior knowledge of these parts would jump at the chance of a breakout. No: he must leave it to the judgement of his captains.

At two, however, it became clear that this was no trivial

weather spat. The rolling cloud was nearly overhead and behind it hung a dark pall. In nearby buildings wooden shutters had been hastily fastened, the last people abroad were hurrying home and all small craft had vanished.

And not one of his little fleet had returned. They had chosen to stay at their post – but if it was the same species of tempest he'd encountered in Australia, would they know of the fiendish wind reversal? Even if they survived they'd be thrown on a deadly lee-shore, driven in by the bluster, and—

A heavy concussion, so loud it shook the stonework of the fort, startled Kydd. Not far out on his right a fork of lightning burst on his senses – then another, leaping between the clouds in hideous display. A further avalanche of thunder pealed out, nearly deafening him.

In the breathless atmosphere it was a devil's display of malice, intense blue-white lightning arcing down in strikes seconds apart, the smell of sulphur clear on the air. Then a squall buffeted him, a chill and malevolent blast – from the south! The wind swung back, fretful and restless, before another southerly gust caught him, pummelling with a force that increased all the time.

Then came the rain. Gusty torrents and afterwards a hammering roar of heavy drops that quickly became a deluge, driving Kydd to take shelter in a corner. His last sight of the sea was of a perfect fury of whiteness. It was a fight for life that now faced his navy, out there somewhere.

Another stupefying round of thunderclaps burst overhead, this time accompanied by a volley of hailstones as big as musket balls that rushed and clattered violently about. Kydd retreated, hurrying back down the steps, now echoing with the storm's frenzy, and returned to his desk. The view from the window was a blur of grey and white through the sheeting rain on the glass, the muted drone and scream of the wind, quite different from the open howl through bare rigging at sea, and his heart went out to the seamen facing the worst in this chaos.

For hours the tempest beat about them, from dead south to more in the west, a flat, hard, savage blast that numbed the senses with its roar and venom.

Kydd was unable to work and sat staring at his papers. Here he was in the warm and dry while others fought for their lives. And was *L'Aurore* in good hands? He knew Gilbey as a tarpaulin to be sensitive to weather moods but for the same reason he could be relied on to make no concessions to comfort and the frigate would be lying to two anchors, jibbing like a frightened horse at the onrush of frenzied seas.

Kydd dozed at his desk but was wide awake at the first sign of light before the winter dawn. The storm had diminished to a sullen bluster, cold and heartless, but the rain had thankfully ceased. The sea was in a fret and restless, and wherever he peered there was no sight of distant sails. Clutching an oilskin to himself he went outside and looked towards the mole to see one craft alongside, and one poling itself in. Just two.

He pretended to exercise, pacing up and down the foreshore in the mud, among the seaweed and debris thrown up, his oilskin ballooning and the cold wind piercing, but of his seven vessels, by mid-morning there was only one further arrival. Unable to keep up the pretence, he returned to the fort but was shortly summoned back.

'Um, just beyond the point, sir,' a soldier said, stolidly leading. It was as Kydd had dreaded. Some way out there was the low, untidy black outline of a washed-up wreck with two figures picking at it. With a catch in his throat he started out to it.

'Oi, sir, don't you . . .' began the soldier, but Kydd was not to be stopped and squelched on over the mud, then into the heavily discoloured water until he reached the pathetic remains, shattered and tangled with seaweed-strewn rope.

'*Stalwart*, sir,' said a petty officer from the fort.

'Any . . . ?'

'Two on 'em only, sir,' the man said, pointing to the foreshore where tarpaulin-covered bodies lay, which he'd overlooked in his haste. He sloshed back and, with the soldier gravely watching, he carefully pulled back the covering on one.

Dougal. Master's mate. The pallor of death but a calm face, a trace of wistful sadness that was so touching in one on the threshold of manhood. Kydd tenderly covered it again.

The other was Lieutenant Hellard, utterly determined to succeed in his first command. His features were heavily bruised but not enough to hide the bitter indignation, the rage at Fate that had been his final emotion.

Kydd turned away. This cursed place was touching so many lives. He felt hatred rising as he stalked back, trailing mud and water into the fort.

In his office he heard the reports of the three vessels that had survived, listening with compassion as the officers recounted their ordeal.

The hard truth of the matter was that two might be made fit for sea but the third was little more than a wreck, brought back by sheer bull-headed courage and matchless skill.

Two – to stand before Colonia and the massing Spanish

Army. It was impossible, but the imperatives of war dictated he try.

Conscious of their tired and strained faces, Kydd nevertheless spoke firmly: 'That's a grim tale, which I'm sure'll be told in every wardroom in the fleet – but here's the rub. You're the only ones left to me. We have to make a showing off Colonia or the Dons will take heart and try a crossing.

'Gentlemen, I desire you'll get your craft ready for sea by any means you can contrive. In two hours you'll put out for Colonia and the blockade where you'll stay to the last biscuit, drop of water and shot. They must not sail! Do you understand me?'

He did what he could, finding seamen to bear a hand with repairs, soldiers to help with the storing and watering, and any small thing he could think of that might in any way make their lot more bearable.

When he went back to his desk a hovering clerk said apologetically, 'Sir, a Mr Serrano t' see you – seems very anxious an' all.'

'Show him in,' Kydd said. That the artist was daring to come to the fort and risk being taken for a spy in the pay of the British must indicate some urgency.

'Good in you to come, Mr – er, Señor Serrano. A tea, perhaps?' The young man was rumpled and unshaven but had an intensity about him, an exaltation even.

'No! Captain Keed – no time. I will tell you, ver' important. I come as quick as I can. Gen'ral Liniers, he coming! He trick you – while your ships scatter because of the storm he's to make a crossing over.'

'When?' Kydd breathed, his tiredness vanishing in a flash.

'Is not when, is where. Not from Colonia del Sacramento, there he knows you will see him. No, he march forty mile along to Punta Pavón. At there is deeper, an' ship can come in close. He can load up his boats wi' soldiers quickly, you cannot see him.'

Kydd rummaged for his largest-scale chart and found the spot, a third of the way back to Montevideo. Sure enough, there was a tongue of three- or four-fathom water the other side of the Ortiz Bank, coming to within a short distance of the uninhabited coast.

'Ships – how's he going to get them, without we see them move from Colonia?' Kydd snapped, cudgelling his mind to take in the implications of the all-too-possible stratagem.

'He leave them there, an' you think he will still cross. He brings boats from Montevideo, many.'

'Mr Serrano, I need to know – when?'

'Not more an' two days. This I hear from the general talking.'

Kydd slumped in despair. Only two to set against a probable armada, and they a good sixty miles off in still rough conditions. And in two days . . .

'This is hard news, Mr Serrano. Are you very sure of what you heard?'

'Is so, sir.'

'And . . . you're telling me the truth, that is to say, no twisters? Do you swear to it?'

'I say it true,' the young man said, set and pale.

'Oh, I'm not saying your flamming me,' Kydd said hastily. 'It's just as how I must now change plans at the gallop.'

'They come, I swear it.'

Kydd looked into the burning eyes, then eased into a smile. 'Thank you, Mr Serrano, I believe you. Can we find you some refreshment? You must be—'

'I go now,' he whispered, and slipped away.

Kydd tried to marshal his thoughts. He should go immediately to Beresford with the news and the grave admission that the Navy was powerless to stop Liniers; the general would have to improvise his own defences, but if only he could report to him with –

Something stirred at the back of his mind. He peered again at the chart. The tongue of deeper water was indeed an extension of the indented sea passage that gave Montevideo its ocean access – the sparse soundings were probably unreliable but it was worth a try. Animated, he snatched up the dividers and stepped it out. Forty-eight miles. Possible.

He shouted for the master's mate. 'Rouse out our fastest dispatch boat – I've orders for *L'Aurore* frigate as will need it to fly.'

It would be a close-run thing but if the frigate met Liniers's invasion at sea it would be a massacre. Grinning savagely, he dashed off the order that would have the frigate rendezvous off Punta Pavón with his remaining two *sumaca*s, *Staunch* and *Protector*. Sobering, he took another sheet and carefully outlined the situation for Popham, setting out his reasoning for working the frigate up to the embarkation point even if it meant stranding the vessel, helpless on the mud between tides.

It would exercise Gilbey considerably to lighten the ship to the extreme as well as the tricky task of feeling his way through the shoals and banks.

Was there anything else? Yes – he should make some showing off Colonia to assure the Spanish that he was still there and blockading, for if they suspected he knew of the real embarkation point they would revert back and no frigate could make it up that far. There was just one snag – he didn't have a ship for the task.

In frustration he stood up and looked out over the open

roadstead before the city. There was a huddle of small fry and one or two larger craft – like the fine-lined schooner close in and the European-looking ship-rigged merchantman. Circumstances demanded a desperate remedy – but what he was contemplating was little more than piracy.

When the master's mate returned, Kydd was ready. 'I want a party of twenty good seamen. Arm them and let me know when they're mustered.'

'Aye aye, sir!'

It was done. Now, with his orders safely on their way across the storm-torn waters, it was time to let Beresford know what he had in mind.

The general smiled thinly. 'I can only suppose you are aware of the legal niceties, Captain. If there is a disinclination to assist and you have a confrontation then there's nothing I can do to intervene or, indeed, shield you from the rigours of the law should they press suit.'

Kydd bit his tongue. That Beresford was honourable and upright was well known; that his high principles would prevent him giving his support to an action that would save his situation was taking it to absurdity.

'I understand, sir,' he replied evenly. 'You have my word there'll be no contravention of the law.'

He had until those ships were boarded to think of something . . .

The men were waiting when he returned. 'Ask the duty lieutenant to join us with our usual interpreter cove,' he ordered, surveying his party. These were good men, volunteers out of the big ships and reliable.

The lieutenant appeared, out of breath. 'L'tenant Herrick. Sorry, sir, I—'

'Stand easy, sir. I've something to say.'

He turned to the little group and stood in an uncompromising quarterdeck brace. 'If you men are the kind of prime hands I think you are, looking for a frolic at the expense of the Dons, then today you'll get your fill. I've word General Liniers thinks to cross secretly from another place. Only we can stop him and it may turn out to be a first-rate dusting.

'Now, *L'Aurore* frigate is on her way to dispute with him. We've *Staunch* and *Protector* but need more sail and I've a notion where we'll find it.'

He had their full attention and as he outlined his plan it turned to a fierce glee. 'I'll repeat – no man to raise a weapon unless he gets my personal order. Clear?'

Diadem's launch was manned, Kydd himself taking the tiller, and they pulled for the schooner.

There were no colours evident – he would have to play this carefully.

'Schooner, ahoy!' he hailed. A frightened face appeared above a hatch coaming. 'I'm coming aboard!'

Her low freeboard allowed him to step directly on to her deck and he wasted no time. 'What flag?' he demanded, miming the hoisting of one.

'Ai-ya, Portuguee!'

Kydd heaved a sigh of relief. The Portuguese were neutral – but this was no Portuguese vessel. In his experience they still continued the old custom of the prominent display of a crucifix on the after-deck to which every officer and seaman made passing obeisance, and here the deck was bare. More tellingly, in his capacity as port captain, he had not heard of any such seeking clearance, their canny merchants keeping well away until the situation was settled. This had to be a local trader seeking to evade port dues.

He addressed the launch: 'L'tenant Herrick and five, if y' please.' From below two more bemused crewmen appeared and then an apprehensive officer. 'Inform this man of who I am, that I suspect his vessel of illegal entry to Buenos Aires,' he told his interpreter. 'And that I'm impounding it forthwith.'

It was unheard of to have the captain of the port himself board a harmless trader at the head of an armed party, but it had the desired effect. The officer babbled nervously, then waited while the interpreter said, 'He say he forget t' get his paper sign. Isn't there some way he can . . . ?'

'Possibly,' Kydd said, stroking his chin. 'Has he a cabin where we can talk?'

Some minutes later he came back on deck and, with a smile, made a mock bow to Herrick. 'L'tenant, this is your new command. I wish you to ship guns and make motions before Colonia until relieved. Good luck.'

Now for the larger ship: it would add presence and should, with its row of false gun-ports, give pause to any troop-laden vessel.

It was anchored further out and the launch began shipping water from the still-boisterous seas. Resolutely they pressed on until they made its lee – but Kydd had noticed that this ship was an altogether different matter: its red flag with three vertical crowns proclaimed it a Danziger, which he remembered hazily was nominally under the Grand Duchy but in practical terms a fief of Prussia, disputed by Poland.

There was no other in sight that was as substantial and he had no alternative but to go through with it. As the boathook seized the main-chains he grabbed the man-rope and hauled himself over the gunwale – to be confronted by a bull of man who stood with his arms folded and feet planted on the deck.

'Kydd, captain of the port of Buenos Aires,' he said, in crisp tones. 'You are the captain?'

'*Ja.*'

'Papers,' Kydd said, making riffling motions.

They were produced in the old-fashioned saloon. As far as Kydd's experienced eye could tell, they were faultless. And flourished last, like a trump card, were the entry papers to Buenos Aires, signed by Kydd's own staff.

He snatched one up. 'This charter party admits you're trading with Spain, sir.'

Another paper was slapped down. It was a form of release, signed in florid detail by the Danzig authorities and counter-signed with margin notes by the British consul there.

'Nevertheless, Captain, you have attempted to land cargo out of bond contrary to port regulations and I must therefore—'

'I haf not broken bulk.'

The bald statement was irrefutable: if the freight had not been broached then the cargo was in the same legal position as that of any ship with part retained for the next port and therefore not subject to duty or exaction.

'I jus' wait for th' Spanische to take back Buenos Aires.'

Kydd had been inclined to let him go, but this remark made him smoulder. A mischievous thought broke in – but if it went wrong there was no going back. 'Sir – I have reason to believe you have been engaged in commerce with France, a belligerent power, in violation of your status.'

A look of open astonishment was quickly replaced by one of contempt. 'So! You vill search me?'

'Yes,' Kydd snapped, and got up abruptly. If he was wrong

in his estimate of the man, it would be nothing short of disastrous. He went up on deck and motioned to his men to come aboard. He whispered instructions to Bolt, the petty officer in charge, then stood back.

Instead of heading for the monkey-hatch to the hold forward, Bolt went straight to the master's cabin, closely followed by the Prussian, who was now spluttering with anger. Ignoring him, the men looked for the small hatch let into the deck in which all captains kept private provisions. It was opened, and Bolt dropped into the little store-room – and, to Kydd's intense relief, passed up three bottles. Of best French cognac, not the usual schnapps.

'Another three down there, sir,' Bolt called up helpfully.

Kydd allowed a look of grave displeasure. 'Sir, I have proof positive that you have been in breach of the law. It is now my duty—'

'*Gott in Himmel* – is for my use on voyage!'

'Half a case? And more elsewhere I dare to say?' Kydd said darkly. 'No, sir. This will not do. Cognac is not to be obtained without you trade with the enemy. I think we must talk together, don't you?'

Well before sunset, standing out beyond the Chico Bank, a small group of odd-looking ships under the flag of King George's Navy made a brave sight, bound for rendezvous off Punta Pavón.

But for Kydd the feeling of elation had faded.

The cold reality was that there were only two effectives, *Staunch* and *Protector*. The schooner was off Colonia and the Danzig merchantman would be there but only as a hired vessel to sail about looking fierce and not to engage directly. Could they stand fast before the unknown number of ships that Liniers had been able to muster? *L'Aurore* had been summoned, but could she be relied upon to navigate the banks and shoals in time?

In his borrowed hammock in the saloon, sleep evaded Kydd. In the morning much would be decided. Into his mind came images of the unforgettable spectacle that he had witnessed – only the previous year – of Nelson's fleet at Trafalgar sailing to glory as they defended England against invasion. Here he was, an admiral of his little fleet, in much the same position. Would he fail, succeed or die in the attempt?

At dawn they made landfall down the coast and spent the morning working up towards Punta Pavón. The shoreline was flat, drab-brown and monotonous, and without any sign of settlement. With tension building by the hour, they approached the point until a little before midday they raised the slight foreland – and not a sail in sight.

It was inconceivable that they had failed to make contact with a wide-scattered flotilla heading for Buenos Aires on the direct course they had taken so the ships and boats for the crossing had not yet arrived from Montevideo. They were in time.

But there was no sign of *L'Aurore*. If the transports and their escorts made their appearance it would go hard for them, but there was nothing he could do about it, other than be prepared to sacrifice them all in an attempt to deter the crossing.

While they waited there was no point in uselessly sailing back and forth and he ordered an anchoring with doubled lookouts.

An hour passed – two. Kydd climbed the stumpy shrouds and scanned the hinterland with his pocket telescope. He saw nothing – the Spanish Army was either on its way, out of sight inland or well concealed.

For now he sent away boats to take soundings all round with the hand lead to give him a picture of their room for manoeuvre, which turned out to be little enough outside their length of deeper water.

Evening drew in, and Kydd deployed the two *sumaca*s to the south by turns during the hours of darkness to give warning of the approach of the enemy, then stood his men down. Another endless night began, condemning him to the sleeplessness of tension and worry.

When a wan sun rose the next morning, it revealed a waste of cold grey but nothing else. He sent the men to breakfast but could not face his own greasy offering and remained on deck, gazing resentfully at the shore.

In the middle of the morning the situation changed completely.

'*Sail hooooo!*'

Heart bumping, Kydd leaped for the shrouds and trained his glass southwards. Barely visible against the cheerless murk was a sight that he could never mistake: the topsails of *L'Aurore* frigate.

It was a wonderful, glorious vision that pricked at his eye: she was under triple-reefed sails and moving slowly ahead, on either bow two boats leading. And no one could deny that she was quite inexpressibly, breathtakingly beautiful.

She came to in the Danziger's lee, correctly recognising Kydd's flag in the bluff merchantman as the senior. He wasted no time in going to her. Blank-faced, the boatswain piped him aboard with what seemed her entire company watching on.

'Well done, Mr Gilbey. You're in time for our little party,' he said, unable to stop himself shaking hands heartily with his first lieutenant. Behind him was Curzon and beyond him Renzi, watching gravely.

'We're glad t' have you back aboard, sir. It's been a rare trial.' Judging from Gilbey's grey face, it had been a nightmare of responsibility for him.

'Officers to muster in ten minutes, if you please – in my cabin.' That longed-for – yearned-for – familiar haven with all its comforts and appointments.

'Dear brother – if you'll pardon my remarking it, your appearance gives pause to all who love you.'

'Oh?' Kydd said. 'Well, Nicholas, I have to confess to some difficult times – er, I do have to say, this claret tastes like nectar of the gods,' he added.

'Just so. We've been hearing rumours concerning conditions in the city that are a mort unsettling. Do you wish to talk, at all?'

'Not now, old bean. The Spanish are mounting a counter-attack. Here – we're to stop them joining with their friends the gauchos on the far side.'

'Then they're not yet persuaded of the felicities of British administration?'

Kydd put down his glass sharply. 'I know how you feel about the commodore and his scheme but I'm to tell you we're seeing this through, b' God.'

'I have my reservations, yes, but they don't prevent me offering my services to you in these . . . entangled times. As you know, I have the Spanish and—'

'Thank you, Nicholas, that's well said. I'm bound to tell you, however, we've enough Spanish speakers and, er, more mouths to feed would be unwelcome, I believe.'

Kydd, however, saw the sincerity and tried to make amends. 'I'm sorry I haven't had time to bear more of a fist with your novel, m' friend, it's just been so—'

'Pay no mind to it, brother. It's done – that is, complete.'

'Finished! Well, now, and you're to be truly congratulated, old fellow!' Kydd said warmly. 'Um, what happens next as will see you a copper-bottomed author at all?'

Renzi gave a half-smile. 'To be truthful, I'm not so sure. A pile of papers into which I've put my heart and soul means a lot to me, but will it to the world?'

'There's only one way to find out,' Kydd said firmly.

'I know. That's why I took the opportunity to send it off in a mail with *Narcissus* and the bullion.'

'What? Without you have some lawyer cove draw you up a legal thing as will save you from plaguey copyists and so forth?'

'I'll have you know the business is too complex by half. It has to be entered at Stationer's Hall and, um, other things, which I'm not to be expected to know, and so I've placed it all in the hands of Mr John Murray with instructions that he may do with it as he will in my interests.'

Kydd sat back, appalled. 'So if he prints it, he may set his own price on the book and give you naught but a pauper's bauble. I'm bound to say it seems to me a wry way to proceed, Nicholas.'

Renzi drew himself up. 'Mr Murray is a gentleman. It's done,' he said defensively, 'and nothing more to be said.'

There was an awkward pause, so he went on, in a different tone, 'Then you are receiving satisfaction from Mr Serrano? A young man of some ardour it would seem.'

'We are.' Kydd chuckled. 'In fact, it was his timely warning that told us of this Spanish trickery. Now, time presses, my friend, and I have to see my officers before the battle.'

Almost light-hearted, he brought them together and explained the situation. The more he spoke the better he felt; even with a warship of comparable strength present to oppose them, *L'Aurore* would put paid to any sally by Liniers.

'Any questions?'

'Sir, when will—'

Curzon never finished the sentence as clear above their talking came the urgent hail of the masthead lookout.

Sail! Kydd leaped to his feet and pounded up to the quarterdeck, fumbling for his glass, which he had up as soon as he could see the southern horizon. At first he couldn't spot anything and began searching more carefully – until the master pointed out that the sail was actually to the north.

Puzzled, he swivelled round and focused in the other direction. In a few minutes he made out that it was a lone sail and schooner-rigged. It couldn't be – but it was. Herrick had abandoned his place off Colonia and was heading towards them at a great clip.

Through his glass Kydd saw that the schooner's sails were ragged with holes, and pockmarks of shot-strike showed dark against the hull. With a growing sense of dread, he waited.

'Captain Kydd, sir?' Herrick's voice floated across the water, its edge of urgency clutching at Kydd's heart.

'Yes?'

The schooner rounded to, brailing up.

'Sir, I've news! The Dons have sortied from Colonia! I did my best but so many . . .'

'Say again!' Kydd shouted down at the powder-stained and bandaged figure, more for time to think.

'I have it from a prisoner that they sailed together for Las Conchas. I brought 'em to action but only winged a few. I thought it my duty to acquaint you without delay.'

Shocked to the core, Kydd felt desolation and fury. There could be only one possible explanation for what had happened: he had been utterly and comprehensively deceived. Cynically betrayed by Serrano, decoyed away from the true crossing point – and now the fate of Buenos Aires was sealed.

Chapter 13

'You've just missed him, sir,' Clinton said. 'He's marched out to meet the Spanish advance.'

Keyed up to explain himself to the general, Kydd searched the marine officer's face but saw no condemnation, pity or contempt. 'Did he leave any orders for me?' he asked.

'None, sir.'

Apparently when Liniers had made his crossing he had joined very quickly with Pueyrredón's gauchos, the *blandengues* and others, and was now advancing on Buenos Aires.

Beresford had wanted to deal with the threat as soon as possible, and had stripped the city of most of its troops and left for the north at a rapid pace. With the number of his field guns much increased by earlier captures, with the discipline and experience of the Highlanders on the battlefield, there was every hope that, even heavily outnumbered, he could at least cause a halt in the advance and gain time for the reinforcements to arrive.

Kydd looked around. The fort was near deserted, the only

men those on guard duty. 'Then who is the garrison commander?'

Clinton grinned awkwardly. 'I do confess it's me, and if it's orders you seek, then they are that I desire you tell me what happened.'

Kydd took a seat. 'I did what I thought right at the time,' he said defiantly, lifting his chin. 'And I vow I'd do it again, should I have the same information as then.'

He had no need to justify himself to his junior lieutenant of marines – but he wanted to get it off his chest, and he suspected Clinton had realised this.

'Whoever gave Serrano his false-hearted lay knew what he was about, and no time for me to send reconnaissance to verify – and it had to be a strike with all my ships. So they came up with a convincing enough tale and a likely place on the chart, and I was gulled.'

He glowered for a moment and added, with heat, 'And that bloody dog did swear on his honour to the truth of it, may his soul roast in hell.'

'Just so, sir,' Clinton said, leaning forward in sympathy.

'It's done, and there's nothing more to be said about it,' Kydd concluded bitterly. 'And who's to say – with a bare handful of sail left to me, would we have prevailed?'

Consumed by restlessness and frustration, he stood and paced about the room. 'There has to be something the Navy can do.'

'There's the Royal Blues, sir. They're with the general now and he's openly declared they're worth a battalion in the field.'

Kydd didn't answer. This was not the best use of a navy – he could think of countless devastating exploits that had changed the course of many a campaign, from bombardment

314

with the equivalent of a regiment of artillery to daring raids by marines.

There was nothing for it – he couldn't just sit around waiting.

'I'm to go to the general, I believe.'

He found Beresford at the edge of the city, with his troops at rest but drenched after yet another heavy rain squall. He looked up dully, his eyes tired and bloodshot. 'Yes, Captain?'

'General, I came to offer my most earnest apologies for—'

'For Liniers's crossing? Don't be. Do you really think you're the first commander to be betrayed by false intelligence? No, sir. I've always thought it to be the mark of a leader that he makes his determination on the best evidence, acts on it and, if it goes against him, does not repine.'

Kydd felt a surge of both anguish and warmth that the man who must take the consequences of his decision had not held it against him.

'Sir, is there any service we can perform for you? Even carronades on our smaller vessels might—'

'Thank you, no,' Beresford muttered. 'Do you see there?' He pointed ahead to where the heavily rutted stony road gave way to a puddled quagmire of red mud. 'After that frightful rain there's no point in trying to haul guns through that, still less the bogs beyond they're pleased to call pasture. No, Kydd, I have my own decision to make and that as harsh as the one you faced.'

'Sir?'

'I will teach you something of military affairs: that all strategy fails if the gods decree that nature aligns with the enemy.

'Consider – we defeated the Spanish and their superior

cavalry numbers in the field because we deployed in line and square as needs must, and none may stand against us. In going as bad as this – aught but a wretched swampy mire – our infantry will struggle hopelessly in the mud. Not so the enemy, for horses will make light of such. Should I send my columns forward, they will find it impossible to move rapidly when necessary in order to draw up in square. My brave fellows will therefore be cut to pieces by their cavalry.'

'You must fall back.'

'To retreat? My duty as I see it is to play out the game to gain every hour I can for those wretched reinforcements to come. Not to mention what a regrettable effect it would have on morale – on Highlanders not accustomed to retreat and on the city, which sees us cowed by General Liniers and his host.'

'Um, then hold position here, sir, deny the enemy entry to Buenos Aires.'

'Even that will not be possible. In a city of this size any half-competent commander will try to circle around our rear and cut us off while they retake it, and General Liniers is a wily sort. French – did you know that? In the Spanish service these thirty years, fought against us before the Revolution.'

'Sir, I beg you'll tell me what else is possible,' Kydd said uncomfortably.

'Nothing. Of these alternatives I must choose the least bad.

'At one extreme I could fall back in the face of impossible odds, leave Buenos Aires to the Spanish and quit the country, but this can never be in consideration. At the other, I could move forward to endeavour to inflict as much damage on Liniers as I can but at grievous cost. This also is not to be contemplated, not for the pity of the thing but that I'd then have too few to garrison the city.'

'Therefore?'

Beresford shook his head sadly. 'Therefore I choose to contest his entry with half my force, the other half to return and secure the city.

'Colonel Pack, sir!' he called out.

Kydd knew what was being said. This was a fighting retreat but a retreat for all that. Liniers would have parties out probing, thrusting, and must eventually drive a wedge in Beresford's forward elements, causing it to fall back by stages. The only saving grace was that even he could see that city streets were not the place for cavalry and the two armies would in these terms at least be on a level footing.

As far as naval support went, a battlefield hidden among the streets would make targeting from seaward out of the question – an impossibility. But surely there must be tasks for the Navy to do.

When Beresford had concluded his dispositions he cast one long look about him, exchanged deep-felt salutes with Pack, his forward commander, then moved off with half of his men, some five hundred-odd only – less than a single battalion to hold a modern city.

The column marched off to the sound of a defiant piper, joined by another until, heads high, the proud Scots were swinging along as if on parade before the world. As the suburbs became denser, so did the onlookers. This time there was little curiosity, only a sullen, hostile stare. From balconies came cat-calls and jeers, then ugly shouts that had an edge of contempt.

There was now a different mood: a surging restlessness, a tension that radiated out from tight knots of people. Others hurried to distance themselves.

In another interminable rain flurry they at last halted by the colonnades of the Plaza Mayor outside the fort.

Kydd followed Beresford, and a conclave of officers was hastily convened; Clinton was appointed second-in-command after Captain Arbuthnot for the internal security of the city.

Beresford went off to begin his dispatches, and Kydd settled down to the task of finding work for the Navy. The front line would need supply: provisions, rum, gunpowder. What better than to ship it in as the line moved forward or back? It would need escort, and his newly released *Staunch* and *Protector* could do the job.

And just as important was the sea guard, protection of the Army from seaward raids. And then, of course, operations against the enemy's own supply lines. As well there was . . . but where was he going to get the hulls? Or the crews – so many good ships and seamen had been lost in the storm.

It was becoming difficult to concentrate – he had been shifted into Clinton's office to make way for others: Beresford wanted as many as possible brought inside the fort's walls.

A subaltern arrived and reported to Clinton that the sentries who had been posted at key points were being harassed – taunted, muskets stolen, threatened. Kydd felt for the young men out on their own in this treacherous and alien place but they had a vital part to play. If they withdrew, they would be giving up the city to the enemy.

His own concerns claimed his attention again. Provisions in the cask were heavy and cumbersome; water was a critical matter. How many barrels could be stacked on, say, those flat fishing craft? He could seize a few and set up a running supply-line, and be damned to the noise from their owners. Perhaps it would be better to preserve *Staunch* and *Protector* for gun action . . .

At a stirring below and raised voices Kydd looked up as an angry Popham stalked in. 'We shall speak alone, sir,' he demanded sharply.

Kydd got to his feet. 'There is no such in this building, sir.'

Popham snorted. 'You!' he snapped at Clinton. 'Out until I say return.'

Clinton hesitated, but left with an awkward glance at Kydd.

'Now, sir. You'll tell me how in Hades you managed, single-handed, to destroy this expedition.'

Kydd reddened but kept his temper. 'I beg to differ, Dasher. My blockade was sound until the pampero and then—'

'You let 'em pass! And now my entire enterprise is under dire threat.'

The 'my' did not escape Kydd. He replied curtly, 'After the storm I was left with just two sail. Even if I'd been athwart their course when they sallied I could not have stopped them.'

'You didn't even try!'

Kydd took a deep breath and replied levelly, 'If I had, we'd now be left with not a single armed vessel to see off attacks or escort supply.'

Popham glowered at him but said nothing. His hollow eyes and haggard face betrayed an inner torment that Kydd could only guess at – forced to stay idle in the big ships that were on watch in the outer reaches of the River Plate while the destiny of his adventure was decided by others, aware that failure was now not impossible, and his was the responsibility.

'Nevertheless, I find your conduct questionable, sir, to say the least.'

'There are those,' Kydd said quietly, 'who say venturing upon an invasion without we have reinforcements assured is—'

'How dare you?' Popham exploded, his face white. 'You – you have the temerity to criticise me! This expedition was soundly conceived but, I'll have you know, brought to hazard by others. I'll not be cried down by the likes of you, my most junior captain, b' God!'

'Sir, you're being—'

'I'll not forget this, Kydd! If we fail, it's to your tally I'll sheet home the blame for the whole bloody thing, be damn sure about that!' He stood for a moment, chest heaving, then stormed out.

After a decent interval Clinton came in, taking his chair without catching Kydd's eye, and busied himself with a paper.

Kydd tried to compose himself. He had nothing to be ashamed of and be damned to Popham if he tried to prove otherwise. There was vital work to do and he wasn't about to let that suffer on his account. He picked up his quill and resumed his order to take up three fishing boats.

As evening drew in, the subaltern appeared again to address Clinton. 'I've a strange thing to report, sir, if you'll hear it.'

Helped by Dodd, whose calm acceptance of discomfort and danger was unfailing, Clinton had been assigning night duties in such a way that nearby support could be summoned quickly if there were any outbreaks of trouble. It was not an easy task and he looked up distracted. 'Er, what is it, then?'

'In the barracks, sir. One of my privates was cleaning his musket when the damnedest thing happened. He was tapping his fire-lock on the floor when it disappeared.'

Clinton sighed. 'You're not making yourself clear, old bean.'

'The musket – it went right through a hole and he lost it. He called over his sergeant and they found that there was a suspicious cavity underneath where it had fallen and beg it be inspected.'

'Not now, I'm afraid. I'm too busy.'

Impulsively Kydd stood up. 'I'll go. Need to stretch the legs.'

'That's kind in you, sir,' Clinton said gratefully. 'Sar'nt Dodd will go with you. Er, a sword would not be noticed.'

They left by the main gate, striding out into the gathering dark towards the barracks, two streets distant. As they turned the corner, without warning a screeching crowd with clubs ran towards them.

Instantly the three drew their swords and, back to back, awaited the onslaught.

It never came. The mob hesitated at the sight of the steel, then, with derisory shouts, ran away down a passage.

'Rum lot, sir,' Dodd said, sheathing a stout Highland broadsword he had somehow acquired. 'The lads never could work 'em out.'

The barracks fronted on to a grand street, and in the quarters for privates, located in the lower part, a ring of off-duty soldiers stood around a splintered plank. They drew back as Kydd approached. He peered into the blackness of a void underneath. A probe with a broom-handle found nothing.

'Tear up the boards,' he ordered.

Out of the gloom the outlines of a small passageway or tunnel appeared.

'Bring a lantern.' It could be nothing but an old bolt-hole for soldiers to slip out into the town – or was it something more sinister?

Kydd held the light over the hole – and there below was a row of round, familiar objects.

He went icy cold: if these really were . . .

'Stand clear, I'm going down,' he grunted, swinging his legs over and dropping into the pit. 'More light.'

321

He went to the first object. Now there was no doubt: thirty-six barrels of gunpowder lay beneath the barracks in a plot to wipe out, in one blast, half of Beresford's army.

Struck dumb by the enormity, Kydd took some moments to recover. He looked about him – the tunnel led away deep into the pitch darkness: were they still there?

'Sar'nt Dodd – come with me.'

Dodd lowered himself in, peering around apprehensively. Kydd asked for two pistols and a lantern to be lowered. Crouching, they set off into the blackness.

It seemed to go on for ever, but the tunnel was straight and the wavering light reached well ahead. It ended in a stone cellar with dusty stores and a wooden ladder going up to a small trapdoor. Kydd eased it up very carefully, light spilling in as he did so – and all became clear.

The little group looking down the hole in the barrack-room floor started with surprise when Kydd and Dodd magically appeared behind them.

'Turn out the guard,' Kydd said briefly. 'We know where they're coming from.'

'Sir?'

'The convent of St Francis opposite.'

Under the protection and assurances of the bishop, the convent and other sanctuaries had been exempted from access by the British – and that trust had been betrayed.

Clinton was concerned at the revelation of the tunnel, but had other pressing problems to deal with. A sentry had been assaulted by a masked figure whirling a *bolas*, the deadly efficient gaucho method of bringing down steers. He'd then been badly beaten. Five men had simply disappeared.

For Kydd there was unsettling news. Four *felucca*s had reached Buenos Aires; they were full of militia from the south, and attempted to land them behind the lines. A small sea battle had ended with their withdrawal, but if the Spanish had the sense to make a massed attack with more, it was certain that Kydd's tiny navy would be overcome.

He fought off a sense of inevitability and doom, and when the victuallers failed to arrive from Rio de Janeiro it was four upon two – the meagre rations of two men now shared four ways.

Night brought with it its own terrors: sleep in the barracks was once shattered by a demented screeching and howling outside that went on and on. An armed party sent outside returned white-faced – wild dogs had been staked under the walls, then flayed alive and left.

And in the morning the naked and mangled body of one of the missing soldiers was found on the foreshore.

Was this the beginning of the end?

Chapter 14

The sound of trumpets echoed up from Whitehall Avenue. Grenville hurried to the window of the Admiralty, quite neglecting the table of grave faces that were discussing the war at sea. 'I say, what a grand sight!' the prime minister exclaimed. 'Come and see, you fellows!'

With a scraping of chairs the others dutifully obliged, moving to the long windows to peer down into the crowd-lined streets. In the distance the head of a cavalcade was approaching, an escort of the Loyal Britons Volunteers proudly stepping out with fixed bayonets to the sound of two military bands.

People were shouting and cheering, urging on the colourful parade in waves of joyfulness. 'My word, but I've not seen the mobility so exercised since Trafalgar,' murmured Sidmouth, the Lord Privy Seal.

Even the torpid figure of Fox, the notorious but ageing foreign secretary, gained some measure of animation. 'An' they've little enough to cheer these last months since Austerlitz,' he grunted.

Since that climactic confrontation at sea Napoleon had raged about Europe, winning one titanic battle after another. This had brought the late Pitt's coalition to ruin, and had rendered England without friends and alone in the war once more. Now, however, they had a victory: better than that, there was plunder – treasure that took a stream of wagons, each drawn by six horses, to make the journey from Portsmouth to the Bank of England.

The thump of drums grew louder and details of the procession clearer. 'What flag's that?' enquired Grenville, noticing a Royal Marine holding aloft a green and gold tasselled banner in the first wagon.

'I've been told it's that of the viceroyalty of Peru, my lord,' Viscount Howick, the first lord of the Admiralty, said sourly.

'And the others?'

'Flags various, taken at Buenos Aires.'

The procession came nearer, the shouts more strident. Each wagon had a large pennant aloft bearing the single word 'treasure' woven with blue ribbons, and drawn behind each was a gleaming brass field-piece taken from the enemy. 'Nice touch,' Sidmouth grunted appreciatively.

The cavalcade came to a ceremonial halt below their window.

A smart party of Royal Marines emerged from the front portico bearing a banner of blue silk with words in gold – 'Buenos Aires, Popham, Beresford, Victory!' – and carried it out to a carriage where Captain Donnelly of *Narcissus* graciously accepted it on behalf of the gallant soldiers and sailors so far away.

'Come now, Charles, why so peevish?' Grenville said. The government could safely be said to be, at least by implication, responsible for this ray of light into the dark miseries of war.

'The man's insufferable, very plausible and has insinuating manners,' Howick blustered. 'Had the hide to dress up a pirate raid on the Spanish as a tilt at liberation.'

'Popham? I'd have thought we've reason enough to be grateful.'

'He sails off on some unplanned treasure-hunting expedition, and then starts badgering me to find reinforcements from somewhere for his whimsy.'

'Isn't that what we want in a commander – pluck and enterprise?'

'He left station without so much as a by-your-leave,' the first lord snorted, 'which for the Navy you can be very sure will earn any commander a court-martial at the trot.'

'Like Nelson,' Grenville responded lightly. The great admiral's legendary and unauthorised race across the Atlantic had necessarily been accepted by the Admiralty.

'Hmm. Popham was lucky – he takes a city the size of Bristol with a handful of men and ships, then trumpets it to all the world like a fairground huckster. Pens letters that puff South America as the next big market after India and gets the City all in a tizzy. Now I don't suppose I can touch him – he's the people's hero.'

In the wide street below, the bands started up again and the parade got under way, heading for a grand climax along Pall Mall. The two men watched it together as it disappeared around the corner.

'I dare say I should get reinforcements out to the villain,' muttered Howick.

The Plaza de Toros, the bullring, was at the Retiro in the north of the city. After dark in the moonless night it was approached from three directions by a silent stream of men and equipment. By midnight General Liniers had an encampment established within the city.

The only British in this district were a sergeant and seventeen men of the 71st, who occupied a derelict house. In the pre-dawn cold a tired sentry was aroused by the sound of dogs barking maniacally. He woke his sergeant, who was in no doubt of what was happening.

'Go as fast as y' legs'll carry you, an' tell Colonel Pack they're on the move,' he told the lad. 'Say I'll hold 'em as long as I can.'

The sixteen soldiers were posted in fours, covering each other. Steel glittered in the early light as bayonets were fixed, and after he'd told them what he expected the sergeant solemnly shook hands with each man, then sent him out.

A well-aimed shot crashed out in the silence and felled the first *blandengue* turning the corner. Return fire was ineffective: the disciplined Highlanders spaced their own to cover reloading, and the advance was halted.

The enemy recovered and spread out before making a first charge. This was stopped within yards, fleeing men stumbling over bodies sprawled in the street. Then they split their numbers, advancing down several streets simultaneously. The sergeant placed his men in pairs to confront them but now there was a tidal wave of attackers.

One went down, the other snatching up his musket, but the enemy saw their chance and closed with them. In a welter of blood, the exulting Spanish hacked and gouged at the bodies as they surged forward.

Pack drew in his outer guard and sent for field guns. These were positioned at street intersections; loaded with grape, they could quickly be wheeled round and fired down any street where the enemy were massing.

That night Beresford ordered a counter-attack. Three parties set out at four in the morning, one to steal along the riverbank while the other two circled around to drive in from the flank. This was, however, a city in a feverish state of alert, and very soon they were detected and found themselves fighting for their lives.

Soon the British had no alternative but to pull back and tighten their defences.

Then at eleven in the morning there came a defining moment. Colonel Pack, at the head of his advance guard, was trying to hold the line in the face of impossible numbers when the firing began to fall off; in less than an hour it had stopped completely. Into the silence came an eerie, distant thumping. It strengthened until a small group appeared at the end of the long avenue. An ornately dressed officer in a plumed hat was preceded by a soldier with a massive drum on which he kept up a steady double beat – *ta ta boom, ta ta boom*. Behind him, two soldiers supported a large white flag of truce.

'Let's hear him, then,' Pack growled.

It was the Virrey Diputado Quintana, who had earlier met them at the gates of the city to proffer surrender. This time he bore a letter from General Liniers. It was addressed to the commander-in-chief of the British forces, General Beresford.

Pack found a close escort for Quintana and he was taken to the fort where Beresford, it seemed, was not about to be impressed.

'The general is in conference and will see you in due course,' Quintana was told, and shown to an ante-room where he sat with his letter, fuming.

When at last he was ushered in he wasted no time. Standing rigidly erect, he intoned, 'Sir. Comandante Liniers is privy to your difficulties in every wise and demands you give up the city of Buenos Aires.'

Beresford gave a thin smile. 'Sir, I'm unaccustomed to demands placed upon my person by others, still less by a foreign officer. Good day to you, sir.' With a brief bow he turned on his heel to leave.

'General Beresford! Sir! I have a letter from the commander-in-chief of the Spanish forces, Comandante General Santiago Liniers.'

'I give you joy of it,' Beresford said tightly.

'Sir, sir – the letter, it contains . . . It is very important!'

'Very well. Read it,' Beresford commanded his interpreter.

It began by pointing out that the British had seized Buenos Aires in the first place by an audacious stroke, enabled by a lack of direction of the population, but these same, inspired by patriotic enthusiasm and led by regular troops under a full general, were now about to fall on Beresford's tiny force. It ended with an ultimatum demanding unconditional surrender by one o'clock.

'Why, this is nothing but a threat, sir,' Beresford said, in mock astonishment. 'But do allow me to consider it for a space, and I shall pen a reply.'

Quintana was led away, expressionless.

'Gentlemen,' Beresford said, after his officers had assembled. 'The Dons are in earnest, I believe.'

Clinton grinned and whispered to Kydd, 'If the commodore knew what's in contemplation, I'd wager he'd have an apoplexy.'

'Do put a stopper on your jawing tackle, William.'

Kydd wondered how the general would style his withdrawal. It was fast becoming clear that Buenos Aires must be abandoned, either now or in the near future. If there were to be an orderly evacuation the rearguard must be supported at the same time as the main body was extracted, but without a wharf or normal port facilities it could be a hard-fought action for the Navy.

Beresford finally spoke, briefly and abruptly: 'I do not propose to accede to this demand. My duty is clear – to hold the city until reinforced, which at this time I expect hourly. I shall not be quitting my post until then, you may believe. Gentlemen, I shall remain here as long as it is within my power to do so.'

There would be no withdrawal? No retreat out of the city, no return to the fleet – just a holding out until . . . Kydd glanced at Clinton, whose expression sobered, then turned grave.

The general issued various orders, then turned to Kydd. 'Sir, I would ask that you find a transport to take off our sick and wounded, to be at the mole before one.'

This was barely disguised advice to any whose business was not at the end of a gun that they should for their own safety leave with them.

Kydd told the general he would attend to the transport directly. But did that include himself? A siege was without question a matter for the Army, which didn't need distractions. For him, with few ships left and no port to speak of, perhaps it were better he left quietly and returned to *L'Aurore*.

Then, accusingly, a vivid recollection came of the time when he was a junior lieutenant at the siege of Acre, fighting alongside the Army. Together they had held out against

Napoleon Bonaparte in person and prevailed, their victory owed squarely to the tenacity and loyalty of the Navy. If only to honour that memory he must stay and do what he could.

Taking Clinton aside, he told him, 'I'm coming back after I get the wounded away – I have some ideas. I'll need a dozen of your Royal Blues, which I'd be obliged if you'd find for me at my return.'

Clinton's gaze was level and calm. 'It'll be done, sir.'

The mole was only a short distance from the fort and there was no firing on the injured soldiers as they were trundled over the mud on the high-wheeled carts and laid gently on the deck of the transport.

Kydd noted with concern that for a hundred yards or so it was open ground to the mole; if their final withdrawal was contested this might be a bloody place indeed.

But he put these qualms to one side for there was work to do. He planned to create a floating artillery platform that could lie offshore and fire into the enemy. This would need to be the shallowest-draught vessel he could find that would bear carriage guns. An empty grain brig, oddly named *Iasthma*, was conveniently at anchor offshore. Kydd bundled out its captain and crew, and set his party to preparing it as best they might.

It was simple but effective. Everything possible was offloaded – sails, furniture, victuals, spars, stores – and on the bare deck cannon were lined up to form a one-sided broadside. To manoeuvre, a kedge would be streamed out forward and another aft. Sail-power would be replaced by hard work at the capstan but now at least they had means to fight back.

He wished them well and returned to the fort, knowing the unearthly quiet would end at one o'clock. A distant trumpet bayed; it was taken up by another out to the left and one more to the south. An ugly, surging roar sounded in response. Coming ominously from all three directions, it meant that Liniers had succeeded in flanking Pack and his line, and now the net was tightening.

The fighting was vicious and one-sided. Although Pack could command the streets with his artillery it was the city buildings themselves that were his greatest foe. In deference to the sultry heat of summer each had a flat roof, edged for safety with a modest wall all round. Enemy marksmen quickly found these an admirable parapet and, firing down, made a hell of blood and death for the English gunners and any who stood to fight.

Iasthma hauled herself up and down the seafront, stopping only to open up with a crash of guns when enemy troops showed themselves. At one point Liniers ordered two of the Spanish field guns down to the shore and a gun duel opened. A hit brought down her mizzen and with it her ensign. Wild cheering erupted from the enemy. A nimble sailor, however, quickly had the colours aloft once more on the bare mainmast, and her crew gave savage cheers as they threw themselves into serving their guns.

Then, for reasons that couldn't be made out from the shore, the brave vessel took fire, flames starting from her after end and rapidly finding naked powder charges, which flared and blazed. Her guns stopped, and in minutes her crew were in the water, making for the land – to inevitable death or capture.

Beresford had no choice: he pulled in his forces so that only the big square, the Plaza Mayor, was being defended, and this with every gun and soldier he had.

'Captain – I've no right to ask it of you,' he said, in a low voice to Kydd. 'If I had any means of landing a force behind their lines to delay . . .'

Justina was one of the few vessels left in the roadstead. She had fulfilled her charter as troop transport and had been hovering, waiting for the rich cargoes promised. Now she was at anchor and deserted, her crew long since fled.

'I shall need volunteers,' Kydd replied, thinking of the gallant Royal Blues, fighting on land. This would be more to their liking and he knew he could count on them.

'The St Helena men have volunteered,' Beresford said, missing his meaning. 'Artillery men all, they begged a more active war.'

Kydd was touched. That far-off island, a tiny speck in the vast wastes of the Atlantic – and since these were East India Company men, there was no compelling reason for them to be in this fearful cauldron.

He nodded. 'Thank you, sir. We'll sail immediately.'

It took a moment or two for Kydd to shift from a land-bound perspective back to the imperatives of the open sea. A respectable north-easterly was building so it would be close-hauled on the starboard tack and the tide safely making, with no doubt, a useful northerly current. It was possible.

Clinton had another Royal Blues detachment mustered ready. There were set faces among them: *Iasthma*'s fate might well be their own but none had been conscripted into the venture and all knew the risks.

An army subaltern reported that men had now been posted to cover the embarkation at the mole and it was time to leave.

'I – I would wish you well of the day, sir,' Clinton said, extending his hand. In his eyes Kydd saw a look almost of pleading and felt a chill presentiment steal over him.

'Thank you, William,' he replied, his handshake lingering. On an impulse he unbuckled his sword belt and handed across the fine blade that his Canadian uncle had provided for him and that he had treasured since crossing the miraculous gulf to become an officer. 'Take care of this until I return, will you?'

He settled the broad baldric of a cutlass across his shoulders, then found a stout weapon, testing its edge, and slipped it into its scabbard. 'Goodbye, my friend,' he said simply, and left with his men.

Outside the fort there was a lethal chaos of bullets and stone splinters. Men ran crouched, while marines at the corners of the building fired up at windows and roof-tops until they reached the boats and pushed off.

Looking back as the boat pulled out strongly, Kydd saw a pall of powder-smoke drifting up from all around the dark bulk of the fort. Battle sounds floated out over the water and a choking atmosphere of war and waste was fast clamping in.

Justina was in a neglected state, rigging slack and hanging, her sails mildewed and dank, but by the time the last boatload of St Helenas had come alongside to join the Royal Blues they were ready to cast to the wind. No one spoke as they passed the city, then bore away to close with the land.

Kydd reasoned that after they'd passed the front line there would be far fewer of the enemy. Beresford needed a distraction in the enemy's rear: if he placed his raiding force at any point from now on it would cause maximum shock and dismay and, conceivably, a lessening of pressure at the front – Liniers would be forced to turn back to deal with it.

They were sailing close to the chill north-easterly and made heavy going of the short, steep waves it kicked up, but they had the tide in their favour. Something niggled at the back of his brain about the combination but nothing crystallised and he shrugged it off.

He tried to find a place for the landing but no spot suggested itself. Possibly that small, tussocked headland? The tiller was brought over and, under brailed course, they nosed inshore. The St Helenas readied themselves, for without boats they would have to wade to the beach.

Then an unwelcome puff of white smoke showed at the shoreline and another: they would have to fight their way in.

The merchantman had only four six-pounders of doubtful vintage but these were plied with ferocity, their rage kicking up gouts of earth around the positions on the foreshore, which then fell silent. Musket fire came from a warehouse and *Justina*'s guns banged out – windows disappeared and black holes peppered the walls before there, too, resistance ceased.

If they were going to make their move, now was the time. 'Ease away,' he ordered, and the ship swung in to a closer angle.

'Foul water!' a seaman shrieked forward.

'Hard t' starb'd!' Kydd snarled. There was a mud-shoal or some such ahead – but the clumsy vessel shied from the wind and slowly they ceased their forward motion.

It was the worst of situations. Not only were they prevented from going anywhere but they had lost that most priceless asset to a ship under sail: her manoeuvrability. And, of course, without boats there was no chance of hauling off. They could only wait and pray that the incoming tide would lift them off.

However, minutes later a troop of cavalry appeared along the shore, cantering along as they spied out the situation.

Justina's guns opened up and the leading horseman went down in a flurry of kicking but the rest increased to a reckless gallop until they were out of range, then turned and milled about in a watchful group.

Kydd had known there would be cavalry in their rear but they had come up so fast. Certainly now all ideas of a landing would have to be revised.

He improvised a hand lead with a belaying pin and went about the stationary vessel taking soundings. Expecting to find it shallower forward at the mud-bank and deeper aft, he found, to his surprise, that it was the same all around.

The treacherous Río de la Plata had betrayed them. One of its inexplicable wind-driven surges had sent the mass of its head-water back against the tide flow and now the broad expanse of mud-flats was beginning to drain – and would leave them high and dry.

The cruel twist was hard to bear and he knew he must make some very bleak choices in the near future.

The cavalry made another pass and *Justina*'s guns thundered, sending up gouts of mud and water that deterred the horsemen, who raced away to regroup again.

But Kydd had seen one other thing. His gunners had slammed in their quoins to their maximum and the guns were now at the extremity of depression. It meant that as the ship settled on its muddy bed it was canting over. Very soon the guns facing the shore would be pointing helplessly at the sky and on the other side directly into the sea and mud.

The cavalry troop was now being joined by a larger mass of horsemen, galloping along the wide strip of wet mud down by the shoreline. In minutes they would notice *Justina*'s plight and then they would make their charge.

And they were completely helpless. Kydd tried to cudgel

his brain into providing some last ingenious trick that would see them sail away but—

'They're coming!'

Led by an officer in plumes and frogging, waving a sabre, the mass of horsemen splashed into the water in a glorious charge towards them.

There were no longer any options.

Kydd opened his mouth to order the colours to be struck – but, of course, there were none, *Justina* not being in naval commission. In an ultimate stroke of irony they were to be massacred because they could not surrender.

He sent a nervous soldier below to find a bedsheet, which was hung over the side just in time. With much splashing and triumphant whoops, the cavalry sheathed their sabres and noisily surrounded the vessel. The officer shouted hoarsely and they obediently fell back to allow him to get through and climb on to the low main-deck.

Snatching off his tall shako he swept down in a deep bow. When he rose Kydd saw a preposterously young man with intelligent and fine-drawn features.

'Teniente Martín Miguel de Güemes, your service, sir,' he said. 'The fortunes of war – and this ship is prize of His Catholic Majesty.' He held out both hands meaningfully.

His cup of bitterness full, Kydd slowly unbuckled and rendered up his weapon, his career as a sea officer ended.

A bullet struck the fort roof parapet near Clinton and ricocheted off; he felt the usual sting of stone chips – but this was more serious. They were being fired on from a higher angle. He looked about the chaos of smoke and dust and spied where it was coming from. The San Miguel church.

'Sar'nt Dodd – we've got to get to those rascals or they'll make it impossible to man our guns.'

The sergeant nodded. 'Oi – you two!' he called, and two marines left their embrasures to report.

'Follow me,' Clinton ordered, and rattled down the steps to the base of the fort. The square was alive with men, guns and noise, and as they raced across to the ornate church at the corner the air was choked with acrid gun-smoke, the whip and zing of unseen missiles.

They reached the massive doors. Dodd tried to force them open but their solidity resisted all his panting efforts.

'Bayonets.'

Their points were levered into cracks and the butts of their muskets used as battering rams, but to no avail. When one of the marines fell with a cry, the effort was abandoned.

'I'll do it, if'n you'll leave me at it!' Dodd gasped, hefting a length of market timber.

'No. Get back and cover me.' Clinton hoisted the wounded marine over his shoulder and stumbled back towards the fort. Other soldiers were racing to get there, too. This must be the last act – every man was being pulled back into the citadel.

With a roar of triumph the crowd pressed forward, but Beresford had positioned guns at the gate and smaller-calibre weapons on the roof – and with the square now evacuated there was a clear field of fire. A double charge of grape erupted, and the far side of the square was instantly transformed into a carpet of dead and wounded, the remainder fleeing.

Musket fire was futile against the thick stone of the fort and under the threat of the British guns there would be no sudden storming.

It was stalemate.

*　　*　　*

338

Beresford stood among his officers, gravely troubled. 'Gentlemen. It now appears time to consider the last sanction. We have done what we can but the reinforcements have not arrived. Therefore I have decided to withdraw. Where is Mr Kydd, pray?'

'I'm sorry to say, sir, that he has not returned from the diversionary raid. We can only assume he is captured or . . .'

A shadow passed across the general's face. 'So many good men,' he whispered.

Clinton spoke: 'Sir, any evacuation by sea cannot now be in contemplation. There is open ground before the mole, and with the state of the tide as it is, then—'

'I understand you, sir.'

Pack said heavily, 'An' there's no route south, the blandengoes are there in strength.'

'And the gauchos to the north,' added another.

It was Beresford's decision and his alone. 'Then I have no alternative. Gentlemen, to avoid vain loss of life, in two hours I shall ask General Liniers for terms. Pray do what you must to prepare.'

In the shocked silence he turned on his heel and left them.

That the British Army, the conqueror of Cape Town and so recently Buenos Aires, was to capitulate to a few Spanish regulars and a ragtag host of militia, cow-herders and townsfolk was an intolerable shame, and tears could be seen in the eyes of some officers.

His mind reeling at the turn of events, Clinton called the faithful Dodd to his office and together they went through papers, adding them to a pile destined for destruction.

As they worked, a lump rose in his throat. It was likely that as an officer he would at some point in the future be exchanged but men like Dodd, through no fault of their own, would now face incarceration in an enemy land for possibly years.

In the heightened atmosphere the thought threatened to unman him; he excused himself and pretended to look for something.

He couldn't let it happen – not to this man.

Finding his pen he scribbled fast on a paper, signed it, carefully folded it twice, then sealed it. The outside he left blank, no address.

'Er, Dodd. I have a last service for you, if you can.'

'Sah.' There was no resentment, no sullen reproach, just a calm acceptance of how things had turned out.

'Now this is a secret dispatch, and it is to go to the commanding officer of HMS *L'Aurore*.'

'Sah.'

'It's of vital importance – do you think it possible you could deliver it?'

Dodd hesitated, his open face working with emotion. 'Sir, if they—'

'You're a reliable, long-service sergeant. Who else may I trust if not you?'

Snapping to rigid attention, Dodd threw off a quivering salute to his officer. 'He'll get 'em, sir. I knows how!'

'Right. Well, go now, and the best of luck.'

The British colours at the flagstaff lowered and when they were raised again they were over a white flag of truce, seeking a parley.

This was greeted by an instant roar of gratification. The square was invaded by a joyous, incoherent rabble cheering and firing into the air – there would be no respectful falling

340

back to allow the principals of both sides to conduct negotiations on neutral ground.

The scene quickly became rudely chaotic, some planting
field guns opposite the gateway and many shouting taunts
and firing muskets at any British they could see, in a wild
and uncontrollable uproar.

A yell of triumph heralded the arrival of an officer. It was
Quintana, who was carried shoulder-high through the seething
mob to the very gates of the citadel.

At a sign from Beresford they were flung open and the
rabble found themselves at the muzzle of two guns and a
ring of steel and held back angrily. Quintana went in, to
redoubled fury and shooting. After the gate had been closed,
he bravely ran up to the roof and, throwing open his splendid
coat to show himself, berated the rabble for their
indiscipline.

Negotiations were brief. In the circumstances there was no
other recourse – immediate and unconditional surrender.

After some hours, regular Spanish troops arrived to bring
order, and Comandante General Liniers made his appearance;
Beresford went out to meet him. After Liniers's sincere
expressions of regret at the behaviour of his men, terms
were agreed and he accepted the general's sword.

Finally the Highlanders left their positions, marching out
together, tears of frustration and rage on many. They halted
and the colours of the 71st Highland Regiment were given
up to the enemy.

The officers were then separated from their men, who were
taken off to the other end of the square where they were
ordered to ground arms. Many threw down their muskets
bitterly before being placed in three ranks under guard.

Such a brave and pitiful sight brought a catch in

Clinton's throat. These few hundred who had achieved so much – then to be overcome by numbers so overwhelming.

They were marched away to cat-calls and defiant shouts, which left no doubt that their captivity would not be easy.

Quintana asked the officers to go back into the fort where they were invited to sign a book of parole. General Beresford stepped forward first, there seemed little point in refusing, and Clinton added his own name.

After that, nothing seemed to matter any more.

Chapter 15

'*Boooat ahoy!*' the forward lookout yelled into the night.

With *L'Aurore* at such a pitch of nervous tension and her first lieutenant pacing the deck like a penned-up hound, it would never do to allow a stranger to approach too near without challenge.

An answering shout came, weak and distant.

Gilbey arrived to stand beside the lookout. 'Tell that lubber t' stand away or he'll get a cold shot in the guts,' he said peevishly.

The hail was dutifully made, but the little fisherman's punt kept on obstinately, a single indistinct figure at the oars. When he was close enough he stood up swaying and hailed back in unmistakable English, '*L'Aurore*, ahoy – one t' come aboard!'

Men scrambled up from below, eager to hear any news, and with them Renzi, who had become increasingly troubled. Since the betrayal at Punta Pavón they had lain at anchor for several days waiting for orders – or even word of how matters stood for their friends and shipmates ashore.

'One to come aboard,' agreed Gilbey.

Slowly and painfully the figure came up the side; by the time he swung inboard an eager welcoming committee was waiting for him.

'Begob! It's Sar'nt Dodd!'

An excited babble broke out and Gilbey thundered, 'Hold y' tongues! Silence fore 'n' aft! Make y'r report, Sergeant.'

Dodd straightened with difficulty. 'Bad news, sir. Th' worst.'

'Get on with it!'

'Well, as we've struck t' the Spanish, sir.'

After a moment of shocked surprise, there was pandemonium. 'Silence!' Gilbey yelled. 'Anyone says a word more goes t' the bilboes.'

He waited for quiet then said, 'Carry on.'

'I've to give ye this,' Dodd said, fumbling for the dispatches. 'Seein' as you're the new captain. From m' officer, L'tenant Clinton, sir, urgent like.' He managed a tired but proud salute.

Gilbey snatched it and read it avidly. He frowned, then reread the paper, his brow darkening. 'What's this nonsense? Do you know what's in this, Sergeant?'

Confused, Dodd shook his head. 'M' orders were t' get it to you wi' all dispatch, is all I know, sir.'

Glaring, Gilbey thrust it at Renzi. 'Can you make anything of this?' he asked angrily.

Renzi took it and read:

To the commanding officer, HMS L'Aurore

In fifteen minutes we shall be obliged to lay down our arms. In all conscience I cannot allow the bearer, Sergeant Dodd, a man I have come to value above all reason in these ruinous days, to be carried off to a vile captivity at the greatest loss to His Majesty's service.

This therefore is the only method I have of ensuring his obedience in quitting his men.

Signed, Clinton, lieutenant Royal Marines

Folding the paper, Renzi replied, 'Well, Mr Gilbey, I see it to be Clinton's thoughtfulness in providing us with one who may give us verbal news of conditions in Buenos Aires, this paper a means of getting him past our sentries.'

'Oh. Well, what the blazes *is* happening, Dodd?'

'Sir. After them Dons got across, th' whole town rose up an' we had t' fall back on the fort. Too many on 'em, the general had t' ask for terms, is all.'

'Where's Captain Kydd?'

'Don't rightly know, sir. Went off on a raid or such, sorry t' say he didn't come back.'

'You mean . . . ?'

'Taken maybe or, er, snabbled.'

Dumbfounded, Gilbey simply stared.

Renzi swallowed, tightly controlling his feelings. 'Then our forces have capitulated?' he asked gently. 'And General Beresford and all others are captured?'

'Must be, I suppose,' Dodd said, scratching his head. 'I got away before, y' see.'

Gilbey came to, and snapped irritably, 'Then how many of the enemy are there now in the city? Come along, man, what's their force?'

'Er, can't rightly say f'r sure, sir, seein' as how m' post was in the fort.'

'What? You've no idea?' said Gilbey, contemptuously. 'You're sent to inform us—'

'Sir. The man is sorely tried after his ordeal,' Renzi came in. 'I'll take him below and see he has something to recruit his strength while I build up an idea for you of how things are.'

'Very well. I'll see you in half a glass, Renzi.'

In the privacy of his own cabin, Renzi teased out the story. Finding a hiding place, the wily sergeant had lain low while the surrender was completed, waiting as the city erupted into celebration. Then, after dark, he had stolen a fishing punt and made his escape, rowing single-handed against wind and the sea's bluster. Mutely he held up his hands: they were piteously blistered and bloody.

Asked about surrender terms, Dodd could shed no light on them, but believed they had been concluded rapidly as he'd heard the men being marched off within less than an hour after the guns had stopped firing.

This implied overbearing force and therefore an unconditional capitulation of the whole city. 'And you've no idea what happened to the captain?' enquired Renzi, feeling a cold pit forming in his belly.

'Sorry, sir,' Dodd said sorrowfully. 'Jus' didn't come back. Don't mean t' say he's not in clink somewhere,' he added, with loyal fervour.

Renzi left the exhausted man wolfing cheese and hard tack, and appreciative of a jug of thin wine.

Gilbey impatiently dismissed the report. 'Clinton should have had more sense than t' leave it to a Royal to get intelligence out to us. Completely useless.'

Renzi bit back a hot retort, while Gilbey went on, 'So Mr Kydd is taken, or more probably killed. It means I'm captain o' the barky now.

'I have m' duty, and that's to get to Commodore Popham an' acquaint him of developments ashore. Likely he'll confirm me in post on the spot, I wouldn't wonder. Should I move into my captain's quarters now, do y' think, or wait till I'm confirmed?'

'As being somewhat more important than we, the commodore will certainly have been advised by now,' Renzi said icily. 'And I believe your assumption of the dignity of captain should certainly wait.'

'Wait? What for?'

On impulse, Renzi rapped, 'Until I've returned from Buenos Aires. I'm going back to find him.'

It had been said, and he felt a fierce glee begin to swell in him.

'You're what? Be damned to it, man, you're proposin' to present yourself in a city new relieved an' swarmin' with poxy Spanish to demand what happened to y'r captain?'

Fighting down the temptation to reveal that he'd done something like that in Revolutionary Paris, Renzi contented himself with a simple, 'Yes, I am.'

Gilbey sat back with a look of bafflement, then retorted, 'You're mad. Even if he's still alive, how th' devil will you find where he is? No! It's lunacy, and I won't have it.'

'I'm going.'

'You're not – as acting captain o' this ship, an' you crew, Renzi, I forbid it.'

'I don't think so,' he said acidly. 'You've not the authority. Recollect – I'm Captain Kydd's confidential secretary, his personal retinue, not a member of the ship's company.'

'But . . .'

Renzi waited for the implication to sink in, then added, 'But I'd be beholden if you'd allow me to call for volunteers to assist me.'

Gilbey recovered quickly. 'No, I will not! Do y' really think a foremast jack will want t' go back into—'

'I'm going alone. These are boat's crew only, to lie to a kedge offshore. And, yes, I do think they'll come forward.'

Gilbey gave him an intense look and snapped, 'You go, then. However, you'll get no men from me.'

Renzi leaned across. 'Then I'd ask you to conceive of your standing as captain among your Jack Tars if it becomes known you'd not allow me even to *try* a rescue of their Mr Kydd! *Comprende?*'

There were many volunteers. Far too many for *L'Aurore's* smallest boat, the gig, which was all a grudging Gilbey would allow. As he'd also been adamant that there were to be no officers or midshipmen, it was just Poulden on the tiller, Stirk in the bow and old shipmates Pinto and Doud to tend sail and oars. All others had to be content with a well-meant and noisy farewell, which inevitably finished in a three times three hearty cheer.

'We sail after twenty-four hours!' growled Gilbey. 'Not a minute later!'

Renzi had no idea how it was to be done when they pushed off into the darkness, the fishing punt in tow. He realised they would need the rest of the night to make passage, lying at one of the many hard sand shoals mid-estuary during the day and closing to within a mile or so of the city the next night. Gilbey would not dare to put to sea before dawn the following day.

A plan crystallised: it all hinged on the traitor – or patriot – Serrano. If he could persuade him with sufficient threat to divulge Kydd's fate, or possibly his whereabouts, it would radically change the odds.

In his somewhat worn, plain shore-going rig, he would be a confused Italian merchant, unsure of what was happening, seeking news, reassurance. It would suffice.

The boat's crew were not to be risked, for this matter was what he owed his friend personally. To pen a sorrowful letter to Kydd's sister without knowing his ultimate fate was unthinkable. They could come inshore but the final dash would be his alone in the punt, brought along for the purpose.

The lights of Buenos Aires were visible miles to seaward, and as they crept in, there were soaring fireworks, gunshots and all the signs of a city very much awake. 'Lie off for me, Poulden. Be sure if I'm not back an hour before first light to return immediately to *L'Aurore*. Is that clear?'

There was some mumbling, but Renzi was having nothing of it. 'I say quit this place an hour before. No later. Compree?'

'Aye,' Poulden said grudgingly.

Renzi stepped into the punt and took the oars, looking shoreward to take bearings for the return.

The punt swayed dangerously. He looked round – Stirk was climbing in.

'Shift y' arse, I'm coming wi' ye,' he announced.

'Toby, you can't—'

'Can't I? Two reasons – y' need a pair o' peepers as'll watch y'r stern, an' blow me down, what'll they say o' the *Billy Roarer* that they lets orficers take th' oars?'

He shouldered Renzi out of the way and shipped oars professionally. 'Give way, sir?'

There was one spot that suggested itself as a place for landing. Below the fort, he remembered, was where the washer-women plied their trade. There would be none there at this hour and Renzi conned the punt in, conscious that they would be under observation – but he also knew that this was the time when flounder fishermen were about in England, and might not the equivalent be abroad in Buenos Aires?

It seemed to work: there were the silhouettes of sentinels

behind the parapets of the fort but they were taking no notice and the foreshore was deserted.

The punt nudged in to the muddy shore; they pulled it up beyond the tide line and prepared to set out.

'Er, Toby – if you'd kindly allow me . . .' He bent down, then came up suddenly to slop mud in his face. Stirk spluttered with indignation but Renzi inspected him critically. 'Perhaps a little more. Just here possibly . . .'

Looking around, he found a pile of fishermen's sacks waiting for the morning and helped himself to one, bulking it out with seaweed and thrusting it at Stirk. 'Ready? Then follow me, my man.'

On the streets knots of revellers drifted by; figures laughed, brawled and argued. They took no notice of the woebegone merchant trudging along with his servant behind.

It was not far to the back street where he had discovered Serrano lived with his woman. Renzi had no real animosity towards the young man, who must have done as he had more out of ardent patriotism than perfidy, and he was the only possible lead to Kydd's fate.

If, however, he suspected Serrano was aware of his friend's whereabouts, he would have no qualms at all about doing what was needed to wrench the information from him. After his time with French royalist agents, he knew the ways.

'Watch my back,' he told Stirk. With a bent wire he prised open the door lock and stepped inside, ready for anything.

Serrano was there, alone, sitting moodily at a table with a single candle. He looked up in fright when Renzi appeared. '*Santa Madre de Dios!* How you find me?'

Renzi remained silent.

'You assassinate me?'

'That depends,' Renzi said silkily, taking a seat opposite, his eyes drilling remorselessly into Serrano's skull.

The artist looked up obstinately. His eyes were red. 'It make no difference, not now . . .'

'Oh? Tell me.'

Slowly it came out. Liniers was now revealed as a royalist; he had gone along with the revolutionary fervour but had cunningly diverted it into a movement to oust the British first. He had been joined by *los patriotas* to whom he'd given deliberately minor roles in the *reconquista* and, now in control, he had hardened his grip with a view to handing the whole back to the Spanish, with himself high in government.

That it was not yet so was mainly because the viceroy, Sobremonte, was still far inland where he had fled, but the fact remained that Don Baltasar and the Sociedad Patriótica were therefore neatly sidelined and destined to be once more hunted rebels in the resumed administration – they had been betrayed and the clock was being wound back.

'Mr Renzi, I didn't mean that Captain Keed is tricked. When they said I had to, I thought . . .'

Renzi let it hang, then leaned across and demanded, 'I want to know what happened to him – and I want details.'

Serrano looked surprised. 'Why, he were caught! His ship go on the mud.'

'So he's a prisoner!' Relief washed over him in a flood.

'Why, no. He sign parole so he in lodging but not the old. They are liking the English too much so he was move to another.'

'Where?'

'I say the captain is a good man, not many as him. I'm apologise for what I do, an' ashamed for my country.'

'Why do you say that?'

Serrano hung his head as he explained. The terms gained

by Beresford were good: that in return for laying down their arms, there would be an immediate evacuation of the British, each man to undertake not to serve against the Spanish until the formalities of an exchange were completed, their passage back to England to be funded by the Spanish government.

Yet even with the terms ratified in writing it quickly became clear that the Spanish had no intention whatsoever of abiding by them. Carts had been rounded up and the brave soldiers were beginning to be marched away, far up-country. They would be followed by the officers. There would be no release.

The ultimate betrayal.

'We don't get t' him, an' main quick, he's a gone goose! Where's he at, y' bugger?' Renzi hadn't noticed Stirk slip in but, given the circumstances, he couldn't have phrased it better himself.

'He's not far. You write to say come, he see your writing an' he come. I send a boy to bring him.'

On parole an officer was released on his word of honour to return and therefore had limited freedom to move about.

Prudently, Serrano disappeared, and twenty minutes later Kydd walked suspiciously into the room.

'Hail, fellow – and well met!' Renzi cried, moved beyond words to see his friend once more.

But instead of an effusive greeting Kydd said abruptly, 'You, too, are taken, Nicholas – how's this?'

'Not at all, dear chap. We're here to take you back.'

Kydd held his breath, then let it out slowly. 'You're on the loose in a captured city – I won't ask how, but it won't answer.'

'I beg your pardon?'

'I can't go back, and you know why. You and Stirk have risked it for nothing.'

'You mean you've given parole.'

'Indeed, as has General Beresford and we all. I would have thought it reasonable, given we're to be shortly exchanged, according to the terms o' capitulation.'

'There's a boat from *L'Aurore* lying off, waiting for us. We must move fast.'

'You didn't hear me. My parole is my word given, which on my honour will never be broken. Can you not see this? And how damn cruel it is, you tempting me like this.'

Renzi swallowed his irritation. 'Dear fellow, I have to tell you the Spanish have broken the surrender terms and are marching all British away up-country as prisoners. Parole is meaningless in the face of such treachery.'

'Where did you hear that? I can't believe General Liniers to be so lost to honour he'd risk the world's condemning. It's nonsense . . . or is it that you're spinning me a stretcher as will make me break my parole?' he demanded, incredulous.

'Not at all, dear friend. I hesitate to hurry you, but urgency dictates—'

'No! They'll only be moving the men to better quarters, I'd think. No, Nicholas, I don't believe a word of what you're saying. I'm duty-bound to stay, and that's an end to it.'

The stalemate was suddenly broken when the bedroom door opened and Serrano came in, pale-faced but resolute.

In open astonishment Kydd looked first to Renzi and then to Serrano. His face darkened. 'This treacherous dog – what's he doing here?'

Serrano replied, in a quaver, 'Captain Keed, sir! Hear me. He tell it right. They are sending the British soldiers off. I here because I, too, am betrayed.'

Seeing Kydd swell with growing anger, he quickly went on, 'Why am I here? Is easy for me not to come, but I come. To

353

tell you – is the truth! The terms are broken by General Liniers. Your soldiers are taken away. Soon you!'

Kydd hesitated. 'To break parole is a hard thing,' he muttered. 'Nicholas, what do you—'

'The abrogation of a treaty by one sovereign nation renders it a nullity for both,' Renzi said firmly. 'I cannot see how an agreement of parole is in any wise different.'

'Then . . .'

'Then perhaps we should exercise a modicum of celerity in our departure?'

Kydd straightened. 'My word of parole is withdrawn. As of this moment.'

'Quite so,' Renzi said, with relief. 'Shall we now—'

'Not yet. Understand I'm not abandoning the others.'

He paused, then ordered crisply, 'This room is now our centre of operations. All British officers are to be assembled here for escape, which will be done by twos.'

'There's only the gig – it can only take, say, five at a time and—'

'I'm not leaving 'em, Nicholas. Now, we have to pass the word to muster here. Um, Mr Serrano, how's this to be done, do you think?'

Clinton, billeted nearby, was the first to arrive, blinking at the sudden turn of events.

They waited in rising tension for the others, but then Serrano burst in, panting. 'Not good! The officers, they being taken – Gen'ral Beresford argue wi' Liniers. Now they come looking for you, Captain.'

They had to get away instantly but it was madness to think that two English officers in uniform could get through. Kydd had a plan.

'Nicholas – you're taking us somewhere, Stirk follows as servant.' This would give them a chance on the main streets, where parole would allow them, a not uncommon sight, but closer to the fort and the foreshore it would be a different matter.

'Ready?' Kydd then turned to Serrano. 'I thank 'ee for what you've done tonight – but if ever you run athwart my hawse again, I'll screw your neck, so help me God.'

The streets of Buenos Aires were still in festive array when they moved out, Renzi affecting to ignore the taunts and jibes and taking refuge in a dignified silence. It seemed to work and they made good progress but he feared it couldn't last, not if they were out looking for Kydd. They were four; such a number was too many to overlook. It was time to make for the back-streets and the waterfront. Their little boat – so near yet so far.

As they came closer to the water the danger multiplied for they had no excuse to be there. The fort loomed; the sentries limned in the diffuse moonlight.

Renzi came to a sudden stop. 'We've a problem,' he whispered, and pointed ahead to the mole. It was guarded. 'The boat is beyond, just around the point, but how the devil do we get past?' There was no slipping underneath the massive compacted stone structure.

Then Clinton had an idea, a long shot, but there was no going back. 'I'll trouble you for your coat, Mr Kydd.' He removed his own and explained, 'It's fever – smallpox. You and Stirk are carrying me, a dead body, and Mr Renzi will chant the offices!'

The coats were turned inside out and arranged over 'the body' and they set off in the dim light.

With Renzi in the lead making the sign of the cross and mumbling away they approached the sentries who lapsed into a suspicious silence, unslinging their muskets.

'*¡Paso, paso – la viruela!*' Renzi wailed mournfully, and resumed his reciting.

There were exclamations of alarm and the soldiers drew back, watching fearfully as they passed. It wasn't until they had gone around the point that the spell was broken. One of the sentries woke up to the fact that the burial ground was in another direction and urgent shouts broke the night stillness.

'Quickly – we need to get the boat in the water!' Renzi urged, looking about with Stirk in the dimness.

Clinton threw off the coats and got to his feet, waiting tensely with Kydd.

'Can't find the damned thing!' Renzi blurted, breathless and angry.

'It ain't here – 'cos the owner's taken 'un back!' Stirk spat.

More shouts came and figures started to run towards them.

'Find another bloody boat!' Kydd demanded – but there was none.

There was only one thing they could do. 'Into the water!' Renzi urged and hurled himself in, splashing noisily out as fast as he could. The others followed, stumbling in the mud, the cold of the sea shocking as they sloshed their way further out.

A musket shot came, then another, but the wild firing into the darkness was no real danger.

The little group moved out deeper and deeper. The line of freezing cold rose remorselessly up their bodies, bringing uncontrollable shuddering and a draining of life-warmth until their minds could hold only the desperate need to press on and on – and then, with water up to their necks, out in the night there was an anxious low call.

'Toby? Mr Renzi?'

Chapter 16

The outlines of a boat emerged from the early morning pearly mist. Two challenges rang out simultaneously from the lookouts in *L'Aurore*.

The triumphant reply roared back, '*L'Aurore!*' indicating that this was no less than the anointed captain of their ship.

It brought every man and boy of the ship's company on deck in a gleeful rush, with a disbelieving Gilbey. Then the boatswain importantly took position at the ship's side with his silver call.

The gig hooked on and Kydd mounted the steps gravely, his dignity respected even when coming aboard in a filthy uniform without cocked hat or shoes. The side-party, however, was all grins: order had returned to their universe.

'Pleased to be back, Mr Gilbey,' Kydd replied, to the mumbled welcome. 'Hands to unmoor ship, if you please.'

He acknowledged warm greetings from Curzon and Bowden and quickly left the deck for that unimaginably desirable heaven: his quarters. He opened the door to see Tysoe advancing with soap and towels, a fresh uniform on the side dresser.

Kydd stood for a moment with misted eyes, then croaked, 'Not now, Tysoe – there's something I have t' do first.' And in front of his appalled valet he reverently knelt down and kissed the deck.

Later, after they had got under way, there was time for breakfast with his officers in the gunroom. It was stout but meagre ship's fare and he recalled, as if in a bad dream, that his last meal had been rancid blood sausage.

He heard of their interminable idleness at anchor, provisions and stores ransacked to be sent ashore, leaving them on woefully short rations and above all, as matters worsened, the complete absence of news.

He heard, too, how Clinton had sent Dodd away with false dispatches and was touched to find that the sergeant had loyally carried back his precious sword as well.

But there were so many faces missing from *L'Aurore*, good men who had volunteered for the Royal Blues and were now somewhere out in the bleak country ranges of South America. But what could he do for them?

Maldonado was raised a day later, the fleet left at just two sixty-fours and some transports in a loose moor. With the frigate *Leda* away, and the small brig-sloop *Encounter* a distant sail, it was no real deterrent if the Spanish Navy ever returned from the north.

Kydd forced the thought away – it was hardly Popham's fault that the reinforcements had not arrived to swell the numbers, but after his treatment the last time they had spoken he found it difficult to summon a warm sympathy for the commodore.

At the flagship he was shown to the great cabin by the first lieutenant. Popham was sitting at a table by the window and raised his head at Kydd's entrance. 'I'd thought you to be taken at the fall of the city,' he said distantly.

'As I was, Dasher, but with the help of shipmates I got away.' Kydd was shocked to see the effect of the last few weeks on the man: features ravaged by care, bloodshot eyes and a pall of weariness about his movements.

Popham stared for a long time out of *Diadem*'s stern window at the hurry of grey sea and the distant bleak coast. 'I'm . . . sorry for what I said to you before, Kydd,' he said, so softly that it was difficult to catch. 'It was churlish of me. I can only plead an extremity of distraction.'

With a surge of feeling, Kydd came back, 'It was a near enough thing, I'm thinking, and if it wasn't for those blaggardly reinforcements . . .'

'Yes, quite,' Popham said bitterly. 'I've pleaded and begged but still none.'

He pulled himself together visibly, and enquired, 'We're all on short commons as you've no doubt noticed – what's the state of *L'Aurore*?'

'In want of water, dry provisions to three weeks, but the barky in good fettle. And I suppose it must be said that, with more than a few in Spanish hands, we'll last the longer.' He paused then continued in a low voice, 'I feel it hard, Dasher, that they're still there while we sail away.'

'Don't be,' Popham said, with something like his old fire. 'I'm staying here. When those damned reinforcements finally come we'll be in a position to retake Buenos Aires and then, in course, they'll be freed.'

'We're mounting a second invasion?'

'We are,' Popham said shortly. 'We're on the spot, we've

achieved so much with so few and, well, we know the way,' he finished, his head drooping again.

Kydd was taken aback. The reinforcements might well be fewer in numbers than he supposed, and to go in again without overwhelming force would in any circumstances be a grave mistake.

'Dasher, I've seen this Liniers. He's stirred up the people with patriotism and high words and I'd wager they'd be much harder to beat this time.'

'Do you take me for a poltroon? I'm not cutting and running! They're for the most part an undisciplined rabble that will crumble before a determined thrust, take my word for it.'

'We'll still need to find many more ships and men than we can expect of the reinforcements, Dasher.' Kydd paused. 'Can we not make sure of it by calling for more from another station?'

Popham spoke slowly: 'I've asked Governor Baird for more from Cape Town but St Helena won't send another man.'

'No, Dasher. I was thinking more of the Leeward Islands station. Ships-o'-the-line, troops, stores – all for us, if we can convince 'em of the value of rescuing this expedition.'

For a long moment Popham remained silent. Then he straightened painfully. 'Umm. It is the nearest, I'll grant you, but I'd hoped not to trouble them in matters concerning this expedition.'

At his words, Kydd realised that he must have refrained from such a move before for one very compelling reason: the far more senior commander-in-chief there would promptly take control of the whole enterprise, its profits and laurels. But higher things were at stake now.

Popham gave a sad smile. 'However, I believe you to be

in the right of things, Thomas. It would make it sure – and that's what counts. I shall pen a letter immediately. I don't suppose you'd object to the voyage?'

Kydd threw off his coat and eased into his favourite chair by *L'Aurore*'s stern windows, accepting Tysoe's proffered toddy.

His friend waited impatiently. 'So, what is to be our fate, dear fellow?'

Kydd finished his drink, then replied, 'To sail to the Leeward Islands station to beg for reinforcements. We're to clap on all sail and spare none.'

Renzi beamed. 'The Caribbean! A little tropical sunshine would be a capital restorative.'

He looked intently at his friend. 'And I'm put in mind of some illustrious adventures in the past on that refulgent main. Do you remember our dear *Seaflower* cutter?'

For a long space Kydd gazed out of the window – and then, for the first time in many weeks, a smile spread.

Author's Note

For readers wondering what happened next – well, the longed-for reinforcements arrived a few weeks after the surrender took place, not from England but from Baird at the Cape. However, they were too slight to effect more than the token capture of Maldonado.

Stung by public opinion, the government had in fact sent out reinforcements but they did not arrive until early the following year, and with them Popham's replacement: he'd been summarily recalled to face court-martial for leaving his station.

The reinforcements were turned into an expedition for the retaking of Buenos Aires. This started well, with the capture of Montevideo, but Whitelocke, a remarkably incompetent political appointee, had been sent out to replace the able General Auchmuty.

The final assault on Buenos Aires was all but over when victory was turned into complete defeat by Whitelocke. Liniers then had the satisfaction of taking the sword of yet another British general. Terms this time were for a complete evacuation, including prisoners from the first incursion.

A year after they had arrived, the British finally sailed away for ever.

The subsequent fate of the main players varied.

Popham's court-martial resulted in a severe reprimand but it seems not to have affected his career, he at the same time being presented with a sword of honour by the City of London for his efforts to open up the markets of the River Plate. In future Kydd tales you shall see more of this intelligent, manipulative, gifted and controversial figure.

Beresford escaped in a manner much like Kydd did, taking the same line on parole. Later, he led in the capture of Madeira, where he so won the confidence of the Portuguese that he was given the command of their armies following the invasion of Portugal by Napoleon. Like so many military in this book – Pack, the 71st itself, other officers – he went on to distinction in the Peninsular War.

The bluff and energetic Baird, however, was caught up in the recriminations and ended under recall, losing his governorship of the Cape. He was never employed at that level again.

Santiago de Liniers, twice victor, was hailed as viceroy to replace the cowardly Sobremonte, but in the growing divisions between loyalists and patriots, as a royalist and French by birth he was suspected of treason and executed barely a year later.

In a stroke of irony, Spanish and Argentinian sources both freely admit that it was the barely known fringe act of empire portrayed in this book that produced the spark that set South America ablaze to achieve independence, by demonstrating the fragility of the Spanish hold on their old colonies, while Miranda's descent on Caracas failed. This struggle for independence beginning three years after the British left saw other *bonaerense* such as Pueyrredón, Güemes and Belgrano take forward roles, and the colonial South America that Kydd knew was quickly swept away.

Buenos Aires, never before and never since under threat from the outside, is now the capital of Argentina. The city bears little resemblance to what it was in those days: vastly bigger and with only the Plaza Mayor itself barely recognisable, the fort long gone and the waterfront an altogether healthier prospect. The River Chuelo, in which seamen swam heroically to build their bridge of boats, is now straddled by a vast dock area, while Ensenada de Barragán is a naval base and the Perdriel ranch has been swallowed by the suburbs.

The northern shore is now Uruguay but Colonia del Sacramento still has a defiant Portuguese colonial feel to it, the little bastion at the water's edge attracting curious visitors.

Of this whole South American episode there are very few relics remaining but in the down-town church of Santo Domingo a visitor to Buenos Aires may stand before the actual colours of the 71st Regiment of Highlanders, surrendered on that fateful day by General Beresford.

As usual, for space reasons, I am unable to acknowledge everyone I consulted in the process of writing this book, but to all I owe my deep thanks. Special mention, however, must be made of Sarah Callejo in Madrid who gave unstintingly of her time in respect of various queries on Spanish sources. I also owe a debt of gratitude to the staff of the British Library and the University of London Library.

And, as ever, my huge appreciation must go to my wife and literary partner, Kathy, my agent Carole Blake and my editor Oliver Johnson.

Glossary

agent-victualler	Admiralty-appointed port agent for supplying naval victuals
aguardiente	rough Spanish brandy
avast	stop or desist an action
aviso	dispatch vessel
balandra	cutter or sloop-rigged South American privateer or fishing boat
beakhead	the ornamented support and small deck around the bowsprit
becket	piece of rope to secure loose gear
Blaauwberg, battle of	defining battle in 1806 that secured Cape Town for the British
blandengues	South American colonial militia
block	a sea-going pulley
boomkin	spar under the bowsprit to take the block to stretch the foresail to windward
bridle	rope span attached to leech cringles to tauten the sail when close-hauled
caballero	Spanish honorific for gentleman, literally horseman
calesa	two-wheeled carriage for notables
canister	small iron balls in a tin case fired by cannon for anti-personnel effect
carronade	short-barrelled, large-calibre gun for use at close range
catblash	nonsense
coxswain	in charge of a boat; captain's coxswain is in charge of the captain's barge

crow	a bar with claws to lever around the great guns in aiming
cruiser	an independent vessel, normally a frigate, sent to annoy the enemy's trade
cutting out	a daring raid by boats into an enemy harbour to capture or destroy enemy shipping
davit	a boat hoist in place of the usual midship stay tackle
distinction	bringing to notice by exceptional courage or achievement
duck	a fine strong white cloth made from untwilled linen, much favoured by sailors
falucho	decked craft local to the River Plate, used in coastal defence and trade
Felucca	small lateen-rigged cargo carrier, corsair
fo'c'sleman	the division of men stationed on the fore-deck; the most experienced seamen
gasket	rope to secure furled sail to the yard
grape-shot	intermediate between canister and solid shot, tiers of smaller balls separated by discs fired as one shot
gunroom	wardroom of a frigate
half-pistol-shot	twenty-five yards range
hawse	the point where the anchor cable leaves the ship
Indiaman	ship of the East India Company
jabberknowl	gossip, rantings of a fool
jonkheer	Dutch honorific for a person of note or high birth
littoral	that part of the land adjoining the sea
maulstick	a wooden stick with a soft head, used by painters to support the hand that holds the brush
mijnheer	Mr in Dutch
moil	close-in scrimmage
mongseer	sailor slang for a Frenchman
negus	a drink of port mixed with hot water, spiced and sugared
pampero	characteristic storm of wind from the Pampas about the River Plate
Panjandrum	high ruler, from eighteenth-century Samuel Foote play
Partidarios Leales	party of the loyalists
patricio	patrician, high-born person
pinnace	one of the smaller of the ship's boats
poniard	small dagger
priddy	seventeenth-century term for prettifying
projector	promoter of a scheme
purser	appointed by the Admiralty for the supply of provision and slops; was an independent businessman
quintal	an imperial 'hundredweight' or 100 pounds in weight

quoin	a wedge of wood at the breech to cause elevation or depression in a gun
real	eight to the Spanish silver dollar
reis	Portuguese *real* since 1480
rixdollar	*rijksdaalder*: main currency of the Cape of Good Hope
sailing master	attends to the navigation and working of a ship under the captain
schildknaap	Dutch honorific – squire
sea fencibles	land-based naval auxiliaries, local to Britain
sea-anchor	device to drag in the sea to orient the ship
sheave	the wheel on which the rope works in a block
supercargo	an agent aboard a merchant ship responsible for cargo and commercial affairs
veduta	highly detailed landscape in the style of Canaletto
Viceroyalty	that province ruled by a viceroy appointed directly by the Spanish king
volunteers of the first class	educated boys intended to be midshipmen but too young
whiffler	slang for glancing blow
wight	a creature, person
yaw	a deviation to right or left of a ship's proper course

The best books live on in your head long after they are finished. As you read, you are turning the pages faster and faster to find out what happens next, only to feel bereft when you reach the end.

If that is how you feel now, you might like to join us at www.hodder.co.uk, or follow us on Twitter @hodderbooks, and be part of our community of people who love the very best of books and reading.

Whether you want to find out more about this book, or a particular author, watch trailers and interviews, have the chance to win early limited editions, or simply browse our expert readers' selection of the very best books, we think you'll find what you're looking for.

And if you don't, that's the place to tell us what's missing.

We love what we do, and we'd love you to be part of it.

www.hodder.co.uk

@hodderbooks

HodderBooks

HodderBooks